N
The Hook
BEEE 2018
NORTHERN THRACS
SHELTONS CRAG
TUNOKA
KARFAEL
Sainthome
TRYSTLAND
AUXIL
SOUTHERN THRACS
Tunoka Grasslands
Karnock Forest
SOARNESTIA
The Crag
Fallowmere Isles
SUNSOAKED
GLYPH GRASSLANDS
Glimmersedge
GODHEAD
Whitmans Point
BRIMMERLAND
THANTOS
CAVERE
CULCHAR
Arrowhead Lake
CAVERE
ACCLARO
SULK
PLAINS
Jingtalla Falls
SELDOR HILLS
ILLUME
TRAVELLED LANDS
WHALESON
SUBLIME MOUNTAINS
STORMWATCH
SCUTTLE
NORTHAIR MOUNTAINS
The Magestic Coast
Bay of Radiance
Scented Isles
Bay of Storms

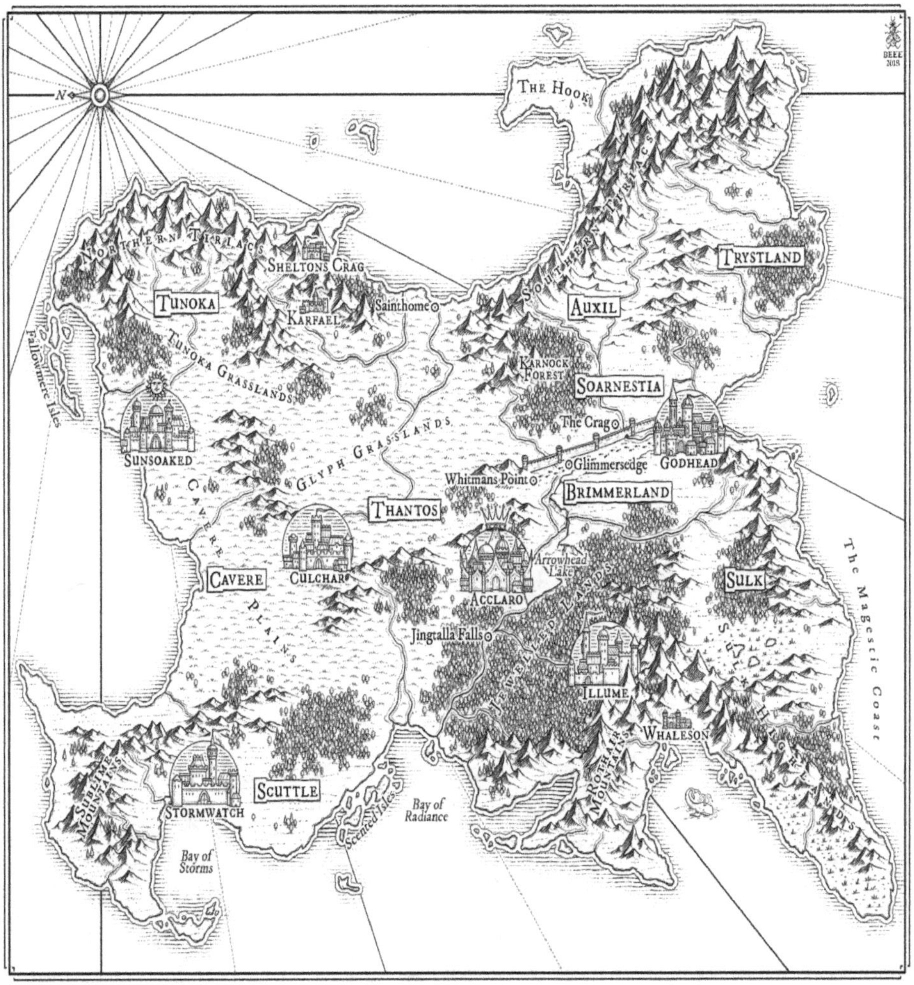

The Severing

Table of Contents

Chapter 1

'She hasn't come...'

The words hung in the air, disembodied and it took Haakon a moment to realize they had been uttered by himself. He yawned then sighed, moving away from the window and its bleak view of the rain battering the town below. The fire was now merely embers so some time must have passed as he had stood there gazing into the storm. Striding over to the wood box, his muscles once flexible and strong, felt tight and unyielding and he wondered not for the first time if the rigors of his harsh life were finally catching up to him. Haakon stoked the fire then began pacing as he pondered his next move. He stopped at the mirror to regard the sight of his ragged reflection with dark ringed eyes peering back at him, and his stubble covered jaw line framed by greasy long hair made him appear older than he was. He cursed and stalked away, once again turning his thoughts to the absence of Latasha who only days ago had sent him a coded message to meet her here. From past experience Haakon knew Latasha was prompt and never kept anyone waiting. That was until now.

Haakon had first met Latasha some nine cycles ago when he had successfully overthrown his predecessor in a violent coup and until then had only believed that she was a figment of the wine-soaked ranting of his late master. 'The brightest flower in the garden, radiant with ethereal light and eyes you would drown in-oh, and the body of a goddess strong and supple. There is no escaping the clasp of those heavenly thighs when they are wrapped around you.' He could still hear the old fool after all these cycles and see the surprised look upon his face as Haakon's dagger tore through his heart and the very life drained from his eyes. With the headache from his investiture as clan lord of the Kenzu only days old, Haakon was notified that a valued client had come to him for a private audience. From this first meeting Haakon knew Latasha was a dangerous woman. She glided into the room, her eyes glittering, taking in all the details quickly. Her smile held barely contained amusement, and her cascading silver hair smelled of summer, immediately marking her as one of the ancients who were adored for their beauty but feared for their charm and cunning. In Latasha's presence chimes passed like moments, and it took all his training to keep his wits about him.

At the meeting Latasha had voiced her concerns that her contract may not be honored and the importance of the task might be lost. As if to highlight the importance of the mission, Latasha had then pulled a small blue bag from her dress, opening it to let the contents spill onto the table. Haakon tried not to look surprised but failed miserably. On the table before him sat a pile of green tear drop pearls amongst a scattering of burnt rubies.

'Uhhh… there is no need of further payment Miss Meldoriel.' Haakon said as he rubbed a hand across his forehead.

'Please consider it as…shall we say, investment protection?' She said with a sly smile. 'So I can be reassured you are not taking me lightly and to remind you, clan master that this contract is your only concern. No questions please. The less you know the better. They say knowledge is power, but believe me there is no power here. Only death to those involved.'

That meeting had been nine cycles ago and over that time the relationship between Haakon and Latasha had grown into a passionate affair. He never knew when he might see her next and imagined he now knew what it was like to be a puppet dancing at his mistress's every word. Those times when Latasha was gone seemed dull and devoid of life. He survived by going through the motions like a hound awaiting the return of its mistress. The fact that Latasha would come and go as she pleased, unnerved Haakon who prided himself on his skills of stealth and subterfuge. Still, he was perplexed at her sudden appearances and exits. When he had raised the issue with her she had laughed, cupped his face in her dainty hands and said.

'These things are of little importance my love let us enjoy what moments we have together free from suspicion and worry.' Her comings and goings went not unnoticed by his men, either, and he had heard her being referred to as an infernal succubus when they thought he was not around. Some had taken to hanging pendants of protection around their necks and adorning rooms with runes to ward off horrors from the infernal realms. Haakon felt the queasy nervousness as he waited for her. The last time they had seen one another was over a cycle ago now when she had taken him to her home and told him she was leaving for a time and wasn't sure when she could return.

Haakon knew he had to act as he had sworn to do and have the coterie of the heart removed to a safe location. But before he did this, he must know what had happened to Latasha. Haakon started to move his body through a series of actions designed to relax his mind and open the energy centers in his body. His breathing became slow and steady as he came to a sitting position: heels tucked under his body, hands palm up on his knees. Using deep concentration honed by sessions of meditation and mental training, he visualized a double of himself standing before him composed of white light. Into this he focused his consciousness. He felt his body vibrating as if from a great distance away. He felt energy tingle up his spine to the crown of his head and then, with an audible click, he was within the energy body, only connected to his real self by a silver cord joining his solar plexus.

Astral training was one of the first skills one was introduced to as a part of an assassin's training. Latasha's knowledge of this realm was nothing short of extensive, and she had taught him how to access the astral world and avoid the many dangers that awaited the unwary, his control was sloppy still, but that took a lifetime to master. With the Severing and the loss of magic, the astral plane could no longer be used to enter the Celestial or Infernal realms. If one had the discipline, mental clarity and intent to will it so, one could travel real world distances instantaneously and observe events from the past and present. He willed his energy body up off the floor and floated up through the roof. Movement in the astral was like swimming through water, but physical effort achieved nothing. Instead mental focus and willpower were necessities if one was to navigate and survive this strange realm. From his vantage point he looked out across the astral landscape suffused with amber light; below him he could make out the multi-colored auras of four guards he had stationed around the cabin. A fleeting shiver embraced Haakon, and he knew instinctively that a storm was on the way and it would be too dangerous to linger here.

Long sessions of visualization had allowed Haakon to perfect the exact image of the glade Latasha called home. It was this image that Haakon formed in his mind as he made the sign of obedience to the astral lords and entered the astral river. A flood of images assaulted his mind taking all his willpower to keep the desired image in focus and not be spun away into the maelstrom of desires, dreams and thought forms that were constantly in flux on this plane. His senses blurred together, causing time to dissolve as he was swept away into nothingness. Dizziness crept over him when his senses returned, and he could see he was floating down to Latasha's home.

Gigantic, translucent everswelt trees ringed the glade. Their branches entwined to form a natural canopy above a pristine pool flanked by yellow wildflower covered grass banks. A small hut sat at the far end of the glade and anxiety gripped Haakon as he noticed its door had been ripped from its hinges and lay in tatters around the entranceway. Haakon paused listening intently, the usual forest noise of its denizens going about their business was absent, indicating that something had happened and intruders had been here.

Using his astral body to his advantage, Haakon opted to move through the wall instead of the doorway, in case it was being watched. He felt a mild pressure all over his body as he pushed through to stand inside the cottage. The one room was stacked with alchemical tools and bundles of herbs hung from the rafters; on a corner stove a blackened pot hissed and the stench of burnt food blanketed the room.

It wasn't until Haakon moved into the center of the chamber that he saw Latasha. She lay naked, face down in a heap on the floor. Clumps of her silver hair had been torn from her scalp and her remaining hair was soaked with blood. Her outstretched arms and legs were bent at impossible angles and had been precisely broken at every joint. A pile of vomit had formed around her face, and she lay in a puddle of her own blood and urine. At first Haakon thought Latasha was dead, but as he knelt beside her face he could hear the faint rasping breath rattle in and out of her battered body.

As Haakon looked upon the only being who had managed to dart past his guard something broke inside him, and threatened to dissolve the emotionally barren wasteland of his heart. He no longer cared about anything else, all that mattered was that he must not let Latasha die. He longed to touch her and comfort her, but the astral body was incapable of that. Despair, widow-black, descended on Haakon as the hardened assassin part of him fought desperately to choke down the scared little boy that represented everything he wasn't supposed to be. Shame clashed with anger and failure crossed swords with detachment, as two parts of his being battled for control of their host.

With a start Haakon realized that Latasha's eyes were open and staring at him and he remembered that ancients could see into and converse with beings in the astral realms. Latasha's eyes locked with his and through a mouth full of shattered teeth she spoke:

'It's a trap…'

His instincts taking over, Haakon thrust the image of the cabin where his material body lay into his mind. As his energy body snapped backwards away from Latasha, Haakon felt something latch onto his back. Strong arms wrapped around him, razor sharp bursts of pain tore through him as wicked claws dug into his ribs and chest, bringing dark spots into his vision. Fetid, foul breath caressed his neck, making Haakon gag. Haakon threw his head back and was rewarded with a grunt of pain from his unseen assailant. Not wanting to give his attacker time to reassert itself, he then slammed his arms downwards and out breaking his enemy's grip around his waist. As whatever had hold of him started to fall away, it snaked out a long, hairless, grey arm and grabbed on to the silver cord extending out from Haakon's solar plexus. With its other arm, the creature started to saw away at the cord with its sharp nails as it grinned up at Haakon through gnashing teeth.

Every part of Haakon fought to remain calm and focus on his destination. Yet if he did nothing and was separated from his astral cord, he could no longer return to his body. The disorientation caused by the river was forgotten as he was immersed in a struggle for survival. The creature had to be from the astral or else it wouldn't be able to attack him in a physical manner. It must be a Jaunt, one of those beings who latched onto unwary travellers and rode their astral body back to their material bodies, where they then separated the owner from their astral cord and instead entered the body themselves as a form of possession. Haakon felt the strength draining out of him from the damaged astral cord and was alarmed to see wisps of mercury drizzling from it into the Jaunt's mouth. The creature's body seemed to grow fuller while he noticed his body was starting to fade.

The cabin came into view, bringing a flicker of hope with it, he pulled himself along the cord then reached down and grabbed the Jaunt by the neck. It thrashed, tearing at his face causing terrible cuts that oozed silver energy. With his free arm Haakon wrapped his astral cord around its throat and tightened it. The Jaunt continued to fight with its talons, slashing down Haakon's abdomen.

A loud ringing deafened him, and his body was starting to ignore his commands. All he could do was focus on the cabin and hope for the best. They crashed through the roof and there was a sickening snap followed by a painfully bright flash and an unearthly howl of pain as Haakon reconnected with his material body. Something around his neck was burning, and his body shook uncontrollably causing Haakon to bite his tongue, filling his mouth with blood. Then darkness, sweet darkness.

❧ Chapter 2

Ishmael was up before the chimes tinkled through the household. Yawning loudly, he slipped on sandals, donned a loincloth, and then tipped the jug of cold water over his head, hissing at the chill.

'Taita, show me my reflection please.'

The crystal wall cleared in front of Ishmael, and Taita the Jaldurial house spirit grinned back at him, her tongue waggling at him rudely. 'Morning, Ish, I trust you slept well? Since your thunderous snoring kept everyone else awake?'

'Taita, I don't snore and, I have no time this morning for your gibberish. So please for once just do as I ask without complaining.'

'What! No time for gibberish? Well then you obviously have no need to hear the important news I have, Master Ish.'

Ishmael rubbed his hands over his scalp… he would shave tomorrow.

'What news?'

Taita ignored him and started to recount information about the day ahead.

'Hot today with clear skies, Johan will be here at two chimes before noon for your Lune riding lesson.'

'Taita!'

'Abbot Linfrey requests your attendance in his chambers for ancient history at the mid-afternoon chime, while brother Tovald wants you in the meditation chambers at twilight to make up for your recent tardiness.'

Taita cocked her head to one side and rubbed her chin.

'The boy needs to practice renunciation, and the Festival of the Lanterns is the perfect time to start.'

Ishmael felt his anger creep up from his belly; he knew that after all these cycles as a brother of Illume he should be able to keep such base emotions in check, but it was difficult.

Slumping back onto his bed he placed his head in his hands, elbows on his knees, and sighed loudly.

'Why me? The festival only happens every five cycles, all the other brothers will be allowed to attend and help guide the people in their prayers for the future, so why can't I?'

Ishmael looked up and caught Taita copying him with an exaggerated frown on her face and couldn't stop himself from barking out a laugh.

'Just tell me the news and put me out of my miscry,' he pleaded

Taita waved her hands, and with a flourish she was dressed as a noble courtier with crimped hair, a tight bodice, frilled trousers, and buckled shoes.

In a slow drawling voice Taita announced.

'Trouble brews in the Tiarioc Mountains. First Flame Commandant Dalwyn Trevlon has ordered his legions to scour the land for Latasha Meldoriel, one of the last remaining ancients who has vital information about the Severing and how magic can be returned to the world. A reward of ten thousand ceta's has been offered for information leading to her capture.'

Ishmael hugged his shoulders and breathed deeply to stay calm. While there were those who sought to return magic to the world he would never be safe.

'Are you all right Master Ish?' Taita asked, concern evident in her voice.

'Yeah, fine, Taita, don't worry about me. It's nothing…'

Ishmael sauntered to the practice hall without the usual spring in his step. This was his favorite part of the day when he could lose himself in the challenging fitness sequences designed for optimum flexibility, mental control and clarity. Even at this early time old Leto sat in meditation, his rhythmic breathing strong and deep. Ishmael removed his sandals and grabbed a burning smudge stick to cleanse his body before his practice. To the east, the sun was just climbing over the wall of night, a golden streak of hope.

Ishmael sat to the left of Leto then settled into his chosen position for meditation, sitting with his shins against the cool wooden floor, calves rolled out hips between his legs. Once a position that caused him great pain and took what seemed like chimes for the blood to return to his feet, it now instantly put him into a state of relaxation and concentration. He inhaled for twenty heartbeats then exhaled to the same count. In his mind, he let the image of a slowly spinning golden disc coalesce, and on this he focused. A soft chiming announced the start of dawn practice, and opening his eyes he saw the hall was now full of brothers. Leto faced the east and led the deep chant to honour the sun the father of life, the only one who casts no shadow.

As if one great entity, the monks of Illume began moving precisely and perfectly through the sequence of creation, their movements telling how Jeda the great eagle of consciousness had argued with the sun over which of them existed first.

The sun said it could burn Jeda up and let itself shine brightly, causing the heavens to boil; Jeda laughed and said he existed to create and consume and nothing could hurt him. They fought, and the sun tried to incinerate Jeda, who flew straight into his adversary to tear out his heart.

Jeda caught fire and plummeted to the earth, but not before raking the sun with his claws. A steady flow of the suns life fell onto the earth where it gathered in crevices and valleys and ran into waterways. Soon after, life crept and crawled from the earth's center to inhabit the world. As Jeda lay dying on the earth his blood mixed with that of the sun, and the races were born with consciousness.

Ishmael, his body lathered in sweat, waited for the hall to empty before he approached Leto as he stood gazing out across the city. The sun's rays seemed to illuminate the old monk with golden light.

'Young Ishmael, your practice was weak today, your mind stuck and unyielding.'

Leto turned and picked up Ishmael's hands in his own.

'You need to let go of your concerns and let the answers come from within.'

'Have you heard the news, Leto?' Ishmael asked.

'What news is that, brother?'

'It's happening, they are looking for me. Taita told me a Dalwyn Trevlon has even offered a reward. Every time that my life starts feeling normal something happens that drags me back to this burden I am forced to carry.'

'Ishmael, we cannot change who we are, to do so can only bring us pain. Yes, you have a rough path in this life. But with that, comes the chance to transcend your limitations and truly be of service.'

Ishmael pulled his hands out of Leto's roughly.

'I don't want to be of service, I don't want the magic that holds my body captive and brings danger while forcing me to live a life of secrecy. You tell me I am blessed for the power I hold, but all I want is a normal life. The magic will overpower my body and rot me, like overripe fruit unless I keep up my practices. It will kill me like it did my father.'

Leto shook his head sadly. 'I really feel for you, Ishmael, but in this you have no choice. When the spirit calls, you follow or perish. Your lineage was chosen as one of the coterie to protect our world's magic until such time as it's safe for its return. Your ancestors and most recently your father have done so with honour, and now it's your turn to follow in their footsteps.'

Leto's eyes softened as he continued. 'No one can make your choices for you Ishmael; your life is your own. Think hard and worry before you make a decision, but once you make it, move on free from further worry. Think of your death when things are unclear. The idea of death is the only thing that snaps us out of the ego and tempers our spirits. To live as a brother of Illume, you have to be crystal clear.'

'Death you say. Leto I feel dead inside already and the one thing that is crystal clear is that this is not the life I want to live!' Ishmael turned away from Leto, not wanting the old monk to see his anguish. He held his palms against his temples and with a cry lashed out, knocking a bowl of scented water from the ledge next to him.

Leto stepped forward to put his hand on Ishmael's shoulder, but Ishmael brushed it away.

'Ishmael, it makes us unhappy to want. Yet if we would learn to cut our wants to nothing, then the smallest things we get would be true gifts.'

'Save your lectures for the people, Leto. I am beyond caring right now.'

Ishmael turned, leaving the hall as Leto's weary eyes followed him wondering what he could do to ease the young man's heart.

Later as the day darkened to night, Ishmael sat in meditation on renunciation of earthly wants and the suppression of passion. Tovald had berated him for earlier transgressions and he was now at least glad of the peace. Tovald was in his reading room down the hall and Ishmael noticed that occasionally he would sneak up to check Ishmael was still here. Half a chime later Ishmael could hear arguing coming from Tovald's room before footsteps ran down the hall. Not the lumbering footsteps of potbellied Tovald, but lighter and faster.

Ishmael looked up as Hofan barrelled into the room laughing loudly, a wide grin splitting his face. He careened into Ishmael, sending them both sprawling. Hofan wrapped his legs around Ishmael's long torso and forced his forearm under his chin, choking him. Ishmael was no beginner to the art of ground fighting, and he turned towards Hofan's chest, dipping his chin and claiming top position.

Hofan gasped with exertion as they wrestled.

'Brother Leto just overruled Torvald and says you and any other brother serving penance are to be excused so they might watch the festival of Lanterns from the estate gardens.'

Ishmael's eyes widened.

'Really?'

'Yeah, really, Ish, and that means I'm free too.'

Ishmael jumped to his feet and pulled his friend up.

'Let's go then.'

They both rushed down the corridor jostling for the lead past a grinning Leto, who nimbly jumped aside. Ishmael and Hofan exploded from the house and into the night. The light of Aspre set the sky on incandescent fire, reflecting off the Jaldurial crystal houses built into the rim of the crater at the peak of Mount Rothair. The city of Illume clung to the craters inside walls in terraced levels, all the way down to the city proper at its center. The upper levels housed the nobility in their Jaldurial mansions, while the middle and lower levels, the merchant class and middle class folk huddled in villas. Underneath the city descending into the belly of the mountain was where the poor and homeless struggled for survival, the ones whose existence the other people of Illume preferred to ignore.

Ishmael and Hofan climbed up onto the stone wall that ringed the garden and sat with their legs dangling over the side. Far below a mass of tiny figures heaved and swayed to the sounds of frenetic drumming that would drive the evil from their lives and cleanse their spirits. Through the human sea a slow procession moved, carrying platforms covered in intricately painted lanterns whose soft lights pulsed like the heart of some large, writhing beast. Ishmael felt an elbow nudge his ribs; he glanced over to his grinning friend, who held out a little bundle wrapped in thick Pakiri leaves.

'A little treat courtesy of Brother Torvald.'

Ishmael opened the parcel to reveal a piece of almond cake, chocolate-glazed cherries and a stick of toffee.

'How did you get these, Hofan?'

Hofan shrugged his shoulders and smiled through a mouthful of almond cake.

'You stole them from Torvald, didn't you?' When he received no answer, Ishmael continued. 'Hofan, what if you had got caught? Huh, what then?'

Hofan had the decency to look a little guilty.

'C'mon, Ish, I was doing the old bugger a favor! The last thing he needs is more food - all that preaching he does on renouncing earthly wants just contradicts the fact that he keeps a hidden stash of sweets in the meditation rooms.'

Hofan sighed theatrically.

'Okay, you're right. I will take them back.'

He reached over to grab the parcel from Ishmael's lap, but Ishmael pulled it away from him.

'You can't return them now; all we can do is hide the evidence,' Ishmael replied popping a cherry in his mouth.

Below, the drumming slowed to a heartbeat and in its place the sounds of ethereal flutes soared through the city.

'Oh I see how it is… you're quick to point out a crime, but happy to receive stolen goods.'

Ishmael frowned theatrically.

'The crime was already committed, Hofan, I took the goods not knowing that they were stolen. In my naivety I trusted you to have strong morals and a sense of pride about your position as a brother of Illume. You of all should know better my son, to steal from others is not a crime against just them but also a crime against yourself as it dulls the spirit and creates more craving.'

Hofan laughed loudly and Ishmael joined in.

'You imitate Torvald so well, Ish, that sometimes I think you are his son.'

Ishmael quickly put a hand onto Hofan's back and gave him a small push.

'HEY!' shouted Hofan.

As he grabbed for the wall, his food fell from his lap.

Ishmael, with his mouth full of cake, pounded his chest, a braying laugh coming from his throat, his eyes leaking tears.

'I could have fallen, Ish…, not funny.'

When Ishmael had recovered he looked at his sulking friend. 'I'm sorry, Hofan.'

'No you're not; if you were truly sorry you would share that toffee with me.'

Ishmael picked up the toffee and snapped it in two; one he popped in his mouth, the other he held out to Hofan. But before Hofan could grab it he popped it in his own mouth as well, grinning broadly.

'You're going to pay for that, Ish.'

'Shhhhhh,' said Ishmael, 'the Lunars are coming.'

High above the city three colossal Lunars slowly drifted downwards in lazy circles. The moth-like creatures had two sets of large, blood-red wings interwoven with white striping and splashes of gold measuring at least thirty feet from tip to tip. The coloring was like nothing Ishmael had ever seen. Most Lunar mounts were dull colored for camouflage. Their riders, encased in their silver armor atop bejewelled saddles, looked like fallen stars. In the moonlight, the two friends could see that the Lunars' eyes had been covered so they didn't lose focus and be drawn towards the Jaldurial crystal houses, or back up towards the moon. The riders guided their mounts down to the waiting crowd, who eagerly tied silk ropes threaded through all the lanterns onto the riders' saddle hooks.

Silence descended on the crowd as the Lunars' riders released the bindings from their mounts eyes. Now unfettered, they beat their enormous wings and rose steadily up towards the moon. Behind them trailed long chains of lanterns inscribed with all the prayers and messages for dead friends or kin that had journeyed to the Celestial realms. They both sat there looking up in awe as the Lunars rose in horizontal formation. The nearest was only twenty feet away. Its rider waved a gauntlet towards the throng of onlookers crowding the estate gardens, and they cheered loudly. Majestically the Lunars flew higher, and the moon Aspre in the background made the scene appear like a painting-too beautiful to be real.

Ishmael continued to track the Lunars progress. Aspre's light reflected off the crystal houses creating a shimmering staircase, guiding the Lunars to the heavens as if the gods themselves had created it. Movement from the west caught Ishmael's attention. Something was moving fast towards the unsuspecting Lunars.

'Hofan what's that?' Ishmael asked his friend who was carefully climbing off the wall.'

Hofan squinted in the direction that Ishmael pointed.

'It looks like a large bird. No wait, there's more than one, and they're angling up under the Lunars.'

Cries of warning echoed around the city as onlookers saw what was happening.

At the last moment, the Lunars sensed they were in trouble. Their antennae spiralled wildly and their keening cries became haunting melodies. The riders tried to get their mounts to bank to the right, but it was too late.

A formation of black-armoured winged Infernals slammed into the unprotected bellies of the Lunars. Within moments two plummeted down their bellies slit open, wings shredded and riders' dead to crash into the side of the mountain.

Somewhere below a bell tolled, calling the night guard into action, but Ishmael knew it was futile. He could see the barracks on the opposite side of the crater was burning. By the time the guard mobilized, the enemies would be long gone. Had the attack on the barracks been coordinated with the aerial one?

The last remaining rider was skilful. He sharply pulled his Lunar upwards, rolled over and down, away from their pursuers. However, the number of attackers and their superior flying soon proved too much. The Infernals swarmed over the dying Lunar and its rider-dark bodies quenching the beauty of their foes, ejecting them from the sky.

Ishmael felt sick, the sweet taste of cherries suddenly soured by the violent deaths above.

Screams erupted below in the city as the shock started to wear off the watching crowd.Hofan shook his head.

'Why Ish? It doesn't make sense. Why would there be Infernals here in Illume?'

Before Ishmael could answer, Brother Leto came up behind them placing a hand on each boy's shoulder.

'Come, brothers, we must go inside until we know what's happening.'

'Does anyone need to know more, Leto?' Ishmael asked as the old monk led them towards the house.

'We all saw it with our own eyes.'

'Does this mean we are at war?' Hofan said turning to Leto.

'Enough questions. I saw what you saw but that doesn't answer anything, so we need to be on guard and wait for official notification from the Council.'

Chapter 3

Zahra clenched her teeth together, the corded muscles of her arms awash with fire as she pulled herself up to the overhead beam.

'Ninety-eight,' she hissed.

'Ninety-nine…'

'One hundred.'

Lowering herself down, she landed softly on the balls of her feet. Her chest heaved as she moved to the window to let the wind wash through her short, sweat-drenched hair. This would be her last night in the tower. She felt a giddy excitement at the thought of being amongst the living once more but also fearful of leaving this place. Her self-imposed exile had taught her so much about herself. Breathing deeply the scent of cedar, Zahra looked over the garden below. The monastery couldn't compare with the exotic, opulent gardens that flourished in the family estates that surrounded it. Yet this simple and reverently tended garden was famous for perfect symmetry and beauty. A dense display of carefully shaped azalea bushes led the eye away from the reception hall, towards a pond centered on a statue of Irdalar the goddess of water. Irdalar stood with arms outstretched gazing upwards to catch the water cascading down from the estate above. A staggered planked bridge crossed the pond away from the goddess set against a stand of blue irises planted along the southern shore. Where the bridge exited on the east shore, a moss garden path split in two, leading south east to the training hall or north east to the main house. This path was backed by cedars and red maples, and in their center; the ancient bell tower that Zahra had chosen as a temporary home sat forgotten at the end of a weed choked pathway.

Except for novice brothers trying to prove their bravery, the bell tower was shunned and only spoken about in hushed whispers. The stone door was bolted and its handle had long ago been removed, leaving a gaping hole through which to peer into its depths. A common dare was to enter the path nicknamed the Fools March and stay until the stroke of midnight, arm outstretched through the hole into the darkness beyond, for as long as you could stand.

Zahra turned away from the window and slid down the wall facing the bell. There was still time, and so with a wry smile she let herself float back over the events of her life since this place had become her home. Nearly eight cycles ago Zahra moved in. Since then, the tower had become home to two ghosts.

The ghost of Sam Towelyn was the precise reason Zahra chose the bell tower as her base of operations. She needed somewhere she could watch over the monastery and Ishmael without being seen. The fact that the tower was haunted made it safe from prying eyes and thus made, Zahra's job all the easier. Not that living with a ghost was easy…

Sam Towelyn was a young monk who had always been the butt of his fellow students' jokes. The ruddy-faced lad was teased about his weight and harassed mercilessly. In time, he withdrew into himself and started seeking comfort away from others. His favorite place had been this tower where he would sit alongside the magnificent bell and imagine being able to fly with the birds, leaving his weak, earth-bound body behind. One night, his tormentors found him there and forced him up onto the window ledge. Crying and snivelling he tolerated their abuse as they whipped his legs with short canes. Sam lost his balance and fell thirty feet to break upon the path at the tower's base. Now he returns every night to the scene of his death waiting to wreak vengeance upon the living.

Shortly after the murder the tower was locked and entry was forbidden, so no further 'mishaps' could occur.

It started the night she moved into the tower. There came heavy stomping up and down the winding staircase, abrupt changes in temperature either to freezing cold, causing her breath to mist, or a dense sweat-lathering heat. Zahra had dismissed the stories of the haunting as a mere tale to scare younger monks, but as the incidents escalated in variety and occurrence, she no longer doubted.

On her second night in the tower things took a more dangerous turn. The wind wailed a sorrowful lament through the trees as the heavens dropped their silvery curtains. Zahra had awakened with a fright, trying to rise from her mat, but a heavy weight pressed down, pinning her to the floor. The blood in her body froze to icy rivers, and her wildly beating heart climbed up into her throat, choking her impending scream.

As the pressure on her chest increased and her breathing became labored, she forced herself to think about the tales she had heard and tried to remember the name of the dead boy.

Zahra reached out across her body, looking for something physical to indicate this was not some supernatural occurrence.

'SAM! Get off me.' She said with as much authority as she could muster.

'I am not going to hurt you. I can help you find peace.'

One of her ribs made an ominous popping sound. Just as she thought they might break, the weight had disappeared as suddenly as it had come. Standing over her was the rotund figure of a boy. His cheeks shone with ghostly tears and a soft light surrounded his body. Zahra stayed where she was. Slowly, as he faded from view, his eyes locked with hers. She remembered that she had felt sadness so deep that it threatened to drown her in insanity.

That had been the only time Sam had attacked her. He manifested more often after that, stamping up the stairs to slowly materialize and sit crying by the bell while looking out the window. Other times, items would move on their own accord or vanish only to reappear days later on her bedding.

Over time Zahra's life became lost in routine. By day she watched the occupants of the monastery, listening greedily and basking in their spoken words. Loneliness had bunked down beside her and kept its cold hands clasped around her shoulders. Plagued by the unforgiving souls of her victims that lay siege to her dreams, Zahra slept only when exhaustion overcame her. Tower life had provided her with ample time to stay fit and she ran daily up and down the stairway until she knew each stair like the back of her hands.

While Zahra was here she knew time would be important to study Ishmael and map out his routines.

Often it was necessary for her to disguise herself so she was able to move around during the day and study Ishmael and the monastery like a battleground. Every full moon a coded message was left for her in the astral, so she would attend that meeting place created by herself and the other sentinels of the Heart and greedily devour the precious messages within. Each day she wondered whether this would be the day orders came for her to intervene and get Ishmael to safety.

She hadn't bothered checking today. After the earlier events of the last two days she knew it was time.

For eight cycles Zahra had studied Ishmael closely. Most missions demanded surveillance, but only enough to find a pattern among the targets routines to enable a successful kill. This was entirely different. Ishmael was not to be killed but kept alive and she needed to know Ishmael so well that in the blink of an eye she could gauge the reaction he would have in any given situation and act accordingly. As Zahra sat there, she thought about what it was about Ishmael that truly piqued her interest. His pale green eyes had a feral intensity to them that softened and revealed beautiful, faint crow's feet when he smiled. Daily back-breaking labor and training had honed his muscles to a chiselled hardness that rippled when he moved. Yes, there was no denying it. The physical attraction was there, and yet there was more to it and maybe that was why she had neglected to reveal herself to him like she was supposed to do as his Sentinel. It was different than the lust that came over her after a kill where she longed to be bitten, ravaged and bruised, to feel pain and ecstasy and know she was alive and not just a tool of death whose only companion was the darkness in which she thrived. That's it! She murmured as she massaged and stretched the tense muscles of her shoulders. Something about Ishmael attracted her. Darkness…

There is a darkness lurking in Ishmael waiting for release, biding its time. Ishmael's secret was killing him, trapping him here.

Sometimes Zahra felt like she was close to unlocking Ishmael, only then to be totally perplexed by his actions. After such a long period of examination she knew Ishmael almost intimately. She knew how he hated the inflexible attitude of his peers who never questioned anything. She knew that he longed for his family who blamed him for his father's death and had cast him out. Knew that he slept curled up on his side and his sheets smelt of citrus and musk. Knew about the jagged scar diagonally down his chest from the right clavicle to his sternum from when his father had died and Ishmael had decided to mark himself, in order never to forget the sacrifices his father had made for him. Knew he hated footwear and preferred to feel the earth beneath his feet and let her heartbeat reverberate through his being. And she knew about the Magic he protected.

Zahra was part of a select group of Kenzu chosen and trained secretly for this purpose: keeping the five most important people of this world alive, and yet still skepticism sometimes itched away within Zahra's mind.

Zahra remembered Master Haakon's words as the five soon-to-be sentinels, including Zahra, sat expectantly waiting to find out their mission.

'What I am about to tell you may not seem believable. History tells us that the world's magic was severed from us, but I am here to tell you differently. Magic was never taken from this world because to do so would be impossible. Magic is a part of the fabric of reality, and until our world dies, cannot be removed.' Haakon raised his hands knowingly to stop the questions springing forth from his students. 'This was the most fantastical of illusions: to have the world believe its magic had been lost. To this day few beings know the truth and now you five are among them. With this knowledge comes more power and danger than you may be able to handle, so I kindly give you one last chance to refuse my offer and return to your life of routine and safety.'

No one moved; all kept their eyes peeled on their master knowing the chance he offered them was death and nothing more.

'Now to answer this obvious question, if the magic isn't lost then, where is it?' When no one offered an answer, Haakon continued.

'Before the Severing every person had some measure of magical ability. There existed a group that had no other ability than storing magic within their bodies. They were energetically configured differently and deemed pariahs by most since their strange skill seemed to serve no real purpose. It was within five of these so-called pariahs that our world's magic was hidden.'

Every tenth day Ishmael met with the abbot whose personal chambers and garden lay at the heart of the main house. They would sit all afternoon talking, and Zahra realized it was vital to find out what happened at these times. The door to the abbot's personal garden was only able to be opened by himself and Taita, the household spirit. The only entrance to be found therefore was by the roof. Zahra lowered herself down into the garden that consisted of raked pebbles and soil interspersed with rock formations that were designed to mirror the soul. The abbot used a primitive form of divination involving raking the garden while in a meditative state. Visions highlighted events of importance and showed him how to proceed. A wooden porch covered a small area around the door from the house, and it was under here that Zahra hid. As they sat talking, she lay beneath them breathing slowly, trying to ignore the insects that crawled over her. Her muscles cramped and dirt and sweat stung her eyes.

'You looked troubled today, Ishmael.'

'It is nothing, holy one, I just didn't sleep well… that's all.'

'Have you been having the dreams again?' asked the abbot as he poured them both tea.

'Not just the dreams, but also voices,' Ishmael said. 'In the dreams there are four other people apart from me, three females and one male. We sit on stone chairs in an earthen walled chamber with no door. A tree is the focus of the chamber and it is not well. Its branches are grey and mouldy without leaves, and the soil at the trees base is hard and dry. The branches react to our voices and strain to reach us, but we stay away from them. We know that together we have some important task to complete here and yet we cannot communicate enough to decide what it is.'

'What about the voices?' asked the abbot.

Ishmael sipped his tea and then put down his cup.

'The voices are the same as the four people in the chamber with me, and just lately I can hear them when I am awake.'

'Have you tried to reach out to them at all?'

'No, I haven't, I just know we are aware of each other now more than ever. I think they are the rest of the coterie. When my father died, and passed on this magic to me, he told me there were four others in the coterie who shared this burden with me. Do you think I should try to reach out?'

'Try to communicate more when in the dream, use your training to stay aware and keep the dream strong so you can find out what is happening. Until you control the dream and it stops controlling you, its meaning will be lost. Let the voices come and go and listen, but don't react until we know more.'

'Abbot?'

'Yes, Ishmael?'

'Do you think something is wrong?' Ishmael hesitated. 'I mean, I hear the others talk about their sentinels, but I don't have one. Maybe something has happened to mine.'

Zahra felt shamed as she realized Ishmael was talking about her.

'I'm sure everything is fine, Ishmael. Just because your sentinel hasn't revealed himself to you doesn't mean you don't have one. Maybe they thought it unwise or unnecessary to do this while you are safe within the monastery. Somewhere I'm sure they are watching or listening to what happens to you.'

Zahra froze in her hiding spot. Did the abbot know of her, know she was here now?

That was the first-time Zahra had heard about the voices. Zahra would have to check with the other sentinels about this. Zahra had felt guilty since then, as Ishmael's sentinel she was supposed to let him know of her and teach him the knowledge he needed to survive. So far, she had done neither. There just never seemed the right time and, well, now too much time had passed and that mistake could cost her, Ishmael, and the world dearly.

By night another obsession took over. She began to record every occurrence related to Sam as it had happened. Sometimes Zahra visited the monastery library to search information to add to the lists she had compiled. It was here she read about the vault of ancestors, where the ashes of every dead brother were stored in earthenware jars. These were sacred to the brotherhood and were believed to form a bridge between the dead and the living. She learnt that during times of trouble or when brothers were promoted to monkhood, these ancestors could be summoned to witness events unfold and give advice.

Zahra turned and looked down at the earthenware jar beside her packed possessions. She felt guilty for stealing Sam's remains from the sacred chamber but knew it was the best thing for his tormented soul. She had meant to do this a long time ago, but as her isolation forced her to confront her inner demons she found herself no longer wanting to release Sam's spirit. He was her rock, the one constant of the last eight long cycles who never judged her or asked anything from her. Zahra believed Sam was the reason she still lived, and on those nightmarish occasions where her victims chased her away from peace and back to the world of the living, she awoke in the damp dark tower with Sam there near her, arms outstretched sympathetically but pointlessly to comfort her. Chimes would pass and Zahra would sit rocking backwards and forwards as she told her ghostly companion of the murders she had committed. These cathartic times were the reason Zahra still lived. Bringing herself back to the present, Zahra picked up the earthenware jar.

Each time she handled it, she was startled by how light it was. The clay bottle was stoppered with cork bound by gold cord. A wax seal covered the front of the bottle and was engraved.

Sam Towelyn
Year of the Drake – Year of the Owl
Rest easy in the arms of the Illuminated one.

Zahra felt Sam before she saw him, the tell-tale prickling of the hairs on the nape of her neck announcing his arrival. He stood facing her, deploring eyes fastened on the jar she held. Zahra's pack rose up off the floor and hovered there. The air felt suddenly charged with energy. She had thought of what she could say to give Sam's spirit the send-off it deserved, but now the moment was here, she felt a lump rise in her throat and her voice deserted her. Her cheeks burned as Zahra realized just how selfish and cruel it had been to keep her tormented friend trapped here. Tears of shame trickled their way down her face. Zahra reached down and grasped the owl-shaped handle of the dagger at her belt then reversed the dagger and drove the handle hard into the clay seal. It shattered to hundreds of pieces that never fell to the floor, but were pulled into a slow orbit around her. Next she cut the gold cord and unravelled it revealing the cork stopper. The stopper pulled free with a tired sigh.

'Safe travels my friend and may your next life be a kinder one,' said Zahra as she upended Sam's ashen remains.

Zahra followed the form of Sam as he floated towards her, his smiling face beaming a look of gratitude that made her spirit soar. Zahra watched Sam as his gaze fixed on something only he could see, then a soft wind reached in and carried him through her and out into the night. Her skin still tingling from Sam's form moving through her, Zahra leaned out of the tower just in time to see his form disintegrate into a burst of fire flies.

It was three chimes before dawn and Zahra's instincts told her that the attack would come soon. She knew this in her heart, because this was when the monastery would be the most vulnerable. Tying her curved sword to her belt a grim smile crept across her face; this would be no easy night for her enemies. She had been touched by death, given the sight to see the dead, and lived. As she tied on her cloth mask over her face, she felt the change come upon her as it always did. Her senses became heightened and power coursed through her body borne by a confidence in her skills no one could take from her. The sensitive, obsessive, and tormented Zahra was forced to sit back and observe, as the killer within her rose to the surface and entered the night, to lead her merry, dance of death…

Chapter 4

Ishmael lay in his room; the dimly lit crystal walls didn't have their usual comforting feel about them. His mind was everywhere, brimming with questions and filling his head with unceasing chatter. The last few days had left him drained but exhilarated. The city of Illume had become trapped in a web of fear following the attack during the festival of lanterns. The Infernals had vanished. Each chime, patrols swept over the city on lunars while heavily armed foot patrols marched through the previously bustling streets with steely determination in their eyes. Residents shut themselves away preferring the safety of their homes and of the crammed taverns, where they could whisper about what had happened, nod sagely, and give their opinions on how the situation should be handled.

Following the attack, life at the monastery continued mostly as normal with the only difference being a sudden increase in the number of chores to be done, and the senior monks seemed to be everywhere at once to hand them out. Ishmael felt like he was a pendulum swinging between dread over what the attacks meant and the excitement that had shattered the dull monotonous routine of monastery life. He ached to leave this place, and yet whenever he came close to doing so, the fear of the unknown outside world froze him. This monastery had become his home and he knew he had a lot to be thankful for. The strict routines of his life as a Brother of Illume gave him an identity that earned him respect and the chance of spiritual advancement that many ordinary professions could not offer. The abbot had taught him a sequence of exercises to control the magic that was stored within his body. If not for these daily exercises, he was sure he would have lost his mind by now. Ishmael knew from experience that to avoid the necessity of that daily ritual would end up with him suffering cripplingly painful cramps accompanied by hallucinations. At those times, he felt so infused with power that his body shook with the effort to control it. His father had warned Ishmael that unless he found a way to harness this energy it would destroy him.

Thinking about his father inevitably led him to the same thoughts of how differently things could have been if he hadn't died. Ishmael wished he could go back in time to tell his father just how much he loved him and how much the business trips and times around the fire sharing stories had meant to him.

As Ishmael contemplated, he became aware of the voices again. Whenever Ishmael concentrated on the voices, they became meaningless babble. He found if he just let them be, then occasionally he could understand them. If he lay down and observed his thoughts without concentrating on the voices, Ishmael found they somehow grabbed him and pulled him into a dream. The dream was always the same stone chamber with no exits and a dying tree surrounded by five stone chairs. The dreams were confusing, and while Ishmael wanted to find out their meaning he lacked the ability to control the dream long enough to learn anything. The other people in the dream often appeared hazy with blurring features and their voices were distorted by echoes. The one thing he felt sure of was that there was something important that they were here to do, and unless their dreaming ability became stronger they would never know what it was.

To avoid more chores Ishmael sought out an old teacher named Zachary who was known for his knowledge in dreaming practices. Zachary was sitting on a chair reading; the old man's knuckles were red and swollen and his hands shook with the effort of holding the book. Usually inflammation affected all his joints and kept him confined to his bed and at the mercy of bed sores and humiliating assisted baths.

'Zachary how about we go to the garden get some fresh air and watch the birds?' Ishmael suggested.

'Oh, yes, Ishmael I would love that! I am tired of this room.' The sky was overcast, but free from the usual biting wind. They sat near the statue of Irdalar where Ishmael dutifully massaged healing balms into Zachary's swollen joints. He told Zachary the recurring dream in as much detail as he could recall.

'Ishmael, we need to recall a few earlier lessons of mine. In order to stay in a dream you need a point of focus that is rooted in everyday life. Something you can turn your attention on, to stop the dream collapsing around you. For this reason you should try focusing on any object or even your hands while you are awake, until they appear in your dreams.'

'Yes I know… from my studies. My hands appear to me in dreams, and I can focus on them easily. What I want to know is how to keep the dream from breaking up when I look around?'

'Ahhhh… only look around with short glances between your surroundings and your hands. The only time you stare at one thing in the dream environment is to use that object as a departure point into a different dream. Does this make sense to you?'

'I think so… I'm not sure.' Ishmael kneaded and stretched out the muscles of Zachary's legs.

'Let me put it another way. Small glances will stop things disintegrating and once you can do this easily you will have enough strength to concentrate on your other senses as well as being able to communicate.'

Ishmael moved to massage the old monks' shoulders but Zachary waved him away indicating he should sit next to him.

'Ishmael, you are quite advanced in the workings of dreams, all you need is patience and practice. However, there are tricks I have learnt that can aid in one's dreaming ability. In your dream focus your energy on that tree; it may be dying but trees are beings that are able to store great amounts of energy. It's dangerous, so tap into it sparingly if you dare to at all. You see, energy from trees can be harnessed in astral or dream states, but if you over extend yourself, the tree can drain the life from you. Trees are ancient beings with a collective consciousness that remembers what men have done to them over time. Given the chance, they will consume you.'

Ishmael as always, had more questions but Zachary asked to be taken back to his rooms to sleep. Ishmael carried the frail man back inside wondering if Zachary was this weak in the world of dreams where he chose to spend so much of his time.

'Lights off, Taita.'

The crystal roof above him cleared and Taita smiled down at him.

'Goodnight Master, Ish,' chirped Taita. 'May your sleep be full of dreams that leave you well rested.'

The room faded to darkness around him. Tonight he would use the advice that Zachary had imparted to him. He directed his breath to each area of his body, feeling his muscles surrender and grow light. As he fell asleep he focused his attention on a spinning coin to lower his consciousness. Slowly his body lost its feeling. The world fell away, the voices were faint but there on the edge of consciousness, and it was to these he shifted his attention, letting them guide him to their location. The tree chamber coalesced around him.

'So far so good…' he thought as he glanced around at his surroundings.

Three of the four others were present, and everything had a fuzziness to it which made it hard to identify who they were. They seemed preoccupied with their own thoughts and the effort of trying to stay in the dream. Ishmael bought his gaze back to his hands again, to focus. Thanks to the long chimes staring at his hands while conscious, they were solid while dreaming, unlike everything else that unravelled if he looked at it too long. Glancing at the tree, Ishmael visualized a cord from his heart center connecting to the tree, then he pushed his awareness along it, probing slowly. It touched something that tugged at his mind, a great anger at his intrusion and yet a shade of curiosity and recognition.

With a rush, energy surged into Ishmael, yet it felt somehow tainted, decaying, dying and Ishmael could feel the trees pain. With the burst of energy Ishmael's senses opened up as in the real world. He could smell the damp chamber and the decay wafting from the tree. Feel the cold floor beneath him and hear someone tapping a tune. Around him the scene solidified. Now what he needed to do was talk to the others so they could finally find out why they were here.

'Where's Raven?' he asked, his voice sounding hollow.

'That's not her name,' replied the sandy-haired man. He was lounging on his chair with one foot propped up on the trunk of the dying tree. Ishmael turned towards him.

'How do you know?'

'All our names are imprinted on the plaques at the top of each chair; each time we come here we appear on the same chair as our name. If you had of been observant then you would know this.'

Ishmael was momentarily stunned at the arrogant nature of the other man.

'Who are you?' he asked.

The man gave a large wolfish grin and rose from his seat. Where his foot had rested on the tree the trunk looked bruised, and a reddish sap dribbled from the gouges his shoe had made. The man looked much larger standing than he had sitting.

'I am Raul,' he said, offering his hand.

Ishmael clasped Raul's hand and couldn't help but notice how the other man's grip encased his own.

'I am Ishmael,' he replied, forcing himself not to wince when the other man's hand slowly crushed his own. Raul's gaze bore into Ishmael's, and as they stood hands clasped, he turned his grip so that his hand was on top. Ishmael realized that Raul was trying to dominate him and started to pull his hand free, but Raul tightened his grip and held on slightly longer than necessary before letting go. Turning away from Raul, Ishmael walked to the chair of the missing girl. Even though he knew he was dreaming he flexed his hand in front of his chest so Raul could not see, to make sure nothing was broken.

The name on the vacant chair read, Brianna Dusk. Ishmael could still feel Raul's gaze on him but deliberately ignored him. He turned to the two women who watched both him and Raul. One of the women stepped forward and offered her hand. She was short and had a homely look to her with a round, slightly pudgy face and long, chestnut pigtails. Kind blue eyes met his as she flashed him a radiant smile.

'My name is Jona and I hail from Acclaro City.'

She paused as if to speak further then stopped herself, her hands patted down the front of her blue dress and she looked embarrassed as she sat back down. Ishmael turned to the remaining woman who was tall and slightly muscled; straight blonde hair mostly covered by a bandana fell about her shoulders.

'Selene,' she said, large doe eyes regarding him coolly. Her voice had a strange lilt to it.

'Where are you from, Selene?' asked Ishmael.

'It doesn't matter where I am from, Ishmael,' she said, a note of challenge in her voice as she crossed her arms over her chest.

'A feisty one,' said Raul from across the room.

'Don't talk to me like some dim-witted maid who you expect to bed Raul,' Selene said. 'You are way out of your league, boy.'

Selene flicked her hair back over her shoulders and Ishmael realized Selene was older than she first appeared. Her sun-bleached skin showed little sign of age, but there was a maturity to her. Raul glared from across the room. His fingers tapped a rhythm on his thighs.

'I could have you eating out of the palm of my hands if I wished,' he sneered. 'You wouldn't last long in my world, bitch. Where I come from women know their place.'

'Is that so, Raul? Well… where I come from men have to earn a woman's respect. We are proud and strong like our men who treat us as equals and our sex doesn't denote our station in life. I know your type, all bluster and muscle and no brains. You are not at your mother's teat anymore boy, so shut-up because your mommy's not here for you to hide behind her skirts.'

Ishmael watched the exchange as they glared at each other. With a snarl, Raul disappeared.

'Coward,' said Selene slumping down in her seat.

Mentally Ishmael knew he should be tiring, but the connection with the tree had allowed that whole conversation with the other Sentinels without the dream collapsing on him. He recalled Zachary's warning and sent his awareness along the bond, visualizing it severing the link like Zachary had taught him, then he panicked. The connection wouldn't shift, it was as if the tree refused to let go.

With the dream beginning to unravel, it seemed to Ishmael that as one of them left the collective dream weakened. Ishmael watched Selene and Jona also fade away, and yet he still felt solid even though half the chamber had collapsed around him.

He made his way to the seat of Brianna Dusk and not knowing what else to do sat down.

Instead of solid stone against his back Ishmael felt the sensation of falling. He panicked for a moment but a feeling of reassurance came over him as the chamber disappeared and was replaced by forest. From somewhere near him a voice whispered one word to Ishmael: 'Witness!'

He stood beneath a huge everswelt tree with rusty chains hanging from its branches. Brianna hung from two such chains, naked and upside down and struggling to escape. A large silver bowl had been placed beneath her, its sides etched with runes. Ishmael tried to speak and move to aid her but couldn't move his legs. A deep singing started up behind Ishmael, and he turned to see a procession of figures carrying lanterns, filing down a slope and into the clearing. They wore white robes with a large red flame over the chest. Despite being close to them, they didn't seem to notice Ishmael, and he realized he was now in the astral and only able to watch this event unfold.

The figures hung the lanterns from the dangling chains then formed a circle around the stricken girl. The swinging lights in the darkness made Ishmael feel sick and giddy. The last two figures moved to stand in front of Brianna.

'Please, I don't know what I have done wrong, let me down… I will tell you whatever you wish to know…why are you doing this. ANSWER ME!' she screamed.

One of the figures knelt on the ground and unwrapped a bundle he had been carrying. He folded it out reverently to reveal a set of knives: silver with inlaid pearl handles that shone in the lantern light.

Brianna's voice was shrill now.

'What are they for? I don't even know you. Please tell me what is going on. Pleeeeeeeease tell me.'

Brianna was sobbing now, and Ishmael ached to help her. The remaining figure slowly pulled back his hood to reveal a kindly face etched with wrinkles and short white hair receding at the front.

'Hush, my child. You are a part of a great event and will take your place in the history of this world. Unlike most you will be remembered.'

Ishmael watched with horror as the man cupped slightly shaking, gnarled hands on Brianna's cheeks and kissed her lightly on the mouth. She tried to pull away, but his grip tightened and he bit down on her lip causing her to scream. The man turned his face away from Brianna and spat something then he removed his robe. Now naked, he accepted a small curved blade from his assistant.

'Escindre, witness this event and know your humble servants act in your stead to restore the world to its natural state of balance. We await your return master, and until then guide us as you can.'

Brianna started screaming again. Blood flowed down her chin to patter into the bowl from her torn lips as the grandfatherly figure proceeded to make incisions down her legs with the paring knife. Bile sat thick in Ishmael's throat as he dry retched. Looking up he found Brianna's eyes on him. Hope flared inside; she could see him... As the old man stood behind her slicing with exaggerated care she found the energy for one last stand.

'Run, Ishmael. They will be coming for you too. Warn the others, we are weak.'

He stood looking back at her and then she screamed.

'RUN BEFORE IT'S TOO LATE.'

Zahra had ceased to exist. She was one with the night, there was no distinction, no separation. From shadow to shadow she flowed, aware of every smell, noise and movement. The night was alive, it cried out for blood, begging her to deliver its due. Through the garden she glided silently, her instincts honed to perfection led her to the north-east entrance of the main house.

As she stormed along the path a figure rose from the bushes ahead. It raised something to its shoulder that looked like a crossbow, and a soft twang split the night. Her curved blade swept out of its sheath with a hiss, interrupting the bolts deadly flight and sending it skittering away. Then she was upon the Infernal, which had dropped the crossbow in favor of its strong clawed hands that sliced out at her stomach and neck.

Zahra ducked the higher strike, held her blade vertical to parry the lower, and let her momentum carry her, shoulder-first into her assailant's legs. Bone snapped beneath her as the creature was slammed to the ground. Before it could recover Zahra rolled along its body turning over once and smashing her elbow down into its face, crushing fangs and skull. Yellow blood fountained, and the shrill cry from the Infernal was cut off suddenly from a reverse slice of her blade across its throat.

Within moments Zahra was back on her feet. Ahead the door to the house stood open, a crystal bolt had been fired into the wall near the entrance. She had used these bolts herself on occasion, a type of crystal that blocked the signal of energy to other crystalline configurations, perfect for negating Jaldurial house security.

'RUN BEFORE IT'S TOO LATE.'

The words hit Ishmael like thunderbolts and he was flung backwards out of the dream into the deep gloom of his chamber. Brianna had seen him, how? Ishmael was lathered in sweat and fear was thick in his mouth, the taste of rusting metal. He leaned out of bed and vomited on the floor. Deep down he knew it was not just another dream. The darkness of his chamber was suffocating.

'Taita light please.'

The chamber stayed dark. The lively house spirit didn't appear.

'Taita, light please,' he repeated, trying to control the panic rising in his voice.

Once again there was no answer. Perplexed, Ishmael crawled from his bed but his hand landed in his vomit and he cursed softly before wiping it on the sheets. He tried to force his thoughts away from Brianna.

I need to talk to the abbot, he thought.

Ishmael took a few steps towards the door and stopped suddenly. The door was open. In any normal house this would not be a problem, but in Jaldurial houses the house spirit used its power to control the doors and maintain security. Ishmael stood staring at the doorway. It looked the same as always except now cloaked in darkness, it seemed menacing. Normally the hallway was lit by crystals but these too were powered by Taita and it seemed she was gone. There was a muffled thump from somewhere in the house. Ishmael held his breath, ears straining to pick up the softest sound…

Maybe I imagined it.

After that dream, who wouldn't be jumpy? He moved to the doorway and slowly peered out into the corridor, first right then left.

It appeared empty and safe, but his animal instincts were screaming for him to get away from here and out of the house. In the back of his mind Brianna's warning repeated itself:

They will be coming for you too.

The quickest route to the abbot's room was through the kitchen and dining hall. Half way along the corridor he felt the hairs on his neck stand to attention and he felt that he was not alone.

They will be coming for you too.

Ishmael shook his head as if he could dislodge the insistent warning. He turned quickly to glance behind him but the corridor was empty. Breathe, he told himself, and purposefully took two deep, slow breaths as he crept to the next passage. He turned left towards the kitchens from where another thud came followed by an erratic thumping noise. Down the passage he could see the familiar soft glow of the fires lit beneath the food cauldrons. Looking back down the corridor behind him the shadows seemed thicker and swelled with possibilities of death and violence.

Warn the others, we are weak.

Ishmael shuddered as goose bumps chilled to life all over his body. He moved quickly along the corridor to the kitchen, the smell of gruel and fresh loaves of bread heavy in the air. He eased himself through the doorway. The large oak cutting bench sat covered in half-prepared food. Two cauldrons were at the top of the square room and the drumming continued to come from near there. Inching forward, Ishmael feared what he would see, and sweat clasped his hands and tickled his neck. He snatched up a nearby cleaver large cleaver, holding it out in front as if it of its own volition could protect him.

Unable to wait any longer, he pushed away from the bench and stepped around to the cauldrons. The cook they nicknamed Crumb lay on his back, with his own cleaver imbedded in his skull. Blood pooled around his shoulders, a crimson cloak of fleeing life and his feet drummed up and down, caught in the throes of seizure.

Ishmael gasped then cursed himself; whoever did this could still be here. He knelt beside Crumb's head. The eyes had rolled back showing the whites, and his mouth had filled with blood that softly gurgled in his throat. Afraid the attacker would come back, Ishmael pulled a towel from beneath the table and placed it under the dying man's legs to try to stop the noise, and then he took Crumb's hands in his own. The dying man's convulsions slowed then stopped and his head lolled to the side.

'Hasten forward, good soul, burn brightly forever with the stars.'

Ishmael was just getting up when he noticed the second body. It lay in the doorway to the dining hall. The monk lay face down with a spear through his back, and behind him a trail of blood led into the dining hall. From where he knelt next to Crumb, Ishmael stared at the surprised look on the dead man's face then looked down at the wavering cleaver in his hands. His hands and feet felt cold, and the full impact of what was happening struck him hard. Two people were dead and there might be many more.

Struggling to his feet on legs that had become as heavy as rocks and threatened to forget how to work, he stepped over the dead body and into the dining hall. A series of muffled screams cut through the night and shocked Ishmael into action. He sprinted across the hall weaving in and out of tables and benches towards the opposite exit. As Ishmael ran, something broke from the shadows to his left. It was spider quick, leaping from table to table, cutting across to intercept his run. Its mocking laughter made his blood turn cold as it pumped loudly in his ears, and his vision began to narrow. Ishmael could beat most in a footrace but this was no normal creature. As they came closer to collision he saw it moved in a crouch, propelled forward on strong limbs. Its skin was translucent, giving view to its disgusting insides. It was the face that disturbed him most. The face of a child twisted and shaped by hatred into a grimace of malevolence.

Brianna's warning shrieked in his head again. Run Before it's too late.

Ishmael rounded the last table, veering to his right, legs pumping furiously… and tripped. The bench for the last table had been carelessly left out in the aisle. Pain exploded across his shins as he flew forwards crashing to the ground, and the cleaver spun out of his hand and slid away under a table.

⁂

Zahra pushed herself harder; she had long ago memorized the layout of the monastery. The hallways were empty in this part of the building with most of the quarters being to the west.

Ishmael chose to stay separate to his brothers so maybe the Infernals would have missed him she hoped.

Then she was there, sword held above her as she slid into an empty room of crumpled bedding and a rank smell. 'Damn! Think, think, think. Where would he be?'

A series of screams came from the west. Zahra sped off back up the passage, this time heading west towards the kitchens. Faint footsteps came from up ahead. Around the corner she ran, blade sweeping down at her enemies. At the last moment, Zahra realized they were monks and turned the blade sideways before barrelling into them. Their screams nearly deafened her.

'Get out…GO!' she screamed at them.

Zahra's mind ran ahead of her. Ishmael would go to who he trusted.

Someone he thought could protect him…the abbot! He's going to the abbot.

The kitchen was occupied by death. Zahra leapt onto the table turning into a forward roll and coming neatly to her feet not breaking stride. He was near. She could feel it like an extension of herself. Into the dining hall she raced, near the opposite entrance a hideous Infernal sat straddled on something. A hoarse cry carried to her, and she reeled. It was Ishmael.

'Ishmael!'

Zahra covered the distance of the hall quickly, and yet it was too slow. The Infernal held a jagged knife and slammed it down into Ishmael below it. Zahra saw Ishmael go limp and the Infernal lick blood from its fingers. As she reached them, the Infernal turned a child's face smeared with blood towards her, and Zahra smashed her blade through its face, knocking it off Ishmael.

'ISHMAEL… Hello! Can you hear me? Please move… Ishmael…'

Chapter 6

Haakon awoke to a world of frantic activity. He was sitting behind one of his men; his arms had been tied around the other man's waist, and they were mounted upon cular lizards. These large lizards were very agile, especially through mountainous terrain such as this. His face felt red raw from where it rubbed against the rider's leather vest, his throat was parched, and when he attempted to speak all that came out was a dry croak.

They were moving fast, and to his right the road dropped away to a steep ravine hidden by the darkness. Slowly he managed to turn his head to the left where far below emerged a sea of glittering lights. The movement made him wince as pain pounded through his head and trembling muscles. Haakon knew this path well; they were in the northern Tiarioc Mountains to the south of Karfael City. This path would take them down to the Tunoka grasslands then two days to the west and the clan house.

Haakon lost his sense of time after that, only dimly recalling the early dawn break where his men dripped cool water down his throat, concern etched on their faces above him. Pungent herbs were rubbed under his nose, the smell preventing him from sleeping. His eyes were so heavy and his body incapable of movement; even so occasional slices of conversation reached down to the inner levels where he had descended.

'Make sure he doesn't sleep; if he loses consciousness we may not be able to call him back… so much damage to his energy body, he may never travel the astral rivers again…'

The next time his awareness cleared they were on the Tunoka grasslands. Haakon recognized the distant lights of Culchar city to the North West and the river they were about to cross was the Shattered river. At some point, they had changed the cular mounts for drakes, which with their long legs and speed were a much better choice for the grasslands. He knew they were close to the grotto now that had formed around the crashed citadel from the age of the Severing that had become home to the Kenzu clan. Haakon had chosen the citadel due to the immediate privacy that the large wooded grove provided. From here they could spot any potential threats from their lofty tree outposts. While not the ideal location for a clan, Haakon had been forced to flee the castle they had previously occupied in the land of Scuttle to the far West.

For days the king of Scuttle had besieged the Kenzu clan, his ballista's and trebuchets demolishing much of the old castle before Haakon had decided to act and depose clan leader Christof then personally deliver his head to the king. Forbidden from staying in the lands of Scuttle, the Kenzu began the slow march to find a new home and had found a suitable one here within the bounds of the old empire of Thantos which was still ruled by King Chez Taloun.

With the change in location, clan leader Haakon used this time of upheaval to cease contracts to focus on the protection of the Coterie of the Heart like they had long ago agreed to do.

The pace slowed as they entered the woods, and Haakon began to notice his sentries as they rode by the well-hidden men. It was near impossible to arrive unannounced to this nest of vipers. Haakon was proud of his people they survived and adapted, his people loved him for restoring honor to the Kenzu, and they would die for him. He knew however that loyalty was a frail thing. One bad decision or failure to act with strength and confidence could shatter that trust. He wouldn't make the same mistakes Christof had.

Haakon longed to ask questions regarding Latasha, but speech just wouldn't come, and his body was overcome with weakness. When they finally halted, strong hands lifted Haakon from the drake onto a stretcher which was hurried away to the physician under an escort of grim looking men.

A large bath had been run, and its steaming water was clogged with the sweet sickly smell of herbs. They removed his clothes before lowering him in. He would have screamed if he could have, but once again his voice deserted him allowing only a hiss to escape. The bath water felt to scolding, and yet his skin had hardly reddened. His muscles began to spasm and Haakon could feel the pulse points of his body beat in time with his heart. The aches in his head and muscles dimmed a little and his eyes and ears cleared bringing sight and sound flooding back to him.

Inwardly Haakon groaned as two large, matronly women entered the chamber with ruddy cheeks and their hair tied up in severe buns. Their sharp tongues made short work of his men that lingered here as they shooed them away. The two women were twin sisters called Avril and Cathleen and while he was here in the clan house they appointed themselves his personal nurses. It wasn't that Haakon disliked them because they were inefficient or didn't show him the customary respect, it was just that they made him feel like a little boy again who was always in trouble.

'Let's have ya up then m' lord,' said Avril as she tucked her arms under his and hoisted him to a standing position.

'An' don't be shy, we seen it all before,' cackled Cathleen as she started to scrub his body with a bristled brush, Haakon put on the most disgusted scowl he could muster and his eyes narrowed dangerously; it felt like the brush was peeling the skin from his body.

Cathleen rapped the brush end smartly against his forehead. 'Don't be lookin' at me with that attitude, m' lord, it's not our fault you're in this mess, it's your own stupid fault aint it?'

Then he was dumped back down into the bath, the water sloshed up over his face, and he swallowed a mouthful that left him gasping and choking.

He was dragged up again. 'Out ya get, m' lord, can't have ya catching a chill, now can we?' said Avril. She clasped his chin in one hand and turned his face to look at her. 'You need a good woman, milord, ya not getting any younger, are ya? High time ya settled down to grow some children.'

Cathleen began to roughly towel down his body.

Haakon managed to croak out one word amidst all the spluttering. 'Latasha!'

Both women stopped and looked at each other, their eyes softening. Cathleen put both her hands on his cheeks.

'All we know is that she in a bad way, and on her way here as we speak, what ya did was a brave but foolish thing, and it might be the last time you travel the astral river. You could have been killed, and what a mess we would have been in then. No disrespect,' m' lord added Avril.

'But she ain't that good woman we been talkin about, always comin' and goin' as she pleases and so full of secrets. Secrets pickle the heart and make it rot,' said Cathleen. 'You need a good human lass, not one of those ancients who you have to watch staying young while you wither away before'm as your body an ya wits fail ya. You can have almost any woman here, m' lord, so why go camping in a distant valley?'

The twins herded him into his bed where they spoon fed him a syrupy mixture that lured him gently to the world of dreams.

When Haakon next awoke, it was to the rich smell of roasted fowl. The double doors to the room swung inward as old Faustus the physician entered carrying a platter loaded with duck and braised vegetables, the tools of his trade hung in pouches from his belt which he removed after giving Haakon his food.

'Food first then business,' grunted Faustus.

As Haakon ate, Faustus crushed herbs with a mortar and pestle. When the hunger within him finally began to dwindle, it was replaced with thirst. Reading his master's needs, Faustus passed him a water skin from which he drank deeply.

His immediate needs now seen to, Faustus ordered Haakon to lie on his back. 'This is wormtile root. I need to apply it to your energy centers so it can help slow the loss of energy from them. Your energy body is very weak and it is slowly draining away, and unless we can stop it you will die a slow death.'

Haakon unexpectedly grinned.' 'Do what you have to Faustus but just keep the twins away from me.'

The old man chuckled as he worked. 'Nothing to fear, even the gods tread carefully if the twins are about.'

'Faustus, where is Latasha?'

'You have been asleep for two days, Haakon. Latasha arrived here with your men last night.' As Haakon began to rise, the old man firmly pushed him down, the corners of his eyes wrinkled as he leant in. 'She's bad Haakon, really bad.'

'I have to go to her,' Haakon said, feeling the anger within him rising. 'Why wasn't I woken?'

'There is nothing you can do for her. Latasha is in a coma, and her injuries are grave. Latasha will never walk again; I had to remove one of her kidneys and a part of her spleen. If she awakes and I mean if, the chances are she will be severely brain damaged due to pressure on the brain from her head injuries...'

The image of the last time Haakon had seen her was frozen in his mind, he had thought her dead.

Faustus finished applying the salve and helped Haakon dress. 'I will take you to her but you must not disturb her; the smallest amount of stress could kill her.'

Faustus led Haakon along the rope bridge walkways, and the proud assassin had to lean on his old friend for support as he was taken to the physician's hut. The afternoon sky was grey and fought a losing battle against an onrushing horde of storm clouds from the west as shade loon bird's laments echoed eerily through the trees.

Nothing in his life as an assassin could prepare him for the sight that awaited him when he entered Latasha's room. He had seen innocents slaughtered in the name of justice or for political advancement, walked through blood-soaked battlefields choked with corpses and in turn he had committed many atrocities himself to further himself and his clan. But here now with his lover lying battered before him did he realize why he had never before allowed anyone to get close to him. It gave his enemies a weapon, a way of hurting him, goading him into making foolish decisions while ensnared in the chains of emotion. Of course, he had managed to avoid this pitfall for many cycles of his life, but Latasha was different. She had commanded his attention.

The blue luminescence of the sun blazer fish tank that lit the room enhanced the fey features of Latasha's face. Although treated and cleaned the comatose ancient's wounds were very visible; her silver hair had been shaved off and her skull was swollen. The bruising of her face had deepened to black and purples that draped over the front of her neck and breast like some obscene necklace.

Haakon swallowed the lump in his throat and moved to her side, slowly examining her as behind him Faustus explained how each joint had had to be broken again for it to be reset. Lovingly Haakon examined her injuries as he forced himself to witness the atrocities committed on the woman he loved. Her soft white belly was now a mass of centipede stitch scars, but the worst was her legs, which had been twisted loose from the hip sockets and shattered. The broken lumps of bone still protruded from the skin in some places and Haakon knew that Faustus was right. Latasha would never walk again; her feet had danced their last elegant steps on this earth.

$$\text{Chapter 7}$$

Haakon ordered bedding to be brought with a pallet so he could stay by Latasha's side. That night he bathed Latasha slowly and carefully with healing balms then massaged creams into her wounds. He talked to her about everything that had happened and what they would do once she was well again and how he would take her far from here to care for her and never let her down again.

The storm that night was ferocious; it tore its way through the darkness like a child searching for a lost toy. Branches above them snapped and Haakon was thankful for the expert work that had gone into building this place. Hail stones peppered the roof tops, and the structures groaned with strain as the storm reached its peak a few chimes before dawn. Through it all Haakon lay watching Latasha, exhausted in his helplessness. Was this to be his lot now? Was he to sit idly in the face of these events, or act?

As the storm calmed, so did Haakon's mind, and for the first time in a long while he admitted to himself he wasn't sure what the hell was going on. It bugged him that even after all he knew about the coterie of the Heart, he knew little about Latasha herself. His former master had commented how she had come to him on his first day as clan master and Haakon wondered how many of the former leaders had also been visited by Latasha. After all, she was an ancient and they apparently lived hundreds of cycles. He had already searched through the contract ledger when Latasha had first come to renew it, and there was little mention of her. As he dozed he thought of the clan book which held the history of the Kenzu and expanded on all the events that had shaped their clan. Later he would search there.

Sleep delivered him to a palace of ivory where he caught glimpses of Latasha disappearing into rooms or rushing away down halls, her tinkling laughter teasing him to follow her and find her. He awoke drenched in sweat with Latasha's laughter fresh in his ears, and reality brought him back to his bleak observation post of the only one that could answer all his questions.

Haakon reached over to Latasha and tucked the bedding tight around her still form. He sat watching her silently until the grey morning light sifted through the shutters announcing the arrival of dawn. Haakon used the water in a basin to rinse the sweat from his body and slipped on a new shirt, and exited the room pulling the door shut behind him.

Fifteen feet ahead through the murky light, a sentry turned suddenly, his hand poised on his sword hilt. Their eyes met and the guard relaxed, ducking his head in deference to Haakon, who let his own smile reach his eyes. Haakon had only caught a guard asleep at his post once, and the poor soul had not lived to tell the story. Haakon had drowned the guard whose frantic splashing had brought others rushing to the scene of the disturbance.

'Never fall asleep at your post. Weakness will not be tolerated,' Haakon had said calmly, as the drowning guard thrashed beneath him, his struggles getting weaker and weaker until his life was washed away. Since that day, Haakon's men had become sharper and more efficient.

You can change much with a single death, he thought to himself without remorse as he headed into the house proper.

Haakon's personal chambers were at the center of the house, enabling his guards to keep a tight ring of security around him. Above this there was another level consisting of only one chamber, which housed all clan valuables. The guards opened the do to Haakon's room as he approached. He felt stronger today, directed by a sense of purpose.

Haakon was surprised to see the hidden door within his chamber open, golden light spilling out. Shaking his head in wonder, Haakon entered the room that was the heart of his clan.

He emerged to the smell of cinnamon tea and sweet breads, which had been laid out between two cushions atop a rug with the clan symbol on it. On the cushion opposite him sat Alexis with his back stiff and a smirk painted upon his hairless face. The teenage boy placed both hands on the floor in front of him and then dipped his torso forward touching his head to the floor as he bowed.

Haakon waited for him to finish before indicating that Alexis should pour tea for them. The chamber was meticulous, not a trace of dust on any surface. Famous clan weapons and armor adorned the walls along with perfectly painted portraits of all leaders the clan had known. At the far end of the room upon a pedestal lay the clan ledger which was protected by several deadly traps. The wall behind the pedestal was a bookcase, full of valuable ancient and modern writings.

Alexis spent most of his time here in this room, recording every event concerning the clan as it happened. It was also his role to be up to date with the latest happenings in the outside world and keep a thorough documentation of clan history.

'How do you always know?' asked Haakon.

'It is my place to foresee what your needs may be,' replied Alexis in his high voice, breaking with puberty. 'I would be a poor choice for this role if I failed to attend to you properly.'

Haakon outlined what he needed as they ate.

'The attack on myself and Latasha changes thing dramatically, and there are certain things that need to be put into action. We knew this day would come where the clan's honor and strength would be tested. The problem is that we don't know which enemy has dared to test us. The sentinels guarding the coterie of the Heart should be on their way to the safe house with their wards, but they need to be contacted anyway.

'Haakon, Faustus told me you may never be able to access the astral ever again due to the injury you sustained.'

'That is true Alexis, and that makes contacting them harder since they will only answer my messages not anyone else's.'

I want you to delve through the clan archives and find any mention of Latasha Meldoriel. I also need information about potential enemies who may have found out about Latasha's connection to the Severing. No matter what happens, the magic cannot fall into the wrong hands!'

Alexis sat quietly sipping his tea as he committed all his orders to memory

'How long do ancients live, Alexis?'

'Most live between two hundred to one thousand years. The most common cause of death in ancients beyond two hundred years old is from loneliness or suicide. They begin to live in the past and wrap themselves in solitude, not bothering about their physical needs but reliving memories of days gone by. Suicide is less painful. What age is Latasha?' asked Alexis. He poured more tea for them.

'When Latasha first visited me to find out if I would honor the contracts, she was careful not to answer personal questions about herself and said that it was safer not knowing the details.'

'Alexis set his cup down. 'Do you want me to contact the Sentinels of the coterie then?'

'Yes, Raul Tomfalen, Brianna Dusk, Jona Felzarun, Selene Winsele and Ishmael Shantari are all in great danger. This is what we have spent so long preparing for,' replied Haakon.

'As you know, Alexis it is only proven members of the clan that know about the coterie and the magic they hold. The remainder of our clan believe magic to be lost for good just like the masses. The huge fortune paid to protect the coterie until magic is released means that the Kenzu need not fear lack of wealth or resources and our best interest is to see these five kept live until the rightful time when magic is released again.'

'So, master Haakon you don't trust Latasha?'

'Latasha has had three hundred years of dealings with our clan, and yet so little is known about her. I know her but not whether she can be trusted.'

'How do we know if any of the coterie have been killed?' Alexis asked.

'Only by the sentinels alerting us since I cannot enter the astral to converse with them. It's possible they have left messages that we are yet to receive.

'Maybe the reason you don't have further information is that when you deposed Christof you killed the only source of knowledge available to you besides our records,' Alexis pointed out. 'It seems to me that at least some knowledge passed on from master to master would be spoken only, never to be recorded.'

There was an awkward silence. Then Haakon spoke, his voice filled with restrained menace.

'And of what concern is that of yours? I don't need you to remind me of clan law. For clan safety I need to know about Latasha and how she came to hold such sway over us, what her last movements were, and with whom she spent time with or was in danger from. If clan laws must be broken to serve our purpose in this, then I will do so and answer for it afterwards.'

Alexis choked on his tea and began coughing uncontrollably while his eyes never left Haakon's and the knife that Haakon was now deftly spinning through his fingers.

Trying to apologize, he started coughing again. Haakon stood up and looked down at Alexis. A part of him wanted to bury the knife in the boy's throat, and yet an unfamiliar part of him mocked him over how easily he lost control these days.

Taking a long slow breath, Haakon hurled the blade he was

holding at the opposite wall and was rewarded with a loud thud as it imbedded itself into the wood up to the hilt.

'Alexis. I will only say this once. Don't ever question my orders again. If you think you are irreplaceable then think again. As for your precious records, it was a small loss compared to the ruin Christof would have delivered the clan into. Do you understand me?'

Alexis coughed and bobbed his head, his eyes wide with fear.

Chapter 8

With the Infernal in its death throes, Zahra knelt down over Ishmael.

'ISHMAEL… Hello! Can you hear me? Please move… Ishmael…'

Of course, he didn't answer her; he just kept mouthing something silently over and over.

Zahra ripped Ishmael's robe open to see the extent of the damage, and she knew instantly that it wasn't good. A large puncture wound gushed blood to the left of his sternum. Two deep gashes split open his stomach, oozing steadily with each labored breath he took. There were other wounds he had been dealt, but Zahra quickly deduced he would not die from them. She struggled out of her backpack as she continued to look around for any more danger. Her fingers trembled with the knot tying her small blanket to her pack, then losing patience she cut it free. She folded the blanket in two and placed it over Ishmael's chest and abdomen, taking careful note of where the wounds were so she could apply pressure to them to stem the bleeding.

Ishmael's mouth gaped open and closed and a trail of blood slid from his lips, winding its way down his chin. His pale green eyes had lost their feral intensity and appeared glazed over as they dimmed to greet death.

Zahra slapped him hard across the cheek.

'You can't go now, you bastard!'

Hot tears of frustration washed down Zahra's cheeks. This was not how their first meeting was to have been. Blood started to seep through the blanket onto her hands, its copper stickiness heavy in the air.

Ishmael's head lolled to the opposite side leaving the white pressure mark imprinted on his pale face

'Don't die dammit!' she pleaded.

Placing her hand against Ishmaels' neck, she could feel his fluttering pulse. He was close to death now and she knew that she could do nothing more for Ishmael. Ahead of her up the aisle came a soft rustle of cloth. Zahra had her dagger in the air before she even registered that the approaching figure was the small and aged abbot. He held a bowl overflowing with some type of plant to his chest; even so with ridiculous ease he deflected the dagger with his robe and shuffled forward.

'Easy, daughter…I am a friend.'

Kneeling at the opposite side of Ishmael's body, he gently removed the blanket covering Ishmael. Zahra started to object, but he looked up at her with such kindness in his eyes that she sat there silent watching. His voice startled her out of her reverie.

'Many have died here tonight, and more will. We can fight back, but if Ishmael dies it have all been for nothing. You cannot let that happen.'

The abbot lifted the large leaves of the plant one at a time, draping them over Ishmael's chest. Zahra noticed that the top sides of the leaves was a rich green but the underside which was being placed over the wounds was a purplish color and it started to quiver as if alive when it got close to the flesh. He continued to work even as he answered her unspoken question.

'It is known as the Maiden's Kiss, a rare but useful plant for protecting deep wounds. The plant thrives on flesh and the parasites found within the bodies of living creatures. The leaves harden and protect the wounded areas from any further damage due to exposure.

However, he can still die from internal bleeding, so you must find help soon. Of course, as with most miracles we encounter in this world, there is a price for the use of such a plant.'

With the worst wounds covered, the abbot started to cover the deep gash over Ishmael's left rib, the stumps of his two severed fingers, and the severely torn bicep muscle of his left arm. Sounds of battle had been steadily coming closer, and looking behind them Zahra could see a cluster of monks backing towards them as they struggled to fight a group of Infernals. The peaceful monks had little real fighting experience though their forms they practiced were based on combat. It was only their superior numbers that kept the hellish creatures at bay. Looking back at the abbot she saw he was unconcerned. The calm radiating from him rolled over her and forced away some of the fear that had taken hold.

'The Maiden's Kiss will not leave its host willingly; therefore it is of vital importance that every part is removed or it will gradually take over Ishmael's body. There are signs that indicate when this is starting to happen. He will start wanting meat all the time and will eat it raw. Cooked is of no use because fire destroys the nutrients the plant needs. Keep a close eye on him for if this plant is left unchecked its need will push him to attack other living beings and the death toll will be terrible.'

More brothers of Illume continued to enter the hall to help defend them and now he was finished, the Abbot motioned to Zahra to help lift Ishmael. They carried him away from the desperate situation of the monks as the Infernals tore into them from both sides. Shuffling down a long hallway, they came to two monks who unbolted the door to the front of the temple. While the two guards watched for enemies, Zahra and the abbot lay Ishmael on the ground. The abbot reached into his pocket and removed some sort of whistle that let out a shrill wail when he blew it. As she stood staring he caught her eye and motioned her to keep watch. She cursed herself as she realized her blade was back in the hall as was one of her daggers. Pulling the other short blade from her belt, Zahra turned to watch the night around them. The guard beside her noticed Zahra's reaction to the strange whistle.

'He calls his mount,' the monk said without turning to face her. 'It is the finest breed of Lunar, you will see.'

Above them Zahra saw a shape gliding from the night sky, the undersides of the Lunars wings covered in beautiful silver spirals. The remaining monks protecting them began retreating from the house towards them. One of the Infernals broke through, leaping high over the defenders and bounding towards Ishmael and the abbot. Its wet, red skin glistened and thick black hair sprouted from its face, legs, and arms.

Rolling sideways, Zahra intercepted its charge and waiting for the Infernal to be almost upon her before ducking underneath and slashing into the soft inner thigh of its leg. The Infernal roared and batted a heavy fist into Zahra's shoulder, knocking her to the ground. Then it fell on her, smashing her again with another punch, its head now above hers as it tried to force her neck back and tear out her throat with its teeth.

Zahra's blade was trapped beneath the brute's chest, she managed to get her right hand up in time to protect her face and neck. As it moved in to bite, she plunged her thumb hard up into its eye socket and felt the soft orb burst. The Infernal thrashed about, raining down blows with its massive fists as it towered above her. Her left arm now freed, Zahra used her last energy reserves to lift up her torso and drive the blade deep into her attacker's throat. The beast moaned then slid off her.

The abbot stood looking down at her, concern masking his kind features as Zahra extended an arm for him to help her up. Pain blossomed sharp and angry along her ribs, and her right collarbone ached terribly while her left eye had already begun to swell shut. He hoisted her up onto the Lunar's back and into its saddle while behind her in a second saddle Ishmael had already been secured.

'Can you fly?' asked the abbot urgently, and she nodded. 'Then go, and may the light illuminate your journey,' he said.

Zahra needed no further urging; she slipped off the shutters on the Lunar's eyes and it rose effortlessly with beats of its powerful wings. As they left Zahra glanced below and saw the abbot fighting three Infernals. Unlike his dead, inexperienced brethren around him, he could fight, and as she watched the mesmerizing dance, she vowed silently to make sure his valiant stand and that of all the brothers of Illume would never be forgotten.

Chapter 9

Above the battle there was one other who watched the outcome with interest. He drifted on the evening air currents, enjoying the turbulent wind on his wings. The attack had failed and though much damage had been caused to the temple and brotherhood of Illume their target was escaping into the night. Zacriel smiled. First Flame, Dalwyn Trevlon would not be happy with proceedings. The fact that he had been forced to collaborate with Trevlon was infuriating, but the man had knowledge that Zacriel needed. Trevlon might be a fool but he was smart fool and only doled out enough knowledge to force Zacriel's acquiescence.

'His day will come,' thought Zacriel. 'And then I shall rend and tear, smash and break him.'

He tasted blood and realized his teeth had bitten through his lower lip. The smell and taste stirred violence within him, and he had a wicked thought. His mission was to observe only and make sure all went as planned; however, blood lust was upon him, and since he could not vent three hundred years of frustration and hatred on Dalwyn Trevlon, then he would take it out on this puny monk and his pitiful protector. Tucking his glorious golden wings to his sides, he swooped down upon his unsuspecting prey.

Zahra directed the Lunar up away from the temple in a course leading over the city, heading towards the jewelled lands that clustered around the foot of the mountain to the east. Her left eye was useless now and the pain from her wounds competed for her attention.

When the silver spirals covering the Lunar's, wings burst into light and a loud keening came from the mount beneath her the hairs on her arms and neck sprang to attention, it could only mean one thing. Danger!

Turning her head fully to the left to compensate for her blindness, Zahra looked up as a flash of gold shot by and something slammed against the side of her head. For a moment, she was only aware of the blood pounding in her ears and a stickiness on the side of her face.

The Lunar frantically tried to gain height, but its efforts were hampered by a buffeting wind. Zahra tried scanning below them for any sign of their attacker.

Nothing. Wait! There…something getting larger, sheathed in gold.

Zahra realized the shimmering gold was the creature's wings. She reached into her boot and retrieved her remaining knife. The attacker moved fast and then she saw before her an Infernal, more disturbingly human than any she had ever encountered. It landed on the mount directly in front of her near the Lunar's head, crouching with its taloned feet digging deep into the Lunar's flesh, its impressive wings spread behind it like a sail slowing its flight even more while holding its prey immobile. Zahra overcame her temporary surprise and slashed the knife at the Infernal's throat. The blade was bashed away with such force it fell from her grasp and disappeared below.

As she looked up into the face of her enemy she was stunned. Never had she seen such beauty. A face with perfect proportions, framed by a strong square jaw line and high cheek bones, slightly arched eyebrows perched above storm-cloud colored eyes that promised pain and torment unfathomable to any living being. Zahra tore her gaze away from those penetrating eyes. It stroked the back of a knuckle down the side of her face, and she spat in defiance.

'What are you waiting for? Kill me!'

The Infernal's other hand slashed down and she felt the saddle's tension release. Abruptly the hand stroking her face grabbed her jaw hard and pushed her sideways.

Zahra slipped from the saddle and would have plunged to her death if her right foot hadn't become caught in the stirrup. Suspended by her foot, she watched the infernal push away from the Lunar, which once freed, pin wheeled sharply away towards the city below. The Infernal had no trouble keeping pace with the wounded Lunar, and Zahra realized it was not enough for this creature to kill them— it wanted them to suffer. Above her in the second saddle Ishmael still sat slumped forward, motionless. Zahra reached up to grasp the stirrup that was painfully twisting her ankle. Finally, on the third try she managed to grab it and pull herself up by the pommel. Secured by only one strap, the saddle slipped and tilted to the side jolting her and wrenching her shoulder muscles. Somehow she managed to get her ankle free and was again holding on with both hands, her right leg draped over the mount's back. Some would have called it fate or the luck of the gods, because as the Lunar banked tightly to the left, Zahra tipped upright onto its back again. Another blinding flash of gold, and blood sprayed her arms and face as the Infernal darted past, gouging a great tear along the Lunar's wing joint. Geysers of blood fell like red hellish rain, and Zahra knew the Lunar was almost done. As they spiralled earthward Zahra managed to guide the dying beast out of its free fall and level out. Down they swept to a height just above the ground, tearing along cobblestone streets, extinguishing lamps as they sped along. Two guardsmen cried out and threw themselves to the ground as they raced past. An occasional glance behind told Zahra that the hellish attacker was hot on their heels, its superior manoeuvrability enabling it to keep up with ease.

They continued to elude their pursuer through the upper and middle levels of the city and Zahra led the chase between crowded villas.

Ahead on the right a cavernous mouth lay open, it was one of the entrances to the city's underbelly and without a second thought Zahra directed them into its oily depths. The Lunar was slowing now as its life drizzled away.

Flying erratically they dipped and swerved through slum clogged arterial tunnels, startling their unlucky inhabitants, who feverishly muttered prayers while signing against evil as they hurtled past. Now the tunnels widened out and branched at a fork. Large signs pointed right toward the lunar caverns where the moth like mounts were bred and trained, but Zahra knew there was little chance of escape as the penned in caves led to a dead end. She chose left and they sped into another cavern.

Zacriel was enjoying himself immensely; the look of surprise and fear on the woman's face, the Lunars terror, all came together to form the perfect experience. He was drawing this out; it had been so long since he had been able to terrorize the living. The woman surprised him with her strength and resistance; she had spat in his face, found the strength to pull herself back up after he tried to tear her out of the saddle and now she led him on a wild chase believing they had a chance of escape. How pitifully misguided she was! He hated to remember he was once like her, full of hope, love, and weakness. He had chosen power, and his life of evil and cruelty had eventually turned the eyes of the dark gods upon him. In recognition of his deeds they had finally rewarded him with the finest honor of demon hood. By the time the war ended he would have left and taken his rightful place in the halls of the damned, but the Severing had changed everything. Magic had been cut away from the world and the gates leading to the Celestial and Infernal lands were locked trapping legions of Infernals and Celestials in the mortal's world.

Tiring of the chase, Zacriel closed in on the dying Lunar. He swept in underneath and flew with his back to the ground as he ripped upwards with his claws, tearing open the soft underbelly of his prey, viscous contents warm with life spilling down around him. He flipped right side up, slowing his pace as the Lunar plunged over him heading towards the cavern floor.

Zacriel gloated with pleasure as the woman in desperation tried to get the dying Lunar to respond to her commands, but it was too late. They plummeted downwards to meet the ground, skidding and sliding through the rubble of some old ruined structure, before slamming into a wall that collapsed around them raising a veil of dust and debris.

Beating his wings to retain height, Zacriel hovered while he watched for movement below.

It was time to end this and return with the monk, making use of him to pave the way for the return of magic to the world.

Wings spread wide Zacriel let his hatred drive him. He could feel her fear now as she tried frantically to release herself and became aware of him still above her. Zacriel expected to see fear yet all he saw was defiance and acceptance of what was to come.

Then the world fell apart. A thunderous crack echoed through the cavern, and the ruins burst into blue light. Molten heat engulfed Zacriel, and he was thrown backwards hitting the ground sideways, rolling to a stop with blue flames dancing over him. Burning… burning! He wanted to scream, but fire gushed down his throat evaporating his cry. His skin bubbled and split, and his glorious wings burst into flames like dry kindling.

Chapter 10

Zahra shielded her eyes from the blazing ruins around her. The Infernal had begun its dive towards her and Ishmael but then it had burst into flames when the ruins had lit up in blue fire. Zahra watched it writhe about, its wings engulfed in fire. Its thrashing slowly subsided as flames still licked at its body, now blackened and permeating the air with the smell of scorched flesh.

This must be hallowed ground she thought with wonder. Around them the ruins had collapsed even farther, revealing an imposing statue among the rubble of a tall man with steely determination etched on his face, hair splayed back as if he was standing before a forceful wind. One hand held a staff crowned with a golden sphere, and the other was thrust out in front of his body, palm out as if to halt an enemy before him.

Struggling to her feet, Zahra moved towards the statue for a better view and realized she was observing a statue of Pasha the god of hope, sanctuary, and love. Pasha was one of the old gods who had disappeared during the Severing. With the rise of new powers in the world and the intermingling of cultures, new gods had risen to power and influence and the other older gods faded away. But none of it matters anymore thought Zahra. The Severing had changed that, and those deities lucky enough to survive were left stranded along with their followers in this realm.

The strange fire in the ruins started to die, but the statue's eyes continued to burn azure blue long after Zahra had turned away to check on Ishmael.

He seemed no worse off than before except for a fine layer of dust settling upon him. Once she was sure he had suffered no further injuries, Zahra removed Ishmael from the saddle. It was hard to see now that the flames had gone, leaving the only light source from the Infernal's motionless body burning quietly from across the cavern.

Zahra removed a wooden torch from her backpack; its end was wrapped in oil-soaked rags. Taking a deep breath she stalked closer, watching intently for any sign of movement. At ten feet she stopped and crouched on her haunches, observing the body of their attacker while trying not to gag at the stench. Desperate for a weapon she picked up a rock. Zahra threw it and watched as it thudded off the Infernal's head and landed next to its body. Feeling braver now, she stepped forward and used the torch to prod the Infernal. There was no unexpected movements or sudden attack, so she held the torch against the smouldering flesh until the rag caught fire.

Heading back to Ishmael, Zahra became aware of a crowd that had gathered outside the ruins. Some had started to creep closer to Ishmael and the dead Lunar, Zahra returning with light had sent them scuttling back to the group.

Groups and crowds made Zahra nervous. She knew people felt empowered to do things that they would never consider if they were alone or numbered a few. Many times she had seen situations boil out of control where mobs were concerned.

At a glance the mob seemed harmless, clothed in meagre sweat stained rags that barely hid their bodies, lathered in grime and dust they looked like creatures of stone. Some carried crude axes and knives and they huddled as one whispering and gesticulating towards Zahra and Ishmael.

Standing in front of the mob, Zahra raised the torch higher to see, but the crowd shrank away from the light. 'I need someone to guide me to the nearest city entry point,' she said slowly, trying to fill her voice with confidence and power but deep in the cavern her own voice sounded hollow and weak.

Her demand was met with odd looks and muted expressions, and Zahra realized as she looked closely that many of these unfortunates were marked with missing limbs and deformities and were possibly unable to speak.

Cautiously Zahra removed a pouch of gold that she held up and jangled around. 'I have gold, enough to buy you all a new life. Just get us out of here.'

A small figure moved around the crowd to stand in front of her. The girl must have been hardly ten cycles old, and she wore a faded black dress and a rusted necklace way too large for a child, thin arms reached out for the bag.

'I will take you,' she said in a croaky voice. 'My name is Nina. Come quickly before their fear of you stops. They say you are a witch and worry whether you will set them on fire like the winged man.'

'I assure you, Nina, I am no witch.'

She didn't like having to trust someone unknown but they had no other choice of finding their own way out.

Zahra held the torch out for Nina to carry, but she had to soothe and encourage the girl before she would take it. Lifting Ishmael over her shoulders, Zahra followed while throwing furtive glances behind at the crowd, which was following from a distance.

Twice that she could recall they stopped and pulled back into the shadows or behind rocks to let patrols pass without being noticed.

Zahra lost all concept of time; with Ishmael's extra weight to carry she could only concentrate on putting one foot in front of the other, as she followed Nina's urgent encouragement. 'Not far now, miss.' Fatigue made her want to yell at the girl for lying, but Zahra knew she was just trying to help and it would not do to scare off their guide. They stopped to share water from a canteen Nina had, and the cool liquid rejuvenated Zahra enough to take note of their surroundings. The walls were smooth here, and the ground cobblestoned like some vast underground highway.

'Nina where are we?'

'This is called the Merchants' road. My father was building it all the way to Whaleson City on the other side of the mountain. He said using Lunars was too dangerous and that we would find a new way and get rich.'

'Where is your father now?' Zahra asked between panting breaths.

From up front Nina stopped and turned to her, eyes bright in the torchlight.

'He is dead and so are Momma and my brother, killed by bad men who want to make the road their idea. I will make sure the bad men get in trouble for what they have done and that it is called Amarl highway for my father.' She held up the purse in her left hand. 'This gold will help me fix everything.'

The bitterness in Nina's voice struck a chord in Zahra's heart. She wished this girl the chance of finding true happiness in life, not just pain and the emptiness of revenge.

The road started to show signs of common use and Zahra saw signs giving directions to the Lunar caverns and new mine shafts. Ahead a pale light slowly grew into a large opening that revealed a mining camp below. The two guards at the exit from the mountain looked barely awake, and the clatter of two silver ketches on the table next to them chased away any questions. The new day was still in its infancy, and Zahra was happy leaving the darkness behind.

'Zahra how did you set the winged man on fire?' Nina asked.

'I actually didn't do anything,' Zahra replied. 'Those ruins turned out to be an old temple to Pasha the god of sanctuary, hope, and love. He is a champion of good, and when the Infernal flew into those ruins to kill us it was actually flying into hallowed ground and well you saw what happened to it. You see, Nina, hallowed ground cannot abide evil while unhallowed ground cannot abide forces of good.'

They stood looking down on the camp at the base of the mountain and the town that sprawled around it. Zahra's stomach growled as the aromas of hot food assaulted their nostrils. Now that they were outside of Illume and on the far side of the mining town she could see the lush forest of the Jewelled lands. This was how they would leave, but first they needed rest and medical aid.

As they made their way down into the camp, Zahra noticed that Nina was no longer with them. She turned to look behind only to catch sight of the girl vanishing back into the tunnel. The camp was slowly awakening, there were the usual wretched souls lying about suffering from a heavy night on the drink, or possibly the unfortunate victims of murder and thievery. Places like this were a law unto their own, and Zahra was only too aware of the dangers.

Zahra and Ishmael stumbled down the poor excuse for a main thoroughfare. Zahra spied a line of wagons chained together a short ramp of stairs at each one led up to a doorway in which stood garish whores trying and failing to seem excited and energetic, yawning and with tired eyes. With what little clothing they had on they must have been freezing. Zahra angled over to the first caravan with the name Yolinda above the doorway. The woman seemed surprised as they approached and she put on a coy look, while absentmindedly twisting her fingers through long chestnut hair. In a voice thick with weariness she outlined her terms.

'A silver ketch for the one o' ya, double it for the two. Don't do roughin' 'cause it just won't do to mark me pretty face, but besides that I'll please ya beyond ya wildest dreams. Anyhow looks like ya friend won't be needin much action.'

'Let's discuss the price inside, Yolinda. The night has been long and daylight is the last place I want to be.'

The interior of the caravan was made up of a large bed fluffed with bright cushions. A small bucket and washcloth lay in one corner below a wall cupboard and above the bed a faded painting of a curvaceous woman was nailed to the wall. Yolinda started to raise her skirts 'Wait!' Zahra laid Ishmael on the bed and turned to the woman.

'We don't need your services, Yolinda, but I need somewhere to leave my friend, he is badly injured and I need to find a healer.'

'Aint the pox, is it?' asked Yolinda, her eyes growing wide.

'No, not the pox, he's just been badly injured. I will pay you well to keep him here for the day and make sure he is given water.'

With hands on hips Yolinda pouted. 'That is a lotta money for the day, lady, I can't afford to miss other customers. 'Her words died off as Zahra handed her two gold ceta's.

Zahra stared hard into Yolinda's eyes. 'You do the right thing and I double it come nightfall, but if you hurt my friend or run with my money I will make you beg for your miserable life and no customer will want you with the scars I will leave.'

'Sure thing, lady, will be the easiest coin I ever earned.' She stood watching as Zahra removed her cloak and revealed a blood-stained shoulder.

'You need help with that dear?' Yolinda moved to help but stopped Zahra's glare.

She unravelled a bandage from her pack and began securing her injured arm across her chest. When she finished she allowed Yolinda to clasp the cloak back on for her. Zahra stopped in the doorway and turned to her. 'I will be back come nightfall, don't let him leave, and tell no one about us.' Then the door slammed shut, and she was gone.

Chapter 11

Manu belched as he rose and left the cookhouse, the taste of eggs and spiced bread still lingering. Today was a good day to be alive; in fact any day when he managed to have breakfast was a good day. The sun might be high in the sky, but Manu had only been up and about for a few chimes. He ducked under the tent door and into the glare of the day. The street was alive with activity now that a new vein of gold had been found below the mountain and glitter greed had taken over the camp. Manu stood there a while watching the activity around him; the latest batch of soldiers from Illume had returned from their forays into the Jewelled lands. There had been many wounded and his makeshift surgery had been filled with the screams of the dying. Many survived his work and most would live long lives even though they were missing limbs and would never sleep the rest of a normal man again. It was the stomach-ripped ones he hated the most. They promised everything they had if he could save them. Manu took what they offered knowing that the blades the Harlequin used were coated in poison that ate a man from the inside and there was little he could do for them.

These unlucky souls he often gave Freya root to chew; if they survived they could curse him for the addiction later. Manu had been a battle surgeon a long time now and he knew when someone would live or die. Not that it mattered a ceta. They were all summoned to the halls of death eventually, the most he could do was delay the visit.

The cries had been getting to him lately, and only gonzola brandy cleared them from his mind. The ones that wouldn't live needed help to cross peacefully to be spared the pain of a slow death and so he had started to purposefully drug the dying soldiers before piercing their hearts using a long stiletto blade. They died instantly with no one knowing enough to discover what he had done. His work had developed a reputation, and many soldiers on their way into the Jewelled lands often made it known that if they were hurt they wished to be bought to Manu. It was said that Manu bartered with the gods for your soul and would at the least win you a painless death. Yet he was far from who he used to be, and the life he wished to forget was kept at bay with the help of the brandy.

The latest foray into the forest had left this morning and the dead had been cleared away from his surgery. He could afford the luxury of having others clean up after his butchering work. They would be finished by now, so he could go home and rest with his one true friend Gonzola and drink the day away.

As Manu entered his home he noticed a backpack upon the wooden table. A half-eaten loaf lay on its side slathered in butter, and a bottle of his precious brandy stood glaringly empty. 'Those fools,' he muttered. How dare they touch my personal store. He would see them whipped for this. He heard the door slam shut behind him as he stormed inside even though he hadn't closed it.

Spinning on his heel, Manu saw a feminine figure in the shadow of the door and stepped forward menacingly. 'I asked for no whore,' he said, and then something cracked into the bridge of his nose, and he was on the ground cradling his face in his hands.

'Manu, long time no see, have you missed me, my friend? I have come to collect that favor you owe me. I hope you don't mind, but I made myself at home.'

Manu groaned inwardly. He had hoped the bitch had died. The day had started so brightly.

All sensation of pain fell away. From somewhere behind him a strong wind was blowing, and Ishmael could feel it's caress on his skin, and it made him want to laugh and shout with joy. He opened his eyes to find himself among the stars floating towards a kaleidoscope of light shimmering through a celestial curtain above him. Without knowing how, he managed to turn himself over to look down and saw the world far below, a pulsing sphere of blues and greens so majestic and beautiful that tears of wonder trickled down his face at the sight. Energy and life radiated from below, and he felt connected to everything, knowing from deep within there was no self, no separateness. He was also aware of its swollen red center, inflamed and raw, and he felt sadness and loss that the world was dying. He floated up as peace came over him, the stars overhead revealed a light that bathed him in love and the promise of tranquillity, the light of Illume. Figures moved beyond that hypnotic glow and voices called out to him. He thought he recognized the voice of his father, and his body reacted as if it were a string on a harp. Not far to go, then no more pain and suffering.

Again, his attention was drawn to the world beneath him and he was in the stone chamber, looking at the dying tree before him. From the tree stepped a woman, her skin pale teak, thin and spidery with veins of sickly yellow ichor. Ishmael realized an almost invisible cord connected him to the woman. She beckoned him with fingers ending in newly born leaves. Ishmael longed for the light and whoever waited for him there, and yet the woman opened her arms, called his name and drew him into her caress, free of judgment and welcoming him home.

✦

Chapter 12

irst Flame Commandant Dalwyn Trevlon reigned in his mount and signalled for the band of warriors behind him to do likewise. Night had claimed the sky and even for a group as large as theirs it would be unnecessarily foolhardy to travel farther where they would be openly exposed on the plains of Cavere. Before dismounting, Dalwyn reached into his saddlebags and retrieved an apple, which his horse, Sigil, gently took from his palm. Dalwyn loved animals, their loyalty was assured if treated right, and unlike men you never had to watch your back.

The inn was busier than he would have liked; even from out here he could hear the stamping of feet, singing, and lutes. After peeling off his riding gloves Dalwyn threw a handful of silver ketches in the dirt at the feet of the approaching stable hand and made his way into the common room with his men. Many heads turned as they entered and once they noticed the flame emblem, the smart ones looked away. Dalwyn strode through the crowd to the bar, ignoring the glances directed at him. He ordered five rooms for himself and his men, throwing in extra coin in advance for a hot meal and drinks for them. Not bothering to eat, he took the keys to a room and climbed the stairs with his two bodyguards following him closely.

His room was bare and pathetically furnished, but Dalwyn didn't care about let alone notice the lack of comfort. From his pack he removed a small chest adorned with frosted amber arcane symbols. Kneeling down, he swept away the dust and dead bugs that littered the floor in front of him, then he lay down a red piece of fabric upon which he placed the chest.

Reverently Dalwyn opened the chest, revealing a gleaming pendant necklace engraved with its symbol of Escindre. It always took his breath away when he looked upon this treasured object. The time of magic might be gone for now, but this necklace reeked of power not meant for mortal hands.

As he had every day since receiving this pendant from his father, he held it aloft.

'Our time shall come again!'

This was his birthright!

This was his destiny!

It had always been worn by the high magus of Escindre, and that station had been held by his father and his grandfather before him. The name Trevlon was a name to be feared in the time of magic. Their lineage had produced the most powerful sorcerers in the land and the family's influence extended from the city of Karfael to the furthest peaks of the Tiarioc mountain ranges. It was his responsibility to regain those days of glory.

The Severing had hit his family hard. His great-great-great grandparents who had lived well beyond the natural lifespan of a human due to various enchantments of longevity, crumbled to dust when magic failed. The flying citadel their family lived in collapsed, falling to the earth, freeing the air spirits that had suspended it above the ground and destroying the city area below it.

The Trevlon family had made magic their life and without it they were nothing. They had built Karfael City, stealing away the land from the barbaric tribes of the Tunoka Grasslands who claimed it was theirs by birthright. For over a century the city withstood the attacks of the tribes due to the magic prowess of his family and its mages, and with the collapse of the Trevlon family the tribes saw their chance.

They came with their stone axes and arrows like a horde of ants devouring all in its path and his ancestors had cowered amongst the rubble of his home as the unlucky ones were dragged out into the streets and brutally slain. The very people who his family had protected for so long now turned their backs on their masters and fled, leaving Karfael City to become what it was to this very day. A city of ghosts.

Dalwyn was so close to achieving the first part of his goal. The Ancient one named Latasha had spilled her secrets as her courage fled from the cut of his knives. The magic still existed here stored within five chosen and now he knew their names and locations. They were the coterie of the Heart. The rest would be easy, or so he had thought.

The few tomes on magic he had salvaged from the ruins of his home were useless to him. There was nothing explaining the possible loss of magic in the world or how to recover it. The contents were empty parchment now, missing the spidery text that once held powerful enchantments, leaving only penned sections relating to historical research and theoretical magic. What he did find out was that magic is inherent to the world, it could not be removed or destroyed.

Initially Dalwyn had thought that if they killed the coterie of the Heart, magic would be returned to the world and the natural order of things restored, but Brianna Dusk had put an end to that notion. Before she had taken her last breath and the ruby life had drained from her body, something detached from her and hovered above her momentarily, luminescent and full of glittering stars. It had swirled and coiled like a snake around and between him and his men, then shot off across the sky, streaking away into four separate parts and directions.

The pendant of Escindre had burst into fiery life as the magic briefly touched it and the crimson power that emanated from it restored the waning belief of his men.

However, having no way to track where this mysterious luminescence went they had continued on towards their destination.

Since Brianna he felt rejuvenated and years younger.

For the first time he had witnessed the very magic he had so jealously read about, and the tiredness had been swept off his shoulders with his dream finally validated. His men were transformed also and no longer looked at him strangely when he spoke about magic. They, like him, could never again question its existence.

Dalwyn put the necklace away and sat back into a position he favored for meditation. Magic may well have been lost for many cycles but thankfully he had the foresight and willpower to keep preparing his mind and body for its return. Effortlessly he slipped into a trance and for once didn't despair at the intrusive thoughts that tumbled through his mind, instead revelling in the glutted images of power and glory he would attain.

Chapter 13

Zahra paced past the operating table where Manu worked on Ishmael drawing an exasperated sigh from Manu.

'In all the past dodgy dealing I have had with you, Zahra, I have never seen you this anxious.'

Zahra watched a drip of perspiration roll down Manu's forehead, which he blotted on his shoulder with a twist of his arm.

'Do you have a point to make, old man?'

'Not really, I just thought it's nice to see you not getting everything your own way for a change.'

Zahra ignored the jibe and changed the subject instead.

'So, can you help him?'

'The plant cannot be fully removed from Ishmael at this time because already it has hold of his nervous system. Whoever had applied the Maiden's Kiss must have had a great knowledge of botany to be able to know its uses and apply it so well. Removing the plant now would be pointless since it's keeping Ishmael together nicely. If Ishmael was one of my patients back from the Jewelled lands with these wounds, I would use Freya root to end the poor man's life.'

'Still using the Freya root, then? Well, I'm not asking how you would kill him, Manu, can you help him or not?'

'Quiet, woman! If you insist on forcing me to help your lover, at least extend me the courtesy of some damn peace.'

Zahra slammed the door in response. It felt good to get back at Manu and get under his skin. She knew she always annoyed him and knew it irked him further knowing he owed his life to her and had in fact sworn a blood oath to return a favour at any time in the future. Zahra busied herself making food as she waited for Manu to finish.

Zahra had said nothing about Manu's weakness for the drink and the fact he had returned to his old ways. Words were unnecessary, for the look of guilt on his face had said it all. If Manu needed to drown away the memories of who he was to get what little enjoyment was left out of his miserable existence, then that was up to him.

Once the food was finished Zahra slipped back inside the surgery.

Manu wearily walked over to the well in the corner and drew up a pail of cold water to wash away the blood from his arms. He spoke as he washed up.

'The whole process took too long, Zahra. I left portions of the plant from the stomach and chest wounds that were too deep to risk any further work on them. The other wounds have been cleaned and sutured, but Ishmael is still in a bad way.' Zahra walked over to Ishmael; his skin was a pallid grey and the tightness around his eyes and mouth accentuated his condition. Taking his pulse, she noted it was irregular and his chest barely rose with each breath that managed to inflate his lungs. Zahra left to prepare the food and could hear a commotion coming from the surgery. Manu was searching through his surgery for the brandy he had stored there but, he wouldn't find it because she had already removed it all. She moved to the doorway and, she watched him searching urgently through his shelves, his breaths coming in gasps and, his hands were shaking badly.

With a cry, Manu swept all the bottles from the shelf with his arm, releasing astringent aromas and spilling remedies and unguents across the wall and floor.

'Are you looking for this?'

Zahra knew Manu expected to be berated and mocked and instead she moved over and draped her arm around his shoulder. In her other hand, she held a bottle of brandy, which she opened with her teeth before spitting out the cork. 'Come on Manu I think we could both use a drink. We have much to discuss.'

Zahra led Manu into the main room where she had a pot of food simmering gently on the stove top. Taking a long swig of brandy, Manu sighed then handed the bottle back to Zahra. 'You will make a good wife one day Zahra; if I knew you could cook I mighta married you long ago.'

Zahra smiled sweetly. 'It's part of the training of an assassin. The best way to kill someone is to cook for them.' She moved over to the fireplace and dished up two heaped bowls of stew, one of which she placed in front of Manu. 'Of course we also spend much time imbibing the poisons we use so we can eat the food without suffering any ill effects. Eat up, Manu, you suddenly look pale! Some hot food will put some colour back into your cheeks.'

They sat talking long into the night. Manu had placed Ishmael into another room in a warm cot, his body now wracked with shaking, and Manu had explained that even after the work he had done there was no guarantee that Ishmael would live through this night.

The drink loosened their tongues and the time for straight answers had come.

'Zahra, I know of the attack on the Brothers of Illume, it was all the talk around the camp this morning. Who is Ishmael, and why are you protecting him?'

'I'm not sure you would believe me, Manu. You see, it involves magic.'

'Why wouldn't I? Did you say magic?'

'Pour us another drink, Manu you're going to need it for this tale.'

Manu rose and stretched; from a high shelf he retrieved a pipe and bowl filled with a blue crushed flower. Sitting down he packed the pipe and lit it with a stick from the fire. Soft tendrils of smoke lazily floated upwards and a sweet aroma carried throughout the room.

'Don't you think it's odd that magic just disappeared, that something so powerful and that permeated everyone's lives…could just be gone forever?'

'Well of course, Zahra. Who hasn't imagined those days and wished we could have had access to the magic of that time, that we would have done things differently and not let the world be ravaged by the abuse of power?'

'Manu what if I was to tell you that the magic we speak of has never left this world but was just hidden within five individuals who were energetically different from the rest and could hold this within them but not use it.'

Manu swallowed another gulp of brandy, his eyes widening as Zahra talked.

'That's not possible.'

'And that is why it has worked so well, because it seems impossible and the perfect ruse for allowing time for our world to heal. Now certain things weren't foreseen like how the magic passes onto the oldest child or next blood relative of these chosen, and that is how three hundred cycles after the Severing, Ishmael and four others hold the worlds magic within them.' Zahra sat quietly for a time to let that sink in.

'What, is there more?'

'Their ruse is finally ended Manu; the attack on Illume City was our enemies searching for Ishmael. They want the five who we call the coterie of the Heart so magic can be bought back to our world on their terms, but to do so before the world is ready would be catastrophic and maybe cause the destruction of our world instead.'

'So how do you enter the situation then, Zahra?'

'The Kenzu clan were chosen to protect the coterie, and a select group were trained for the very purpose of protecting each member. I asked no questions, in fact I was just content to be given a mission that for once didn't require me to kill. This was the dream job, to watch and protect and if trouble comes, get Ishmael to safety.'

'Where is this safety?'

'I can't tell you that,. Manu, it's safer if you don't know. I am taking Ishmael to a safe house where we will meet the other coterie members and their sentinels before deciding what we do next.'

'And what if you die? What happens to Ishmael then?'

'That is something I would rather not think about now. Pour me another would you?'

Zahra sat and rotated her injured shoulder, wincing as pain stabbed up the side of her neck. The salve Manu had put on the wound helped, but now a deep stiffness had set in. Her eye was still swollen but was nothing but annoying now. She accepted a full drink from Manu and studied him closely as he sat down.

'What?'

'You don't seem to have aged since I saw you last, Manu.'

'What can I say?' He shrugged his shoulders. 'Time has been kind to me, and I keep a great supply of creams for the skin.'

Zahra snorted. 'What aren't you telling me? You act older, maybe even wiser if that is possible, and yet you appear to be physically as you were last time we had the fortune of travelling together.'

'I think you should leave the rest of the drinking to me, Zahra; it appears to be addling your brain.'

Zahra rubbed her eyes and sighed. 'Secrets, damn secrets, Manu. Why do we insist on keeping them?'

'Because the truth is too brutal, and so we create illusions of who we think the world wants us to be. If we don't keep our secrets our illusion could be shattered and the world will see the type of person that we really are.'

'That's very observant. Is that why you're not sharing?'

'I'm coming with you Zahra! Being here is no longer safe for me now that you have come.' Zahra started to say something but Manu talked over her.

'If Ishmael is who you say he is then it's only a matter of time before someone comes looking here. There are no secrets in this camp, and everything gets noticed by someone.'

'Manu, you have a life here you can't leave...'

Manu placed the empty bottle on the table. 'I can and I will! And look around, there is nothing I can't do without; people are dying everywhere, so work is no problem and healers are welcomed with opened arms. Actually Ishmael, is still in a bad way, and I know someone who can help do what I can't.'

The drink made Zahra's head feel heavy, and she shook it to try and wake up a little. 'Where is this someone? What is his name?'

'In the Jewelled forest is a shaman of incredible power, and he will be able to draw Ishmael's soul back from between worlds. There is power in names, and I am sworn to never reveal his to anyone. I have always wanted to go there before I die, so why not now? But know this, Zahra, my debt to you is paid and so I travel with you by choice.'

Zahra stood up to warm her hands on the fire.' How soon can we leave?'

'I will need a day to finish up and organize passage; we will be travelling by barge down the Winding River.'

'So you plan on taking us into an area devastated by war?'

'If you want Ishmael to live, then the answer is yes. We will have the safety of Illume mercenaries about us, and so we won't have to fear attack, and anyway we will not be heading to the front lines but will hire a guide to take us to our destination.'

Chapter 14

The heavy morning mist rising from the river obscured the plumes of smoke that snaked up steadily from many fires that raged throughout the city. Zahra and Manu had woken well before dawn to the hustle of workers trudging up into the city to help with the fires. All talk was of Infernals marauding through Illume killing at whim and burning everything they could. The council had finally agreed that the attack was aimed mainly at the Brothers of Illume and related to the attack during the Festival of Lanterns. The famous Illume blades had been mobilized and the defence of the city turned over to them.

Manu strapped Ishmael onto a travelling stretcher, his wounds still an angry red, and Ishmael's breathing was still shallow, and he had a fever. The sight that greeted them at the river was unexpected. The river where it flowed past the jetties downstream was choked with boats packed with fresh soldiers, food and medical supplies bound for the front line of the war with the Harlequin.

'Must be trouble further downstream.' Manu mumbled out load as he scratched his backside. 'River traffic is usually flowing pretty easily at this point. Looks like we'll be waiting with the rest of the poor blighters, just need to find a boat that will be happy to carry us is all.'

'No! We cannot delay. I will go without you if I must,' answered Zahra, her voice terse with finality. 'The more distance we put between Illume and Ishmael the better it will be.'

'But there is safety in numbers,' Manu countered. 'If Ishmael is still hunted then we will have the protection of soldiers. Alone just the three of us, one unable to defend himself would be easy pickings.'

Zahra stood facing Manu, her hands on hips. 'Manu, usually I would agree with you but you did not see the Infernals that attacked us. The one that pursued us into the caverns could slice through these soldiers like chaff. They will expect us to seek refuge in numbers.'

A few soldiers on a nearby barge turned to look at the commotion with curiosity. Manu moved closer to Zahra to avoid being overheard. 'Then what choice do we have Zahra? Look! This mess will not clear for chimes.'

Zahra was about to admit she had no answers when she saw a familiar figure upstream at a single plank jetty. It was the whore Yolinda. Yolinda was now garbed in long jade trousers with a tight yellow top that struggled to contain her ample bosom. She seemed to have caught everyone's attention, and as the soldiers wolf whistled and hollered at her, Yolinda lugged a large case along the plank jetty looking all the while as if she would end up in the water. As the case fell onto the small boat, a loud cheer went up from the soldiers; Yolinda turned to them flashing not just her beautiful smile but also her breasts before hopping aboard the boat herself. The only other person on the boat was a man locking in a set of oars and pointing up river.

Zahra picked up her end of the stretcher. 'It looks like we have an answer to our problem.' She grinned at Manu. 'Come on, old man.'

Zahra rushed along the river bank to the jetty just as the boatman was untying the craft from its mooring.

'Wait, please wait!'

The boatman paused then continued untying. Yolinda turned to watch Zahra run along the jetty, she said something to the man and he halted nodding his head.

'Yolinda, is this your boat?'

'No, miss, it aint, just bought passage is all, what's got you all in a huff then?'

'Noticed you were heading upstream and I was hoping you may

know a way to avoid the bottleneck here. We need to get down to Acclaro City.'

Yolinda beamed a stunning smile. 'Well that's where I be going, but you'll be needing some o' that fancy coin to keep Murk happy.'

Zahra turned to see Murk eying her suspiciously. 'Don't care who you are, girl, you and yours have to do as I say on my boat when I need you. Cost is one ceta for each of you now and another when we reach Jingtalla Falls.'

Zahra plucked the money from her belt pouch. 'You're the boss, Murk, and thank you for this kindness.'

'Don't thank me yet girl you're not there.' Then he spat over the boat's side into the water.

Zahra hurried back to the expectant Manu, explaining their good fortune, but Manu didn't share her enthusiasm.

They got Ishmael on board and put him within the small canvas tents erected on the deck at one end of the boat. Yolinda looked Manu up and down and raised her eyebrows suggestively, which bought a red flush to his face. He shook her outstretched gloved hand and sketched a sloppy bow to her.

'Nice to meet you, miss.'

Yolinda giggled throatily. 'Oh my, a true gentleman.'

This comment sent Manu scuttling away to talk with Murk, Yolinda and Zahra looked at each other and burst out laughing.

Manu approached Murk, just glad to be away from Yolinda and Zahra. As he drew closer to the big man, he watched as Murk pulled a small blade from his belt and slashed it across the inside of a forearm, muttering under his breath and clenching his fist so blood dripped into the murky waters. Manu purposefully paused, allowing the man to finish his blood offering to the river god Aril the Great Slumberer.

Manu gestured to Murk's bleeding arm. 'Let me bind that for you.' In return Murk just nodded and studied Manu intently.

'Is there something wrong?' muttered Manu as he worked.

'Nah, not wrong, I just noticed the look of disdain on your face when I spilt my blood is all. I take it you don't bend to the gods?'

Tying off the bandage. Manu lifted his head and met Murk's eyes. 'Once yes, but I believe the time of the gods has come and gone, now they have less power than a mortal man. With magic gone they are merely mortals like us.'

Murk climbed up onto the jetty then untied the docking rope and clambered back aboard before answering. 'You seem mighty educated in the affairs of gods. You some sort of priest as well as healer?'

'Let's just say my faith is dead and I shall rely on the gods no longer. Now since I am a guest on your boat I shall also give the river an offering.' With a smile Manu pulled a clay jug from his knapsack, unstoppered it, and poured a generous amount over the boat's side. Then he offered it to Murk who sniffed suspiciously at the rim before raising his eyebrows in delight. 'Gonzola! I think our journey will be a fine one indeed with you aboard Manu.'

They both drank deeply from the bottle then Manu helped Murk with the long poles to help push the boat upstream against the current.

Chapter 15

Nina paused before entering the tunnels again. Childish laughter reached her from below in the mining camp. She moved to the edge of the sharp decline and lay in shrubs and sharp rocks watching as two girls held a rope while a third jumped and repeated a rhyme.

None of them even saw her watching from above. A lady came out of the small hut near the children and scolded them for playing in the morning chill, then ushered them inside for breakfast. Even after the years away from the mouth-watering cooking of her mother, Nina could recognize the smell of bacon and baked bread. Her mouth salivated and she let the lure of the mining camp draw her down, intent on a hot meal. She had gold now, but her lack of cleanliness and good clothes made her stick out like a fox in a chicken coop.

A group of older kids ran over to her. The boy who appeared to be the oldest stepped in front of her pointing at the money pouch she held.

'What ya got there, girlie?'

'Nothing for you,' she said as a wisp of fear coiled up inside her stomach, clutching her gold tight to her chest. Nina pushed past him.

Instead of letting her pass he stepped around in front again, balled his fist, and drove it into her stomach.

With a surprised grunt Nina fell to her knees, wincing at the pain, involuntarily her hand opened releasing the precious gold to fall to the ground. As the boy bent to steal the money the thoughts of a hot meal became a distant memory. Nina repeated her silent mantra. 'I won't cry!' She pulled her knife and slashed at his arm, slicing deep into the muscle of his forearm.

He squealed loudly and fell to the ground, clutching his arm in shock. Keeping her knife between the boys and herself, Nina grabbed her gold and backed away then scrambled up the embankment into the tunnel. Curses from the two half-asleep guardsmen at the gate followed her into the darkness as she sped past them.

The common name for where Nina called home was Slumsville, a town with houses made out of crates, lit by greasy smoke billowing oil lanterns and a place to trade stolen goods. This dangerous community of outcasts and thugs had become her home since her family died. They had accepted her easily into their midst once she had proved she was no easy target and good with a knife.

Nina had even started to feel safe in this place, she didn't have much but earnt what she needed through odd jobs. But now she had gold and things were different. The slummers looked at her differently, not even bothering to disguise their glances at the money bag at her waist.

Nina knew they would come for her while she slept and so once inside her crate home Nina climbed the rock back wall of her abode and stashed the bag of coins into a hole she had carefully worn away over months for this exact purpose.

'Money is power,' her da had always said. He also said that people strived their whole lives to attain it and once they finally get some they worried about losing it or what they would purchase with it.

Then she waited knife in hand, heart hammering in her ears and cursing her stupidity. They would not take her money! Nina had taken to staying away from the other slummers. After two days of moving around sleeping where ever she could find a warm place, Nina decided to return to her home.

I should never have come back here, she thought.

But where would I go then? Even amongst the brutal laws of Slumsville she knew these people were all she had.

Chapter 16

The Mother showed Ishmael the world before the Severing. How magic was used to create magnificent structures, explore hidden realms, heal the dying and sick. Ishmael watched as the power contaminated Mother Earth's children bringing greed and fear as it was misused to wage war and hatred. Civilizations rose and fell before his eyes along with the gods and their religions, all taking their piece of the Mother life with them, uncaring about the consequences of their actions. With surprise, he saw how the races were created to be her protectors but they had forgotten their connection to her. Even the gods who were her oldest children abandoned her instead choosing to glut themselves on the faith and worship of their followers. These powerful beings forgot that without the Mother and their followers they would cease to exist and instead they mirrored the actions of their earth-bound creators and waged war on one another, jostling for influence and power.

The Great War came, and Infernal hordes battled Celestial armies, both summoned by covens of immense mastery and fighting a war whose original purpose lay forgotten. The magical power unleashed and the effects it had on the world were catastrophic. Immense waves of fury patrolled the seas, smashing all in their path and breaking coastal cities to pieces like they were made of paper. The sun had not risen for days, its light and warmth choked by the immense clouds of smoke as the land was consumed by the grasping tongues of uncontrolled fires.

Ishmael watched as with a thunderous crash the forces clashed once more in their final battle at the forest of Karnock. The ancient forest had regrown on blood, flesh and bones ground together. Even though the forest regrew the land around it had become sick, a wound that would never heal. Celestial knights fought a deadly battle in the skies against winged Infernals; underfoot a host of armies fought its way forward against waves of concussive and devastating spells tearing into their ranks from the mountainous fortress above them. Elementals strode the battlefield, venting their fury on the enemies of their conjurers, and the air was thick and tense with energy as cadres of mages strained to break down the shields of their foes.

Ishmael felt the fear of the Mother as she was split apart, her power boiling up and bathing the world in blinding radiance and vehemence that stopped the fighting, mortal, Infernal, and Celestials alike watched the energies roiling above and around them in horrid fascination. The energetic pressure burst eyes and ears and screams were drowned out by the tempest of magic now covering the world as both innocent and guilty paid for the crimes against their mother. The Mother was shaking, forcing to their knees the creatures she loved and fought to protect. Only now that it was too late did some realize their mistakes and the magnitude of their actions. Others wailed that the gods were angered not realizing these gods had been cast out of their heavenly abodes.

As the living cringed upon the shaking Mother in pain beneath storms of might, a silence descended; the calm amidst the storm or pause before annihilation, and a word rang out strong and clear: sunder. The whirlpool of magic's churning in the sky shivered then, elongated into a spiralling spout that toppled down striking the fortress above the remains of Karnock forest in the land of Auxil.

There was a feeling of being cut, and then all at once an overwhelming pain as the inherent magic that abided with in every living creature and was as much a part of them as their life's blood was severed. Millions died as magical enhancements created to increase powers or abilities or prolong lives collapsed and delivered death with his rightful quota. Magical flying citadels nosedived to smash into cities below, the divine connection to gods was severed and ancient beings of good and evil were suddenly freed as their bindings melted away. The world was plunged into darkness, unable to rely on the magic they had come to lean on so heavily. The Severing had begun.

Commandant Dalwyn Trevlon watched as the squadron of Infernals landed before him, the horses though picketed farther away whickered with fright, trying to tear free of their tethers. Their eyes wide with fear and mouths dripping froth reminded Dalwyn of the fear of those unlucky to be chosen for his knives' attentions.

Once landed the Infernals' leader faced Dalwyn and fell to one knee, head bowed.

Speaking in their natural tongue Dalwyn addressed the one who stepped forward.

'Where is Zacriel?'

The Infernal lifted its tusked face and fixed contemptuous eyes on him. 'Zacriel ignored your orders, human, to pursue the target as he fled the monastery. I chose to return and inform you myself of these unforeseen circumstances.'

Dalwyn threw his hands up in frustration, and his soldiers closest to him involuntarily took a step back, wary of the temper that he was famous for.

'So where is he now then?'

'Beneath the mountain. He chased the monk and his bodyguard who fled upon a Lunar mount. There have been no sign of either since.'

'So you knowingly let your leader fly into danger without your support?'

A loud rasping came from the Infernal's throat. 'He is not our leader, and you yourself gave us strict orders to observe only.'

'That is correct, spawn; alas, I forgot you creatures have no initiative to make important choices by yourselves and now one of the targets may…'

Before he could finish, the Infernal thrashed its wings, stepping forward with a wicked axe in its clawed hands. Dalwyn's bodyguard surrounded him their blades drawn, shields raised.

'Never forget your magic is no more, mortal. You no longer control us, we are allies at best but make no mistake, we don't need you.'

Dalwyn pushed past his bodyguard. 'Yes, you are correct but you fail to mention that you have not lived up to your side of the bargain. I had thought we shared common goals, Infernal, but it seems you are content to stay here on this side of the planes as mortal as us humans. I suggest you find this monk Ishmael and return with him or our pact is at an end.'

Dalwyn spun on his heels.

'Break camp; we move now!'

With a roar of fury the Infernal slashed with its brutal axe at the one beside it, blood fountained from its neck and it collapsed to the ground and its brethren lurched in to feast upon the unfortunate victim.

With no leads to follow concerning magic, Dalwyn Trevlon decided to head south toward Acclaro City, the magic had sped off in all directions but it seemed to him that it was concentrated in that direction. There was little for him to do in the meantime but wait to be notified of the outcome of the other planned attacks.

They had one more major stop over the next three days while upon the plains of Cavere, the city of Culchar lay ahead and his men were due some downtime before the hunt began again.

Chapter 17

The memory of them both had been burned into his mind at the same time his skin was burnt from his body and his glorious wings destroyed, leaving only the membranes and a cruel memory of what he had once cherished. It was the image of Ishmael and that meddlesome assassin that kept Zacriel in the world of the living. His need for vengeance was so strong that the pain that wracked his body barely registered. They had left him to die; the fools would regret not finishing their handiwork when he finally had them back in his grasp.

The darkness soothed him and whispered promises of retribution that gave him the fire and determination to be patient. In the past he had always had the last laugh with his enemies. But these two he had underestimated and should have destroyed when he had the chance. Instead he had become arrogant and distracted.

Zacriel would not make the same mistake twice.

The passage of time here was warped, it seemed that his saviours had no concept of it since their existence was spent amongst the bleak darkness of the caverns away from the light of day. So he lay here as much a captive as a guest upon a bed constructed of bones and sinew built to appease him. With every movement the bed rattled, and Zacriel found the sound strangely comforting.

Word had spread like the wind through the belly of the mountain beneath Illume and the lost, forgotten, discarded ones flocked to see him. They were calling him the fallen god come to lead them from this forsaken place.

All he could do was submit to their assistance, and his body was recovering well with the salves they applied. He had examined himself with his hands, feeling the twisted burnt remains of his body, taking care to feel the damage done so he might repay his enemies tenfold the pain he had suffered.

More worshippers arrived daily, crowding around his bed with torches to see their god and kissing his twisted fingers while pledging their lives for him. They were a primitive people once a part of the thriving city above, but their kin had been driven underground for varying reasons and now the next generation were growing up full of hatred for those living above and in need of a leader.

An army at his disposal to do his bidding. He smiled at the thought, no longer disgusted by the taunt strain of scar tissue around his mouth and nose.

More and more his thoughts returned to Ishmael and the assassin, he had spent many chimes pondering how he would break their bodies and spirit, but pondering was not enough. Now he wanted their blood.

A soft scuffing sound announced the arrival of Cinerus, the leader of this underground world. The hairless, ashen-skinned man was blind, but his ears picked up every sound as he swivelled his head from side to side, so he moved through the caverns with little trouble. As he reached the bed, Cinerus lifted Zacriel's hand and placed it on his forehead.

'Instruct me master.'

Zacriel pulled himself to a sitting position, the bony framework of his wings now nothing but a nuisance. In time they would have to be removed.

'Where are they?'

'They are all around us, master.' Cinerus scratched his arms as he spoke tearing the scabs off the deep furrows that had been dug into his muscles there.

'You are lucky that I need you, Cinerus. I meant the other two visitors not your damned bats!'

'Sorry master, the bats and I are one: I feel what they feel. I did not mean to anger you.'

'Come here Cinerus, come and sit with me…that's it, there is no reason to fear me. Closer! There you see that's not bad is it?'

Zacriel lunged and caught Cinerus by the neck. He was yelling now, and the fear on his face excited him.

'WHERE ARE THEY GONE? They did not just walk out of here, so find them! I don't care how, but do not return to me until you have what I want.'

With a grunt, he released Cinerus and watched as the pathetic man, if one could call him that scuttled out of the chamber.

Zacriel turned his thoughts to Dalwyn. The fool would be cursing his failure by now. No matter, Zacriel knew the destination where Dalwyn would be heading, and there was still time to capture Ishmael. All that needed to be done was to find out where they were headed. That's why he needed the girl who guided them out of these tunnels.

After so many cycles he would finally be able to take his rightful place in the Infernal lands, and it would be because of him that the portals guarding the Infernal and Celestial realms would be reopened when magic returned to the world. What name would he take? He mused silently, the only sounds were the clunking of bones as he shifted his weight to his right side. 'The Bone Lord!'

He said it out loud to hear it roll off what remained of his tongue. Yes, that would do nicely.

He would claim his due, earned through villainous deeds and forge an army to strike at the heart of the Celestial realm removing their influence and plunging the world into despair.

Already the dark gods had rewarded him with wings of such beauty and speed that he knew his ascension into the courts of hell was assured. Then the Severing had taken all that away, leaving him and the small army of Infernal followers he had drawn about him still trapped in the material world.

Sipping from a jar of water, Nina started to relax until her eyes came to rest on a large bat hanging from her makeshift clothesline on the opposite wall. The rust coloured bat was nearly invisible in the gloom as it's stretched out its wings. More movement caught her eye as the doorway came alive and countless bats flew into her makeshift home.

Nina shivered with revulsion; she hated the creatures, especially these rust coloured ones whose screeching caused headaches enough to drive her crazy.

Not knowing what to do, she waited. There were too many to wack, and if she did their bodies would crunch into the floor. YUK!

The bats began chittering loudly, and she thought their milky-white eyes focused on her. Someone had told her that bats were blind, but she didn't believe that. Nina covered her ears and closed her eyes and hoped they would just go away, but she knew why they were here, knew he would be coming too. Finally she opened them; the bats were still there but had quieted down.

Crouched in the doorway knelt a bald, slender figure with scars for eyes and large ears; as she stared a beetle scuttled in front of him, his hand shot out, snatched the beetle, and popped it into his mouth chewing slowly. His body was covered in a black robe but failed to hide his skeletal frame.

'Nina, I have been looking for you.'

Not trusting herself to speak she nodded.

'Come with me, Nina.'

'I don't want to.' She fought to control the trembling that had taken over her body.

'The fallen man wants to talk to you, not hurt you. I will make sure he is nice to Nina.'

'The fallen man, she had never heard of before, but then before today she had thought that Cinerus was just a made-up monster. When she first came here she had been told Cinerus was the lord under the mountain and was more bat than man. *If I live through this* she promised herself silently, *I will leave these tunnels and find some way to live above ground.*

An angry clicking of teeth came from the doorway.

'He is awaiting you, Nina.' Gone now was the smile on his face which had now changed to a creepy grimace.

Realizing she had no other option, Nina nodded her head and retrieved her money. As she walked the bats swivelled their heads towards her. Money in hand, she faced Cinerus.

'I am ready.'

'Good, he will be pleased.'

As she stooped at the entry, Cinerus grabbed her wrist to lead her. His strong hand hurt her, but she was thankful for the pain because it cut through the same feeling you got when a beetle ran over your skin, leaving an itch of revulsion. The bats followed, fanning out above them, a flowing cape of bodies. The slummers stayed back at their approach and Nina noticed some dash off towards her little home. At least her money was safe.

These people were never her family; they never knew what love was stuck in this place deep in the bowels of the mountain, where the light of Illume would never shine upon them.

Cinerus led Nina down through the cavern to a sloping tunnel she had always avoided, where the stone was slippery and oozed water. There was a natural spring nearby.

Cinerus ranged ahead, leaving her to make her own way, and she caught up with him outside a roughly made wooden door.

Cinerus cocked his head to the side, listening to something beyond her senses and then he turned to her.

'Go, Nina, he awaits you.'

Nina stepped through the door and down the tunnel until she reached the chamber. Lichen smothered the walls giving the room a green tinge that held the darkness off. The chamber crowded around a huge bed made from bleached bones and tied with hair to one another with skulls adorning the bedposts. The bed squatted like some long dead beast in a tomb. So taken with the sight was Nina that she didn't see the figure reclining upon it until he spoke.

'Anyone ever told you it's rude to stare?'

Nina didn't jump at the sudden voice; her already wrangled nerves had most likely had enough scares lately.

'I just have never seen a bed as ugly as this. That's all.'

In a fluid movement the man on the bed rose to a sitting position. In one hand he grasped a leg of fowl or some other meat, juices dripping onto the bed covering. Yuk it wasn't even cooked properly.

This close she could see in great detail the burns that discoloured his body with twisted scar tissue along his arms, neck, and face. He stood then turned with a slow flourish like the dancers her momma had once taken her to see. She noticed the two holes in his back below the shoulder blades and suddenly knew who this was.

The fallen man heard the gasp and now stooped to cup her chin with a gnarled hand.

'Do I scare you? Are you disgusted, repulsed by what I have become?'

'I don't know what you were before, so how can I know what you are now?' she said. He didn't answer so Nina continued.

'They call you the fallen man. You were the one on fire that day when the others came but that's not why you are the fallen one, is it?'

'Some may call me that name. However those who walk the paths of power would know it's more like ascension. The gods have rewarded me for my efforts in this life to further their cause, and in return I will take my rightful place by their sides in the Infernal lands.'

'I think they call you the fallen because your wings are gone. You don't look powerful to me, you look frightened and sad...'

Zacriel grabbed her by the throat, hoisting her up off the ground and cutting off her words. 'You are just like the rest of them, despising me, making me the butt of jokes. I will show you what life is about. Yes, that is why our paths have crossed. I must enlighten you and pass on my knowledge before I ascend from this world.' Anger turned his face a bright red and spittle erupted upon her face from his mouth.

'What would you know of fear, girl? You have barely lived a speck of your miserable life, a life without meaning, forced to grow old and face your regrets. There is an alternative, the one I took to give my life meaning. DO YOU HEAR ME? MEANING!'

Nina could no longer breathe; she squirmed and batted the arms holding her with tiny fists.

It felt like Zacriel would squeeze the life from her frail body; snap her like a twig.

Chapter 18

Haakon watched Faustus check Latasha's injuries and listened to the old man's comments as he worked. 'Hmmm, swelling continues to recede around the cranium which is promising, breathing is still shallow with a slight whistling on inhalation. That must be addressed in case of farther damage to the lungs. The radius and ulna bones are healing well but due to extensive damage to the shoulder capsule she will never really be able to fully extend her arms again. The heads of the femurs in both legs were torn free from the Acetabulum so violently they can never be repaired. But look, I was able to reinsert the tibia and fibula in both legs-they still won't work and are knobby to be sure. But hey, better than they were, don't you think, Haakon?'

'I think you can leave now, Faustus. There is nothing more you can do here today.'

Faustus raised his eyebrows comically at Haakon and barked out a sudden laugh before turning away.

'Is something funny, friend?'

'No, it's not funny, milord,' the old physician replied with a sneer.

"Not funny one little bit" is the fact that two weeks have passed while you sit here whispering sweet bullshit to the almost corpse of Latasha fucking Meldoriel while your people wonder where you are. Haakon, your enemies think you are vulnerable right now, and nothing but ruthless commitment to the clan will keep them at bay. You have scrolls in your study from over a week ago demanding replies, and our people need your guidance. Obviously you don't give a frig about what happens to the remaining coterie, you just care about the love of your life and that's okay, but either step down from the clan lord position or step up and lead.'

Faustus smoothed his moustaches to the side and rested aged spotted hands on Haakon's shoulders before exhaling dramatically.

'Return to work, my friend and master. Latasha wouldn't want you to be affected this way and you have a job to do so do it with such aplomb and power that you exceed your every expectation in the matter. Do it for Latasha.'

Haakon had never heard Faustus be that vocal before and as the old man walked slowly away Haakon realized how stuck in the situation he had become and the danger to himself, the Kenzu, and Latasha by not acting. Faustus was the only one who could be trusted to tell Haakon what he needed to hear and not just what he wanted to hear.

As usual Faustus was right and Haakon marvelled at the uncharacteristic outburst from the physician. Haakon arranged the bedding around Latasha then stepped out into the day. As he walked through the grounds tired, and unkempt he forced himself to be cheery and to walk with determination. The eyes of many within the clan would be following him as he walked. They would be judging his every move and waiting for him to flounder and at any sign of weakness they would be upon him, the swine.

Saluting the personal bodyguards outside his chambers Haakon sent a servant for clean water, a razor, and hot food for two.

The private chambers of Haakon were sparsely furnished with a lush wool pallet strewn with cushions in black and white. An altar in the north wall depicted the clan symbol carved in obsidian on one side and the laughing visage of the death jester in marble on the other. Antique blades and scabbards hung from the walls, and a leather chair along with a small table on which three scrolls sat unopened occupied the center of the room. Haakon slumped down into the chair then reached for the first of three scrolls.

The scroll was sealed with a wax raven, which was the symbol used by the five assassins he had selected to be trained as sentinels for coterie of the Heart.

Clan Master Haakon:

I write this to notify you of two things, master. My charge, Brianna Dusk, is dead. I was taken by surprise and overwhelmed, they left me to die, and when I awoke she was gone. My attackers wore no insignia and came at dawn; they seemed to be waiting for us.

I tracked Brianna to a place called Shiver's Top and there found her remains. The bastards had bled her out and she would have died slowly. Our mission is compromised; they will know about the others in the coterie and Brianna would not have been strong enough to be able to resist them.

My last act was to warn the others in the astral and bury Brianna's remains so she might at least bathe in the glory of the Illuminated One.

These tasks accomplished, I will now take my life for failing the clan, and I only hope this is payment enough for my incompetence and that you will look after my family.

In this I humbly beg your forgiveness.

Your frail servant, Clem Ludwell

Haakon screwed up the scroll and threw it against the wall. The attack against them had succeeded after all, and now one of the coterie was dead, and it was his fault. Sweet Brianna Dusk had suffered at the hands of her enemies and Haakon had failed to protect her. 'She should have been on the way to the safe house, dammit!'

Haakon turned to the other two letters. One was from Benjani Dutoolo who was the sentinel of Jona Felzarun and the other from Selene Winsele's sentinel Ansar Pel.

Master Haakon,

I have received notification from Clem, advising me that he has failed us and his charge, Brianna Dusk, is dead. Now that things have taken a turn for the worse I will be heading to the safe house. Jona is safe with me. No messages have been forth-coming from Zahra, Ansar, or Kaitlin as yet so it remains possible they also have been compromised. My own messages have received no replies and yet I remain hopeful as to their safety as well as yours. May time be kind to us both, milord, and see us soon sharing many mugs of ale, until then I will try to track the whereabouts of the others via the astral. I will keep you informed of my findings.

In you I trust.

Benjani Dutoolo

Haakon mused over Benjani's letter. The other sentinels would also be trying to contact him from the astral as well as by letter. His energy body was still too weak to revisit the astral realm and leave the coded reply, but if they didn't receive a message from him then communication was now a problem.

Haakon took a deep breath, ran his fingers through his hair, feeling the tension of his jaw he consciously relaxed it before picking up the remaining letter from Ansar Pel.

Clan Master Haakon,

Our mission is compromised; Benjani has advised me of the situation with Clem, may his soul find its rest. I will be leaving the ocean behind me soon to head for the safe house. Trying to contact you from the astral, but there is no sign of your astral symbol or you. I can only hope all is well there but my fear tells me it is not. Master! The storm is brewing; where are Zahra and Caitlin? With Brianna's death our enemies may be closer than we know. My other concern is what happened to the magic when Brianna died? Does our enemy somehow hold it? There are too many unanswered questions, old friend. We need your instruction more than ever before, Haakon.

I await your reply.

In you I trust.
Ansar Pel.

Until the coterie and their sentinels reached the safe house, Haakon realized he would find it nearly impossible to make contact and advise them of his situation. Of course another of his men could leave messages in the astral for them, but they would be ignored. Only Haakon's personal symbol or those of the other sentinels would be read. The only option would be for him to meet them at the safe house personally or send someone in his stead.

The servant returned with hot water to fill his bath along with the razor he had requested, and Haakon bathed and shaved as he pondered his best course of action. Once finished he sent for Alexis, eager to hear what the young man had found out about Latasha.

Haakon ascended to the clan room above his quarters. The boy was late in coming, but when Haakon saw the red-rimmed, baggy eyes and pale skin he already knew the young man would have been burning the candle at both ends with the tasks he had been given plus all his normal duties.

Haakon indicated the seat across from him, and Alexis slumped down on to it with a groan. The food the cook had sent up was accompanied with piping hot char which was commonly used to stave off tiredness and fatigue and was actually quite tasteful with sugar. They ate and drank in silence until the char started to work on them and their stomachs stopped complaining.

'Haakon, it seems that someone certainly had been searching for Latasha. East of Karfael is a town called Shelton's Crag. A nobleman by the name of Dalwyn Trevlon posted a reward for information on her whereabouts.'

Haakon started to interrupt but Alexis stopped him with an outstretched hand.

'Now this is where it gets interesting. The name Trevlon has a rich and powerful history; they were the power behind building the city of

Karfael which angered the barbarian tribes of the Tunoka grasslands who view the city's location as a sacred site. As you know Karfael was razed by the hordes once the Severing occurred and those of the Trevlon family that didn't perish once their sorcerous magic's wore off were slaughtered except for one woman with child. Dalwyn's great-grandmother. She fled to the mountains with the remaining Trevlon soldiers and they applied for sanctuary in Shelton's Crag, a rough lawless town that came under regular attack from brigands. The town council agreed to let the survivors stay as long as they pledged their allegiance to Shelton's Crag and helped defend it. Our spies say that Dalwyn, like his recent ancestors, is tireless in his pursuit of returning magic to the world. Maybe one month ago Infernals were seen in Shelton's Crag for the first time, and they have allied with Trevlon who now rules the town with his garrison of soldiers.'

'When you say garrison, how many are you saying, Alexis?'

'I can't give you exact numbers at present, master, but our spy has estimated eight-hundred battle ready troops. However with Dalwyn's absence from Shelton's Crag, his one and only sibling, known as Dillon, has taken over power during his brother's absence. Already the young man is being called a military genius. Dillon has made treaty with the surrounding bandit lords, supplying them with food, weapons, and armour in return for their forays down into the barbarian-infested city of Karfael.'

'The barbarian clans from the Tunoka grass lands are gathering downriver from Karfael, this talk of magic returning has them spooked.

The emperor of Cavere, Magnus the third, has proclaimed that his empire will not be drawn into the escalating conflict around the supposed return of magic to the world and yet he has bolstered all his frontier garrisons with extra cavalry while drafting any man over the age of fifteen and able to fight.'

'Enough news Alexis, do we know where Dalwyn is now?'

'Yes, master, our men sent notice that he is on the Cavere and heading to Culchar. He plans to meet with an ally named Virgil who is the last living descendant of the Svette family that used to have estates in Karfael.'

'I need you to keep our men in Culchar on Dalwyn's trail; we need to track his movements at all times. Send a man who can talk the tribal languages of the Tunoka to Karfael with the news of the allegiance of the bandit lords and the Trevlon family and explain to them that we seek nothing but the knowledge that together we share a common enemy.'

'What about Zahra or Kaitlin, any news of their whereabouts yet?'

'Of Kaitlin and Raul, no. They seemed to have just vanished from the eyes of our clan, but Zahra was seen leaving Illume in the company of two men, one who had to be carried on a stretcher. They left by boat on the Winding River the day after the attack at the monastery, but no sign of them since then. There has been a high number of claims stating people have witnessed miracles or seen ancient artefacts from the age of magic come to life momentarily infused with magical light then fading away. The news of these events has travelled so fast that now all the worlds' powers are manoeuvring for position should they be true.'

Haakon stood, stretched his arms out, feeling the tense muscles fight against him, and then turned back to Alexis.

'Walk with me Alexis.' Haakon descended down the ladder past the startled guards into the day,

Alexis came stumbling after him slipping on the gravel path outside.

Haakon stood looking down at Alexis in disapproval until the red-faced boy stood brushing the dirt from his clothes.

'It seems young Alexis that certain aspects of your training are lacking. Remember that at your heart you are an assassin that might need to act in any moment to defend himself or his clan; second, you are the clan scribe.'

'Yes, master.' He fell neatly in alongside Haakon as he strode along the path.

' Now I have been thinking that this return of magic when it finally happens is going to be an event of such magnitude that it affects every living thing of our world in a way that we can have no idea of what to expect. Will it go back to how magic was in the age of magic, or will it be in some different form? The fact simply is that no one actually knows what will happen when magic is returned to us. It is simply our role to make sure the coterie are protected until such a time and not get side-tracked by the politicking of the nations around us. We serve no one in this situation except to honour the contract.'

Alexis was silent for a moment.

'What is on your mind, Alexis? Don't try to deny something is bothering you, I know the signs too well.'

'May I speak frankly, master?'

'If you must, then yes.'

'It seems to me that one way or the other magic will be returned to the world. Whether the coterie restore it when they choose to do so or they are all killed and the magic leaks out, it will be returned. We need to think about the future, master, possible alliances to protect us in the new emerging time to come. This is the perfect time to strike at our enemies while they are distracted. We could easily disguise our men to cause in fighting amongst the nations to our advantage. The possibilities are endless.'

Haakon stopped to face Alexis.

'You are young, Alexis, the youth want war, action, excitement. I was the same. However our entire clan was contracted to protect the coterie of the Heart until the magic is returned to this world. So we may not be assassinating leaders or causing political upheaval but this is more important than any contract we could ever have taken. Financially we are beyond wealthy which in itself will ensure the longevity of our clan.'

'But, master no one knows who we are, and the other clans almost believe we no longer exist. We should be proud of our clan, make sure everyone knows us to be the most effective option for hire. We have so many men doing nothing but waiting on your word to strike.'

'So you think I'm not proud of the clan?'

'Master I don't doubt that you are, but your men need to be proud too, and sitting around playing spy games doesn't allow them to achieve that. Could I be so bold as to suggest...'

A scuff of sandals on the path ahead signalled the arrival of Faustus. Alexis broke off suddenly bowing his head to the old physician.

'So bold as to suggest what?' asked Faustus?

'Our young scribe thinks we are wasting resources by no longer accepting contracts until the current one is concluded. He feels that many in the clan are not given the opportunity to be proud of their heritage and recent events are the perfect setting to announce ourselves again while securing powerful allies for the future.'

Faustus shook his head at Alexis.

'It serves us best to not exist. That is when we become untouchable or traceable. Never have we failed in a contract. Haakon shall not be the first to do so, and it is his choice on how to use the clan resources not yours, so learn your place boy. Run along, now, the adults need to talk.'

Alexis's head bowed, his reddened face neutral as he turned walking slowly back the way they had come.

'Haakon, watch that one; he is dangerous.'

'Who, Alexis? Bah, he's just a boy; I doubt he has it in him.'

'Yes, well, Nicholae failed to heed the warning about you too, Haakon.'

Haakon ignored the comment; instead he guided Faustus out along one of the jetties before turning to his old friend.

'Faustus, we need to relocate the clan house again. My injuries keep me from the astral world, but my sentinels protecting the coterie will not follow any orders but mine in person since I cannot leave messages astrally. They need me there. I'm going to need your guidance and support.'

'Of course, Haakon, but be aware I have a bad feeling about all this.'

They clasped each other's shoulders before continuing on their walk, unaware of the figure standing stone still amongst the plant shadows nearby.

Chapter 19

Nina regained consciousness during more of Zacriel's ramblings; as something crashed against the wall near her she decided to pretend to still be asleep even though her throat was sore and bruised and she ached for cool water to soothe it. Something had been put on her wrists; through slit eyelids she saw them to be manacles.

'You think I had a choice?' rasped Zacriel.

His back was to her and Nina wondered who he was talking to. She decided it was himself. Maybe he was like what Daddy used to say about Mommy; that all women have multiple personalities and that's why they were so difficult to deal with.

'You think I didn't try to be good, but it wasn't my fault my parents hated me. They were evil and so I was born evil. I am evil!'

'You don't have to be bad!'

Before she could stop it Nina had blurted out the words, she lay there on the bed cringing and slowly opened her eyes.

Zacriel stood facing her, eyes wide. 'What did you say?' he whispered. Then he sprung onto the bed. Nina tried to scramble away, but the manacles reached the end of their tether and jerked hard on her wrists, causing her to cry out.

Zacriel straddled her and pulled her hair back, forcing her to look up at him. 'I asked what you said,' he yelled at her as he raised a fist.

Nina was crying now, great sobs that kept coming and coming and between them she screamed back. 'I said you can choose! No one else has the power to choose for you.'

'Child, you speak as if you have experience in life, but I can tell you are just repeating gibberish learnt from your aristocratic parents who probably had everything handed to them on a platter, just like you!' He emphasised this statement with a hard poke to her chest with his index finger.

Her cries now had turned to shrieks 'I have had nothing handed to me but sadness.'

His face still close to Nina's, Zacriel laughed derisively.

'Get used to it, Nina. Make the pain your friend and turn it against those who wrong you, claim back your power, and stop being WEAK!'

'Through her large, blue eyes with tears painting her cheeks she spoke to him in an urgent whisper. 'Let me go. You can change now, can you please let me go?'

Zacriel gently stroked her hair back, used his shirt sleeve to dry away the tears on her face, and spoke in a voice as cold as winter. 'Child, I cannot let you go, you have much to learn and so little time.'

⁂

The smell of guano soothed Cinerus as it always did when he visited the Spiral. Other smells were layered beneath it, and he detected the musky incense sticks burnt for sacrifice days and the fading smell of fresh air as he delved deeper into his realm. Fluttering wings were gathering for his visit as he arrived at the spiral's edge and stopped.

The bats swooped down and around him, shrieking and brushing along his body. The love he felt for these creatures swelled within him, and briefly he imagined it must be the same for any parent seeing a child after some absence.

He stood on the edge of the spiral like he had that day long ago ready to be sacrificed to the god of the mountain as his family and friends looked on hoping his death would bring about the return of the gods who had deserted the world. Except Cinerus hadn't died that day like those who had gone before him. For reasons not yet known Cinerus had been saved by the bats.

The caress of his children lasted longer than usual but he was content to let it be so. Much time had passed since he had visited the site of the prophecy he had discovered so long ago and he needed time to think about all that had happened. Naturally he ended up here.

Cinerus let himself fall forward into the depths of the spiral, feeling the air snap at his robes and he gasped as adrenaline flowed through his veins. Soft bodies formed a blanket beneath him as sharp claws and fangs latched onto his skin and robes slowing the decent and lowering him to the cavern floor alive with hundreds of tiny flowing wounds.

He welcomed the pain they brought and allowed it to cut through the clutter of his thoughts to focus on this place of sanctuary. Though blind, Cinerus could recall exactly how the chamber looked, from the pure silver torch sconces to the mysterious mural covered walls that told a story of prophecy. He remembered that terrifying day after his sacrifice and the lights from above had dwindled. His loved ones left him to his fate down in the Spiral, confused, alone, and in pain. That day he had fished inside his clothes to find the moonstone his mother had given him amongst her tears of anguish as he was led away from her. As he waited for the death that never came, Cinerus used that light to search his surroundings and found not only a trove of treasure left from previous sacrifices but the prophecy etched and painted on the caverns walls.

Since birth Cinerus had endured problems with his eyes, and by the time he was to be sacrificed to the spiral his vision was already clouding over but in the soft green light of the moonstone as he followed the etched story of prophecy in a state of fear and awe his vision was as clear as it had ever been.

Letting his fingers trace the scenes on the cool walls, Cinerus became one with its story following it to the end where it depicted the coming of the fallen one from the heavens who would lead them back to the surface and to victory against those who had wronged all the pitiful souls forced to live below the mountain. The twisted runic script read, 'When the fallen one's wings are lost forever, then and only then will the forsaken rise to throw down their oppressors, earning their return to the realm of stars.'

When Zacriel had arrived, Cinerus was so sure he would fulfil the prophecy, but at times he experienced doubt creeping into his thoughts. Was Zacriel the fallen one as he had so readily accepted, or had Cinerus made a grave mistake?

The mighty, arrogant Zacriel certainly accepted the position of saviour and yet had done nothing but take from his rescuers, never showing any knowledge or interest of the prophecy or the plight of this tunnelled realm. With news of Zacriel's arrival, people from Slumsville and its neighbouring towns flocked to see this fallen god. They brought delicacies of food and wealth, some even of flesh to heap upon their saviour and Zacriel had taken it all. He was still yet to show why he had been chosen to lead them forth from the darkness.

Thanks to the quick actions of Cinerus and his people, Zacriel had recovered relatively quickly from his injuries. The town of Slumsville housed a number of talented healers and apothecaries whose skills had reduced the damage to Zacriel's body considerably. Now no longer bedridden Zacriel had begun making demands of Cinerus and talking about the army that was forming beneath the mountain as his own. The twisted creature had also turned his interest to little Nina, an orphan struggling to shine her light within the devouring darkness of the streets of Slumsville. Nina had led the woman named Zahra and her monk companion out from the tunnels to the river and that was the only reason Cinerus could fathom as to why Zacriel desired the girl stay by him. Cinerus had heard Zacriel telling the girl that he intended to show her the path to power and shed her weakness forever. Did he also have that in store for the people below the mountain who had rescued and healed him?

Zacriel began taking Nina with him on his forays to inspect his growing army, and Cinerus the bat-loving idiot had surprised him with his efficiency and contacts. Cinerus still insisted that as he stood a willing sacrifice all those years ago on the edge of the spiral awaiting his death at the claws and fangs of the bats, but instead was dropped softly to the floor at the spiral's base. The blind fool had taken him to this spiral, and Zacriel had played along with him faking amazement and awe as he looked into the darkness of a dusty cavern stinking of musk and bat shit, the place of prophecy apparently.

Few things excited Zacriel anymore, but this day he thrilled to be up and about, though pain still taunted him when he walked.

He strode along whistling, dragging Nina with him, enjoying the muffled grunts of pain when he jerked the chain around her neck. She thought she had beaten him by refusing to eat, drink, or converse with him, and it was the last that riled him the most. He was preparing her for ascension, but she was ungrateful, self-important, and weak. Their battle of wills was just beginning though and she would learn just like his parents had taught him. *Her walls will be broken down and then I will rebuild her, show her that we cannot truly change but only embrace that which is our true nature.*

Coming to a ledge, Zacriel dragged Nina to him, scooped up her small form, and jumped to the corridor below. Two of Cinerus's men waited here, holding reins of a magnificent beetle, green and black in colour. Atop it sat a large saddle and Zacriel climbed up and hoisted Nina up behind him.

The beetle moved quickly, scurrying through the maze of corridors before eventually stopping amongst the huge rocks of a fallen structure. At first Zacriel thought they had bought him to the temple where he was struck down, but then he realized the differences. A heavy stone door was being pried open by two soldiers who grunted and shook with the effort.

Zacriel leaped nimbly from the beetle's back, dragging Nina with him. Unfortunately for her she was not so nimble and the useless child fell hard with a stifled yelp. As he strode towards the opening a piece of darkness detached itself and stepped out to meet him. 'Cinerus?'

'Yes, Zacriel, it is I, back from my visit to the spiral, and I have a gift for you.'

'A gift, you say?'

Cinerus gestured to the now open door to a narrow set of dusty stairs.

'This leads to the holy tower of Shail. It will be the perfect vantage point for you to conduct the fall of Illume… oh, the irony.'

'Wasn't the gift I was expecting but thank you anyway, Cinerus, I guess.'

Cinerus grasped Zacriel's arm. 'Go up the stairs it waits for you there.'

'What? Take your damn claws off me!'

Cinerus pulled Zacriel closer, and Zacriel was surprised at the thin man's strength.

'Do you have so little faith in us, my lord? Climb the stairs and see what your people have done for you.'

Momentarily taken back, Zacriel allowed Cinerus to lead him and Nina up the cramped, narrow stairs to a door that opened out onto a balcony and looked down over the city of Illume. It was beautiful up here. To his left something moved and he turned swiftly, expecting danger, but in front of him lay sleek figure curled on the stone wall, its fine ebony form blending with the tower stone. It was a Lunar. Cinerus nudged him, and he looked down to see the man was offering a wooden whistle.

'Try her, Zacriel, she is yours now.'

Zacriel unchained Nina, handed the chain to Cinerus then stepped forward to plant a hand on the Lunar's flank. Its antennae whirled, and it gave a bleating noise at his touch. He blew the whistle softly and climbed in the saddle upon the Lunar's back. Once he was strapped in, Zacriel, blew a long note and the Lunar pushed up off the tower banking away, and once again Zacriel revelled in the joy of flying.

Chapter 20

Zahra trickled water into Ishmael's mouth then sat at the side of the boat, fingers trailing in the cool river as she studied the passing forest. The river had branched off into a side tributary to the east and Murk had told her it would continue to wind back on itself until it met back with the Devouring River. With luck they would bypass the problem and come back out on the open river.

The forest here was lightly powdered in thin pink crystals that clung to leaves and branches and crumbled if touched. She imagined it must be like snow even though she had never seen it herself. Zahra had to think of what to do next. She had no way of safely getting in contact with the clan and had specific orders not to return to the clan house with her charge.

By the gods, she didn't even know if the other coterie had been attacked or if Ishmael was the sole target. His condition had changed everything. There was no point travelling in haste to the meeting place while he was comatose. They would attract too much attention.

Then there was Manu. Zahra hated to leave their fate in his hands. Sure, he had kept Ishmael alive, but getting information out of him regarding this mysterious healer in the Jewelled Forest was like prying coins from a beggar.

Turning slightly, Zahra looked around at her companions. Yolinda lay in one of the hammocks, snoring softly alongside Ishmael's frightfully still form. Meanwhile Manu and Murk seemed to be getting on famously with the help of two flasks of brandy. Zahra knew she should be annoyed, but Manu was a big boy and right now she was so tired; as she drifted away into sleep the slurred words of Manu and Murk offered some comfort of just knowing there were friends around her.

Sometime later Zahra awoke with a start as Yolinda gently shook her shoulder. Instinctively her hand reached for the knife at her side, but she released it as Yolinda smiled at her warmly and passed her a bowl of what smelt like stew with a large, crusty piece of bread. Behind Yolinda by lamp light Manu was tending to Ishmael while Murk carefully steered the boat slowly through the fading light of the day. The stew was good and soon gone. Zahra scanned the banks of the river for any sign of danger but could detect nothing but the continuous croaking of the large Calipo frogs that seemed to have gathered in packs to watch their craft pass by. Standing and stretching her sore limbs Zahra moved over to Murk's side.

They both sat quietly as the suns dying rays reflected off the white and blue crystals that covered the forest's trees. Where before they were thinly coated in crystal, here the crystal was thicker and grew in fungus like clumps that held in the last sun rays long after it faded and left the river and forest bathed in a blue-and-white luminescence. Murk's deep voice nearly startled her.

'It's said that the farther you travel toward the forest's center the more the crystals coloring changes and becomes more rare and beautiful. So too do the Harlequin's colouring change to reflect how dangerous they are. The white Harlequins, for example are said to be merely workers and servants while the black or onyx are the lords and leaders among them. Have you ever seen one, Zahra?'

'Not alive,' she answered. 'They have always fascinated me. Not long after being in Illume for the first time I witnessed the return of a mercenary from the Jewelled lands. He bought back a Harlequin body with him, flame orange in colour. On the river bank near the jetties he caved in the Harlequin's chest and pulled out the orange, glittering heart to sell for use as a Jaldurial house spirit. Once the heart had been removed the body collapsed, its colouring faded right there in front of me leaving what appeared to be a pile of broken glass. It somehow felt wrong to see its body desecrated like that.'

Murk switched arms on the tiller. 'Let me tell you a story that one of the Harlequin once told me.'

Zahra perked up to listen.

'When the world was still young, the god of water, who was then known as Unkta the crying god, stopped crying. The world started to dry up. People across the land prayed fervently to the gods and sacrificed much, hoping in return for rain. Diseases were rampant, war over water broke out, and the death toll grew daily. A Jingtalla child from the tribe that lives not far from here at the Jingtalla falls decided to contact Unkta. He travelled through the Jewelled lands, which then was called the dew lands, and climbed up high to the top of the Rothair mountain, above even where Illume now sits. Once there he called out to Unkta to hear his plea.

'For four long days and nights the boy sat there calling upon the god. Finally out of annoyance Unkta assumed the form of a giant moon-touched raven and landed beside the child, threatening to tear out his belly if the summons was not important. The god heard the boy's plea and replied. "Alas I can no longer cry, my life here is fulfilled, and I know no sadness." The child collapsed then, and as he lay dying a funny joke came to mind that his father had once told him. He beckoned the god over to him and told the joke.

'A great roaring was then heard followed by claps of thunder. Unkta laughed so hard that he started crying. He fell from the mountain top and smashed into the side of Rothair, and forming the crater which the city Illume is now built into. Unkta lay at the base of the mountain crying for weeks, and water flooded the land once again. The child returned home a hero and became a great chief.

'The Harlequin then explained to me that when the god fell and hit the mountain, large pieces of it crashed down into this very forest around us and from the crystal found in this stone and with the heavy rains the Harlequin were born.' Zahra sighed. She looked out over the water, smiling.

'That is a beautiful story. It really captures the peculiarity of the Harlequin. I have also heard that the Harlequin cannot survive long away from water, and are at their most powerful beneath the rain that forms the crystal that covers these lands. The rain is reported to aid in healing them and reforming their bodies after injuries.'

Murk glanced at Zahra. 'I don't know anything about that except he was the oddest creature, utterly alien with intensely judgemental eyes that made you feel as if you were a child again.'

'How much farther until we meet up with the main river? Asked Zahra.

Murk shrugged. 'I would hazard to say only a day now that we are flowing with the current. However we still have to pass the ill-fated passage of the drowned'

They stopped as the sun broke through the trees that morning so Murk could rest. Murk looked weary after guiding them through the night, but before he slept he gathered the motley crew together. 'Today we pass through the passage of Drowned and we will be tithed by the river trolls there. They require fresh meat, fish, and whatever suits their queen's liking at the time. Let me do the talking and we will be fine; give the proper respect to Jayne and we will be leaving in one piece. We will leave again at midday.'

Chapter 21

The hunting was good here. Zahra smirked in satisfaction as her latest arrow struck the boar in the side of the neck. The beast fled straight into a tree and toppled down with bloody froth bubbling from its snout. It struggled to rise as she approached with her knife, and she stood above it peering down trying to glimpse what that final moment before death was like. Was it painful or did something within the body release a natural painkiller. What was like a low growl came from her left? Not even ten feet away crouched a large cougar that hissed as Zahra locked eyes with it. The great cat crept forward a step, a long growl rising from its throat, ears pinned back.

Zahra felt the change come. Quelling her instinct to back away, she dropped the crossbow and drew her knife from its sheath. 'Catch your own meal, you bitch!'

The cougar slashed out a paw narrowly missing Zahra's outstretched arm but she twirled away from the blow and let her spin bring her close to the animal. As its head snaked out, teeth ready to maul, her blade dove down into its face. The blade met air as the cat leapt back into a crouch, teeth bared, and its wide eyes locked on hers; the two predators weighed each other up. Then the cat was moving, fleeing away into the bush searching for easier prey elsewhere as a twig snapped nearby.

Zahra walked over to the boar carcass. 'Come help me, Manu there is some butchering to do.'

Manu squatted down beside her as she started to skin the beast.

'You going to help or sit there like a sack of shit?'

'You okay, Zahra?'

The question made her pause then she continued to skin.

'Of course I'm all right. Skinning animals never bothered me.'

'You just stood there laughing at a cougar, Zahra. By the gods, you're lucky to be alive.'

Running his hands through his hair he then pulled a flask from his belt. 'Strangest thing I ever saw, a cougar fleeing a girl armed with a knife and laughing like a mad woman.'

She shrugged her shoulders. 'The cat saw its death in my eyes so it fled. What is so strange about that?'

'It seems to me you throw yourself into danger with reckless abandon almost as if you would be happy to die.'

Looking up, Zahra studied Manu, blood spots flecked on his face gleaming in the filtered sunlight. 'I surrender to death when I am in danger; there is nothing else at that moment but to be who I need to for survival. Long ago my master told me that death had marked me as one of his own and he had seen that I was like him, and that is why he took me in.'

'You seem so haunted, Zahra.'

'We all have our burden to carry, Manu. If I knew any better I would say you actually care about me.'

'Maybe I do…, after all you are the closest thing to a sister that I have. An ugly sister to be sure and none too bright, but…'

Zahra burst out laughing, 'Well you hardly help the situation? Any potential suitors I may have are scared to death of the freak with me.'

'Yes, threatened by my manliness, they realize it would be useless to stand up to me over a woman.'

Zahra pretended to retch. 'You're going to make me hurl if you keep this up. C'mon help me carry this meat back.'

Manu walked ahead whistling merrily, and Zahra smiled at his antics. His joking had bought her back to herself allowing a moment to forget this greater situation she was faced with.

They emerged from the forest to see that Yolinda had put together a sizable package of bright cloth, a large painted lantern, a glass jewellery box, and pots of spices. The meat was wrapped in large pom frond leaves and tied with vines.

'I always thought Jayne of the river was superstitious nonsense,' muttered Manu as they worked.

'She's as real as the blood that flows in your veins Manu,' Yolinda replied. 'I have only passed through the passage twice before with Murk, and she is quite a character and unpredictable too. It is said she is over two hundred years old, and believe me, she looks it too. She surrounds herself with other things to pretend she is young still and holds court like any queen.'

Early that afternoon with the sun high in the sky they were on the river again. The foliage had changed to a darkish blue and purple that seemed to Zahra to drain away some of the excitement of what was to come, replacing it with an unfamiliar nervousness, the feeling something wasn't right. Things were taking too long; she needed to get Ishmael to the safe house or they would believe him dead and she had failed. What was he going through? Was he even alive and aware inside, or was the damage already done?

Chapter 22

Nina had thought about escaping to the surface, try to find Zahra and warn her of Zacriel. Cinerus seemed to read her thoughts and had kept her with him. In all the time spent down here beneath the city, Nina hated the way the man would just stare at her, with empty holes boring into her soul, and she felt there was no hiding from Cinerus.

As she accompanied him on his inspection of the growing army she noted the effect Cinerus had on the men and women who were preparing to fight for Zacriel, the so-called saviour who had fallen from the skies. By the sun's grace! Didn't they realize he was just another Infernal, a nasty, mean creature who used to be a man and now was pretending to be a fallen god? Cinerus ran his underworld realm with iron rules that brooked no mercy if broken, and yet he would also take the time to help his people where possible. Often his goons would be seen providing some charitable act to make sure families didn't go unfed or providing shelter and protection for those found worthy. So why was he so blind to the manipulations of Zacriel? Nina guessed Cinerus had become desperate for his prophecy to be true.

Nina was no soldier, but even she was impressed with the growing army that had amassed in such a short time. They even had some weapons of steel, shiny and sharp, ready to kill at a moment's notice.

They stood upon a circular smooth rock above the soldiers working below. Some of the soldiers saw Cinerus and began chanting his name, and as more and more joined in Nina thought that surely if they continued this racket even the surface people would hear and come see what was happening beneath their mountain.

Cinerus had called for those who he had allocated the roles of leaders who showed their adoration for him with hugs before he impatiently signalled for quiet.

'We are children of the mountain, we are on the brink of a new age, and our time to crawl from the crevices and tunnels is nearly at hand. Our saviour is among us to fulfil the prophecy that foretold his coming. It is a time of contemplation, and for you leaders to remember what we have been forced to sacrifice and endure beneath the oppression of this society that is referred to as civilized. There is nothing civilized about a world that shuns others less fortunate, forcing them to crawl away into the crevices like bugs, to seek refuge in the darkness away from the light. My leaders, you know your roles in this war. We are many, and we will strike where the city is most vulnerable. In a war we cannot openly defeat our overlords, but we can bring them down with one well-placed strike that destroys the council and disables the Illume blades. In ten days' time we strike while the city still lives in fear from the events of the Festival of Lanterns. Zacriel now puts the final touch on his own preparation to lead us, so go now and distribute the food my men have prepared for you all. Our liberation is soon at hand.'

'Do you really think Zacriel is the saviour from the prophecy, Cinerus?' Nina asked

Cinerus said nothing for a moment but stopped walking and turned to her. 'Yes, I do, Nina, his coming was foretold. Do you doubt it?'

'He doesn't care for us people here. He only cares about revenge. He won't stay to fight with us.'

'You will see child that he is the one, and in ten days you will see why.'

'If he isn't the right one, what then?'

But if Cinerus had heard he didn't respond and instead started walking away.

Later that night Zacriel mounted his new steed and took to the night sky. The Lunar turned out to be a chameleon breed, it's now ebony skin almost undetectable. The flying was nowhere as fluid as when he had his own wings, but the Lunar could complete tight turns and dives easily or glide upon winds if needed. The act of flying again boosted Zacriel's mood immensely, and when he had finished he went looking for Nina. He found her reading some book, once again chained to the bone bed.

'What is capturing your attention so fully, Nina, some children's book?'

'Nothing that would interest, you Zacriel,' she replied closing the little book. 'It's a book on how it's not important what things happen to us but how we react to them, an idea you don't understand.'

Zacriel laughed loudly, interrupting her.

'You said you wanted justice for the murder of your family, Nina, so why not seek it out yourself.'

'I will see my parents' murderers brought to justice the right way, within the rules.'

'Ha, the laws are enforced by powers beyond you or me. Do you honestly feel you would be able to bring them to judgement and win? The man that killed your family is a high-ranking member of the trade guild and sits upon the council of Illume. They will never take your word over his.'

Nina stuck out her lip petulantly.

'I will find a way to avenge my parents and open the highway to the coast, to see my father's dream that he died for come to pass.'

'Then let me help you, Nina,' Zacriel said. 'You can't do it alone. Let us show this killer what it's like to be the hunted, peering wide-eyed into the shadows, always looking over his shoulders never knowing what's coming next. You will get to see the hopelessness and fear in his eyes, not to mention his comprehension of his impending demise.

Your parents were idealists, but this is far from an ideal world; instead the strong prey on the weak, and you must choose where you fit in. Do you want to repeat the mistakes of your parents?'

The passage came into view. It was considered a natural phenomenon; the trees had spread their seeking fingers from the banks and met above the river to twist together forming a natural passage. Crystalline blossoms graced the opening of the passage and curled around the rusted portcullis, and green lights stretched off into the darkness within.

A village lined the river banks, and a group of young trolls ran splashing into the river to swim alongside the boat, hooting and whistling as they came. 'Ware the boat, you grey-scummed bloated fish guts, keep your greasy mitts out of the goods or you will get nothing. Lead me to Jayne then I have some special treats for...'

Murk never finished the sentence. A spear arced out from the bank closest to the boat thrown by a loping troll. It struck Murk with such force it pinned him to the deck as it re-emerged from his body. On both banks other trolls were now rushing the boat. Yolinda was screaming; Manu had moved to help Murk but couldn't pull the spear from the deck to lower him, and each tug drew a grimace from the boatman. Ishmael lay on the deck so vulnerable to spears falling like rain around them. How long before one struck him?

Zahra moved to Ishmael and stood above him waiting for the first troll to come over the side. A young troll climbed over the side, wicked talons digging into the timber next to her searching for purchase. Zahra neatly severed one of its hands, and it fell back screaming into the water; spinning on her heel she sank the dagger into the throat of a second troll looming above her. Everything around Zahra seemed to slow down; she saw Manu batting away at trolls climbing onto the boat with an oar which was then torn from his grasp, and he was swarmed. Yolinda was still screaming, and Murk slumped awkwardly on the impaling spear haft his blood draining along the deck.

Zahra stepped over to the troll above Manu and slit its throat, kicked another with such force it fell back off the boat into the river, only for it to be replaced with three more trolls knobbed with barnacles and eyes glittering with hatred. They couldn't win here, she thought desperately as a huge figure climbed aboard the boat beside her. Turning, Zahra looked up at the troll that now towered above her, tilting the boat with its weight. Breathing heavily, Zahra ducked under a clumsy grab from the troll and jammed her knife up into its armpit, then she slid between the beast's legs avoiding the troll's slashing claws. Now behind the troll Zahra produced a garrotte from her belt, leapt up onto its back then looped the wire around the throat of the troll and let her body be the weight that tightened the garrotte.

The troll fell to its knees as the wire tore through its throat, black blood fountaining from its neck, and the troll fell back into the river.

Strong arms grabbed Zahra from behind trapping her arms and pushing her to the deck where her arms were bound. In front of her Yolinda was still screaming as a young troll yanked her hair; Manu lay dazed and Murk was still pinned by the spear, standing back arched, gasping silently like a fish out of water.

As the craft now crewed by the trolls slipped to shore, Murk's life also slipped away leaving a smiling corpse. Maybe the famous orange carp of Aril had come to take him after all thought Zahra.

Chapter 23

The three prisoners were dragged off the boat and marched through the village to a small castle. Two trolls dressed in the livery of guards opened the doors to a long hall of white- and-blue floor tiles that ended at a throne of shell, inlaid with precious stones. Two naked human girls perched in a shallow pool beside the throne, pouring buckets of water gently over the wizened figure that sat upright upon it.

Jayne of the river sat tall upon her throne, a gown of silvered fish scales, stunning black hair coiled into a bun to allow a view of the necklace fashioned from silver and amber stones. The effect was stunning until one looked closely at her skin, which was dry and cracked, then the horror sunk in as those eyes turned upon Zahra, hungrily darting over her and drinking in her visage. Jayne was laughing softly, not unlike a clashing of stones as she regarded Yolinda.

'Well, come here, Yolinda, don't you know how to behave when greeting old friends?'

One of the trolls pushed Yolinda, and she stumbled forward sketching a rough curtsey.

Jayne stretched her hand out, grasping Yolinda's and pulling her close, ignoring the tear that slid down the woman's cheek and the visible shaking of her lower lip.

'Why frightened, little one? Jayne won't hurt you.'

Yolinda gave a short sharp laugh. 'Don't sit there saying that when one of ours lie dead upon our boat. Jayne, is this how you greet visitors now, with spears instead of words and trade?'

Jayne's eyes narrowed, and one desiccated hand grasped Yolinda's chin drawing her close.

'Murk and you made certain promises last time you travelled this way, and these promises turned out to be empty. Murk's death was unfortunate but necessary, for I cannot let those who defy me to freely wander around bringing disrespect to my name.

'Enough, later we will talk of you and your future, for now sit here beside me, Yolinda. I find such pretty companions are scarce in my kingdom.'

With Yolinda sitting in the water next to her, Jayne absently twirled her fingers through the woman's hair and turned her gaze to Manu and Ishmael then back to Zahra.

'What is your name, girl?'

It is of no consequence to you. My companions and I are caught up in some feud we want no part of. With your leave, my lady, I would gather my injured companions and be on our way. We brought tribute and seek no trouble in your kingdom, just permission to travel through your lands, my lady.'

'You can't leave me here, Zahra,' shrieked Yolinda before a rough jerk of Jayne's hand in her hair broke her words off.

Jayne grinned manically in a sick imitation of Yolinda.

'You can't leave me here, Zahra.'

'Why leave Zahra? Stay here and work with me, I will give you everything you desire and more…'

'Cut the bullshit, Jayne I have no time for lies.'

Her words were cut off by Jayne's powerful voice. 'Remember where you are human. The next time you choose to tell me what to do, I will not be so forgiving. Guards! Bring her to me for judgement.'

Zahra was dragged forward by two trolls to the edge of the pool, her head forced back by the hair to see Jayne's face just above hers.

'I, Jayne of the river and sworn queen of these realms, do hereby swear you and your companions as enemies to the kingdom and thus sentenced to death by drowning.'

Zahra was briefly aware of the roar of approval from the assorted members of Jayne's court before having her head thrust below surface. As she struggled, the wire binding her wrists dug in painfully. Pressure mounted on her chest and head as darkness crept into her view.

Zahra was heaved up by the guards again, coughing and gasping.

'Oh my, poor thing, don't struggle; now, just relax and surrender. This doesn't have to be painful.'

The ancient face bent forward, kissing Zahra's brow. 'I forgive, you child.'

Then Zahra was below the water again, straining to fight and escape even as strength faded from her already battered body. Again they pulled her out letting her thrash on the floor weakly. Awaiting the next and probably final dunking, Zahra's hearing started to return. From where she lay Zahra watched as an incredibly tall man climbed the stairs. His eyes briefly rested on hers then looked away, discarding her fully.

'Mother, let me have these humans. I have foreseen this visit, and it is necessary that I return the life to that one there,' he said, pointing to Ishmael's prone form, 'and these others I will need to attend me in such matters.'

'My son. So you choose to visit your mother at last, and the first words out of your mouth are demands? There is the simple matter of what's in it for me.'

'In return for this boon I will offer my services to you once only for no charge.'

This must have been some discount, thought Zahra as the deal was made. At her new master's gesture she stood and started to follow him then turned back to Jayne. She was kneeling before Yolinda and untying the girl's dress and letting it slip from her shoulders.

'I won't leave without Yolinda,' shouted Zahra.'

A hand spun her around and the tall man hissed. 'You are lucky to be alive; it's too late for your friend, now come.'

Looking back at Yolinda who was now being molested by the ancient troll queen, Zahra caught Yolinda's eyes. The girl mouthed, 'Don't leave me here!'

Then she was being pulled away by her saviour. They collected Manu and Ishmael and stowed them comfortably into a cart. Zahra sat up front with the tall man driving the cular steeds.

The man turned his attention to Zahra showing white teeth in a horrible grin. 'I am Ramon the river wanderer at your service. You have questions, I know, but now is not the time. When we get to my hut then you shall have my answers also.'

As the cart lurched away from the village and the river, Zahra felt sick to her stomach. They had left Yolinda there in that disgusting bitch's hands to do as she wanted with her. As they travelled, Zahra kept replaying that moment over and over in her head.

Don't leave me here.

The mission is too important, she rationalized silently, don't lose focus of your true mission. The casualties were to be expected, the girl as good as dead already. Touched by death, Haakon had said. You will bring deaths to all you love and care for, forced to watch those lives twinkle out of existence because you, my little raven, are touched by death.

Soon the rhythmic movements of the cart drew her into a disturbed rest.

In the rear of the cart Manu opened his eyes, tongued his swollen lip, and wondered. Events had led them here, and if he was not wrong then this Ramon was the shaman they searched for. He just thought the shaman would be human. He had said that this meeting was foreseen, and Manu wanted to know what else Ramon had seen.

Chapter 24

Nina awoke to Zacriel shaking her. 'Come, Nina, I have a surprise for you, you're going to love this.'

Still disoriented from sleep and trying to gather her wits, Nina found herself dragged to a small circular chamber in which a hooded figure sat tied to a chair. Muffled yells came from the hood; it was a man. Whoever the man was he was huge and wore a shirt the size of a tent, cut of expensive silk with tight black trousers and high, leather boots. Both hands were adorned with expensive rings of turquoise with one large one sporting a seal in the design of an owl for sealing documents.

At the sight of this ring Nina felt began feeling anxious. She knew that ring and that it belonged to Ezekiel Perdomo, the man who had murdered her family.

Zacriel stood beside his hostage and removed the hood, revealing the man's tear-streaked face, his jowls wobbling with his silent sobs.

'Why, Zacriel? What did you bring him here for?'

'This is what you wanted, isn't it, Nina? This is the part where you slake your vengeance on the man who took your parents from you. Kill him and it will set you free to get on with your life.'

'Zacriel, just because this man murdered my parents, killing him won't bring them back.' 'Yes, but their death will be avenged, Nina which is what you want. Isn't it?'

'Well, yes, but not like this. I want people to know this man's crimes, not for him to suddenly disappear.'

'Kill him and be done with him,' Zacriel told her. He deserves no less for what he has done to you. By leaving him alive you allow him to prey on others. Surely this is an evil that must be stopped. It would be wrong of you to let this man go.'

Nina looked intently at Ezekiel. He seemed only a shadow of the man she had witnessed laughing and joking about her father's death. He was fatter now and draped with so much jewellery he rattled as he sobbed.

Zacriel nudged her shoulder, and she turned seeing the blade he proffered to her. She reached down and grasped the handle; the metal was cold.

'It's easy, Nina just stick the blade deep into his chest,' whispered Zacriel by her side.

'Do it, be strong. Others have taken from you all your life haven't they? Now is the time for you to take and fight back, Nina.'

Ezekiel's eyes were on her now, tracking the movement of the knife.

'Girl, I don't know you, but I am sure we can come to some arrangement. Obviously you have me confused with someone else...'

Nina pushed the point of the blade into a fingertip, watching the ruby bead form around the blade as it pierced her skin.

'Listen girl, Nina, is it? I have a lot of gold. If you release me now I give you my word that you will walk away with more money than you can imagine. My word is my bond, let us be friends rather than enemies.'

Nina slowly raised her gaze to Ezekiel's face. Her breathing had become laboured and shallow, and her hands shook slightly. 'Your word is your bond, huh, how honest was your word when you murdered my family?' She grabbed his chin, forcing him to look into her face.

'Look closely; do you see whose daughter I am? YOU KILLED MY FATHER! Why would you do that? They never hurt anyone, and you murdered them.' The rage inside her blurred her vision along with the tears. With the hand on the chin she forced his head back, exposing his throat, and held the knife to the soft flesh there.

'Yes, Nina, do it!'

Images replayed in her mind as she held the blade there, of her baby brother learning to walk, her father's happiness at winning the contract that would connect Illume to the coastal port of Whaleson, creating jobs for the poor and wealth for all, her mother kissing her goodnight and the pair of them dancing to the minstrel's voices that carried up to the estate from the taverns below. Then the image of her parents arguing over what was the right thing to do after they caught a thief in their household. Her father exclaiming that two wrongs don't make a right and there was no excuse for taking another's man's life then giving the thief money and food before escorting him off the premises.

The blade descended, and Ezekiel's shrill scream was like music to Nina's ears.

The rope fell to the floor. Ezekiel kept blubbering as he realized he was still alive. He had soiled himself and the stench was awful. 'I don't ever want to see your face again. One day the Merchant road will be opened in honour of my father, and you will rot in the darkest, dirtiest jail for your crimes.' She turned to Zacriel who stood aghast, hands over his mouth. 'I will not kill him because you say to. I am not bad like you.'

Nina turned and slowly walked out of the room past Cinerus, who stood outside the chamber following her movement with his head at an angle, face unreadable.

Chapter 25

Even with the swaying of the cart Zahra managed to get some restful sleep, and when she awoke the forest crystals had turned an orange-red and the cart had stopped.

'We are at my home,' Ramon said. 'Tonight when the moons rise I will consult the spirits regarding your friend. Bring him inside while I light the lanterns and build a fire.'

Once they had Ishmael placed safely inside the hut Zahra stripped the clothes off him and bathed him in a blend of herbs provided by Ramon who insisted the mix would make Ishmaels spirit easier to locate within the spirit world. Ramon then painted peculiar symbols on Ishmael's skin just above his navel and upon his cheeks before retreating to the shelter with Zahra and Manu.

As Ramon and Manu squatted by a fire stirring a clear viscous liquid in a clay pot, Zahra joined them.

'Ramon, earlier you said you had foreseen our visit. What else did you see?'

This close to Ramon, Zahra could easily see the resemblance to his mother, his size and the greenish tinge to his skin. Ramon leaned forward and slowly stirred the bubbling liquid before answering Manu.

'I came to this moment we share now within the spirit world, and this is how I knew you would be coming here. The Earth mother has shown me the importance of your friend Ishmael in my dreams and as a care taker of this world I was sent to intercede and bring him back to this body.'

'Wait, you mean you have lived through this moment. How does one do this, Ramon?'

'In the world of spirit, or the astral realm as some people call it, every event has an imprint. One can travel to any imprint within the past or future if you know how to access it. It requires strict training to acquire the pure intent needed to locate specific people and times, especially in the future because the imprints are future possibilities only and are not so clear. As a shaman, I can ride the astral rivers confident my intent will take me to events that have importance or may be decisive in the future to shape the world around me.'

'So how will you bring him back, Ramon, and where is he?'

'To avoid dying, he has connected himself to the Earth tree. Her energy has kept him alive and for a reason that only she knows she has chosen to let him live. Ishmael has spent too long in the spirit realm any longer and he may forget his human life. I will bring his spirit back to this existence, which will be hard and very painful for him, almost like being reborn. There is a great journey ahead of Ishmael, and his choices while on this path will shape and mould the world forever. It remains to be seen whether he will do the Earth mother's bidding or use his power to do as he pleases. The signs say the time is close and the Earth is healed enough to allow magic to return.'

Later, under the moonlight, Zahra and Manu watched as Ramon carried Ishmael out onto a bed of smouldering branches chosen from selected power plants. The freshly killed carcass of some kind of animal lay next to the branches. Ramon laid Ishmael's head close to the carcass. They both noticed that the remnants of the maiden's kiss plant the abbot had used to close his wounds had risen to the surface of his skin. Like a swollen serpent, the plants tendrils snaked beneath the skin seeking to escape their temporary home. As they watched the plant started to come out Ishmael's nose and mouth. Ramon knelt beside Ishmael, carefully pulling the plant from his body and placing in upon the fire to shrivel and die even as it tried to move towards the bloody meat.

The process was slow, and Zahra had to get up and walk around to stay awake. Her own wounds were painful, and sight had barely returned to her eye that had been damaged while fleeing the winged Infernal. Manu sat mesmerized, watching the shaman as he worked, and Zahra didn't want to distract either of them. She knew nothing of the healing arts so was content to stay away. Chimes passed before Ramon rose to his feet and using a spear hoisted the dead meat onto the fire.

'The plant has been removed from Ishmael's body and now we wait for the tincture I have been brewing to thicken. Then I will travel the astral realm and try to bring Ishmael back to us.'

Zahra slept beside the fire as they waited. It was the first place she had felt safe since fleeing the monastery.

Manu watched as Ramon removed the tincture from the fire. He sat it down to cool before he turned to Manu, staring at him intently. 'I just realized that you don't cast a shadow.'

Manu stayed silent. He wasn't sure what to say and so said nothing.

'No need to fear anything, Manu, your secret is safe with me. Do your companions know the truth about you?'

Manu shrugged and poked a stick into the fire watching it alight.

'Who can say? I have never met Ishmael and Zahra knows a lot more than she lets on, but I don't think she knows. I once thought I knew who and what I was, but that was when I was young and foolish. Time has shown me that I may never find out the answer, and these days I'm no longer sure I want to know.'

Ramon nodded before answering.

'Sometimes it is enough for us to know we are a part of a great mystery that we will never solve and know there is no need to search for any answers but just be.'

They sat there for a time not speaking, just staring into the fire lost in their own thoughts. Zahra was asleep and occasionally tossed and muttered words Manu couldn't make out. She was like this night after night since they started out on this journey. Her dreams were haunted, and he wondered what nightmares she had that would cause her such unrest.

Nina slept fitfully that night, she dreamt she was sitting down sharing dinner with her family and everything was nice until Nina noticed the deep bruising around her father's neck and crushed windpipe. He whispered hoarsely while her mother sat there vacantly staring. Her father put down his utensils and leaned towards her, and she could smell the rot on him. 'Nina, it's up to you to regain our family's honour. Justice must be served at any cost. My dearest child, we are stuck here until vengeance is wrought, our spirits trapped with unfinished business. Now eat up, love, you look skeletal.'

Reaching out for the plate of chilli crabs, Nina recoiled as she saw the food was moving and writhing with worms. Jumping to her feet she threw the food away from her and then looked to her parents, who now were motionless skeletons in rags. With a gasp Nina awoke from her bedding on the floor, Zacriel kneeling beside her to release her restraints. He smiled wolfishly at her, teeth gleaming.

The room was in shatters with the grotesque bone bed the only piece of furniture still whole. Nina sat on that bed glaring defiantly at Zacriel, who paced back and forth amongst the broken remains.

'Nina you were so close to turning your life around. I really thought you had it in you, but I was wrong. No worry, though; you are young and we have much time ahead for you to realize the way to enlightenment.'

'Did you kill him, Zacriel?'

'Why would I do that, Nina? You wanted him to live and with that comes responsibility for your actions. Who can tell what acts of depravity he will do next. You had the chance to save others from his tyranny but sadly he was allowed to walk away.

'For now, you will stay here. I must go or the wretched sight of you will make me ill.' Zacriel left the room and though Nina hated him she didn't want to be alone, and so she sat, unable to cry or sleep.

~

Manu scooped soil into a body-sized mound. He had totally immersed himself in the work, and perspiration gave his face a feverish glow. Beside the fire Ramon sat skinning the bark from a length of wood with a knife chanting softly as he worked.

Manu felt honoured when Ramon asked him to help with the ritual. The staff had been stripped of bark then buried for one chime in the Earth. Following this Ramon had cleared off the soil and run the length of wood through the fire until it was slightly scorched. Finally with a hiss Ramon submerged the staff in a trough of water before hanging it in the wind.

'Now the elements have been sanctified and the elemental lords will not hinder my search for your friend. I will need you to keep watch on my body and that of Ishmael, for if something were to happen to our bodies here we will both be swept away on the astral winds forever. Of course you know all this I am not used to company, and so I speak the obvious eh?'

'In that you and I are alike, Ramon,' Manu replied. 'I also am a solitary being these days, and yet in my youth I longed to be at the centre of attention involved in the ebb and flow of the world. Now I long for home.'

'Manu we are coming to a time of, ah, how do I say it? Convergence where many things are coming to an end; a new time is emerging but with that will come upheaval. Maybe you will see your home one last time in this life.'

Ramon glanced up at the moons. 'It is time.'

Ramon entered his hut and returned with a long bundle that he unwrapped on the ground. A mixture of oddities lay inside including a cat broach with glittering rocks for eyes, a white stone woman and black stone man and a clear flask of golden fluid. Ramon selected a small brown pouch and pulled out a number of vials filled with coloured sand. Then Ramon carefully applied a small circle of the sand upon the energy centres on the front of Ishmael's body. 'Manu, I will now begin my journey, but do not touch either me or Ishmael at all and in my hut you will find blankets. Ishmael will be cold and weak when I bring him back so get the blankets ready to cover him.

Okay, Ramon, and good luck, my friend.' Manu looked over to where Zahra was lying, but all that remained was an empty crumpled blanket where she had been. No time for keeping tabs on her now, he thought, and so squatted to keep vigil on Ramon while he journeyed to find Ishmael.

Ramon retrieved the staff then sat at Ishmael's head, holding the staff across his knees, and closed his eyes.

Chapter 27

The city of Culchar was considered the southern gate to Thantos. Trade from both Acclaro and Illume was strong, and many came here to make their fortune. It was said in many parts of the world that this was the city of dreams where common people came to exchange their lives for a better one. One such man was Gill Trellis, or Grim as he was commonly known, and his life since coming south a cycle past to Culchar had most definitely suffered.

'Dreams of gold and glory and a dick of steel will not assure greatness,' his father had told him the day he had turned his back on their life of herding goats within the Tiriac Mountains.

'Well, papa, isn't it better to strive for a better life than this ordinary existence we live here? I want to feel alive, not dead inside. I look at you and see misery, a life wasted...'

The slap of his father's backhand caught Gill in the mouth, splitting his lips, and he had looked into his father's eyes for the last time before collecting his sword and bed roll and leaving those forsaken mountains. With his mother's crying loud in his ears and his father's stare burning behind him, Gill had marched off to a better existence. Of course not able to resist getting in the last word was childish and stupid that day and once again it had been the same problem that had cost him so dearly here in this city of opportunity.

He swerved down the road towards his house, belching loudly, Gill silently admonished himself for eating too much. When he first came to this pox-ridden city, he was slim and the muscles of his body cut and hard, but now his gut hung over his belt and it was harder each night to unlace his boots. He had become soft!

'Just down on me luck is all,' he huffed out to the night. My break will come, you bastards!'

Tipping the bottle up he shook the last precious droplets of wine into his mouth then dashed the empty bottle against the wall. He was puffing now from the walk and silently swore to get back into training tomorrow. 'Here we are, home at last.' Leaning against the wall, Grim tugged his key from a pocket and promptly dropped it to the ground. 'Oh you drunken whore, the pox take you.' His questing fingers grasped the key from the cobble stones and as he straightened he noticed a cloaked figure a few feet away. The light here was too dark to see who had approached him.

'Can I help you sir?' said Gill, squinting.

Gill heard the twang of the crossbow before he registered the danger, and the bolt tore into his gut, he stood dumbly looking at it sticking from his stomach.

'The time for help is over, Gill, you are no longer welcome here. Should you survive this unfortunate business it would be best you went far away, never to return.'

He knew the voice but couldn't pin down the owner. The figure leant down. 'Not going to need this, now, are you?' it said as it pulled the key from his grasp. It turned, walking away, the urgent clapping of heeled boots fading in the darkness.

Strange, thought Gill, I always expected there to be more pain. His hands now sticky with his own blood, Gill staggered onto the main street crying weakly for help. A light post loomed before him, its cobwebbed lantern squeaking on its chains, and Gill leant against it sliding to a sitting position looking down freedom way.

'It so cold, I'm so cold,' he said, shivering.

Something was happening farther up the street: spheres of light were floating towards him. Lampposts that had stood untouched since the Severing now burst into blue light accompanied by a tinkling of bells as the spheres moved down the road.

Gill watched the spheres roll past him, one coming so close the heat from it was tender on his skin. He peered into its center and saw a confusion of images; then the sphere brightened, forcing Gill to avert his gaze. One moment they were there and then the next they were gone, speeding off down the road away from him. Dogs barked in the night as the lights faded, once more plunging the street into darkness, and Gill shook his head. He pulled himself to his feet to look down where the spheres had gone only now realizing the absence of pain. With his fingers he investigated the wound finding only jagged flesh where a new scar had formed.

Gill had never been blessed with high intelligence but he was sure he had just witnessed something truly amazing and could only be one thing. Magic! But how?

The chimes until dawn went by in a haze of disbelief and fear. After the night's strange events he had expected to want a drink, but in fact the mere thought of drinking anything but water made his stomach churn. Could it be true that the old curse had returned to the world? If magic had returned then everything would change. For the hundredth time, he pulled up his shirt and inspected the scar on his stomach where the bolt had struck him. Afraid and with nowhere else to go, Gill started walking East from Culchar. Now his feet ached terribly and his throat was dry with dust, but he felt compelled to walk.

Gill breathed deeply, feeling the tension leave his body as he stared at the mountains far ahead. His father was right they didn't belong in cities, they were tribal people who lived on the land. Living in cities stole one's heart and ability to commune with nature, becoming deaf to her messages, but neither was their place in shanty villages perched in dangerous ravines and valleys.

Whatever it was that healed him had to be magic, there was no other explanation. Now he was tainted with the ancient curse and he felt different, filled with a sense of purpose that he thought lost. These changes might be sorcery, but he intended to use them to his advantage and further the cause against magic and those who would see the world beneath its power again. Why would the gods prove to him magic was returning unless they wanted him to do something about it?

No matter what was coming, Grim knew that magic could not be allowed back into the world.

The gods had disapproved the abuse of magic and caused the Severing. If it had returned, what will that mean for his people?

Chapter 28

Ishmael felt like he was floating, his mind tumbling from the amount of vision he had endured from the Earth Mother. Throughout his time at the monastery Ishmael had been taught by great teachers like the abbot and old Leto. Yet even with their wisdom available to him, he had never really used it to help him understand the magic within him. They had tried of course again and again to help, but he had refused to see the magic as anything but a burden he longed be free from.

The Earth tree which Ishmael now realized was also the Mother had changed that when it had reached out to him through their connection as he lay dying in the mess hall, and not severing the connection with the Earth tree had kept him alive. He had been comatose and visions constantly bombarded him as the Earth showed him that the power he and the coterie held would shape the future of this world. It was up to them when and how magic would return to its rightful state. However, those who hunted the coterie would not rest until the magic had been torn from each of them. They thought this would bring the magic back, and maybe it would. With the danger confronting him and the coterie, Ishmael had come to realize that this danger was the catalyst for the emerging dream skills. What else would emerge? Even here, which he believed to be in the astral due to the amber light that pervaded everything, he could sense Raul, Jona, and Selene.

Being here was like floating within a great ocean far below the surface. Ishmael tried to move but found he couldn't. After some experimentation he realized that any movement could be directed by the intention of what he wanted to do and so it took a lot of concentration just to turn his head. Spinning slowly he looked out across this strange amber world. A silver cord linked him by his solar plexus to the biggest, most majestic tree he had ever laid eyes on. The Earth mother. A deep, green glow emanated from within the tree, whose branches moved gently as if seeking something.

He didn't know how long he had been here and if he would ever return to the world of everyday life, which had always seemed mundane to Ishmael. He would give much to be safely back in the monastery once again before the attack, but it was no longer safe and he doubted he would ever see the place again.

Every now and then flashes of what had happened flickered alive inside his mind like the Infernal sitting astride him, its childish face contorted and grotesque above him. Then it had been cut down from behind by a woman in black who kept telling him he couldn't die.

Ishmael's mind jumped to a memory of his father's bedside as he lay close to death. His father had beckoned him to move closer and pulled Ishmael into a tight embrace.

'I never saw him until today, Ishmael…'

'Who Papa?'

'Quiet, dammit, son! I need to tell you this before I die, so pay attention.

'When my father told me about the sentinel, he said there is someone looking after you because of what you are and what you carry. You may never see this person, and with the blessing of the gods you never will. This watcher will help keep you safe in times of need. I never believed him of course until today, when I awoke to find a strange man here. The shadows shrouded his features, and at first I thought an assassin had come but then he started talking, reciting my life to me, even things I had shared with no one but your mother. He finished by saying he was the sentinel and my time was drawing to an end and that soon the magic would need to pass to you, Ishmael, and that I was to prepare you for it.'

'What magic, Pa? You are making no sense, everyone knows that magic no longer exists.'

'Shut up, Ishmael, my time is running out. Look at me, son. I said LOOK AT ME!'

Ishmael looked into his father's eyes. They were bloodshot and seemed larger than normal, something moved behind that gaze and it scared him; he tried to turn away but couldn't move, and then his father's eyes became brighter and brighter.

As if from far off he heard his father's voice one last time.

'I love you, Ishmael, and I am sorry to give you this burden.'

His father grabbed him by the shoulders. No words could ever describe what happened then as the light burst from his father's gaze into his own. Ishmael felt violated, but it kept going until he shook with the weight of it all until eventually the light dimmed in his father's eyes and disappeared. The weight of his father caused them both to topple off the bed to the floor. Ishmael tried to call out for help, but he was overcome with exhaustion. Something roiled through his insides as if something living was thrashing about.

From where he lay he heard footsteps running towards the room, then saw from beneath the bed the door swing open and his mother ran in.

'Julian, are you okay?'

She rounded the bed looking down upon him and his father, then put her hands to her mouth and screamed. She stepped over Ishmael and knelt, cradling his father's head in her hands, weeping. Ishmael managed to pull himself into a sitting position.

By then his sisters had arrived and joined in the wailing. They started to help him up but their mother turned on them.

'Leave him, he did this to your father; it's his fault.'

So, weary and confused, he had crawled from the room to his own and found comfort within a deep sleep. The watcher never came, was his final thought.

Chapter 29

Nina started to plan her escape from Zacriel and Slumsville. She wished she had gone with the lady Zahra, but she had been scared and thought of Slumsville as her home.

Zacriel mostly ignored her lately now he had his lunar. At least there was a saddle for it now so both she and Zacriel could easily secure themselves on the lunar's back when in flight. Cinerus seemed to be everywhere looking at her with those blind eyes, and he always knew where she was even if quiet. A few times Nina tried to sneak past Cinerus or hide from him but always he would be looking straight at her or just say in that voice devoid of emotion, 'I know you are here, Nina.'

Zacriel had called her weak for not killing Ezekiel, but she didn't feel weak at all. Yes, it had felt good to scare him, and letting him know he was only alive because of her felt better.

Nina worked as she thought about a plan. This chamber she was chained in was littered with food scraps, parchments, dirty clothes and empty wine bladders. A clean tidy environment encourages great ideas, her parents used to say, and Nina agreed. If she was to be trapped here, then at least it would be pretty.

'Guards! Guards?'

The guard looked tired when he came in.

'What is it?'

'I need a broom to clean this room up and something to put rubbish in or wood for the fire so I can burn it.'

'Sorry, don't have a broom. See Cinerus, not me.' He started to leave.

'I guess I will just have to tell Zacriel that you wouldn't let me clean up then,' she said, slumping on the bed.

The guard stopped and looked at her questioningly. Nina nodded her head yes at the unspoken question.

'I guess getting you a broom to clean can be done.' Then he left.

Once clean and swept the chamber looked much better especially the new fur rugs covering the bed and the glorious cushions covered in scenes of merriment that were also procured by the ever-helpful guards. Now finished there was nothing she could do but wait for Zacriel's return. Zahra was famished but knew no food would be coming because weak people needed little sustenance… or so Zacriel said. The bowl of water used by Zacriel to clean his fingers after a meal along with the scraps of meat left on bones always seemed like a banquet when he allowed her to have any at all.

Cinerus walked into the chamber, his hands were clasped before him and following behind was a soldier wearing one of the new uniforms of the city guard that someone had stolen in a raid last night on the barracks. He carried a box that even had a ribbon tied around it. The man stopped before Nina and extended the box to her, which she took with surprise.

'What's this for?'

'It's a gift, from me.'

'Derrrrrr, but why? It's not my birthday.'

'Well tonight is a special occasion and you will be accompanying me and Zacriel when he gives them the final address before we strike the surface tomorrow.'

'Oh, is that all?'

'Look, Nina, at least you will look and feel good for this most boring necessity…'

'But he's not the one.'

'What did you say?' said Cinerus leaning closer.

'I said he is not the one in the prophecy.'

'What do you even know of the prophecy, Nina?'

'Well at least I know he isn't the one you're searching for; maybe you missed a scene of the engraving or something because you are blind.'

'I recorded the prophecy while I still had my eyesight.'

'Well, you're still wrong.'

'If you're so clever then tell me why Zacriel is not the saviour of our people?'

'Okay, well firstly, an Infernal as your saviour? It just doesn't happen that way with Infernals. Zacriel only cares for himself and getting revenge, it's always revenge. Why can't you see that Cinerus?

'Secondly, just because the prophecy says something it doesn't mean that is what it means. I thought prophecies were meant to be tricky.'

And when the one who falls from the sky loses his wings, or whatever. Zacriel has wings, prophecy says wings, so it must be him. What if it was the monk or that lady Zahra? Finally, if this was a true prophecy, everyone would have heard about it not just us down here.'

Cinerus gestured to the present she held.

'Well open it, Nina it won't open itself you know.'

Nina pulled the ribbon out and slowly lifted the lid. She gasped and lifted out a gold dress and matching pair of shoes, the type you could only ever gaze at through the frosted windows of shops in Abundance square, knowing you will never touch let alone own a pair.

'Well don't just stand there,' she said to the soldier. 'I have to change, you know.'

Smiling awkwardly, the soldier left the chamber and Nina turned to Cinerus.

'Cinerus?'

'Yes, Nina.'

'I won't wear it. It's too beautiful and I'm covered in dirt, I will ruin it unless I have a bath.'

'Oh, I didn't think of that,' he replied.

Nina lathered her hair with soap enjoying the sensation of her whole bath in the bathing chamber where warm water bubbled up from a number of deep cracks in the ground and roof. She couldn't get her nails clean but that would be okay she guessed. Who would be looking at her nails, anyway?

Finally after a series of loud complaints by Cinerus, Nina scrubbed herself again then towelled off. Then she pulled on the dress. There was one problem though, she had no underwear, which she most definitely would have preferred. The dress was stunning and was adorned by gold buttons and sequined floral patterns, even the shoes fit well.

Cinerus walked in.

'How do I look?' she asked and then burst out laughing at her silly joke.

I'm sure you look just fine, child.'

Nina rushed forward, embracing the waist of Cinerus.

'Thank you so much, Cinerus, for the dress, but I so wish I was wearing it to the Gawker's ball.'

'Get off me, Nina.'

When Cinerus and Nina returned to the bone chamber, Zacriel was busy preening himself and making small adjustments to his attire. Since his arrival here his golden hair had regrown but was nowhere near its usual lustre. His burn scars lent his neck and face a stretched, melted look; the rest was hidden beneath his white lace shirt, blue trousers, and high leather boots shined to perfection. A guardsman stood behind him, strapping on an elaborate silver breastplate.

'Nina, so glad you could join us. What is that awful dress you're wearing?'

Nina stared at him, refusing to speak. Zacriel was nothing but an ugly, horrid man and nothing would change that.

Zacriel's breastplate was strapped on now, and he picked up a sabre from the bed with its pommel worn from use. With a soft ring the blade came free of the scabbard and Zacriel made a series of swift cuts through the air before sheathing the blade once more and belting the scabbard to his waist.

'Well, Cinerus, lead on, my blind friend let me see this great army of mine.'

The three set off to what was known as the chamber of echoes, a cavern pocketed with smaller cave like roosts in the ceiling rock that Lunars used to breed in but now stood empty and created echoes. Cinerus led the party silently through the tunnels to a stone platform at the end of a narrow passage with candle lit stairs ascending to a stage from which the great Zacriel would address his army. Even from back here the thousands of voices talking from within was impressive, and Cinerus had to move beside Zacriel to talk loudly in his ear. 'Let them know you are proud of them, Zacriel, they have trained hard to come to this moment and your praise will seal their loyalty to you.'

Zacriel placed his hand on the chest of Cinerus pushed him away. 'I don't need someone like you to tell me how to be a leader, Cinerus,' he hissed.

Nina noticed the look of barely contained fury that masked the slum lord's features. Zacriel grasped Nina's hand, taking her with him up onto the stage with Cinerus following behind. When the crowd saw them, there was a deafening roar and the thunder of clanging shields.

Cinerus extended his arms out to the side basking in rapturous glory at the voices raised up at Zacriel; this was surely the prophecy's reference of the correct saviour.

For cycles the homeless, widowed, poor and outcasts of Illume had cowered beneath the city like roaches. Forgotten and uncared for, their number had multiplied within the mountain's belly. Now among the cheering Cinerus believed his vision had come to life.

Zacriel stood arms on his hips head thrown back dramatically as if performing for a large audience, which Nina supposed he was. The crowd chanted his name over and over, and the intensity raised the hairs on Nina's arms. With a dramatic flourish Zacriel flung his arms out, signalling for quiet.

'Silence! People of the mountain, you took me in, attended to my grave injuries, told me I was your saviour as you were mine. But today I stand before you not as your leader or saviour but as one of you.'

Zacriel had to pause then as the roar of approval drowned him out.

'Due to unforeseen events I found myself indebted to you for your kindness, so now it's time to repay you with something I know a lot about. REVENGE!'

His voice dropped to a rasping whisper.

'They treat us like rats; attempt to trap us, forget us, hide away the ugliness of a reality they cannot face for then they would be forced to admit that as a society they were failing. You know where to strike, so together we shall boil up from our nest, disable the Blades, and destroy the council to gain the city, and the cobblestones will run red with Illume's blood.

'Strike first, strike hard, and strike true, and know I will be beside you, so go now; ready yourselves for glory, and when darkness falls we act. Tomorrow many of us will be dead, have no illusions for it will not be easy, but those who live through tomorrow will if not ever before witness the sun rise once again.'

Nina obediently stood alongside Zacriel watching as he controlled the crowd with masterful charm; beside her Cinerus babbled and laughed insanely, drunk on elation.

Nina was forced to cover her ears from the applause as Zacriel pulled her from the stage behind him.

~

Zacriel marvelled at his own performance, he could be among the best if he had wanted to, the object of every woman's desire and the object of men's envy. Tonight he would lead this army of rats up into the city but then his part in this war would stop. If they were content to cringe like vermin then let them be treated as such. It was not his fight.

As they headed back to the bone room Zacriel stopped and turned to Cinerus. 'I am going to see to my mount.'

Cinerus cocked his head on an angle questioningly. 'You won't need a mount for the battle.'

'Well, since you're the genius here, Cinerus, pray tell us how you will direct the battle across the city and give orders. You say I am the saviour, so let me do the saving, hey? From above the city I will pass orders to your other riders for them to dispatch, no one has my battle experience or knowledge of tactics.'

Zacriel left them standing there and strode away.

'He is not your saviour, Cinerus.'

Cinerus knelt beside Nina, hands resting on the girl's arms and smiling.

'I think we all saw that there are maybe six thousand warriors who disagree with you. Your words nearly killed my hope, but now, here I know that he is the chosen.'

Chapter 30

Commandant Dalwyn Trevlon was awake with the dawn as was his daily routine, except this day he lay in his small tent a while instead of rising to pray to Escindre.

The plains had been exhausting for him and his men. Gruelling days of riding across Caverre had bought them to within sight of Culchar. The heat made the sight blur and melt in the distance and was one reason why the sprawling metropolis had earnt the name city of dreams. As he lay there his thoughts turned to home or what was left of it since the barbarian hordes from the Tunoka grasslands had taken Karfael for their own. One day he would lead the other families of Karfael into the captured city to purge the barbaric scum with the fury of Escindre and return the city to Dalwyn's family's rule.

Dalwyn forced himself from the bed. Immediately his lower back muscles and knees began their customary ache and for a few moments he paused knees bent, face twisted into a grimace until the spasms of pain subsided.

'Damn this body!'

With each passing day, the aches of his body deepened as if deaths bone claws were piercing him. Not even magic could defy death its eventual victory, as many mages had found out when the Severing happened and they disintegrated as their longevity magic's failed.

Dalwyn stepped from the tent amidst the busy dismantling of the camp around him. Someone passed him a cup of bitter tea that scorched his tongue and lips. In the distance stood Culchar; they could have easily reached their destination last night but had camped here in order to have his men fully alert when they entered the city of dreams. They would stay in Culchar for as long as it took to repair and resupply as well as letting the men have some well-deserved down time.

It annoyed Dalwyn that he needed to rest his men, but he had realized a long time ago they weren't like him. They did not share the same bloodline he did and didn't have the same motivation and drive he had. However, Dalwyn knew all too well the danger of unhappy warriors, and so he relented. Since he had personally viewed the release of magic when Brianna was sacrificed the urgency in him to capture the other coterie members had intensified. The long chimes each night had since been spent delving into what books he had managed to carry for this journey and surprisingly it had not all been a waste of time. A text from Honourus the third had claimed that 'magic is a part of the whole and it cannot be separated from other matter and in its purest energetic form it is attracted to itself and thus will strive to join like particles.'

This now made perfect sense to Dalwyn. If they could track its path, it would lead them to the other members of the coterie that Latasha Meldoriel had mentioned and then they would have them all.

Dalwyn was terrified of dying. It was not so much the act of dying he thought as he sipped tea, but the uncertainty of what came afterwards. From tomes of Escindre he had read repeatedly that when a soul leaves the body it is carried away upon the winds of magic by the individual god or goddess to their abode where they are judged before being sent either to the Infernal realms or to the Celestial realms. But that had been written before the Severing. Now there were hordes of Infernals and Celestial beings trapped in this world with no way to return to their planes of existence. So the question was, what happened to those souls of the dead now that magic is no longer here, and how did those souls reach their destination? For all they know, there could be no more life after this one due to the Severing. With no way for the soul to make its final journey, how could one be reborn. So that left nothing but emptiness and that was what scared Dalwyn. That his life was drawing to its natural end and his soul would not make the journey to the halls of Escindre to celebrate his worthiness but instead would remain trapped here until its essence faded to nothing.

Discarding the empty cup, Dalwyn pulled the amulet of Escindre from its case, placing it around his neck and holding it up towards the sun peeking just above the horizon.

'Escindre, may this day see you returned to all your glory, ready to lead us, your faithful. In your stead witness our struggles to do your bidding and know we await your return and forever hasten events to achieve that end.' His usual hour of daily vigil at dawn would not be happening this day. They needed to reach the city before the next chime, there were friends that would find his news to be very interesting indeed. Maybe, just maybe, then they would realize he was right and not insane as was widely whispered behind his back. As the illusionary city coalesced into its real shape Dalwyn led his soldiers towards the city of Dreams.

Zacriel had chosen to spend some time alone. Now two chimes later he sat perched on a ledge above Slumsville. His speech had whipped up quite a frenzy for the Slummers who now celebrated in their town when they should be resting. The truth was that this army stood little chance of taking over Illume even with their swelling numbers, because they lacked the discipline and cohesiveness they would need come dawn. Something large and dark swept past where Zacriel nestled startling him. He could smell oil.

Peering down, he saw more dark shapes flying above the town and noticed armoured figures converging from the sides of the cavern.

Lichen towers burst into light around the town perimeter, and then Slumsville caught fire.

Zacriel ran through the honeycombed tunnels to find a better vantage point. He found one that confirmed his worst fears. The Illume blades had found the Slummers and had them surrounded. Wearing their fine chainmail armour and wielding the glowing white blades, they cut down anyone trying to flee the flames.

They had been betrayed. Cinerus had assured him the city guard never ventured this deep below the mountain; however, now he realized they had stupidly chosen to ignore the fact that the city council might know of their existence. The plan was ruined and even though Zacriel had never intended to lead this makeshift army into the city and on to victory now he would miss the chaos that would have befallen the self-proclaimed capital of the civilized world. One particular figure caught his attention and he hissed. Perdomo!

Having seen enough, Zacriel wheeled away down the tunnel. It was time to leave this place. But first get Nina, she has no one else but me.

Chapter 31

Nina looked around the chamber. This dark, cold room with its bed of bones had been her prison since Zacriel kidnapped her. The room had at first frightened her with the rats sifting through scraps on the floor, the rattling of the bone bed every time she moved as if some great beast were beneath it. Hollow-eyed Cinerus had tried to make it more comfortable with lichen plants that gave off a soft green glow and a small chest of drawers he had salvaged for her to put in her personal items. Not that they were many, mind you. Her money pouch was always there when she checked along with a silver hand mirror, and Ezekiel Perdomo's owl signet ring she had prised from his fat sausage finger. They would be leaving soon, and yet Nina would still be Zacriel's prisoner no matter where they went. Escape would have to wait until Zacriel made a mistake and then she could get away from the wretched creature. Maybe she would find a family who could take her in and love her as their own or even better find the lady Zahra. She would be a great momma. Nina pulled out a small doll from beneath the bed. 'At least I have you, Deidre.' She brushed a cobweb from the doll's hair. 'Oh my Deidre, you need of a bath, young lady!'

The doll didn't answer of course; instead Deidre's one button eye regarded her coolly.

'Don't fret, little one, everything is going to be fine, I promise, okay?'

'We going to be in a real battle, Deidre, but don't get too worried because you won't be fighting anyway and Zacriel would never give us swords because he knows I would stab him, and, Deidre, I would too. Don't be silly, he will never just let us go, Deidre. We are his prisoners and even though I told him everything about the lady Zahra and her sick friend, he still doesn't believe me. It's just lucky for you that he has never seen you or else he would want to question you and make you cry. 'Nina heard noises coming from the corridor outside but couldn't make out what was happening.

'Deidre, wake up, it's important you be quiet because if he finds out about you we won't be able to stay together, okay? Good, quick, get under the covers; someone is coming.' Nina stowed Deidre away, patted her dress down, and sat quietly on the bed waiting. It was not Zacriel as she expected or Cinerus but the nice guard who had given Nina the doll, Deidre. Something was wrong with him. He had his hands clasped over his tummy and a big red stain blossomed around them. He collapsed and a figure stepped around him from the chamber entrance.

'There you are Nina. I have been looking all over for you, did you miss me?'

Nina screamed and scooted as far away as the chain would allow her. Ezekiel Perdomo stood with his face slick with perspiration and wheezing loudly. With a grin he gleefully pulled the chain towards him.

'Come here, you little bitch, I hate unfinished business.'

'Just leave me be; I will scratch your eyes out if you.'

Ezekiel's ham-like fist smacked into the side of Nina's head, and she fell against the bone frame, splitting her lip open. Nina felt herself give up, she didn't care anymore. She just wanted her mommy.

Nina was rolled onto her stomach and felt her dress tear as it was wrenched up around her waist and then Ezekiel was above her, breathing in her ear and fumbling at his trousers. Nina began to cry.

~

Zacriel sped down the tunnel into a small battle of soldiers fighting Slummers. Not stopping he drew his sabre, smiling at the feel of it in his hand once again as he cut down two enemy from behind and slipped through the mayhem into empty space again. The soldiers were Perdomo's men, how had they got here so fast from the caverns?

Zacriel jumped from the back of the beetle. One of his guards lay dead and a trail of gore led into the bone chamber.

'Nina?'

Not breaking his stride,' Zacriel entered the room, sabre ready. Inside he found Ezekiel Perdomo, half naked and straddling Nina's limp body trying to manoeuvre his massive body above her.

The sabre's blade slipped into the white fatty flesh easily, causing Ezekiel to howl in pain and look up just as Zacriel slammed it home again and again and again.

'Don't you touch her, you filthy scum. I will show you a glimpse of the hell you're destined for.'

Zacriel wrenched Ezekiel off the bed by his shirt, and the fat man scuttled away but Zacriel was right behind him slashing mercilessly.

'Where are your guards now, Perdomo? Nina didn't kill you, but I have no such hesitation in watching you die. When I ascend we shall meet again, pig man, and then you will have eternal torment.' Ezekiel had slowed now, and Zacriel used all his strength to roll him over.

'Tsk tsk now look what you have done. I have blood on my shirt.'

Zacriel calmly walked over to the bed and pulled down Nina's dress to cover her body; she was still breathing but her face was bruised and swollen.

Zacriel removed his shirt, twisting his neck to the side until it cracked violently and then turned back to Ezekiel and with a howl leapt on him.

When his blood lust was sated, he breathed deep gulps of air then forced himself to crawl to Nina who now lay curled tightly into a ball.

"Nina it's me Zacriel.' He touched her shoulder gently, but she stayed curled up tightly sobbing, so Zacriel picked her up in his arms and turned to leave. Cinerus stood in the entrance.

'Cinerus, we are undone.'

'Zacriel, it's time to lead your people. We still have a chance; their soldiers are tired and our reinforcements are now pushing them back and in the process of flanking the overconfident scum.'

'Stand aside, Cinerus I need to get Nina away from here.'

'Zacriel, all we have planned for is now here, and we can attend to her later after the battle. Your men need you.'

'You don't get it do you? I don't give a damn about your precious prophecy or your people, for me you are just a means to escape this forsaken place. I am not your saviour, you mad freak.'

Cinerus grabbed Zacriel by the shoulder. 'We need you, Zacriel, don't do this to us. I won't let you do this after all we have done for you.'

Zacriel slammed Cinerus into the wall, cracking his head against the smooth stone. He slumped to the floor, and Zacriel rushed past cradling Nina in his arms.

Chapter 32

Ishmael moved closer to the trunk of the Earth tree. The visions had stopped now and this was the first time he had been able to observe wherever this was. Next to him he noticed a large cocoon like shape connected to the tree like he was. Something inside the cocoon moved,' causing it to spin around slowly. Willing himself closer, he flowed forward to the cocoons side and tried to peer inside it. His hands moved over the thin jelly skin of the cocoon. Looking closely, Ishmael felt that whatever was inside was also trying to look at him, the sensation cold and alien, making him shudder. He pushed away from it and looked around among the amber shadows of the tree for anymore cocoons but couldn't see one anywhere. He moved past the cocoon and saw it turn to follow his progress.

Could it be that he was meant to help whatever was in the cocoon? Could it be evil? If it's connected to the Earth tree then it couldn't be something evil. But that made little sense because as he had been taught, there is no such thing as good or evil in nature.

Ishmael plunged a hand into the cocoon, digging furiously and pulling away gobbets of the gelatinous substance and soon he had dug out a sizable hole. Maybe whoever was here knew how to get out of this strange world. The Earth Mother had shown him everything but what was the point of knowing how to act if he was trapped here. Ishmael worked feverishly; he wanted to know who was inside.

Finally he tore the covering from head to foot then peeled it away from the edges. There was something inside, a pale and unmoving female. He scooped the jelly away from her face, revealing long, silver hair and strangely pointed ears with a sharp jaw line and high cheek bones. A pulse had started to beat within his palms and temples; Ishmael felt a great heat stirring within his lower stomach and groaned as he tried to relax and breath the feeling away. Gritting his teeth, he went to push away from this creature to focus his mind on controlling the surge of power within him, but a slim hand clamped tightly around his wrist.

The creature's eyes opened, a startling, feral yellow. 'Do it t'thaal, release it!' Her other hand grasped his chin and turned his face to meet hers. It was like she was trying to draw the magic out of him, and Ishmael could feel it surge up across his chest and into his arms and neck.

A voice boomed from him. 'Ancient one, you have no right to such power any longer, your time of such ownership has ended!'

Ishmael could only guess the Earth Mother had spoken through him. The figure before Ishmael was now weeping openly.

'Forgive me, you must forgive me, I am not myself and my body can't resist what you carry, I need the magic you carry.'

'I am a friend, and just knowing some of you are alive has given me great hope.' Ishmael replied.

'Who are you?'

'Now is not the time for talking. They come for you.'

A tugging began at Ishmael's solar plexus, and he felt himself moving closer to the gigantic trunk behind him like a fish being reeled in. As he was pulled away a radiant smile lit up the woman's face. Already the cocoon around her was rebuilding as small branches extended down through the membrane, rebuilding it from within.

To Ishmael it seemed he was absorbed into the tree, and a deep purple-tinged hole grew brighter from the darkness in front of him. A flickering form stood before him holding a staff, talking rapidly and beckoning Ishmael towards him.

Then the darkness tore, spilling light that hurt his eyes. A man stepped through the tear, blocking the light momentarily, and slashed a blade at Ishmael, severing the cord protruding from Ishmael's solar plexus. Ishmael started to float away, but the figure grabbed him, and for a moment he was face to face with the man who'se eyes were as large as saucers and filled with a terrible intensity; then they were rushing down a tunnel, spinning so fast Ishmael wanted to vomit but couldn't.

The sensation changed as they exited the tunnel into an opaque world that felt as if he were under water and swimming up to the surface with light diffusing down from above. Thwack. With a crack Ishmael went through the surface and straight into his body which now felt alien to him and throbbed with the pain from many injuries. He gulped for air that burnt his throat, and his eyes were open but couldn't focus. Voices around him spoke quickly and urgently, but his senses were too addled to comprehend anything even though the sounds here were amplified and stung his ear drums.

Everything came rushing back, memories unwanted, and Ishmael screamed long and hard until he could scream no more but just lay there as someone wrapped him in something warm.

There was little fanfare as Dalwyn rode with his men into Culchar the city of dreams. The day was still young as they pulled up to the large gate main gate leading into the city. A guard stepped from a small gate house looking smart in his blue tunic with yellow pants ballooning out above his knees showing off polished blue sandals with straps wrapping around his calves. Smoothing down his moustache he motioned for Dalwyn to stop. 'What is the nature of your business, sir?'

'Visiting business partners, family in fact, they're one and the same. I have my business papers here along with employment papers for these soldiers who accompany me.'

The guard accepted the papers from Dalwyn, then began examining them slowly, thoughtfully nodding his head.

'What appears to be the problem?' Dalwyn snapped curtly.

There was a sound of chairs sliding from within the gatehouse as two more guards stood up from a table and stepped with their hands on curved swords out into the morning.

'Its okay, Jant, they're just tired is all; I'm sure my friend here didn't mean any disrespect, did you?'

'None at all, it's been long hard days in the saddle for us so we just want a bed beneath our bodies with a full belly to sleep on.'

'See,' said the first guard motioning for his other two brutish companions to stop.

With another stroke of his moustache he went back to the papers.

'Hmmm it all seems to be in order except I can't be sure about the date of expiry on these papers. It appears smudged beyond recognition, so…'

'Would there be any way at all friend that we could assist you in speeding up this process of yours?' interjected Dalwyn through clenched teeth.

The guard turned towards his large friends, extending his arms and shrugging. In reply the brutes nodded their heads, smiling widely.

'Well, luck is on your side today, Mr Trevlon, my esteemed colleagues here have accepted your proposal.'

'And what proposal would that be exactly?' questioned Dalwyn, the look on his face darkening by the moment.

'The one that states you will pay a ten ceta fee for us passing expired paperwork. Also, my friends don't like to be interrupted while playing cards, so throw in another two cetas for drinks after they finish this long exhausting day. That should do it.'

Dalwyn forced a smile onto his face. All he wanted to do was ram a sword up this fool's arse to stop his snivelling pompous attitude, slice his throat, ceasing the patronizing rubbish that oozed out from it. Instead he swung down from his horse, loosened the strap from a saddle bag, and counted out twelve cetas then pausing, before adding an extra two.

'For your generosity, sir,' he explained handling over the money.

The moustached guard beamed as he accepted the money graciously before returning Dalwyn's papers.

Normally Dalwyn would never accept to stooping to this level, but the guards of Culchar were known for the tough 'never back down' attitude that served as the spine of their men. He had no wish to fight this early especially against well trained soldiers that wouldn't crack at the sight of blood and guts and were itching for a dust up.

They entered Culchar through the north gate, which opened up into the merchant quarter focused on all things to do with money, social clamouring, and the trade. Inevitably it attracted all manner of poseurs amongst political intrigue.

The second quarter was simply known as the commons, whose poorer inhabitants battled daily to escape the gangs that stood over them. Then there was the law quarter, where the city guard housed their barracks, training grounds, and also kept a prison whose criminals were forced to work in chain gangs throughout the city. The final quarter hadn't been in use since the Severing; it was the magic quarter whose gates were barred until such time that magic returned.

Dalwyn led his men into the merchant district, meandering through the gathering crowd past exotic shops whose owners were already haggling deals, threatening, cajoling with sugar-coated tongues. They stopped at The King's Ransom Inn where foppish man servants ran to see to the needs of their mounts while thickly powdered whores leant from an upstairs balcony baring long legs and heavy cleavage to passers-by. His men were already jangling their heavy purses up at the ladies above along with whistles and promises of love.

Dalwyn slipped through the front door of the establishment smiling at the plush interior; he had stayed here so often that the expensive trimming was a comfortable familiar sight. He shrugged off his heavy coat before sitting down at the bar where a hot spiced tankard of mead already sat awaiting his attention. He took a long pull of the mead then looked up when a loud voice called out to him from behind the horseshoe bar.

'Trevlon, you old dog, you still roaming around, eh?'

The old inn keeper walked slowly out from the kitchens, his one arm outstretched in greeting, hair once black as night now iron grey along with his impressive moustache.

'Virgil, my friend, it's been many nights since I stayed beneath your roof. Business is booming as usual, I see.' They shook hands, then Virgil moved his hand beneath the fine black shirt he wore and pulled out a pendant similar to Dalwyn's own. He kissed it reverently then repeated the ritual words, 'May Escindre guide our ways.'

Dalwyn pulled his friend into an embrace. 'Come my old friend let us speak where we won't be disturbed, I have some interesting news for you.'

Dalwyn let Virgil lead him through the inn's kitchen down into the cellar where an old table was surrounded by rare vintages of wine. Once they were alone, Virgil closed and bolted the door. Dalwyn pulled the cork from with his teeth from the bottle Virgil handed to him then poured two liberal amounts into the cups. They clinked the glasses together.

'Escindre, may his return cleanse this world once again.'

The wine was a little too robust for Dalwyn's liking, but refusing to drink would be an insult so he slugged down the glasses contents with a smack of his lips and a smile.

Virgil wiped his mouth with the back of his hand then leant forward on his elbows.

'Dalwyn it is fortuitous that you happened to pass this way. There have been rumours that magic has once again been witnessed in the world. There is one shop owner who has been telling all his customers he saw it with his own eyes. By the gods Dalwyn could it be true?'

'Firstly, Virgil may I ask if this person has been interviewed regarding the matter?'

'Not yet, but the news is all across the city with some hopefuls actually waiting outside his shop in the hope they may also see what he did.'

'What type of business does this man run anyhow?'

'He deals in the rare artefacts from days gone by. I am not sure exactly what he has been saying but to make such claims seems impossible and may be just a ploy to suck unwary customers in.'

'Why the big shit-eating grin, Dalwyn?'

'Well, I never thought I would be saying this in my lifetime Virgil, but that fool is right. I have witnessed magic myself with my own eyes only ten days' past, with Tumul as my witness I swear to you this is the truth.'

Virgil sat opposite to Dalwyn speechless as he tried to make sense of what he had just been told.

'Dalwyn, I must know everything.'

'I will tell you what I know, but first I need you to do something for me. We have known each other most of our lives. Hell, it was your grandfather who helped my mother escape and relocate, and for this we are eternally thankful.'

Dalwyn's voice took on an urgent tone.

'This is it, Virgil, your chance to restore your family back to the honoured status that made you one of the most powerful families in the known world.'

Dalwyn's eyes gleamed with fervour in the lamp light.

'We will be the ones who restore magic to our world, but I have to know I can count on you, that's why I'm here. With your resources and contacts, our cause will be greatly simplified. What say you?'

'I'm in, Dalwyn, you can count on me.'

Dalwyn removed his pendant, laying it on the table between the two of them. With his knife he slashed it across his palm, letting his blood pool on the ancient jewellery. He passed the knife handle first to Virgil.

'I know I can count on you, friend, I never doubted it for a moment.'

Virgil picked up and examined the blade silently, then looked up to Dalwyn's expectant gaze; he drew the blade across his palm. Blood pooled along with Dalwyn's then both men dipped a finger into the warm blood, making the sign of Escindre on the other's forehead.

'Now sit Virgil, while I tell you a story that will amaze you. Escindre has chosen us to help bring magic back to this world as well as returning him to his rightful place. May Tumul shine the crimson light upon us.'

Chapter 33

Two chimes later Dalwyn staggered from the inn. He should head home to sleep off the drink, but the excitement of the morning had bought with it haunting memories of someone he really had no right to visit. But it seemed that today was to be time for throwing caution to the wind. The soft wind carried the sounds of merriment from numerous taverns along with it as Dalwyn strode along the empty streets up to the noble district where three burly guardsmen played dice in front of a large closed wrought iron gate.

They wore the yellow and blue of the Culchar guard with one exception; they also had house insignia on the chest as well as the arms of their tunics. The noble district insisted on using their own men to protect the district, which inevitably created tension between the city watch and the family guards since the city watch still had the ability to enforce the law in the district but allowed the nobles to provide soldiers on their own estates and to man the gatehouse. Dalwyn marched to the gate, pulling out the papers that Virgil had supplied him with. 'Good day fellows!' he said, handing the papers to the nearest guard, who casually looked over them.

'Says 'ere you're a wine merchant, so where is your wine?'

'I assume you know about the upcoming wedding of Lady Tia Urvile?'

The guard nodded his assent.

'Well, she has asked to see me privately regarding a special request for that special day of hers coming up, and it didn't require me to bring any wares. But you will be happy to know that should this meeting go the way I am expecting it to then I will make sure you guardsmen are fully compensated with fine liquor for your efforts.'

'Usually the lords send messages to us if they are expecting any guests, but we have no mention of your visit. You will have to wait while we send a runner to confirm with Lady Urvile.'

'I know how to get to the Urvile household, there is no reason to inconvenience yourselves at all. You see, time is money, gentlemen and I am a busy man with no time to waste playing beggar at the gate. I'll tell you what I will do.'

He dipped into a pocket, pulling forth six shiny cetas which instantly got their attention. 'Since I bought no fine drink with me, here are two big ones each for when you finish your shift okay?'

Two of the guards looked eager to take the money but the third played thoughtfully with the pommel of the sword in his belt.

'Lady Urvile finished organizing her wedding months ago; she hates being unorganized and has had no guests regarding her wedding for some time now, so why are you suddenly showing up without the correct clearance?'

'Okay, so be it, but I can dally no longer, so please pass this message to Lady Urvile for me. Tell her that Mr Luis Quail regrets that he could not get to see her regarding her request…ummm oh, and that I doubt that I shall be in Culchar again before your big day so best wishes from myself on behalf of Quail Refreshments.'

Dalwyn spun on his heel, flicking his cloak over the shoulder. He managed three strides before he heard the words he needed.

'That won't be necessary, Mr Quail, I guess this once we can let it pass, but in future follow the correct channels of protocol.'

'Yes, sir, I will but you know how women are eh especially noble ones.' He thumbed his nose meaningfully then handed each man two gold coins. 'As you see I'm a man of my word.'

The guards grinned back at Dalwyn as he strode away in the direction of the Urvile manor.

Access to the Urvile manor was too easy. The guards looked over his papers then sent him through into the manor hall where a foppish man servant in pristine tight white breeches, a black velvet shirt, and highly polished black shoes proceeded to lay out the rules.

'Now there are just a few little points to mention, sir, when approaching Lady Urvile. Firstly, be courteous when she motions for you to approach. Don't speak 'til you are given leave, bow when she first looks at you, and stay that way until she bids you rise. My man here will search you for weapons.'

A guard moved his hands over Dalwyn's body doing a very efficient pat search that almost bordered on intimate.

'Do you want to fuck me or frisk me?' he asked the guard who flushed crimson then stepped away hurriedly.

'Umm, sir, that sort of behaviour will not be tolerated.'

'Just fucking send me through, or I will tell Lady Urvile how you endeavoured to keep me from seeing her regarding a very important matter.'

'Okay, sir, but just know that any trouble then you will be evicted from my lady's presence.'

Dalwyn just stood there staring at the man servant until he nervously fumbled open the door to the hall. Then with a wink at the guard and a blown kiss he walked into the Urvile hall to see the love of his life. The future lady Tia Urvile sat tall upon a lavish chair that could pass suspiciously as a throne with all its inlaid gold and silver. A balding man stood at the end of a royal purple carpet that led up to the lady's chair. A thin, well-dressed merchant stood before Lady Urvile, pleading his case.

'My lady, there is still the matter of my daughter's murder; she was only seventeen summers old.'

The man had to pause then as sobs filled the hall. The lady sat looking down at the man, her displeasure plain for all to see.

'Her murderers must be brought to justice.'

'My good man Soloman, as you know the three accused have

alibis for the night and time of your daughter's murder. They were on shift that night here guarding my home. That was why the court saw fit to find them not guilty.'

'Yes, my lady, I am most aware of the situation as I was there. There were witnesses to the abduction of my girl by the three guards and…'

The now shrill voice of Lady Urvile drowned out the merchant.

'And since they have disappeared, no doubt remorseful of their lies, they have slunk away to wallow in their shame therefore deciding not to testify such false accusations.'

Just as Dalwyn was ushered onto a stone pew to await his turn, the good man Soloman lost his temper.

'You know your soldiers raped then murdered my daughter, you lying piece of shit, and you also know the witnesses were paid off to keep their silence. I hope your house falls down around your ears and I am around to witness it.'

He then hocked loudly before spitting an impressive wad of saliva that landed upon the equally impressive cleavage of Lady Urvile, who looked down at it in horror.

'Guards, arrest him!'

Within moments good man Soloman was lying beneath a pile of guards who pummelled him into unconsciousness.

As Soloman was bundled out of the hall, Dalwyn stood quietly awaiting his chance with his head bowed.

'Get this spit off me, and get me some tea!' screamed the lady.

Dalwyn smiled inwardly. It seemed that Tia had lost some of her calm and composure as she got older.

Just when he was growing tired of waiting, he saw from his peripheral sight the lady notice him for the first time.

'You may approach, old man.'

Dalwyn did, stopping at the carpet's end before he bent into a deep bow holding his position.

'You may rise.'

'My Lady Urvile, may I present Merchant Quail who is here to see you regarding your urgent request.'

'Quail? I have never heard of any such merchant family, Mr Quail, so I doubt that you were asked to come here. So the question remains, old man, why are you wasting my time?'

Dalwyn raised his head, looking upon her still golden hair, those grey eyes smouldering with anger locked onto his. Then the anger on her face turned to surprise as she recognized him. Tia coughed into a hand, hiding her surprise well.

'May I speak Lady Urvile?'

When she said nothing, Dalwyn took that as an invitation.

'Yes, my lady, it is I, Dalwyn Trevlon, at your service, but before you throw me out into the street like good man Soloman, may I beg a personal audience with you regarding a matter of great concern to us both?'

Lady Urvile rose from her seat, brushed down her skirts then signalled for Dalwyn to follow her.

'Joseph, please ensure that we are not disturbed. We will be in my library so refreshments can be bought there.'

'Okay, my lady, but you still have a queue of people who are waiting to see you so should I act on your behalf in those matters.'

'That won't be necessary, Joseph, just tell them I will see them tomorrow afternoon at one chime after lunch.'

The lady Urvile strode through the hall at a fast walk out in front of Dalwyn, who used the moment to keep his eyes on her waggling bottom while smiling to himself because he knew he had her flustered. When they reached her library she opened the door with a large silver key then ushered Dalwyn in impatiently. Behind them the two guards took up position outside the room.

Once the door was shut and locked, Tia rounded on Dalwyn eyes flashing furiously.

'Dalwyn, by the gods what do you think you are doing here?'

'Well I was in the neighbourhood, so I thought it was worth seeing you because we need to discuss something very important.'

'Dalwyn, you are not a part of my life anymore, you already know that. I don't want to see you.' As she said this Tia drove her index finger into Dalwyn's chest after each word.

Dalwyn caught her wrist in one hand then pulled Tia in close against his body which earned him a slap hard enough to spin his face to the side.

'Let go of me or I will call my guards!'

'Oh come on, Tia, we both know you won't do that.'

'Dalwyn, I'm not joking, get your hands off me. If Trey saw you here he would murder us both.'

'Trey? I'm guessing he is your husband then and obviously a noble considering your rank not to mention this estate. You have done very well, Tia, but then you always did seek out the wealthiest man so you could wring the wealth from their bones.'

The next slap caught him across the lips with one of her rings, drawing blood that trickled from the corner of his mouth down over his chin.

'Don't you even dare go there, Dalwyn. I sacrificed everything for you and that bloody search for magic, even my inheritance was squandered looking for something that hasn't existed for hundreds of years and probably never will again.'

'But that's where you are wrong; it does exist, I have now seen it with my very eyes. I know you have never believed me and I promised a long time ago you would get that money back. That promise still stands. But first I really need your help just one last time for old time's sake. You know after all these cycles I still care for you even after you ran away from me thinking I wouldn't find out where you were.'

'Dalwyn, you left me no choice but to run away when you stopped caring what I thought. Wasting both our families' money in your damned search for magic as you gallivanted around the land while your supposedly happy fiancé sat in the damn mountains under the close supervision of your personally picked chaperones. I only ever wanted you, you great fool, but I will always be second to this search of yours, so that's why I left.'

'So did you miss me then?' Dalwyn asked with a smile.

'Of course I did but that was long ago. Now I love Trey, he treats me better than I have even been treated and is a good man with honour.'

Dalwyn ran his fingers through Tia's hair as she spoke to him. Her scent, even after all these cycles, was still of a summer evening, which drove him wild.

'I don't give a damn about your husband, Tia. You belong to me, or did you think you could just break the pledge of love we swore that night under the light of Tumul so easily? Tumul never forgives transgressions against his name.'

'I'm sorry, Dal.'

'SHUT UP!

Now listen to me carefully, Tia there is something I need you to do for me. If you do this then I give you my word on my Mother's grave that I will leave you and your foolish husband alone.'

There came a loud knock on the chamber door.

'Milady? Are you all right?'

Tia looked at Dalwyn then the door.

'I'm fine, just a heated conversation, that's all.'

'Now sit down, Tia, like a good girl and listen carefully to me. I am not asking much from you, just a small favour for old time's sake; then I will be out of your life.'

Dalwyn sat beside Tia on a seat close enough that their legs touched.

If you don't cooperate with me, then things between us might become tense. You know how much my search means to me.'

'Dal can you just leave please, I promised already I would help you, didn't I?'

'Yes, of course you did, Tia, I knew I could count on you.'

Dalwyn smiled warmly at Tia as he slid a hand up under her skirts finding the inside of her thighs. He tried to kiss her, but she turned her face away from Dalwyn to hide the tears that had begun to streak down her face.

Dalwyn strode out from the Urvile household as if he owned the place. He had to admit, Tia was still in great shape. She had always been great in bed, but today she was simply boring. He may as well have been fucking a corpse. At least she was terrified of not doing as he had asked. Of course, her husband, Trey, might cause a problem or two if she told him what had happened and a part of Dalwyn wanted Trey to confront him so then he would have an excuse to kill the man who was with his rightful wife.

Chapter 34

When Nina became conscious of the world again, she was sitting with her back to a stone wall which seemed to be a balcony. Between iron rails Nina could see a city stretching out below her that she soon understood was still the city of Illume due to the terraced garden estates that lined the edges of the great crater on which the city had been built. Nina stood then, looked up to see a high crystal spire brightening into fire with the morning sun. The spire must be the Tower of Illume, she thought, where Shae was laid to rest. How did she get up here, and what had happened before that?

Nina's legs wobbled as she walked along, using the rail to guide her unsteady steps. As she paused waiting for the moment of weakness to pass, she tried to mentally go over the events as she remembered them, desperately needing to fill the emptiness of that gap in her memories. The last recollection she had was of that pig Perdomo entering the chamber where she was chained to the bed and him striking her face, but after that, nothing. Nina knew she sure didn't sprout wings and fly up here, so how had she found her way to the highest point of the city. Following the rail led her in a circle around the tower chamber to a solitary entry. From the inside there came a clattering then a curse, someone was coming. With nowhere to go, Nina stood just inside that doorway trying to adjust her eyes to the darkness untouched by the dawn. A figure slid into view from the dark recess of the chamber, pulling itself wearily up the stairs. Its twisted face found her there in the doorway glancing at her fiercely. Nina stepped back in alarm.

Zacriel. She wasn't free.

'Nina, it's all right, we escaped.' He smiled back at her, trying to look comforting but failing. Zacriel slowly came forward out of the gloom, arms laden with food, a blanket, water skin, and gold trinkets hung around his neck.

'Nina, I am so happy you are back. I thought you had been lost to madness.'

He must have caught her glance as she looked to the water skin he carried along with food wrapped in a sheet of cotton. He placed it at his feet then handed her the water, which was sweet to drink. She lowered the water skin, wiping her mouth with the back of her hand. Zacriel offered her some bread that was smothered with honey and Nina took it, thanking him with a smile then tried to eat it slowly so she didn't get what da called indigestion. The bread was dry but she didn't care, it just felt good to eat. When she finally finished it, Nina burped terrifically, which bought a shy smile to her face at the comical look on Zacriel's face.

'How long have we been here?' she asked.

'Just over one day. The slaughter of the Slummers beneath the mountain is over and once again Illume is in lockdown, so we are safe here for the time being. We were fortunate to escape the inferno down there, especially with the Illume guard at full alert. I decided to wait here until things settle down.'

'Where will we go then?'

'To Acclaro, and we will see if your friends have been there. As I recall, it was you who told me that's where they were heading.'

'Why can't you just forget about them? What terrible thing did they do to you?'

Zacriel laughed then, a low chortle that Nina didn't like at all. She took a step back warily, noticing a glimmer in Zacriel's eyes. He frowned then walked to look over the balcony.

'They are responsible for this deformity I am forced to live with, the burns you don't like looking at or the truly amazing wings that I had, which gave me freedom. Besides that Nina, the monk is one of five very important people needed to bring magic back to this world. When that finally happens then I can take my rightful place in the Infernal lands, healed from these terrible inflictions I carry.'

'My da once told me that the magic going away was a good thing because it was used in a bad way that caused the world to start dying. He believed that only once the world was fixed then magic could return, so why can't everyone just wait until then?'

'Nina, you have never seen the wonders that magic brings.'

'Yes, but you are ignoring the bad things it brings too,' she countered.

'Bah, I refuse to argue the intricacies of magic with you when you have never seen it for yourself,' Zacriel said. Let's eat some more; I'm famished.'

'Okay but just remember that if everything was to go back to how it was before the Severing then nothing will change and we will end up in the same old big mess we were in before.'

They both tucked into the remaining bread and honey along with some dry but yummy sweet pastries that Zacriel had also found. Nina thought it was almost nice if she could ignore the bird droppings that covered the hand rail and that her companion was some monster right out of a book of nightmares.

At times Zacriel seemed almost normal but then would change to a cruel, hateful twisted thing that terrified her. Nina knew she just had to wait for the time he would trust her too much then she could escape. She needed to believe that because that was all she had along with her dreams of revenge to keep her going. Zacriel had told her that they shared something in common, revenge, and had laughed when she yelled, I can never be like you. So we do share something in common then, revenge. How could she make sure her Da's dream of creating the merchant road come true if she was a slave to Zacriel?

With their bellies full, Nina sat alongside Zacriel, content for the moment to listen to the sounds of the waking city waft up from below. A patrol of Illume guards zipped over the city, their blackened armour dull against the bodies of their wasp mounts. When the attack had come on the night of the Festival of Lanterns, the Infernals had taken the time to fire bomb the hive barracks of the Illume guard, which was why the sky guard was so long in mobilizing and even then had lost most of their trained mounts. That now seemed such a long time ago. Time beneath the mountain was different, or so it seemed, and Nina couldn't recall how long had passed since Zacriel had crashed into her life. Nina rubbed at the corner of her eyes.

Zacriel had been to the tower of Shail many times since Cinerus had bought him here. He had explored the chamber where once the body of the goddess had lain after her collapse to be looked after by her priesthood. Zacriel had half expected Shail's body to still be there asleep on the bed, but there had been nothing. Most likely she had perished or the priesthood moved her body every night to a safer location, but that seemed like a lot of trouble to go to. There wasn't a holy box holding her remains that could be used in the future as relics for her followers. Zacriel watched Nina fall asleep, draped a blanket over her small form, and gently picked her up and carried her into the most holy of chambers in the city. Lying amongst the lavish pillows and silk sheets, Nina even looked like a goddess in that chamber. As Zacriel turned to leave the chamber, he realized he was smiling. The last time he had genuinely smiled was a lifetime ago.

Chapter 35

Zahra awakened as Manu and Ramon were preparing to retrieve Ishmael. She toyed with the idea of returning to rescue Yolinda and slay Jayne but knew the task would take too long, and she needed to be here for Ishmael. It was her sacred duty, and after all Haakon had done to give her a new life she owed him her best. Now was not the time for weakness. This was more important than dwelling amongst her personal regrets. Zahra stole off into the night, and as she moved she noticed that the clearing that Ramon's ugly house squatted in was devoid of the thick orange-red crystal that clung to the surrounding foliage and tree trunks. Moving deeper into the tangerine night, Zahra found a nearby hilltop that afforded a view down to the winding river far below. The sight was majestic and briefly took her breath away. The two moons appeared close enough to touch. Breathing deeply, Zahra let her surroundings overtake her senses until the krill beetles chirping echoed around her and the faint smoke on the breeze tickled her nostrils. The air here was so fresh and her body welcomed it as if it they were old friends reunited.

More sensing something than hearing a sound, Zahra let her eyes flicker open and glanced to her left. Five feet away a figure crouched, regarding her. Its humanoid form must have been at least six feet tall if it had been standing, and its skin was a hard polished ruby red that faded to orange along its slender crystalline limbs. The hilts of two blades protruded above both shoulders. Zahra slowly turned to face the being that could only be one of the mysterious Harlequin.

She lowered herself into a crouch to mirror her visitor. Fiery eyes stared back at her, and despite her training she flinched when a clear musical voice carried to her with a hint of wind chimes in it.

'You are not like other humans; why is that?'

'What do you mean? What are you called?'

She managed to blurt out, trying to regain some sense of composure

'We have no individual names but only recognize each other by our markings. You don't have the stink of death on you like all the others I have been close to. You fascinate me…'

'Zahra,' she finished for the Harlequin.

'You travel with one of the Earth's chosen, Zahra, yet you yourself are not one of them.'

'I am his sworn guardian, chosen from my clan to protect Ishmael and what he carries.'

'This chosen Ishmael was near death when the warlock bought you here. We worry that maybe you are not skilled enough in this role due to the current state of your charge.

What do you think?'

Zahra bristled at the suggestion.

'You think you can do better, Harlequin?'

In answer the Harlequin drew a blade in a lightning-fast motion, slashing horizontally at her throat. To avoid the cut Zahra let herself fall onto her back, and then as her foe closed the distance lashed out with a foot, kicking the legs out beneath the Harlequin. Zahra flicked a dagger from its forearm sheath into her hand, stabbing towards the exposed side of her foe that arched into a backbend before springing its legs over its body into a crouching stance and lunging forward, sword point towards her abdomen.

Zahra reacted with pure reflexes, batting aside the sword blade as she rolled to the right into a crouch and dropping the other dagger into her empty hand. The Harlequin's attacks rained in fast to drive Zahra back. She was aware of the cliff face close behind her as one dagger pommel caught the Harlequin's blade, turning it down and thrusting with the second. The Harlequin leaned back incredibly, kicking up with his lead foot towards her sternum. The move caught Zahra off balance, when she twisted away it connected with her shoulder and spun her to the side. Then her foe was there again, crystal blade dancing at her, changing levels, never allowing her to find a pattern in its attacks. Zahra knew she was no match for this foe; it was time to fight her way.

As the Harlequin moved in for the attack, Zahra feinted a slip and went down to one knee, ducked beneath the slashing blade that scraped the side of her head as it passed, then stood upright, meeting the Harlequin face to face, daggers locked against the sword barely holding it back. She smiled then and spat the needles in her mouth she had pulled from her sleeve when ducking her opponent.

Zahra was rewarded with a look of surprise from the Harlequin, who wrenched its head to the side, the needles pinging off its crystal cheek. They wouldn't have damaged the Harlequin, but they did enough to distract it. The Harlequin backpedalled defensively and Zahra dropped her blades, pulling her bladed sickle from the small of her back, blade in the left; she twirled the weighted chain in her right lashing out at her opponent when it tried to close on her. The chain lashed out, weighted end curling around the Harlequin's sword arm, who braced his feet and pulled hard towards him. Zahra went with the pull, twisting inwards and slashing the sickle up at the Harlequin's face, who at the last moment got his blade up to intervene. Zahra tried to twist away again, but the Harlequin stepped with her, crashing its empty fist into her face. As she slid away she lashed with the sickle, letting the chain extend, and it connected with the Harlequin's shoulder, tearing off a large chip of crystal before pulling the chain blade back to her hand.

They circled each other, and as Zahra felt the blood down her left cheek she saw the first sense of uneasiness in her foe's movements, as if it was no longer certain of its skill to win this fight. Stepping forward suddenly, she swung the sickle in a figure eight pattern, holding the chain weight to parry. The Harlequin stepped into the pattern, twisting away from the sickle but barely avoiding a downward swing by falling to his right knee. And Zahra's blade jerked back to her hand as she triumphantly stepped in, holding the curved blade against the Harlequin's neck.

It was then, as her opponent's laughter rang around her, she noticed its left hand held a shorter blade that was now jammed up against the hollow of her throat. Zahra laughed then also and couldn't stop for some time. She dropped her chain sickle and fell to the ground the tension releasing along with the Harlequin's amusement.

Blades now sheathed, the Harlequin regarded Zahra.

'Few have bested me in combat, Zahra. Your prowess is remarkable.'

'I didn't beat you, we fought a draw. If time favours us then maybe one day we will meet again and cross blades.'

'Zahra, I came here to be sure the chosen is well protected; we normally refrain from interfering in human affairs, but events unfolding will affect all races. The hive is now content that at least this Ishmael is protected.'

Zahra tried to show no surprise. From the Harlequins words he was telling her they existed as hive like insects, and as far as she knew this had never been documented.

'Then come with us and help guard Ishmael, friend Harlequin.'

'Magic is necessary for our crystal bodies to function well. Since the Severing as you humans call it, our crystals fade and we cannot stray from our homeland here without slowly dying'

'Then why are you helping us instead of trying to kill the chosen, which would release magic back sooner?'

'It is not a matter of just releasing magic, Zahra, there is a right way and time to do it. The state of mind of the chosen when they release their power will forever forge the form that magic takes, and so it is vital that the chosen are not viciously slaughtered. That would create a chaotic entropic world racked by magical storms and unpredictable effects from the use of these forces.

'The responsibility you protectors and the chosen carry is of such great magnitude to all the children of this world that when we knew of your coming here we decided to aid you in two ways.'

The Harlequin rose gracefully, moving into the undergrowth and returning with something wrapped in large leaves. He unwrapped it revealing a white crystalline curved blade that here in the moonlight seemed to suck white light from Aspre high above. Deep within the blade a red pulse seemed to answer the red glow of Tumul, the blood moon.

'Carry this blade well, Zahra and known you are the first to be gifted a blade from the Harlequin. Her name is Moonbite.'

Zahra took the blade, noting immediately its fine balance, it looked so fragile and felt weightless, and as she stood and put the blade through a series of thrusts and slashes it felt like a natural extension of her arm.

'Zahra, my time is short here, so on behalf of the Harlequin take this gift. It will aid you to protect Ishmael. You will hear from us again soon.'

Zahra had many questions to ask, but when she looked up the Harlequin was gone. Hearing movement coming up the hill behind her, Zahra turned as Ramon moved to her side, his saucer eyes hypnotically gazing at her.

'You have had a meeting with power this night, assassin, be sure to use the gift well.'

'How much did you hear?'

'Nothing but I recognize the work of the Harlequin and feel their power when they come close. They never let me meet with them, for I feel they fear me. Come along now, Zahra.'

'Ishmael is awake already then?' asked Zahra, who had thought maybe a quarter of a chime had passed.

'A chime or more has passed since I entered the astral and bought Ishmael back.'

The first thing Ishmael saw was the sky above him, soft rain pattered down to fall on his skin, and he lay there just enjoying this simple sensation. By Illume, he was happy to be alive, he thought to himself and tried to rise off the makeshift bed he was lying upon. Ishmael regretted the decision as pain flashed through his body, and a deep burn engulfed him from his stomach area. Emotion welled up inside of him as he cast his thoughts back to what had happened in the monastery when the Infernals attacked. What had become of his friend Hofan or the abbot? It had all been his fault that the Infernals had come to Illume- he knew now that it was him they had set out to kill, and if he hadn't been at the monastery then there would have been no slaughter there. More burdens to carry.

The pain and confusion became almost too much. Then a man was looming over him his bushy eyebrows creased in worry above cool grey eyes. The man yelled something out but Ishmael couldn't hear anything at all. The world had become strangely silent. His body thrummed from the inside, and it felt as if he would burst from the energy that suddenly engulfed him. This was it, thought Ishmael, the cursed magic he held was trying to force its way out of his frail body when he was weak and unable to control himself. But no matter what, he couldn't let that happen now, it wasn't the right time. From what seemed like a dream state he lay there watching as the saucer-eyed man came into view above him talking rapidly. Someone had hold of his legs and arms holding them while saucer eyes painted something on the front of his body. The man seemed to be chanting as perspiration dripped from his brow. Whatever had been applied quickly cooled down the fire in his body and dulled the pressure he felt inside of him. Ishmael felt himself sliding away again and tried his hardest to stay conscious, but to no avail.

Zahra spent the remainder of the day at Ishmael's side. After the strange fit that had overcome Ishmael, Ramon had insisted that someone stay with him. She dribbled cool water across his forehead and bathed his face, checked his injuries which now included seven angry blistered circles down the front of his torso, throat and forehead. Ramon had explained that this was where his energy centres were and the burns had been caused from the magic he held trying to escape. She tried to think of how it must feel to hold such power and whether or not Ishmael or any of the other conduits ever felt like just opening themselves up to let the magic do as it sought to and escape.

Ishmael had been awake for some time but kept his eyes closed as he listened to the strangers. He tried to put faces to the names, but as far as he could determine they belonged to.

'He should awaken soon, Manu, it's only a matter of time now, and he's been dead to the world for a day already.'

'Yes Zahra, but these things cannot be rushed. If he isn't allowed to heal as much as possible first then it could mean a lot of complications later.'

The female apparently named Zahra tried to say something, but the man Manu spoke over her. 'Yes, I know what you're thinking and that it's important for you to get Ishmael to safety with the others but the important thing is we get him there alive, isn't it?'

'I just feel so helpless, I'm no good at waiting. It's time to act, and every day we stay here the danger grows stronger.'

'Zahra, we need days for Ishmael to heal before we can be off again.'

'The sooner the better it will be,' said Zahra. She lowered her voice to a whisper.

'I don't trust Ramon. I know he's been a great help, but he is the son of Jayne.'

'If it wasn't for Ramon then all of us would be dead by now, so I think you need to be realistic about our situation here,' Manu replied.

'Be realistic, huh, well how's this, we are stuck in the fucking Jewelled lands with a half-troll shaman whose mother killed our guide and took a friend as a slave. The Harlequins are close and watch us, but we don't see them unless they wish us to, and we don't understand them enough to decipher their motivations. Lastly, we are hunted by Infernals and the safety of this world falls partially on our ability to get Ishmael to safety.'

Ishmael heard the sound of Manu moving away muttering under his breath.

'Damn, women never make things easy.'

Then Ishmael heard Zahra come and sit by his side.

'You can stop pretending you're asleep now, Ishmael.'

Ishmael just lay there motionless, breathing slightly but otherwise not moving a muscle.

'You are most likely wondering who we are Ishmael. None of us here are going to harm you, but we are actually trying to get you to safety. So if you are awake then we need to talk urgently about the situation we now find ourselves in.'

Ishmael opened his grey eyes, locking them onto Zahra's.

'Where were you?'

'When are you talking about?' replied Zahra.

'I'm talking about when I was being pursued by Infernals

through the monastery, caught and gutted like a fish by a baby-faced monstrosity. You must be my sentinel, but you were not there when I needed you. I guess I expected more from someone charged with protecting my life. My father told me I had a protector, and yet you never made yourself known to me?'

There was silence while Zahra and Ishmael studied each other.

'That's a fair point, Ishmael and you have every right to be angry at me. Yes, I am your sentinel, chosen to keep you safe and yes, I nearly failed in that, but make no mistake. If you had of died, my life would have become forfeit. However you didn't die, and I intend to ensure you don't either. I truly understand any animosity you have towards me, and that's fine. You don't need to like me, but if you value your life then from this point on I am in charge and you need to trust me so I can do my job properly.'

Ishmael decided in that moment that he didn't trust anybody, but he nodded his head in agreement anyway. He would find out more about these people who claimed to be his rescuers. Realizing that arguing wasn't going to change anything that had happened, Ishmael pulled himself to a sitting position, noticing for the first time his severed fingers.

'Why didn't you ever reveal yourself to me then?'

'Before your safety became my concern, my predecessor told me he hadn't revealed himself to you because you were safely ensconced in the monastery, which is most likely the safest place for you. Or so we thought. I decided a number of times to approach you, and yet each time I didn't follow through with it because it did not feel right. I followed you everywhere to learn your routines while also learning where you spent your free time, but the right time never came and I guess I just decided to leave it. Then the attack on the monastery occurred. All that is left for me is to forget my near failure and succeed in getting you to safety.'

'What happened to the others, the abbot and my friends?'

'I'm sorry, Ishmael, but I don't know. The abbot was alive when we escaped, but the next morning the news was that the monastery had suffered a high death toll.'

From across the clearing Ishmael saw the man approaching them.

'So you're awake then, lad, I was starting to think I wouldn't see you awake in this world. No don't try to get up, I'm Manu, an old friend of Zahra She bought you to me when you were close to dying but there are some things that are beyond my natural abilities in healing, so we bought you here.'

'What do you mean by that?'

'He means that some injuries are beyond the physical but are concerned with the spirit.'

Ishmael slowly turned towards the speaker, who would have easily towered over most people. His skin was tinged with green and wore many fine bracelets and necklaces of what appeared to be crystal that jangled as he walked.

'Ishmael, I am known as Ramon, and while you are here my home is your home. There is much you need to learn, but for tonight rest; then soon we start your training.'

'What training?'

Ramon cocked his head slightly at Ishmael and seemed to be looking over his left shoulder.

'You really need to be aware of the dangers face you, Ishmael, you and the other chosen need to work together to save this world. Alone you will all fail to restore the magic if you decide that's what you will do. Without the training I can give you it will be hard to stay in contact with the others like you. The astral world is dangerous to the unwary traveler, but there are some skills that will make it easier and then you can be in contact with your fellow chosen whenever you choose.

'But that's enough of that for now, my friend; I have gathered what food I have so let's feast together this night in acknowledgment of this small victory.'

The food was simple but delicious with grilled fish stuffed with rice and vegetables; thick, brown, grainy bread lathered with crushed fruit and washed down with strawberry wine.

They ate as if it was their last meal in this life while praising Ramon for the food provided.

Time passed slowly for Ishmael. At the monastery he had chores and routines to distract himself, but now he was injured and could only rest to regain his strength. It was a miracle that his internal organs were unharmed, or so his new companions said. At least this time gave him a chance to sort out in his head everything that had happened since the attack and the death of Brianna Dusk. His memories of the time in the astral realm were confusing, and he didn't really understand what had occurred with the creature in the cocoon. Ishmael longed to contact the other coterie members, but he had promised Ramon to wait until he had a chance to share his knowledge of that realm. Ishmael realized that something within him had changed since his near-death experience. The Earth Mother had shown Ishmael why the magic had to be taken away, and he had learnt the importance of his role as one of the coterie. Ishmael found that if he concentrated on the others he could tune into their moods, or sometimes he had glimpses through their eyes.

His new companions were still strangers; there was Zahra who he now knew to be his Sentinel. She hadn't spoken much to him over the last few days and seemed absorbed in her own thoughts as she worked tirelessly around the camp or in her training, which he watched with interest. He longed to start his own physical training again, but nobody would allow him. Since encountering the cocoon in the astral realm Ishmael was now very aware that the magic would easily rise up within him, trying to escape. Normally the exercises that he practiced within the monastery kept the magic quiet, but in times of danger or of emotional upheaval it seemed to rise up within him, clouding his mind and threatening to burst out, maybe breaking him apart for all he knew. No one had any experience with what would happen if the magic he and the other coterie members held managed to escape, and personally he didn't want to be the one to find out. How were they expected to know what to do about the magic when they were finally gathered together, anyhow? When the Earth Mother had been communicating to him in the astral it was as if he was dreaming- the images came to him, reassuring him that at the time he would know what to do, but he was not convinced. Currently the magic was coiled deep inside, and he could feel it like a snake content to hide within him until the next time it surged up to try and find release. How long could he hold it before it overwhelmed him? The dreams came and with them knowledge of what to do. He dreamt he was with the other coterie members: Raul, Selene, and Jona, and they sought five crystals needed to reshape the world. He knew this was something he should share with his captors or rescuers, but he still didn't trust them yet.

Chapter 37

Dalwyn headed back to The Kings Ransom inn. Already his men were deep in their cups, so he picked the least drunk of them.

'Snake, you're with me, get your blades then wait for me here.'

'Yes, sir, can I finish my drink first, sir?'

'No, it will be a better idea to stop now. The last thing I need is a rollicking drunk bodyguard. I will personally pay for your drinks when we return, Snake.'

'Yes, sir.'

Dalwyn moved through the crowd with Snake in close pursuit. They entered the merchant district at the wrong time, so the crowds were impassable at times. The directions Virgil had given him were precise, so once they had passed the worst of the crowds it didn't take long to locate the shop of Kumar the magician and arcane diviner. Just as they arrived at the shop, a robust man with an impressive steely, grey beard along with flint eyes to match was just locking the door.

Snake knocked loudly, waving his hands to get the man's attention. 'Excuse me, sir!'

The man mouthed, 'We are closed.' Then he turned to walk off.

Dalwyn removed his gold pouch then held it up where the man could see it. The man swung open the door with a smile that almost engulfed his face.

Silkily Snake stepped forward into a deep bow.

'O great Kumar, please forgive us for taking up your precious time. May I introduce my master, Lord Trevlon, who has travelled far to converse with you regarding a certain extraordinary event.'

'You along with your master may enter my humble shop, but please refrain from touching any of the items you see here; they are very rare.'

Kumar ushered them inside then locked the door. He took them into another room where a large crystal ball sat upon a metal claw pedestal near a lit fireplace and runes were painted on the walls. 'Be seated while I do the necessary closing.' Dalwyn sat with Snake standing behind him as Kumar produced a piece of chalk from a voluminous pocket of his robe then began mouthing gibberish while drawing a circle around his guests.

'By all the powers that be, listen to your master…'

Dalwyn had seen enough; with a nod from him Snake grabbed the mighty Kumar, who squawked loudly as he was forced to his knees in front of Dalwyn.

'You can't do that to me! I shall rally the forces of spirit to drive you from here.'

'Listen to me very carefully, Kumar. Unless you tell me exactly what I want to know I will end your charlatan act, burn down your shop, then break your legs so the only career you will have available is as a beggar. Do we have an understanding?'

'I am not about to bow down to threats from the like of you, street scum.'

Snake rammed Kumar's head into the floor with a thud.

'You say you're a magician, well let me tell you, oh powerful Kumar, that Snake here is a magician also. Show him, Snake, how you make things disappear.'

Kumar began to struggle against Snake until Dalwyn smacked his face into the floor again, pushed him onto his stomach, and then sat astride the man's back.

Snake licked his lips in anticipation, showing his split tongue off to Kumar as he stretched the man's arm out.

'Please don't hurt me I will do as you ask, I promise.'

'That's great news, isn't it, Snake. Now, Kumar turn your face so you can see your hand.' Kumar did as requested. He was breathing heavily now.

Snake raised his arms theatrically. 'Watch me closely.' He slipped a hand behind his back then produced a knife with another ridiculous flourish.

'Now, Kumar, just so we both understand each other, Snake here will show you a disappearing trick.'

'Abracadabra!' Snake sliced down hard, severing Kumar's right thumb, which he then tossed into the fireplace. Amazingly the great Kumar didn't cry out because he had fainted. Snake retrieved a chair from another room then tied Kumar into it. They slapped him back into consciousness blubbering like a baby.

'Now, Kumar the word getting around is that you claim to have recently witnessed magic and are claiming to have your power returned to you. So I would like to know what happened.'

Kumar took a deep shuddering breath. He was shaking now, blood pooling beneath his now deformed hand.

'I was working late with a client who wanted to contact her dead mother. I know I claim to be a magician, but I am not.'

'Really, I would never have known otherwise,' Dalwyn said drily.

'I know I look the part, but my parents told me I would have inherited magic because it's in our blood. My mother's mother owned this shop originally; she was renowned for rune magic as well as necromancy. So now it's passed to my hands. That night as I was contacting the spirit, the crystal ball there on the stand burst into blinding white light, the runes on the wall lit up as well. You can imagine my surprise, not to mention my client's.

'It lasted for some time then left as suddenly as it appeared. My client who had walked with a limp from gimpy knees left like she was a young lass all over again. Of course I took the credit; you would have too. Since then I have been swamped with clients clamouring for healing and news from the spirit planes. That is all I know, so can you leave me alone now?'

Dalwyn nodded at Snake, who swiftly pulled Kumar's head back, slipped his arm around the man's neck, and with a deft twist the great Kumar's neck broke with a sickening crack.

Dalwyn hocked up some phlegm. Spat it onto Kumar's body which now lay broken on the floor.

'One thing I hate is charlatans.'

Snake rifled through the pockets of Kumar, located some money and quickly hid it in one of his many pockets, looking up innocently at Dalwyn as he did so.

'Now, my lord how about those drinks that you mentioned?'

'Not yet, Snake we still have a body to dispose of.' Dalwyn grabbed a bottle of lamp oil he found inside a cabinet while looking for another exit. He doused the body then splashed oil over the curtains along with the other contents of the room. At the doorway they threw the lamp so it smashed in the middle of the room.

Dalwyn watched eagerly as the flames danced over the oil, swiftly turning the room into an inferno. Then he turned, leaving by the back door he had located where Snake waited impatiently for him holding a large sack over one shoulder.

'What? Just a few keep-sakes, sir, I even found something you will like.'

Chapter 38

Now that it was decided that they would be staying here with Ramon for quite some time Zahra was at a loss of what to do with herself. Her mind was still reeling after the duel with the Harlequin. The blade they had gifted her with she had kept hidden within her bedroll and she longed to get it out to train with but there was one small matter that was stuck in the back of her mind like an itch she couldn't scratch. It had caused her to be in a foul mood for days now so much so that her companions avoided her company as she stalked around methodically completing chores and keeping to herself. That small matter of bother had festered within her mind poisoning, her values and beliefs as she tried to ignore it. But it could no longer be ignored and it might be too late to fix, but Zahra knew she had to at least try.

The night was cold. Even the moons had decided to abscond behind their cloud-covered curtains and plunge the Jewelled lands almost into partial darkness.

This suited her well, for this night it was time to right a wrong and possibly face consequences of going against her intuition and better judgment. That makes two, she whispered lightly as she flitted from shadow to shadow. Two wrong decisions made that could have cost the lives of two people. She already had too many ghosts in her closet, be damned if she would let there be more.

Ahead the stone wall loomed up out of the darkness. No guards patrolled the parapets above her. The defences were poor; someone had been lax in not doing their job properly and for that they would pay. In two places the boughs of trees that stretched their twining arms above the canopy of the forest reached almost to the edge of the wall, allowing possible access. Scampering up the tree, Zahra leapt nimbly down onto a path. There was still no sign of guards? It showed such arrogance that she had gained easy entrance to the small fortress. Below the planking was a large courtyard that Zahra recognized from before when they had been dragged through it into the bitch's hall. The courtyard below was unguarded. The supplies that Zahra and the others had bought as a tribute to Jayne lay in one corner, discarded, and empty barrels smelling of sweet wine littered the area. That would explain the lack of guards. Zahra crept down the stairs to the ground, pausing to listen but not hearing any sounds of alarm. The ornate double doors were shut but swung quietly inwards to the throne room, which also showed the remains of celebration except for one addition. A human figure hung by chains before the throne; it wasn't moving, and with some relief Zahra noted the dark brown hair that hung down over its face. It wasn't Yolinda, then so maybe there was some hope after all. The woman here was dead, thick bruising covered her neck, which hung like a broken marionette, thought Zahra, and she had to stop herself from letting out a shrill laugh.

Two passages exited the room and Zahra selected the one behind the throne through a set of purple curtains. The floor before the open door was covered in a large puddle of water. Drawing Moonbite, Zahra inched through into another large chamber, this one set with an enormous table laden with food if you could call it that. It certainly wasn't food for human consumption. The head of Murk had been placed atop a silver candelabra, wide eyes staring. The rest of Murk's body lay half eaten on the table alongside a small cauldron full of what looked and smelt like blood even from this distance.

Zahra felt the bile well up in her throat and turned away, fearing what they had done to Yolinda. The only other door from here led into a huge kitchen. Retracing her steps, Zahra went back to the throne room, and took the easterly passage this time which led to an armory stocked with an impressive array of dusty weapons and armor. There were no other exits, which baffled Zahra. The trolls had to sleep somewhere close to water or else their bodies dried out and became hard and brittle with a type of rigamortis before breaking apart into dust which usually took a day or so. Once again Zahra retraced her steps to the door to the dining hall where the puddle of water sat. Zahra inspected the stone floor, couldn't see any reason for the water being there. No dripping water had been falling from the high roof, and it was too much water to have been spilt carelessly from wayward waiters.

The small pool of water in which the throne sat showed no evidence of a water trail leading to the mysterious puddle; the flagstones here were bone dry. Somewhere nearby Zahra knew that the trolls were hidden.

Trying to recollect any information she had on the ecology of trolls from her training, Zahra soon realized she had no inkling of whether they slept on land or were forced to sleep in water. So if they had to be close to a water source, Zahra mused, then it would make sense to have somewhere inside here to act as an escape route while doubling as a hidden passage to that necessary source of water. Moving back over to the puddle, Zahra got down on hands and knees, running her hand over the flagstones not in the water but around the water itself. In one spot she detected a slight breeze, and within a short time she had marked the outline of a square that obviously opened to a secret area. The problem she faced was locating the trigger to open the trapdoor. Starting to become irritated, Zahra took a few long deep breaths. If she was the famous arrogant Jayne of the river, where would she put the trigger?

Glancing around again, Zahra noticed that only one wall had a piece of art on it, a painting of none other than Jayne herself sitting upon her throne trying to appear regal but looking like nothing but a drying out husk adorned with gaudy jewels.

Zahra approached the painting, pressing against the canvas with her hands trying to locate some sort of indentation. The painting had been mounted on the wall with metal bolts. When Zahra ran her hand over the crown on Jayne's head, the canvas there gave a little so she pushed harder. A loud grating noise came from behind her, and she turned to see the square of flagstones slide back to reveal a slimy wet staircase descending into the darkness. Kneeling down at the top of the stairs she sheathed her sword, shrugged off her backpack, and then removed two of the torches she had inside along with two flasks of oil.

Once the backpack was on again, Zahra stuck one of the torches through her belt along with an oil flask, poured a touch of oil on the second, and lit it from the still smoldering fire pit in the main hall. Zahra pulled her mask up over her lower face then with torch in one hand and oil flask in the other she started to descend the stairs slowly, feeling the giddy excitement in her belly. It was time to pass judgment. Immediately there was a flicker of movement at the foot of the stairs below her.

Behind her mask, Zahra smiled. She had been expecting a sentry, and if there were more, one may have left to sound the alarm. There came movement below her as a troll surged up the stairs three at a time, long arms extended towards her, its eyes shining.

At the last moment Zahra ducked the troll's grasp then threw oil on to its face and chest. It had closed the distance faster than she had expected though ramming a knee into her head as she rose. Somehow Zahra stayed on her feet and slammed the lit torch against the side of its face, which erupted into flame. Suddenly the troll wasn't interested in her. Its shrill scream echoed eerily as it sought to escape back down the stairs, but Zahra was upon it in an instant, beating her torch against the back of its head. It burst apart like a melon, black blood fountaining. Zahra splashed more oil over it from behind as it fell and tumbled to the base of the stairs, now crawling towards a large pool of water. The torch descended again, and again until it stopped moving and Zahra crouched to regain her breath. The torch had gone out during the beating but from the light given off from the troll's body she saw the chamber was a large pool. It didn't look natural, so they must have created it. Spilling oil over the torch again, she lit it from the burning body then stood, raising the torch to see the chamber better.

The torch light revealed an oval chamber that narrowed at the far end to a tunnel. The rough stone floor was covered with green algae, causing Zahra to step slowly on its treacherous surface. Zahra could see what appeared to be large lumps like rocks beneath the water, the algae that covered the floor also covered the ceiling above the pool. When she moved closer it seemed to grow brighter like some sort of sensor. The eerie light showed the rocks more clearly, and Zahra saw they weren't rocks at all but trolls covered in barnacles, their long arms coiled around bodies, some of which were starting to uncoil, possibly due to the light above them.

'By the gods!'

At a quick count Zahra numbered them to be at least twenty. Quickly she upended the remaining contents of the open flask into the water and took off her backpack again, pulling out the other three oil flasks she had stolen from Ramon's grotto, four total. She threw one high into the middle of the roof above the pool, smiling in satisfaction as it shattered, raining black droplets onto the water. Another she ran along the pool edge, pouring the contents onto the water to make sure when the trolls surfaced they would have no oil free passage to get to her. Then she lit the oil.

Zahra was surprised when two burning bodies burst up out of the water to land on their feet close to her howling in pain and anger; the sickening smell of charred flesh was terrible. One teetered forward then collapsed into a writhing heap just before Zahra. She simply kicked him off the edge into the burning water again. The second made it to Zahra, who ducked under a lazy slash of claws before tearing out its groin with her knife then smashing a burning torch into its face.

Now more trolls were swimming rapidly under the surface of the flames to come up at the pool's edge, scampering out towards her. Zahra lit the next torch, moving back onto the stairs where she could always retreat back inside the throne room. However, from the corner of her eye she saw the stone door had slid shut again, leaving her now trapped between its cold stone and the raging tide of trolls stumbling towards her.

It was time to make a stand. Zahra stood at the top of the stairs, torch in her left hand burning brightly while holding Moonbite the crystal blade in the other. Its blade gave off an intense, white glow in the fluttering torch-light, causing the nearest trolls to shield their eyes.

Then she was amongst them, slashing the blade in an attacking pattern before her, lopping off arms and legs, tearing open abdomens to spill out their ropey contents on the already slippery floor. Never before had Zahra wielded a greater blade in combat; it was light in her hand, its razor edge carving a bloody swathe through the ghoulish troll ranks before her. No doubt a lot of them were already dead on their feet from the fire damage to their bodies, but still if there was someone to witness her at this time then songs would be sung about her prowess. This was how she liked to fight: up close and gritty, the blood singing in her body, her face set in a grim smile wreaking havoc amongst those who didn't deserve to live and trolls did not rate highly on her scale of acceptance. Once the fighting was done, Zahra paused to orient herself, intentionally slowing her breathing as she moved between the burning trolls prone on the ground. She doused them in more oil before lighting them up.

Still there was no sign of Jayne or Yolinda, but Zahra was sure they weren't far away; it could have been Jayne who closed the entrance trapping Zahra down here. The draft at least let her know there was an exit, but after examining the remaining area she was sure that the exit lay across the water down through the tunnel entrance that led into more darkness. That would mean swimming in the deep water, which still could be hiding any number of trolls below its surface. Jayne was very cunning and had managed to stay alive for over a hundred years, and Zahra didn't want to have to fight her in the water where Jayne would have the advantage.

As Zahra pondered what to do, a scream rolled across the water followed by a lengthier one a moment later.

'Great! It just gets better and better.'

Suddenly coming here alone didn't seem such a great idea. If she was to stand any chance at all of escaping this predicament then the less she was forced to carry the better her chances would be. Zahra removed her backpack then strapped Moonbite diagonally across her back where she could still draw its blade if needed. If she had to use a weapon in the water then she would have to rely on her smaller weapons. Now with knife clenched between her teeth Zahra slid into the water trying to stop from making any splashing. The water in some places was still burning, forcing her to weave between them; the heat compromised her vision as her eyes attempted to adjust between the darkness and flames around her. Charred bodies bobbed against her, the stink repulsive but maybe it would stop her scent carrying to Jayne.

At any moment, Zahra expected to be dragged down beneath the oily surface by trolls to be held immobile as she drowned with only the horrible visage of Jayne leering in front of her but soon she made it to the opposite bank, scuttling to the safety it offered from her paranoia. From here Zahra could see some length down the tunnel in which a rusty portcullis stood open. Crying echoed down the passage punctuated with sobbing words.

'Please, Jayne, noooooo, oh someone help me.'

Zahra was back in the water, all ideas of restraint gone as she surged towards Yolinda's screaming, which just continued on and on growing ragged like some tortured animal. Ahead the tunnel joined an intersection at which a small boat sat rocking erratically with Yolinda in the water bobbing up then down beneath the water to come back up coughing, spluttering with sobs, 'I can't swim.'

Treading water, Zahra looked but couldn't see Jayne anywhere. Soft shafts of grey were starting to stretch through the natural, twisted wood ceiling peppering the passage with streaks of awakening dawn. A rope secured the small boat to an iron ring on the wall, to the right the passage widened into open water while to the left darkness stretched away curving into darkness.

Zahra reached the boat amongst the choking coughs from Yolinda as she surfaced again. Her hands had been tied behind her back while a chain around her neck stopped her from swimming to shore. Pulling herself into the boat with a grunt, Zahra reached back grabbing Yolinda by the hair with one hand as the girl slipped beneath the surface again. Straining with Yolinda's weight Zahra managed to sneak an arm beneath each armpit as she attempted to drag Yolinda into the boat beside her. 'Come here, you...'

Leaning back almost in a standing position, Zahra heaved Yolinda onto the boat, then she was falling backwards as the small boat rocked violently. Zahra fell backwards into the water her arms flailing, a fast blur and strong arms dragging her to the rocky bottom. Something sharp hit against her spine, pain shooting along vertebrae.

The murky face of Jayne momentarily appeared in front of her face, and Zahra grasped futilely at it, then Jayne's head slammed into Zahra's cheek, not doing any real damage but stunning her for a moment. Jayne raked claws down the front of Zahra's chest, releasing rivulets of blood to float up past her own face.

Zahra knew she was in trouble. Her heart beat rapidly in her ears, her chest burning with the need to breathe. Only her training prevented her from panicking but Zahra had only moments before she would need air. Jayne's leering face appeared again, and with one last effort that may be her last act in this life, Zahra thrust her nails up at Jayne's face.

Jayne began to pull away now, black blood mingling with Zahra's. Zahra shot upwards. Breaking the surface, Zahra gulped air down as she hung weakly to the boat's edge. Yolinda lay in the boat, her eyes distant.

Then Zahra was dragged back under by the ankle. As she was pulled down she managed to grab the chain securing the boat to the wall, and it came free in her grasp. Zahra noticed with great detail the bubbles flowing past her face as she exhaled slightly, the chain manacle floating before her. Manacle! Obviously this was not just a mooring chain. She turned as Jayne dragged her down, letting go of the ankle and instead grasping at Zahra's head but slipping off the short hair and closing onto Zahra's throat, trying to squeeze the life from her. Zahra bought her chin down to stop Jayne's hands from tightening farther and pulled Jayne into a close embrace. Teeth slashed Zahra's shoulder, ripping flesh away, but she ignored it, instead reaching behind Jayne's neck and securing the manacle around her throat and clicking it shut with a soft but audible click.

Immediately Jayne let go, hands going to her throat, and Zahra lifted her legs, pushing off Jayne's chest with them away from her back up towards the boat above using the thrust to break the surface and scrabble inside the boat once again. Jayne followed her, claws raking along the back of Zahra's calf as Jayne lay half in the boat screaming with rage. Yolinda was cowering at the end of the boat as Zahra grabbed the dagger she had dropped, smashing its handle once, twice, three times against Jayne's head, splitting the flesh.

A kick sent Jayne howling back into the water, where she disappeared below, only the dragging chain against the boat giving away her possible location. Thankful for the moment of respite, Zahra sat dagger in hand looking around nervously. Yolinda still sobbed at the other end curled tightly into a ball. Zahra tore the sleeve of her shirt down to examine the wound on her shoulder.

It was bleeding freely but wasn't deep, so she tied the torn sleeve over it using her mouth to help pull it tight. The chest wounds from Jayne's claws were worse, seeping darker blood, which could be a real problem. The chain rattled against the boat pulling tight then releasing.

What do we do now?

Zahra knew she had to do something; the longer Jayne was left in the water the more quickly her wounds would heal. The fact Jayne had not resurfaced seemed to indicate Zahra had hurt her badly.

Zahra shook Yolinda gently. 'Yolinda, it's me, Zahra.'

There was no answer. The girl just cringed and covered her face protectively. From her peripheral vision Zahra noticed something bobbing just on the surface nearly unseen; it was Jayne watching them like a predator watches its prey, her eyes gleamed with hatred.

'Listen to me, foolish girl; you can't escape me, so let's just work something out. You can even take the girl, she means nothing to me.'

'Fuck off Jayne, it hardly seems like you can bargain your way out of this. Not this time. This time you die.'

'You really think you can kill me, Jayne of the river? Many have tried to do that, assassin, but only end up on my plate for dinner. You won't be the last to try.'

'Yeah? Well none of them were me!'

With a flick of her hand Zahra threw her dagger. It struck Jayne in the cheek, and Jayne disappeared under water again.

Zahra scanned the water for her, seeing nothing but the chain growing limp. A faint scratching noise started; it appeared to be coming from beneath the boat.

The bitch it going to try sinking us.

She grabbed Yolinda by the arms, pulling her roughly around to face her. The girl's hands slapped feebly at Zahra's face as a small mewling escaped from her mouth.

'Yolinda!'

There was no response.

'YOLINDA!'

Now grasping her by the face, Zahra tried to get behind the eyes.

'Yolinda, listen carefully to me. If you want to live through this I need you to help me. Jayne is trying to tear a hole in the bottom of this boat, and if she does we will most likely die. I need you to help get the boat to the shore, but first we need to drag this chain up so Jayne can't get beneath us, okay?'

Yolinda began to turn away, but Zahra slapped her hard against one cheek, she raised her hand to do so again but saw the first glimmer of life behind the girl's eyes since she had rescued her. 'There you are, Yolinda.'

The scraping noise was louder now, more persistent too; they both glanced towards the boat's bottom. The wood still held for now, but it wouldn't be long until water started to break through.

'We can't let her sink us, Yolinda. All I need from you is to help me drag this chain up then row us to the bank near the passage entrance; can you do that for me?'

Yolinda nodded.

'Good girl.'

Zahra lay the sword next to her then both of them heaved on the chain, looping each foot around one of the oar holders. Water was now seeping into the boat from a number of tiny holes as they heaved the chain up. There was little resistance at first, then Jayne fought to halt them, thrashing around in the water like a great catch that only tales told of. Muscles burning Zahra grunted with every heave, reducing the chain's length and drawing Jayne up against the boat's side. Jayne changed her tack then lurching up from the water half-way into the boat, claws slashing, and narrowly missing Yolinda who swung the oar against Jayne's head twice. Blood sprayed, dotting the face of the girl before Jayne fell back into the water. Zahra grunted with the effort, using her feet for leverage then pulled Jayne tight against the boat securing the chain around the oar stop. The bitch could only swing her claws up a little now but not close enough to injure either her or Yolinda.

Grabbing both oars Zahra panted heavily, ignoring the burning pain across her chest. She locked the oars in place then began to row back out of the passage into open water. The going was slow now she was tired, but they were nearly at the shore. Yolinda was rocking back and forth again now, eyes partially glazed but still wild. With a final heave the boat jammed up onto the shore. Yolinda scrambled from the boat running up onto the land then, plucked a fallen branch from the beach holding it in two hands looking around fiercely.

After a moment, Zahra climbed from the boat, cold but elated at being on solid ground. She began dragging the boat up the sand along with Jayne, who lay slumped against it, all the fight gone from her, eyes darting from Zahra to Yolinda, long tongue flickering over lips.

Zahra stumbled up the beach into the fortress courtyard where she had earlier seen their tribute discarded. She pushed through the pile, finally locating a flagon of wine. Greedily she tipped the contents into her mouth, choking as she swallowed too much and falling to her knees with ruby rivulets running down her chest. After she had slaked her thirst, Zahra walked back down to the beach. The sun was rising in the sky now, but she still felt chilled to the bones in the wet clothes. Yolinda lay on the beach asleep, her eyelids flickering with faint groans.

They stayed like that for some time, Yolinda slumbering like the dead; Jayne trapped against the boat, wounds half healed, head misshapen with swelling, her skin already showing signs of drying out. Zahra ached from unknown amounts of scratches, cuts, and bruises whose only positive effect was to keep her awake to finish the work she had come to do.

A chime later Zahra staggered from the fortress, which was now burning brightly, black smoke billowing up into the morning sky. Before she had doused everything she could in oil she had collected new daggers from the armoury along with clean clothes a little too big for her and Yolinda. Then on the way out found a stash of gold hidden among piles of clothing and other supplies most likely from other unlucky travellers. Bone tired now, Zahra shielded her eyes as she moved back down out of the burning castle onto the beach then stopped dead, her mouth falling open in shock.

Zahra sat in the sand before the misshapen tree, tears sliding down her cheeks. In front of her a pair of white sandy feet dangled gently in the breeze accompanied by the creaking of the rope that Yolinda hung from. A rasping, hacking laugh bubbled from the boat where Jayne lay, skin parched, black blood flowing from cracks in her skin now tarnished red from the suns heat.

'Nothing more than she deserved. She was just a whore.'

Zahra stood up then began climbing the tree where Yolinda hung. She cut Yolinda's body down, and it crumpled into a heap like a sack of potatoes. All the while Jayne cackled away.

The two-chime trek the night before now turned into a six chime return trip. Zahra's old injuries had begun to heal but the fight with Jayne had caused her shoulder wound to flare up, and her left eye was swollen again. At least the chest wounds turned out to be superficial.

When she reached the hill leading up to Ramon's grotto, she paused. At the top of the hill stood Ramon looking down at her then up over her shoulders into the distance from which thick smoke still billowed. He stayed that way until she drew level with him at the grotto entrance. Neither of them said anything. Zahra was lost for words and Ramon's knowing eyes told her that he knew exactly where the smoke came from. At one point Ramon turned his gaze slightly over her left shoulder seeming to see something there, and his eyes widened before he turned away, spitting a wad of saliva onto the ground then walking ever so slowly away into the undergrowth accompanied by the wind rattling the branches crystal coating against each other. Manu looked up as she stumbled into the camp, his face widening into a grin before clouding over with worry as he saw her wounds.

'Zahra? By the light of Illume, where have you been?'

'Its better you don't know, Manu, just leave me be. I'm okay.'

'Well you might be okay, Zahra but you're not the only one involved in this journey, are you?'

She tried to step around him, but he stepped too, blocking her route. Ishmael, who had been stretching his body, stood watching the two of them.

'Manu, I will ask you once only, move, please!'

'I won't move yet; I have something to say first. We are supposed to be a team here, but it seems to me that you just go running off to attend to your own agenda. Now I know you have things you keep to yourself, we all do, but I'm sick your little disappearing acts. I was worried, Zahra.'

She said it so low that at first Manu didn't hear it, but she repeated it louder then.

'I killed Jayne.'

'What do you mean Zahra?'

'You heard me, Manu, I said I killed Jayne and oh, since you want to know everything then you should also know that Yolinda is dead.'

'Wh-What? How?'

Zahra slumped down onto a log by the fire. Manu poured her some cool water that soothed her throat. 'I went back and found out where the trolls hid through the night. Jayne used Yolinda as bait to lure me to my death. I managed to trap her with Yolinda's help, but as I attended to destroying that abominable fortress I returned to find Yolinda had hung herself. I waited for the sun to rise and cook Jayne to a crisp before I returned here.'

'Oh damn, Zahra are you okay?'

'Zahra giggled a little too highly then, 'Yeah, Manu, I'm just great.'

She stood again wincing from her wounds, her legs already stiffening up from the tough demanding trip back.

'Zahra?'

She turned to Manu, who was now stirring the food in a pot. 'It's not your fault, you know. You can't be blamed for her death. At least you went back for her.'

'Yes I did, but the damage was already done.'

Zahra moved to her bed roll, lay down, and was asleep almost immediately

Chapter 41

Ishmael awoke early while it was still dark. The night had been full of restless dreams that finally chased him out of them into the still morning. The embers were the only light in the sleeping camp. Then he saw a figure moving silently about the grotto, placing things into a bag and was about to raise the alarm when the intruder raised his head then looked straight at him. The saucer eyes of Ramon bore into his, then he went about his task again. Ishmael gingerly got to his feet. His wounds were repairing well now that he had been able to rest and recuperate for an extended time.

'Ramon?'

The Shaman ignored him for a moment, choosing instead to place contents of containers and bottles into pouches before he turned to Ishmael with something in his hand extended towards him.

'What's this?'

'A map of how to get to Acclaro.'

'Why are we going there?'

'Not we, young Ishmael, just your companions and you.'

'But Ramon, where are you going then?'

'Away from here to a new home. I can no longer help you, Ishmael, though I promised to. Let's just say there is now a conflict of interest between myself and one of your companions.'

'What about my training then? You warned me that I have little knowledge of how to use the astral plane.'

'You will need to find that knowledge yourself now, Ishmael.

Just remember to use your heart and follow it when making decisions. Your companions are good people for you to count on. For you there is some greater purpose to fulfill. One day when magic returns to the world I will know you had some part in allowing the Earth to heal first and will count my blessings and sing of you in acknowledgement of your service to the Earth.'

'But…'

Ramon put his hand up to Ishmael's mouth.

'Now I must go.'

'Goodbye, Ra.'

'Haaaa, No goodbyes, they are too final; instead we simply say, til we meet again.'

Ramon then began a slow walk down the hill out of the grove with Ishmael watching until the strange half-man vanished. He knew he should awaken the others but chose not to without really knowing why. His companions had been hospitable and looked after him as if he were kin. However, he knew little about Zahra or Manu, and he missed the monastery and his friends. Life with the monks had been simple, methodical, and peaceful, yet while he was there he had longed for the freedom he now had. But what price he had paid? Ishmael felt bewildered. Ramon had begun teaching him about the astral world and its dangers just yesterday but now he had gone, but why the change in his demeanour and what did he mean about a conflict of interest?

Ishmael added kindling to the embers watching as the flames crackled to life then placed the teapot onto the coals to wait for it to boil. Across the fire Manu stumbled from his blankets, stood rubbing his eyes then let rip with a loud fart when he saw Ishmael sitting by the fire.

'Sorry, lad but sometimes you just gotta let it out, eh?'

Despite himself, Ishmael burst into laughter.

'Morning, Manu do you want tea?'

'You got any brandy? Oh, well, then tea is fine. What has you up so early?' Manu asked.

'Ramon is gone. I awoke to someone sneaking around the camp, it was Ramon collecting his valuables. Then he left.'

'What, without saying anything?'

'Well he did mention a conflict of interest with either you or Zahra; do you know what he meant by that, Manu?'

Manu accepted a mug of tea from Ishmael.

'It means that he no longer wants to help us because yesterday Zahra killed Ramon's mother. She was one of the most evil creatures in this world, but she was still kin to Ramon.'

'So what do we do now, Manu?'

'We wait, my friend, for all three of us to be present then we will see what options we have. But now we rest and get some food in our bellies.'

'I almost forgot, Ramon gave me this map so we can find our way to Acclaro.'

Manu took the map and carefully opened out on the table. It was very detailed and included the lands from Illume all the way to Culchar and Acclaro.

'Well, this shall certainly help; Ramon has marked several paths we can choose from.

With the help of Manu, Ishmael made them a simple breakfast of omelettes from the remaining food in the camp. Zahra still hadn't emerged from her bed roll, so Manu inspected Ishmael's wounds. In all the days he had worked as a medic Manu had never seen wounds heal so quickly. Ishmael still complained of a painful gut, especially if he ate a lot of food, so there was certainly something still healing within him. He should have been bed-ridden for months, and instead here he was whistling away as he cleared away the meal. In his life before being a medic he had witnessed miracles of healing, from a time he would like to forget but maybe never would.

It wasn't till midday that Zahra awoke from her slumber with a loud cry, sitting bolt upright her chest heaving, wild eyes looking around her.

Both Ishmael and Manu both leapt to their feet in alarm. When they moved towards Zahra, she held up her hands.

'I'm okay, it was just a bad dream.' She smiled weakly, but the look of fear that haunted her face told a different story.

Ishmael passed her some tea and an omelette, receiving a tight smile in return.

While Zahra ate Manu scoured the camp, checking what had been left by Ramon. Secretly he had hoped the shaman would leave his supply of healing herbs, but anything of medicinal value had gone with him. They were going to have to fend for themselves again now.

'Where is Ramon?' asked Zahra with a mouth full of food.

'He left early this morning once he knew you killed his mother,' replied Ishmael looking over at her.

'The bitch should have been killed a long time ago,' spat Zahra.

'Maybe so, but Ramon was my only link to learning how to use the astral realm. Surely there was some other way to sort things out in a non-violent way?'

'Holy shit, I've heard it all now, Ishmael. For over a hundred years Jayne kidnapped and murdered travellers on the river. The only way to deal with someone like that is violence. That's all they understand. While you were comatose Jayne's merry band of trolls murdered our boatman, and Jayne kept a lady named Yolinda as a slave. I went back to save Yolinda and I burnt Jayne's filthy hovel to the ground after I killed all her trolls. Then I left the bitch to dry out in the sun. That is how I deal with scum like that, so if you have a problem with me ridding the world of a sociopath like Jayne, then too bad.'

'Sorry, Zahra, I meant no offence.'

'I know you didn't, Ishmael, but you need to accept that you are no longer in the monastery meditating and praying to Illume. You are in the real world where things are not so black and white. It's time to grow up. A lot more people could die before we get you to safety.'

Zahra turned to walk off then stopped.

'By the way, you need to start learning to fight. I watched you training in the monastery, so it's time to start putting it to use, because we may not always be around to protect you.'

After Zahra had disappeared into the undergrowth, Ishmael turned to Manu, who had a knowing smile on his face.

'Is she always so surly, Manu?'

'Oh only about ninety percent of the time, but at least she is on your side, Ishmael; believe me when I say you don't want her as an enemy.'

'So how do you know her Manu?'

'That's a long story, Ishmael. I was working as a medic in the Cavere army. Zahra was one of my patients who was recovering from a near fatal poisoning. At that time I had nearly lost my soul to drink and even had my own stash within the hospital itself. No one seemed to catch on to the fact that most of the time I was wasted except for Zahra, that is. As you know she doesn't pull any punches, so she confronted me about it when she returned to my care for a shoulder wound that required some surgery. Her exact words I believe were, 'don't even fucking try to open me up when you're pickled to the gills on that shit, you drunk quack.' Hahaha she sure has a way with words, doesn't she?

'Anyhow, suffice to say that someone else did the surgery. Later Zahra happened to be close by when my stash was found by the superior matron. Zahra came forward to tell the matron that it was hers and that she was a hopeless alcoholic who could not be trusted to stay free of the shit. So my job was saved and Zahra let me know that I now owed her a favor should our paths ever cross again.' That was maybe nine or ten cycles ago. Since then Zahra has a habit of turning up in my life at the most unexpected moments. Ishmael, if anybody can get you to safety, Zahra can do it, but you need to trust her.'

'I know I need to learn to trust both of you, but it's not that easy to do that with people you have just met,' Ishmael said

'Yes, I agree, but if we meant you harm you would have known by now. From my understanding, you and this coterie are important to everybody who inhabits this world, and to try and harm any of you before you return the magic would be truly foolish. What is it like to carry the world's power within you?'

'I'm mostly unaware of it, but if I neglect to do the practices given to me by the abbot then I get a pressure throughout my body as the magic tries to escape. It starts as an aching then becomes a burning pain all over my body. Leading up to the attack by the Infernals I started to become aware of it inside of me, almost like a serpent moving up and down my spine. Ramon says the magic is held in by my energy centres and will be released once all seven centres are open. At the same time I also became aware of the other coterie members in my dreams, and now if I concentrate I can actually tune into the others at any time, but it is exhausting.' Ishmael sighed. 'To be perfectly honest, Manu, I never really took the whole magic thing very seriously at all. Ever since I learnt of it from my father when he passed it onto me, it has been nothing but a great burden I would rather be rid of.

'That all changed when I nearly died though. The Earth Mother showed me everything from the birth of the world when magic was a normal part of life until the war and the Severing. The sorcerers who cast the final spell did the right thing, and now the Earth is almost healed, but the return of magic will cause so much upheaval which is why our job of choosing when to release it is difficult. We have no idea if it will take the form it did in the past or if it will affect the world in a totally different way. Not even the Mother Earth knows what will happen.'

Zahra returned from bathing, her hair dripping as she moved gingerly back into the camp. Manu called Zahra over then they both began perusing the map Ramon had left them.

'Zahra, I really don't feel good about us leaving here while you and Ishmael are still injured. We would be too weak if attacked. What do you think?'

'As much as I hate to admit it, you are right, we need rest.'

'I'm glad we agree,' Manu said. 'Ramon didn't leave any of his healing stores, but there is plenty of food here and we can forage if need be. This will also give you time to get Ishmael training again.'

Ishmael spoke up. 'Are we safe here now that Ramon has gone?'

'Nowhere is safe, Ishmael, especially here, but at least this camp was chosen well,' Manu replied. 'Its height gives us great advantage if we should need to defend it. We have plenty of food available as well, so this looks like being our home for now.'

Chapter 42

That night the rain came again; the three lay in Ramon's hammocks and for the first time since this whole ordeal started Ishmael found himself almost comfortable. As he dozed, the hypnotizing patter of the rain around the camp set his mind free, and the sounds of the night faded to be replaced by the voices of the coterie. There was the softly spoken Jona, the no-nonsense Selene, and also cocky Raul. Ishmael focused in on Jona by strengthening his concentration on her and fading out the others.

'Jona, can you hear me?'

'Ishmael, it's you! I thought you might be dead. You need to be less forceful when you send your thoughts, you nearly blew my head apart '

'Sorry, I will try. It seems our links are stronger now.'

'Yes, Ishmael, who knows what we will be able to do in even a few days from now. The sentinel told me that the danger we face will uncover abilities within us. We are all learning, and if we can master these latent abilities then we have a better chance of surviving. Where are you Ishmael? '

'We are in the Jewelled lands, near the Winding River. The monastery where I have lived was attacked by Infernals looking for me; my sentinel got me to safety, but barely.'

'Let's try something Ishmael. Picture the location as vividly as you can and hold it in your mind then project it to me kind of like pushing.'

'All right, like this?' Ishmael concentrated on the image.

'You are surrounded by soft orange lighting and it's raining. It seems you are on a hill top, but I'm not sure. Now it's your turn, Ishmael.'

'Hmm… you are inside a room with a fire; you're alone with a book on your lap called When Trails Converge.'

'Yes, you did it, Ishmael. That's exactly what I'm reading.'

'Where is your sentinel, Jona?'

'He is trying to get a message to his clan leader by the astral. So far he hasn't been able to contact the clan, and with no messages getting through the astral it seems that something bad may have happened.'

'Let's try to contact Selene.' Together they focused on Selene, sending a quiet call. At first there was nothing, but then a scene coalesced inside Ishmael's mind. Selene was standing on a large rock looking out to the ocean, and behind her stood a solid, capable looking man with a sword strapped to his back. Selene suddenly looked up then her voice burst into their minds.

'Ishmael, Jona, how did you do that? It felt like you were inside of me looking out just now.'

'Owww, don't yell,' they both sent in unison.'

'Sorry,' giggled Selene but I never knew we could do this.'

'Neither did we till just a little while ago, Selene.'

'Have you tried to contact Raul at all?' said Selene, the acid clear through her thoughts.

'No, we started with you.'

'Shall we try?'

'Yes, let's give Raul a chance; he is still one of us.'

This time they agreed to concentrate on Raul; however, Jona suggested they first push their minds together before trying any contact. It was an unusual feeling doing this, reminding Ishmael of a time long ago when his father had taken him and his sister to Illume city and they had been allowed to climb one of the unmanned sky towers. All the way up Ishmael had been terrified. His hands sweated profusely while a sick feeling burnt the back of his throat and then he had looked down. If his father hadn't of been there Ishmael would have fallen as the vertigo made him lose balance. It was this feeling that swept over him as his mind melded with Jona and Selene's. The sharing of minds briefly allowed Ishmael to see great distances, and he sensed he was above the glade where they camped looking out across the lands. Ishmael became aware of the very uncomfortable sensation of Jona and Selene in his mind, and he found he could switch view points from his own natural sight to the sight of the other two or combined sight of the three of them which was crystal clear, but the focus to hold it was more difficult. Selene's calm voice slid through his mind.

'Now just focus on our combined sight while picturing Raul, how he was that day in the tree chamber when Brianna died.'

As they concentrated a scene emerged from the haze within their combined minds. It was a dark chamber lit only by a few candles, an old water-stained picture of a horseman wielding a sabre whilst astride a rearing horse hung lopsided on a wall above a bed. Looking down Ishmael saw a woman, pretty with black hair moaning, her skin shiny with perspiration then suddenly Ishmael realized what was going on. Someone giggled, it sounded like Jona.

Then Raul's presence was there in all its fury.

'Get out of my head!'

He must have said it out loud, because the woman's eyes opened.

'What did you say, Raul?'

Then they were hurtled back into their own bodies. Ishmael opened his eyes to the campsite where Manu sat by Zahra, whose naked upper body was decorated by a heavy pattern of scarring. He found his eyes drawn to her breasts then looked away hurriedly with the feeling of what Raul had been doing fresh in his mind. Ishmael looked over again at Zahra where she sat as Manu softly applied a salve to the claw marks over the shoulder and across her chest. The fire light danced over the curves of her hardened body. He was completely taken by surprise when she turned to look his way, catching his stare. Embarrassed at being caught Ishmael turned over to put his back to Zahra. He lay there a while trying to reconnect with Jona and Selene, but the earlier effort had drained away his energy, so he soon drifted off into sleep.

Chapter 43

Manu poured himself a steaming mug of tea, looked around to make sure Zahra wasn't watching, then slipped a dash of some homemade liquor that Ramon had left behind into the mug.

Sipping contentedly he moved over to the small clearing at the side of the grove that was until recently covered in green grass but now lay torn and trampled by the daily fitness sessions of Ishmael and Zahra.

These sessions hadn't interested Manu at all, but todays would. This time they would spar with each other for the first time and having been on the end of a few of Zahra's beatings himself, Manu felt a tinge of pity for young Ishmael.

They fought without weapons first. Zahra lunged forwards with a straight jab that Ishmael ducked beneath then tried to take Zahra to the ground, but before he could grasp her in his arms her knee met his face, dropping him hard. Zahra stepped back allowing him to rise, expecting to see defeat in his eyes but was surprised to see anger there. A trickle of blood ran from Ishmael's right nostril, and when he smiled at Zahra she could see more blood stained his teeth.

Ishmael turned his body so that he no longer provided such a large target. Trying to remember his training he began to slow his breathing to gain control of his anger, but Zahra wasn't about to allow him to rest. She came in with a low kick of her shin to his mid-thigh, drove a fist into his stomach then danced away with a short elbow strike as he stepped close. This time Ishmael waited for Zahra to attack, she kicked his opposite thigh, causing the knee just below to buckle slightly, then she followed through with a left hook. He caught the punch on the outside of his forearm turning his wrist over to grasp Zahra's wrist from above then pulled down hard pulling Zahra off balance and past him. As she turned, Ishmael stepped towards her driving a kick at her face, but she simply ducked beneath the kick then rewarded his actions with a stiff palm to the groin causing Ishmael to squawk then fall over. From the camp site Manu cackled loudly slapping his knee.

'Zahra, take it easy on him hey. He still carries some injuries'

'I won't take it easy on him, because the enemy won't. He's just gotten lazy in his fighting that's all, he's too predictable.'

Zahra patted the still-gasping Ishmael on the head then helped herself to some water. She had being trying to contact the other sentinels via the astral plane, but for some reason no one had come to the meeting place, so she left a message. Something felt wrong there, and the unease made Zahra suspect a trap. She had thought of asking Ishmael to try to contact the coterie with her message to see if that would work. There was still the problem of trying to contact Haakon, who would be waiting with advice if she could just get to him by some avenue of communication. Ishmael was walking now timidly towards where she had sat with Manu.

'Ishmael, do you know what you did wrong?'

'Yes, I do, I got out of bed.'

That bought a laugh to all three of them.

She would never admit it to him, but Zahra was impressed with Ishmael's attitude. After all he had been through, he was still quite positive with strong self-belief. There was no complaining that he was injured, he just got back up again and again until she told him to stop.

Ishmael was sore from foot to head. He couldn't remember the last time he had been pain free. The stumps of his missing fingers ached every day, and what was worse was the feeling they were still there or the itching that the missing fingers caused him. He still found it hard to eat much since Manu had stitched his stomach up. Something just didn't feel quite right but that wasn't going to stop him. The Earth Tree had saved his life to give him a second chance that he couldn't afford to squander. He was enjoying the challenge the training had bought, although he had to admit his ego took a bruising every time Zahra hit him. Beaten by a woman was hardly good for the ego, but then Zahra was no ordinary woman. Just after he sat down, Zahra made him get up again for weapon training with two staffs cut to sword length. With no actual weapon training allowed for monks of Illume, Ishmael was battered by Zahra, who hardly seemed to break a sweat during the session.

Later Ishmael wandered down the worn path to the river. The daylight had already begun its slow exit and the orange crystals were already glowing softly. Ishmael imagined it was like being at the heart of a bushfire without the heat. He stripped off his sweaty clothes and folded them neatly before entering the water. For the first few days Ishmael was unsure about bathing in the river, but now he had become accustomed to the area along with the animals that inhabited it. It felt good to be exercising again; his muscles had complained painfully at their work out, but the training had done more for his mental health as he was able to unload all the frustration he had endured since the attack at the monastery. At least now normality was creeping back into his life, he thought as he lay back floating in the cool water.

Suddenly he felt as if he were not alone, and he opened his eyes in time to see Zahra wiggle free of her clothing and slip into the water. She dove beneath the surface then came up alongside him with a grin.

'What, haven't you ever see a girl naked, Ishmael? Do I look that bad?'

'You look fine, Zahra, I'm just not used to being around women: you know there were none in the monastery.'

'You have been moving tentatively since training, but it won't take long to build your strength. You learn quickly too, which is great because I won't have to carry you in battle. I can't recall you being in any fights while at the monastery.'

'Unless you count being mauled by an Infernal, then no I haven't.'

'They train you in unarmed combat but why not in weapon to weapon combat?'

'To be a brother of Illume means you will refrain from harming another being. The use of weapons within the monastery grounds is forbidden to us monks.' Ishmael paused. 'Zahra, can you tell me what happened after the Infernal gutted me?'

He listened patiently as Zahra recounted the events from the attack, by the time she had finished the night was settling in amongst the flaming crystal ambient glow, but the water had grown cold now so they swam ashore to sit for a while.

'What happened to my brothers and the abbot?'

'Well, the abbot fought alongside the other monks to get you to safety, but I didn't get to see what happened to them, just that they fought with such courage to hold the Infernals back against overwhelming odds. The truth is that I only heard that there were a handful of survivors. Looks like your brethren went against their own laws to fight for your safety.'

They dressed in silence, Ishmael facing away from Zahra so as not to see her naked body, which bought a snort of laughter from her and a blush to his face.

Back at camp Manu had been busy making dinner from the fish he had managed to catch earlier in the day.

'You know if we weren't on a mission so important I would make this spot my home. Ramon sure knows how to pick a great place to live. Yep, me, myself, my fishing rod as well as the bugs would get along just fine.'

'You forgot the Harlequin, Manu, they would be your neighbours.'

'Bah, they would be my servants to wait upon my every whim, protect me so they could pass along their secrets through me to the masses.' From beyond the fire light a voice carried to all three of them causing them to stand in alarm.

'Humans will never understand our secrets.'

The three of them surged to their feet. Zahra grabbed a branch from the fire, holding it high she turned slowly illuminating the edges of the clearing where now hundreds of Harlequin of all colors stood motionless, watching them.

'Don't pick up any weapons,' she murmured to Manu and Ishmael.

'If they wanted to harm us they would have done so by now.'

Ishmael stared. He had only ever read about them in books or seen pictures of them but in reality they were so much more beautiful. Their crystalline bodies set the clearing awash with multi-colored fire as they moved silently closer to the three companions. Manu stood grinning as he looked around them.

'Children of the soil, we welcome you to our temporary home, enter and be free from worry or harm.'

From the ranks of Harlequin stepped a dark purple figure almost black, smaller than the others who made way for it to approach.

'One who knows the old words of greeting, it is fitting that Earth and Sky meet this night far from our homes. The elements are gathering to make the mother whole once more.'

Then the figure beckoned Ishmael forward. They could see it had something cradled in its hands. Ishmael paused until Manu pushed him forward along with a nod. When he stood before the purple Harlequin, all the others bent on one knee.

'Ishmael Shantari you are one of the coterie of the Heart. The life of this world hangs in the balance, and as keepers of the Earth we finally are able to complete our task of safe keeping. This crystal represents the element of Earth. Now it is your responsibility to carry it. Long we have waited for this moment. Your coming has set in motion great energies, and we pray you choose well how you use it.'

'But what is it for, can't you help us?'

'In time you will learn its secrets, but we cannot interfere. Our allotted task is complete.'

With that the Harlequin held out what appeared to be a clear rock crystal to Ishmael, who took it in both hands and inspected it.

Ishmael lifted the crystal towards his face. There was something inside the rock that caught his attention like a shape or symbol; then there was a click from what seemed inside his head and the familiar terrifying feeling of the magic bursting up from within his body, except this time it was stronger. He used all his mind to push it back down, but the force was too powerful for him, and burst forth from his fingers into the rock with such power that he shook until his teeth rattled. Was this his death? Had he failed because he couldn't control the power he held? Then it was gone as the magic slipped back inside his body. With a cry he fell to his knees in wonder, his body thrumming with power. Ishmael could feel the life around him like never before; the vibrant lifeforms of his friends and the land, even the Harlequin He was aware that the special moment was shared with the coterie and he could faintly feel their questing presence.

As Manu watched Ishmael take the crystal from the Harlequin, a wind sprung up seemingly from nowhere right before a fierce, blinding light consumed Ishmael and forced Manu to turn away. Ishmael's body was so infused with power that Manu could feel it dance along the hairs on his body, waking up every nerve fibre within him. That amazing feeling made Manu cry out in joy, he had never thought he would feel it again, but then it was gone again, leaving him feeling empty more now than ever.

When Ishmael was consumed by the light, Zahra instinctively stepped forward to grab him but it was too intense and she was forced to turn away. Zahra cried out his name, but it was like screaming into a storm. Her body reacted to that light, making her feel more alive than she could ever remember, lost in that moment she became aware of her surroundings again only once the light had retreated inside of Ishmael, leaving her in a state of awe. So that was magic?

The purple Harlequin took Ishmael by the shoulders.

'This is good, Ishmael, the crystal has acknowledged you as the chosen to bear it.'

'What is it? I need to know what I am to do with it.'

'We cannot help you, for we don't know, but trust in the Mother and she will guide you. Now it is time for us to leave; we wish you the best in your quest. With you the Earth has chosen well.'

With that the Harlequin simply stepped back into the darkness, leaving them alone again. Manu took a swig of the strong liquor he had found then passed it to Zahra, who also downed a healthy swig.

'Well, I never expected that I should ever meet Harlequin at all let alone twice,' Zahra said.

'When else did you see them?' asked Ishmael, looking at her incredulously.

'While Ramon and Manu were getting you back to your body from the astral, I went for a walk up to the hill there. One of the Harlequin approached me. It questioned my ability to protect you, so we fought. We fought a draw, and lucky for me too because I really think it would have killed me. Anyhow the Harlequin gifted me with a blade made of crystal; it also said I was the first human to be given such a blade.'

Manu shook his head in wonder. 'So you're telling us you were given a Harlequin blade? Where is it, Zahra?'

Zahra retrieved the blade from her bed roll, unwrapping it before returning to show Manu and Ishmael.

'Its name is Moonbite.'

Manu examined the blade curiously, testing the sharpness on a branch, watching in wonder as it sheared the wood easily in half.

'It was said to me long ago that Harlequin blades harness the light of our two moons and that their sharpness can never be dulled. So did you even think to tell us about this meeting as well as the sword or did you just think we wouldn't be interested?'

'Don't get pissed off, Manu it wasn't like that at all. Things just got in way like the business with Jayne. I just managed to forget about it okay?'

'Of course it's alright, these things happen every day, don't they?'

'Quit the sarcasm, Manu,' Zahra said, making a face. 'You're just upset that you didn't get a sword or crystal, obviously you're not as important as you thought.'

Manu smiled. Strange events are happening now he thought.

The meeting with the Harlequin had woken the three of them up and they talked long into the night about their next move.

As they headed to their bed rolls Zahra knelt beside Ishmael.

'Ishmael, I have been trying to access the astral realm but I don't feel it's safe to leave a message there for the other Sentinels, and I badly need to get a message through to my clan leader. I have heard you talking about how communication between you and the coterie is sometimes possible. Can you see what you can find out, please?'

'Sure, Zahra, I will.'

Chapter 44

Ishmael used his breathing to relax his mind then he sent out his thoughts to Jona, but all he received were a bunch of images of a small house with children running around beneath an azure sky. She must be dreaming, Ishmael realized, then he switched his thoughts to Selene only to find himself immersed in images of the ocean as well as a large floating city of interconnected boats. Rather than try to enter her dream, Ishmael switched to Raul. Received an image of a bar room then with a rush found himself there in the bar looking through Raul's eyes. Unlike the last time, Raul didn't cut him off but instead talked into Ishmael's mind.

'So you three are making a habit of prying into my thoughts, are you?'

'Raul, we are just trying to test our skills in seeing through one another's eyes, it's new to us. You are avoiding us, so this seems the only way we can contact you. Try it yourself.'

There was a pause then another presence was inside Ishmael's head. Raul!

It was not like the soft transition when Jona or Selene had looked through his eyes. Raul's presence felt hard, crushing, almost overpowering him completely as if forcing himself out. Ishmael pushed a message back hard.

'Don't do that, Raul!'

'Or what, Ishmael? Did you think I would just allow you to enter my mind whenever you like? You are no match for my strength, so I warn you now don't ever try this with me again.'

The pressure in Ishmael's mind lifted to be replaced with anger.

'What is your problem, Raul? We are supposed to be working together, but all you want to do is try to intimidate the rest of us. Can't you see that if we are to survive this then we need to be able to trust each other? We are a coterie.'

'Why should I trust you, Ishmael, I hardly know you or the others. You barge into my mind like you have some right to do so but you don't. I realize this skill is very useful, but if I need to I will contact you or the others. If you do this again I promise you, Ishmael, you will be bringing down more trouble than you can handle.'

Ishmael felt hot with the anger now pulsing through him but forced himself to breathe deeply instead of unleashing the tirade of abuse he wished to direct at Raul.

'Raul, I apologize for the intrusion, it was wrong of me. We were only trying out this new found ability. We did not mean to upset you.'

'Well it's a little late for that don't you think?'

'Raul, one last thing, I need you to pass a message onto your protector, Zahra says not to use the astral meet point, something feels wrong there. Can you give Kaitlin that message?'

'Yes, Ishmael.'

Then Raul was gone, leaving Ishmael still tense from their contact. No longer tired, Ishmael lay back trying to put everything that had happened in perspective. He knew they would be leaving this place soon to head down to Acclaro, the city of his birth. It has been ten cycles since he had looked upon his mother or sisters, surely they had realized by now that it wasn't Ishmael's fault that his father died. Maybe I can have a family again, thought Ishmael, maybe they will realize it wasn't my fault.

Chapter 45

The next morning Ishmael awoke before first light to the sound of packing. He wiped the sleep from his eyes, yawning loudly. 'Get your flabby, lazy ass up already,' Zahra said,' we are leaving at first light so pack only basic necessities.'

'Breakfast?'

'You can eat as we walk.'

Ishmael washed his face from the water skin then rolled his bed roll up around his mere possessions taking care to make sure the piece of crystal given to him by the Harlequin was carefully hidden in the backpack.

The Harlequin had said the crystal recognized him, but how could that be? Up to that moment when the magic surged within him as he held the crystal he had thought he would be able to keep it under control, but now he knew that wasn't the case and that scared him. The visions that the Earth Tree had shared, emphasized that if magic was returned before the right time it would end in the destruction of the world. The coterie were like blind men without guidance. Ishmael realized that no one knew what to do and now it was up to him and the coterie to usher this world-changing event into existence with as little turmoil as possible.

A chime later they were on the march through the faded dawn. Zahra led the way with Moonbite, using the keen blade to slash through foliage, and Manu followed, map in hand and whistling to himself.

'Why are you so happy, Manu?' asked Ishmael walking alongside him.

'I have been in Illume for two cycles, this is a great adventure may even be my last so I plan to make the most of it.'

'Tell me, Ishmael do you truly believe in the wisdom you were taught while in the monastery? As I see it the brotherhood of Illume are all about shining the light of Shail, whose light washes away the evil of the world. Not once have I heard you mention Shail.'

'Manu, I am young with limited knowledge of the teachings of Shail. Of course I know the legends along with everyone else, but those mysteries are reserved for the highest of the order of Illume. Only those senior monks can ever be allowed to climb the Spire of Illume, where her body awaits its rebirth.'

Manu chewed on a plant stem as they walked, the crystal covering foliage here was now changing to a dark blue that seemed to hold the daylight away.

'I saw her once, did you know, Ishmael?'

'Who?'

'Shail of course. Well, her body anyway. Many years ago I came to Illume full of vigor, hope and pain. I thought that seeing Shail's body might miraculously give me the answers I needed at that time of my life. I was wrong and found something very different to what I had expected.'

'How were you able to even get the chance to enter the Spire?'

'It doesn't take long for your name to get around if you are a good healer, and of the holy sisters had heard about my efforts regarding my patients and had decided to seek my help for their oldest sister who was known as Mama Lauren.

'Once we made to the top, I was let into the tower, which smelt of death. It was not what I thought it would be like. I had pictured brightly painted mosaics on the walls since the chamber celebrated the lady Shail's continued existence. Instead I found a dark unpleasant chamber where an old lady lay coughing blood onto the stained kerchief she held against her trembling lips. She was dying, we both knew it. Her eyes had long ago closed from cataracts, her hands and joints horribly swollen with arthritis. As I took her hands in mine and sat beside her, she thanked me for coming to guide her from this world. Not having the heart to tell her that I wasn't a priest, I mixed her some medicine to alleviate the pain. Every day for over a month I called upon Mama Lauren to administer medicine for her pain. We became something of friends in that time.

'Her chosen successor was quite the opposite with me, saying I was only causing Lauren hardship by taxing her health further. Quite often Mama Lauren would send her young successor away so we could sit alone. One morning after her medicine had been administered, and Lauren dozed I decided to climb up to the chamber of Shail. One hundred rungs, as the legends say to the chamber. At least this small chamber was more like what befitted such a powerful goddess. Everything in the room was white with precious metals inlaid on all surfaces. Shail's coffin sat open facing the east for the sun, her body beneath a gold shroud. Up there alone, I felt as if I were committing sacrilege, but I was in a state of confusion with my own life and believed by being there I could answer some questions regarding my own existence. I pulled back the shroud fully expecting to see Shail's youthful body laying silently as if sleeping, but all I found was dust.'

Ishmael stopped walking. 'But it is said in our records that her body still lives on and a gods body will never rot because they are not like you and me. Tell me you are joking, Manu?'

'I'm sorry, Ishmael, I can only tell you the truth of what I saw, I swear it by our friendship, maybe the body is held at another location.'

'You can keep your dirty lies to yourself; I don't want to hear them.' Ishmael ran to catch up to Zahra, ignoring Manu's call. Zahra was cutting a path through thin foliage for them and now stood, machete in one hand looking back at them. From somewhere he could hear the rush of water, the river must be close.

'Ishmael, what happened back there?'

'Nothing, Zahra, just an old man's lies. Just because he has lost his faith he expects we all have. Well I'm not like him, I refuse to believe Shail is dead.'

'Whoa settle down, just relax, I'm sure Manu didn't mean to upset you. Here, if you insist on being angry then put it to use.'

Zahra passed Moonbite to him. 'Head that way towards the water, soon we will be at its bank. Hopefully the two canoes marked here on Ramon's map are still there.'

As she watched Ishmael slash away, Zahra looked back questioningly at Manu who shrugged apologetically.

'Ishmael was confused, he wasn't quite sure why the story made him feel angry. Grunting with the effort of swinging the sword and trying to ignore the light infused glitter bugs landing on his skin he bent into his task. What did Manu mean, he only found dust? The abbot and his other teachers had taught that Shail cannot die and she would be unconscious until magic returned to awaken her from her slumber. If Shail's body had been reduced to dust, it could only mean one thing. The goddess was dead. Was it possible that all the god's were dead? Uncertainty flickered within Ishmael. It was taught that the Severing cast the gods from their planes of existence to be trapped in the mortal realm of their followers along with the hordes of Infernals and Celestials. He pushed the thought away then redoubled his effort of destroying the foliage before him. Ishmael thought back to the near death experience he had endured, especially the vision that the Earth Tree had shown him when the magic had been torn away.

The Severing had changed the way man as well as the other races of the world thought about the gods, who were now vulnerable. Could it be that the races and cultures were merely going through the motions of worship to their chosen deities whose power was now only equal to the common man next to him? Ishmael didn't know how the world would be affected with the gods losing their power. Would new gods be born if the old ones died? He slashed away at a particularly thick branch across the path, and as it fell away he saw an embankment that looked down upon the Winding River below. Ishmael heard Zahra's voice over the waters roar.

'Can you see any canoes down there Ishmael?'

He leaned out over the drop to see below and there, sure enough, tied up against the trunk of a gnarled grey tree on the bank stood two canoes. They climbed through the undergrowth down to the canoes. Manu passed Ishmael a knife to cut open the long packages that each canoe held wrapped in leather. Inside they found the oars, a flint and tinder box, fishing line with hooks as well as another map of the river system.

Zahra shared a canoe with Ishmael while Manu rode solo with his heavy pack that contained their food and medical supplies. The canoes were well crafted from heart wood that was a deep cherry red. The flow of the river swiftly pulled them out to the middle of the river, which looked free of any dangerous obstacles. From beneath the thick trees overhead they emerged into a glorious day with the sun sparkling off the river around them. The flow of the river was fast here so the current carried them. Ishmael lay back, day dreaming with his eyes closed while he trailed his fingers in the water. Even Zahra whistled away to herself as they meandered down river. Ishmael turned when Manu called to him just in time to catch a face full of water as Manu splashed him.

'You will pay for that, old man,' Ishmael yelled, his anger at the old man forgotten as he received another face full of water. He coughed and Manu laughed so hard he almost capsized his canoe. Zahra laughed and also joined in the splashing. During this time Ishmael caught himself thinking of how he had come to like his companions. It was about time they had a chance to leave their worries behind for just a little while because deep down Ishmael knew that danger would be coming fast on the wings of Infernals that wanted to skin him just like what the old man had done to Brianna Dusk. But even that one gloomy thought didn't penetrate through the joy he shared then with Zahra and Manu out on the river that day. They swept down the river for most of the morning until they emerged into a strait where the water slowed. It was shallower here enough so that they pulled their canoes along behind as they made for an area up ahead where they could beach the canoes. The crystals on the trees here were a blue green, game could be seen coming down to the river to drink and as they ate they watched the life continue around them.

Chapter 46

Once back on the river the sky darkened quickly from a brewing storm. They beached their canoes and waited for it to abate.

The heavy rainfall lasted a few chimes, and then the companions were back in the water paddling harder now that the mist was thinning out. Their surroundings ghosted into view as the Winding River carried them towards the Unkta Falls, a holy place to the Jingtalla people. The sun finally emerged to dry them off as they entered what Manu said was the fastest flowing point of their journey. Gone now were the crystal encrusted trees which had been replaced with bare river banks revealing villages with docking points at which traders would stop to buy and sell wares with the villagers there. The Jingtalla tribes were the sacred keepers of the falls that could be heard faintly. Zahra felt uneasy, usually the Jingtalla people would wave and hoot at the rivers passengers, their children running along the bank yelling and laughing, but there was none of this. Instead their passing was marked by silent watchers shaking rattles or beating drums.

'Why are they doing that, Manu?'

'I wish I could tell you, Ishmael, but it is the first time I have seen them do this. It's as if they think we bring evil with us.'

Ishmael looked on with Zahra and Manu. As they travelled farther towards the great falls the villages became more deserted as if some powerful force had whisked away the inhabitants here leaving an empty world in its wake. They didn't talk much in this eerie place as they let their canoes drift on the current.

Late in the afternoon Manu pulled the other canoe close so he could talk to Ishmael and Zahra.

'It will be dark soon and I can't speak for you two but I am not camping anywhere here.'

'I'm with you Manu, this place gives me the chills. I feel we are being watched even though the villages are empty.'

'Ishmael stop the dramatic bullshit there has to be an explanation for all this. But I do agree with you both that we cannot camp here until we know what is going on.'

'I have an idea,' said Ishmael.

'We can use the crystal to provide us with light as we travel. Our flint and tinder are soaked through and we have no torches. This way we can get away from this place. It's funny, you know, because I have always wanted to see the famous riverside markets of the Jingtalla and yet we are greeted only with deathly silence.'

Manu put his flask to his lips to drink before remembering it was empty. 'Well, it looks like we are up for a night-time journey then.'

Ishmael unwrapped the crystal, which gave off a soft white light at his touch, illuminating the three and their canoes. He braced it amongst his belongings for stability and they continued on their way.

Zahra awoke to the chorus of her aches and pains. She opened her eyes then hurriedly closed them as the sun striking the crystal forest momentarily blinded her. Something was bumping against her canoe, and once her eyes had righted themselves she recoiled in revulsion. All around them were bloated grey corpses wearing the uniform of Illume mercenaries. The river before them had narrowed and was choked with bodies and the rotten stench of decaying flesh. Zahra turned and shook Ishmael, who came awake instantly.

'What, what's wrong?'

Zahra, who now was holding a cloth over her nose, indicated the water-logged bodies. Ishmael looked then puked over the side of the canoe.

'Oh, god what is wrong with you, Ishmael, haven't you seen a dead body before?'

Zahra picked up a chicken bone from her left over meal last night and threw it at the still-sleeping Manu where it landed neatly on his chest. He grunted, wiped a hand across his face, and slept on. Zahra threw a half empty water bag that hit him flush in the face. He came awake with a yell, nearly capsizing his canoe as he stood then he screamed hoarsely as he saw the bodies surrounding them.

'By the gods what happened?'

'It must have been the soldiers that were backed up on the river when we left Illume. I imagine the fight with the Harlequin didn't go their way.' Ishmael gave a shudder. Who would want to fight an enemy like that?

Manu wiped the sleep from his eyes. 'At least that explains the strange behavior of the villagers, but the question now remains as to what the hell we can do to get past this mess.'

'We can't just leave them here to rot in the sun,' said Ishmael.

'Like hell we can, Ishmael. This is no business of ours and we don't have time to spend another day burying the dead from a battle we were no part of.'

Zahra reached over to put one hand on Ishmael's shoulder. 'I know you mean well, Ishmael, but we can't allow our enemies any extra time to find you. These men deserve better than this, but if our enemies catch up with us then it will be our bodies added to this floating graveyard.'

The three of them tied clothing over their noses and mouths then slowly paddled through the corpses. They made it to the blockage that was stopping all the bodies from continuing on their way down to the falls. At some point a large branch had dislodged itself and flowed down stream to get caught amongst other debris in the rocks lining the river's edge. From the other side of the river they could see some sort of boat had sunk, which blocked off the rest of the flow. Dead mercenaries now bobbed up and down amongst the froth as the river's denizens fed upon their flesh.

Not wishing to stay amongst the stench any longer, they beached the canoes then dragged them past the blockage before re-entering the water. All thought of breakfast was forgotten as the three were just happy to be away from the grisly sight and smell. They rounded a bend in the river and saw up ahead the great Unkta falls, its watery roar getting steadily louder. They angled over to a deserted jetty and soon had tied off the canoes.

'I would kill for a hot bath,' said Zahra as she stretched out her arms with a yawn.

Ishmael pointed over to some huts amongst the trees.

'Look, there are people in the houses, you can see smoke coming from many of them.'

From one of the houses an elderly man emerged, stooped over with age and leaning upon a tall staff. When he reached the three companions he nodded at them then stood there breathing heavily.

The old man, the spokesman by the look of him spoke in common tongue thick with age between chewing his heavily scarred lower lip as if not sure of himself.

'I am called He Who Knows! Why do you bring death to our homes, strangers?'

✦

Chapter 47

Manu stepped forward. 'Honoured one, we don't bring death, it follows us on our journey always over our shoulders and just out of sight. The dead soldiers that block the river farther back upstream are not our doing but the result of a battle between the mercenary recruits of Illume and the Harlequin.'

'That may be so, but if you are going to Acclaro then this death that surrounds you is an omen I would take the time to examine, my friends,' He Who Knows answered. 'Was a time when Acclaro was called the crown jewel of the world and one reason why these lands became known as the Jewelled Lands. In that time they say evil could not stay beneath its walls and the city thrived, teeming with trade and endless crowds. Now they say Acclaro is a dead city, its people lost in despair. I don't say these things lightly, and I personally have witnessed strange things that can't be told but need to be witnessed to believe.'

'Well show us, old one, we don't have much time,' said Zahra.

'Not now, impatient girl, but at sunset when the door between worlds is very thin, then you shall know what I know.'

'Another day wasted? I don't think so, now let's go.'

'The trip down the falls can wait, Zahra,' Manu said. 'There is something going on here, I can feel it, and at worst we will be well rested tonight when we resume our journey.'

Zahra glared over at Manu so Ishmael stepped between them and placed a hand casually on her shoulder.

'Let us wait here, Zahra, we can help drag the bodies from the river blockage while we wait.'

Zahra shook her head.

'Great, I can't wait to get started.'

The clearing of bodies took the rest of the afternoon and the two canoes came in useful as they dragged the bodies to shore where the Jingtalla natives had built a bonfire to burn them. Ishmael noticed they weren't talkative as he worked with them pulling bodies from the canoes to dump on the embankment. The tribesman, who were stripped down to loincloths, were careful not to get to close to the three travellers, and when Ishmael tried to talk with them he was met only with smiles, no words.

After the loathsome task of clearing the river was finished, they sat together eating bowls of beans and vegetables with melon slices. The Jingtalla sat in groups away from them and seemed to be discussing their visitors with wild gestures to the spokesman who sat through it all slowly chewing his food.

'Why won't they interact with us?' asked Ishmael.

Zahra turned to face Ishmael.

'It's because of the death we bring with us, they believe that if they come to close to us the death that surrounds us will harm their village and families. Can't say I blame them either.'

'How do you know that, Zahra?' Ishmael shoved her a bowl of food. 'You should eat something too before we set off again.'

'I have picked up a little of their language over the cycles on river trader boats. After that work I have no appetite left.'

The afternoon was spent alongside the river edge sleeping, oiling and sharpening, weapons and swimming. The three were eager to be on their way but also heeded the warning from the old shaman and knew any information they could get regarding Acclaro would help them immeasurably.

Finally as dusk began dimming the sky and Jingtalla mothers started herding their children inside their homes, He Who Knows returned.

'Come, my impatient guests, an interesting sight awaits you. Come!'

They were led up a steep trail that wound away from the roar of the falls to a wooden platform that afforded them a clear view down over the Glyph plains and to Acclaro. The crimson moon Tumul was barely visible beyond the bright glow of the second moon Aspre whose light fell directly on the city below as if highlighting it just for them.

They stood gazing out to the distant city whose outer wall and towers formed a crown and were connected to the royal castle by long sky paths. Airborne shapes flitted around these constructs like moths would a flame.

Ishmael wasn't sure what he was looking for, he turned to He Who Knows.

'I see nothing but a bunch of birds circling around the castle, so what is your point?'

'No, those are not birds, they are Infernals!'

Manu grasped the man's shoulders. 'Are you sure? Above the city, unchallenged? What the hell is going on in there?'

'I myself have spent many nights with the others of our tribe watching Infernals flying above Acclaro. Something has awoken in the city; the king is silent and Infernals fly from his castle. We have had news that outsiders are questioned, that you will be watched closely the moment you enter the gates. They are looking for someone or something; could it be you? Your road is none of my affair, but it is my duty to make you aware that if your destination is Acclaro it would be wise to avoid it completely.'

'Unfortunately, friend, we need to go to Acclaro City before continuing on our journey, Infernals or not,' Manu said. Armed with this knowledge you have kindly provided we now know what we could be stepping into. Forewarned is forearmed, wise one, so we thank you for your concern, now we must be going.' Manu turned to Ishmael and Zahra. 'Let us hasten on our way, for we have much to discuss.'

Zahra turned to follow Ishmael and Manu, but the shaman's eyes grabbed her and she felt trapped beneath his gaze as he stepped over to her.

'When you first appeared at our village I recognized that you are like me, one of the untouched. It's my time, and I have seen it enough in my dreams to know this is how my days end, my final battle. I see by your reaction this sort of thing is not new to you, so then you know what I ask?'

'You want me to bear witness to your death at such a time when the world and these people of yours need you.'

'Others will step forward to carry on my work, but now it is time I undid a wrong that was thrust upon the Jingtalla people, and you must bear witness. Now come, it is better you are at the bottom of the falls when this all begins.'

'What was that all about, Zahra?' asked Ishmael as she joined them.

'I'm not sure, but something is about to happen and we need to be away from the falls when it does.'

Ishmael was first to climb into the woven basket that would lower them down to the ground. He Who Knows clambered on board as the basket started its descent. Ten feet down, the shaman nimbly jumped off onto a ledge that led to a cave blocked off by an iron portcullis. He stopped at the winch mechanism and fitted a pole to turn it. To Ishmael it appeared the cave was filled with gleaming, shining lights, but as he watched it moved, it was a glittering creature that had been locked away.

Manu peered at the cave as they passed. 'I can't believe it, that is a Jewelled One, maybe the last alive?'

'Who are the Jewelled ones, Manu?'

'There once were many, and they are giant arachnids emblazoned with all the colors imaginable. They lived among the treetops where the touch of their bodies left a trail of crystal afterward. Man of course feared them and their allies, the Harlequin, and began to hunt them down. The King of Thantos orchestrated an elaborate attack into the Jewelled Lands that culminated in the capture of the Jewelled Ones' queen, and the Harlequin agreed not to attack traders between Illume and Acclaro.'

'Until recently that is,' said Ishmael as he also watched the shaman at the cave.

'Even now the treaty stands, Ishmael. The only reason the mercenaries were attacked is because they are operating outside of the treaty. I have seen many injured from the skirmishes with the Harlequin, and they all say that it's only once they entered the forests that they are set upon.'

'Then why weren't we attacked?'

Zahra glanced at him then away again. 'I believe we were left alone because of you, Ishmael. The Harlequin visited us twice while we lived at Ramon's glade, once to test me as your sentinel and twice to gift you with the crystal and recognize you as one of the coterie of the Heart.'

It occurred to Zahra as she watched He Who Knows that they were the only ones aware of what he was doing, and finally cries of alarm sounded from above as the portcullis was winched higher. Whoever was lowering the baskets chose that moment to stop, leaving them swinging close enough to see what was happening but with still a considerable distance to the ground. The portcullis was only half up when the Jewelled One squeezed beneath it onto the ledge. Two Jingtalla men had arrived also with javelins at the ready and one flew past their shaman, narrowly missing him.

The Jewelled One rose to its full height, its coloring flared as it reared back on four legs over the three Jingtalla, then it fell upon the two armed men impaling one with a leg that exploded out the man's back and biting down with such force on the second man that

Zahra could hear bones crunch. He Who Knows fell to his knees before the great arachnid and was speaking rapidly. It seemed for a moment he would die too, but strangely to Zahra it seemed that this incredible creature was actually listening to him. Somehow all the javelins missed their targets, and then they were too late as the Jewelled One leapt, covering hundreds of feet to land high into the huge blue-crusted trees on the far side of the river. It paused there a moment then scuttled away into the colored foliage leaving only branches and bushes shuddering with its passage.

He Who Knows ran over to the winch, and the basket began to lower again, carrying them out of sight of what happened next but they could still hear the scream and see the body of the shaman as it tumbled past them. Half a chime later they were at the base of the falls. It was a chaotic mess, groups of Jingtalla had prostrated themselves on the ground around the supposed remains of their shaman as groups of Jingtalla talked animatedly together, leaving the three of them to quietly slip away.

'We need to get away from here before we are blamed for what's happened,' said Manu, already striding away. Ahead they caught up to a cart led by large bulwar beetles and driven by a portly red-faced man. Manu hurried over to him.

'Excuse me, friend, are you headed for Acclaro?'

'Sure am, actually anywhere to get away from here. Something has the Jingtalla all wound up, and I have no wish to hang around and see what them damn natives are up to. Never trusted them anyways.'

'If I sling you a few cetas can we ride with you?'

He cast his eyes over the three of them slowly. 'Sure, friend, the company would be appreciated, it's only a day to Acclaro, but these beasts aren't much for conversation.'

Chapter 48

Dalwyn sat lounging within his room at the King's Ransom Inn. Rumors were rife in the city regarding his lack of manners. It was custom that nobles visiting from other cities announced themselves to the Five who made up the council of Culchar. Dalwyn not only ignored this custom but had also ignored two letters sent by the Five to attend a summons at the council chambers. Now in front of him sat a third letter sealed with a wax insignia. Beneath it was a calling card from House Urvile that Dalwyn had received that morning. Things were progressing well since his arrival in Culchar. People were saying that his arrival was linked with strange sights within the city and that he had bought magic back with him; however, he was happy to let mouths run false truths and had even added embellishments to the stories where possible.

Dalwyn stood and stretched, cursing at the stabbing back ache that still ailed him. His men had told him about a healer in the common district that they would visit when at Culchar. There was no fee, just a donation to the house that aimed to provide healing to all who came.

'Oh their hands are magic, Lord Trevlon. It's painful the way they manipulate your body to stretch out muscles, but the relief the treatment provides is truly remarkable.'

'Well, have one of their workers call on me here then, Snake.'

'No can do, Dalwyn, they don't take appointments or do house calls. If you want to be seen then you line up at dawn with the rest of those seeking relief.'

'If you think I intend on waiting for chimes in line within the common district you are mistaken,' Dalwyn snapped.

'Lucky for you, Dalwyn the people here are quite easy to persuade…if you take my meaning, sir.'

'So be it, Snake, I will go to this pleasure house tomorrow morning at dawn, so make sure my escort is ready.'

As Snake left to organize an escort for the next morning, Dalwyn finally picked up the letter from the Five.

Lord Dalwyn of family Trevlon.

It is to our dismay that you have neglected to advise us of your business in our city. Since you know our custom here in Culchar, it is with great regret that we pronounce your unlawful presence in our city. However being reasonable citizens, we hereby give you two days to settle your business and depart from Culchar. We hope in future your visits to our city will see you abide by our customs and laws.

THE FIVE.

Dalwyn crumpled the letter then flung in onto the unlit fire grate. The calling card from Tia had one short message:

Dalwyn, your request has been completed. I trust this means I shall never have to look upon your piteous face again.

Reading this message made Dalwyn laugh out loud. Trust the bitch to still be upset with him after the night he had posed as a wine merchant. They had rutted like animals. Since then Tia had been unavailable to see him each time he chose to visit, no doubt wishing to avoid tarnishing her future marriage any farther.

Dalwyn wondered where Zacriel was. He knew his welcome here was almost over, but he was loathe to pack up and leave until he had news from Zacriel regarding the monk he was pursuing.

Later that day Dalwyn was inside the inn taproom where he and his men had made a habit of claiming the best area for themselves. He stood back to the bar absently drinking from his cup. Now finished, he waved away the offer of another drink and called over Snake to escort him upstairs. The drink had affected him more than he thought, the music seemed louder to his ears than normal, and with a pleasant numbness had spread over him. Back at the room he fumbled his key from a pocket to unlock his door.

'No need to join me, Snake, I'm sure there's some lusty wench you would rather spend some time with. Yes, that means you can go. Just send up one of the men to guard the door.'

He finally got the door open just as the guard Snake had sent up reached him, saluted, then fell into position. Dalwyn entered the dim room; sleep would be a welcome distraction from the bone-grating pain in his hips. After placing his money pouch on the bedside table Dalwyn noticed the small movement of the curtains, he slid the dagger at his belt into his palm before turning slowly.

The curtain that was closed earlier now stood open, billowing softly from the light wind outside, but it was the hooded figure beside the window that took Dalwyn's full attention. With a shake of its head the figure pushed back the hood, revealing a reptilian face with luminous golden eyes. It raised its scaled hands in greeting, showing itself to be unarmed.

'Master Trevlon, I am sorry if I disturb your rest.'

'Well, are you going to talk to me then, spawn?'

The Infernal smiled then, showing jagged teeth.

We spotted Zacriel leaving Illume on his way to Acclaro. It seems he has had a run of misfortune recently and is now but a shadow of his former self. He regrets to tell you he cannot travel to see you here due to unforeseen circumstances and that you should advise him of a suitable time and location to meet within the capital.'

Dalwyn threw his hands up in exasperation.

'He has his wings, doesn't he?'

'Well, no, master he doesn't anymore; they have been burned off. He has acquired a lunar mount.'

'It just gets better and better then. Pity he didn't do us the favor of dying. Give Zacriel this parchment; it has the details of where he can find me and when. You may leave, but next time if you dare approach me in my chambers your life will be forfeit.'

'My apologies master, but my kind are not welcome in this city or in daylight and I thought it best to be discreet.'

The Infernal then pulled on its hood and stepped out of the window.

Dalwyn looked out to see him land nimbly on the ground below like a cat. The creature's golden eyes glanced up at him before loping off into the darkness. Dalwyn shivered. Infernals always gave him the shivers even after working with them. He examined the window's wooden shutters, which had been pried open. Dalwyn sat on the bed, he was tired of all this crap, it was only the fact that they were close to returning the magic that kept him going. His mind was becoming frail along with his body. Once there was no way anyone would have gotten close to him, but now his senses were slowing, drying up. How long before someone took advantage of his weakness?

Chapter 49

The next morning arrived too soon for Dalwyn's liking. Virgil had kindly given him another room that stunk of mildew that even the fresh lavender hanging in the corners couldn't disperse. Even the bed was terrible and more like a bed of rocks.

Through the cold bitter morning they walked, footsteps echoing off the flagstones. Snake led the way while behind Dalwyn marched with four of his guards. The streets were quiet with the only other people they saw melting away into the alley's or buildings as the small group approached. Dalwyn walked slightly bent forward; otherwise, if he straightened hot pain shot across his lower back and through his hip bones that forced out a hiss or gasp whenever he had to step over refuse or up and down stairs. At the common quarter they were stopped by guards at a checkpoint who seemed more interested in their hot charr than his permit.

The common quarter was bustling even at this early chime, where groups stood with hands stretched out over fire pits, lost in their thoughts. Whores plied their trade in alleyways along with cut purses, mixing with those hardened people trying to sell their meager goods in the hope of enough coin to buy their next meal.

Snake laughed loudly, gesturing to scenery they walked through. 'And they call this the City of Dreams.'

The House of Pleasures was a plain building that had been recently rebuilt. They had arrived so early that Dalwyn was sure they would be the first, but he was dismayed to see the long line of people who had probably slept there all night to assure their spots. Snake led them to the front of the queue, where the maimed, injured, old and completely insane looked ready to defend their spot with their lives. Snake withdrew a large handful of silver ketches, which he threw on the ground away from where the line was. There was a rush of bodies cursing and screaming as those in line lurched forward, trying to collect as much money as possible. Dalwyn and his entourage used this moment to step into the line.

It wasn't long before the doors swung open to emit a horde of people wearing green tunics and trousers. 'They're the volunteers; many now believe that if they help Gianna with the sick that they will be assured a place in the kingdoms of their gods when they return.'

A lady approached their small party, her face full of kindness. She carried a tray of steaming mugs containing spiced tea and little cakes. 'The physicians will be able to see you soon, meanwhile, have something to eat and drink. Now, so you know you can't bring any weapons into the House of Pleasure because it is a place of healing with no room for instruments of death. What ailment brings you here, friend?'

'Some god-awful back pain that I can't shake. Just so you know, I won't be staying to help but will make a considerable donation if I'm happy with the service,' Dalwyn said.

'Oh, the joys of getting older. If it's any conciliation I know the feeling, okay?' With a nod and a smile, she moved onto the next person.

When Dalwyn was ushered into the House of Pleasure, he was taken to a simple room where a single wooden bench stood in the center. Off to the side stood a table lined with jars of ointments and herbs and a mortar and pestle. The walls were adorned with charts of the human body. Dalwyn removed his boots then lay face up upon the bench as he had been instructed to do.

Soon a figure appeared in the doorway. She had the longest hair Dalwyn had ever seen of the palest blonde color, and her brown eyes welcomed him without saying a word. 'Good morning to you, sir,' she said as she crouched beside him.

'You may call me Gianna. It is my honor to treat you. My aides tell me you are here because of back pain, is that correct?' He nodded slowly.

'Are you the Gianna?'

She laughed at that as she rolled up the sleeves of her green tunic.

'Now turn over so I can see this back of yours.'

Gianna was stronger than he had thought, her movements gentle and deliberate as she placed his body in certain postures then with a deft twist or push she would cause his spine to crack loudly, bringing with it a sense of overwhelming relief. Soon she had finished, then she moved her hands over the points of his spine that corresponded to his energy centers, pausing for a while at each then moving on. Some sort of scan, he thought dreamily.

'What are you doing?'

'Nothing you need worry about. Quite often it is something from another dimension especially the astral realm that causes a person's body to be out of alignment. By looking into the astral plane at your body I can see if that is the case.'

'Is it the case with me?'

'No, it isn't sir, the problem I suspect is sleeping upon lumpy beds hastily erected before dark along with long chimes in the saddle.'

'So your little test told you all that about me then?'

'No, but my eyes can see what everyone else can also; was I far from the mark?'

'You were spot on.'

'Now stay here as long as you need, my aides will assist you once you exit this chamber. You will be sore, there is no avoiding that, but soon you will be right as rain. It has been a pleasure to serve you this day. Farewell.'

Her last words fell on deaf ears as Dalwyn drifted deeply into sleep.

Chapter 50

Gianna Satori wanted to run but instead forced herself to walk. There was no need to bring attention to herself more than was necessary. Quickly she changed into her normal clothes, ignoring the questioning glances from her aides. Then she simply left by the secret side entrance. The clan would be pleased, it had worked.

Gianna had known Dalwyn from the moment she set eyes upon the old man's face. They were not kind eyes like that of a friendly grandfather but those of a rat, beady and dangerous. Here was a major player in the search for magic and a dedicated follow of Escindre, may his name be forever cursed she muttered making the sign of protection. The clan had told her Dalwyn was here in Culchar and since then Kenzu operatives had watched Dalwyn closely. They followed him to the inn of his friend Virgil, To the Urvile manor and learned of his plan to visit her pleasure house. It had been her knowledge of healing, the astral realm and alchemy that made her an easy candidate to be selected for initiation into the Kenzu. While treating Dalwyn, Gianna had lied to him about her intent with the astral realm. From the astral she could see the swirling red around the third eye area that was commonly linked to madness while the energy center over the heart wasn't spinning but appeared mired in grey sludge that closed his heart off to affection. The crown energy center which was named due to its location at the top of the head had been black with an intense orange flash through it that had told her he was totally fixated on one thing which he would not be able to let go of until his death or until that ambition had been realized. It was into this swirl of madness she had peeked, knowing all too well the dangers of entering a patient's energy centers from the astral, but this had been important so she had done what was needed.

In Dalwyn's energy centers one scene played over and over as if he often turned to it for some kind of clarification. What had only been moments as she looked into the crown center seemed to drag out as she watched this seemingly old harmless man strip naked then cut the skin off a poor girl named Brianna Dusk. The girl had died and luminous balls of energy had flowed from her corpse to hang lazily in the air before floating off. As Gianna watched them float away she noticed that the trampled grass over which it moved seemed to repair itself back to a standing position, a small bird lying dead shivered then it twitched as its eyes flicked open. Magic! She had seen magic in all its raw glory. One of the coterie was dead, and Gianna needed to leave before the trouble started.

Dalwyn felt totally relaxed, as if he was suspended in the air; his spine felt tender but the nagging pain in his muscles and hip bones was gone for the moment allowing him to rest deeply. It had been many days since he could say he had slept well. Therefore when he sensed rather than saw someone in the room with him he assumed it was one of the physicians or their aides checking in on him.

Then his head was wrenched upwards by the hair as something sharp was held along his throat. Dalwyn tried to cry out, but his assailant had pulled his head right back, arching his body from where he crouched behind him.

'I have a message for you from the Kenzu; stop the hunt for the coterie of the heart!' The stink of his attacker was strong in Dalwyn's nostrils. There was a noise at the door then his head was slammed down into the bench dazing Dalwyn momentarily before the dagger hilt smacked into the back of his head. Dalwyn managed to raise his head hoping to see his attacker before he passed out.

He saw what could only be one of the aides in green squaring off against Snake. They both held knives and circled each other grunting, parrying with the spare hand seeking for some grip of their opponent to twist them into the path of the blade. A few moments was all it took before Snake collapsed to his knees, his belly torn wide open. A stunned, almost comical, look was frozen upon his face. The attacker grabbed Snake's hair then slashed across his throat splashing the wall behind with gore. He turned to Dalwyn and approached knife before him.

The sounds of heavy boots running towards Dalwyn were mixed with alarmed cries from the aides.

'Stop, you can't bring weapons in here.'

As the assassin lunged towards him Dalwyn simply rolled to the side off the table and onto the stone floor, jarring his body as it hit. His men burst into the room and the attacker was cut down immediately before Dalwyn could tell them to keep him alive.

Dalwyn knew he had been stupid to come here, and he had failed to take his enemies seriously, which had nearly led to him losing his head. Today's visit by the assassin had proven that his enemies could get to him if they wished. This called for different measures if he was going to survive.

'Stay here with me,' he told the guards as he tried to hide his shaking hands.

He rose, found his clothes, which he had trouble putting on now that his neck had been wrenched around. The pain was back, worse than before, but Dalwyn wanted to leave this place. His men surrounded him as they left the pleasure house amongst outrageous looks from the idiots who worked there.

'Sir, I am aware of this terrible attack but I must insist your men sheathe their weapons immediately.'

'If he speaks again, kill him!'

They moved out of their way, and they swept out into the street.

The whole way back to the inn Dalwyn cursed himself for being so stupid. Twice in the space of a day his security had been blown right open. Escindre didn't reward foolishness. Back at the inn Dalwyn chose a quiet giant of a man that the other soldiers called Knuckles to be his new second. Not as smart as Snake had been, but he knew how to follow orders and fight. Dalwyn spoke to Knuckles privately then handed him a penned message with his seal along with a note of credit for a phenomenal fee that could be cashed in only through a certain money lender within Culchar. The one thing that his enemies wouldn't be counting on was a quick retaliation.

They thought they were safe just as he had thought he was, but he would show them he was one man not to trifle with.

Dalwyn spent the entire day in his chambers abasing himself to Escindre and the blood moon Tamul. He meditated on his next act, but his mind was in a state of turmoil. Had it been merely coincidence that he was attacked following Gianna's treatment? It seemed strange that she had disappeared so suddenly. Dalwyn refused the meal his guards brought him, choosing to read from an ancient leather-bound book titled The Astral, a Trap for the Unwary.

His astral skills were sorely neglected and he had long ago lost interest in that strange world but realized that there was no better way to find the Coterie of the Heart that by the astral.

They left Culchar with the grey of dawn but Dalwyn was sure the eyes of the Five and the Kenzu clan watched along with the ordinary folk of Culchar. The mist blanketed their departure, and Dalwyn smiled at the surprise his enemies would receive in a day's time. In two days, they would be in sight of Acclaro. He longed for the mountain abscess that had become home to him but knew his ancestors wouldn't give up, and neither would he. Dalwyn wanted to leave a legacy to future generations that he was the one who rightfully returned the world's magic and elevate his family back to their rightful place above the masses.

First he would deal with Zacriel who, although an insipid self-important piece of crap would at least make their task within Acclaro easier to complete. They travelled at a comfortable speed as his men shared increasingly exaggerated tales of their time spent in Culchar that entertained even him.

Chapter 51

Haakon had listened closely to his old friends' concerns as he always did. He was impressed that old Faustus had also seen what he himself had noticed over the past month. There was a growing division within the ranks of the Kenzu. It would seem some of his people were sick of the direction in which he was guiding the clan. They knew about the contracts that had been entrusted to them by Latasha, who now lay comatose. They just don't really believe it, thought Haakon. Just like most of the world, they thought it was a story. Haakon knew there were those who thought the clan needed to be more aggressive and become more competitive against the other clans. To a point he agreed with them, yes, he had been distracted since Latasha's near death, now his perceived weakness would be tested by any who had their sights on usurping him.

Maintaining the fine balance required to successfully keep ahead of all his possible enemies was tiresome, and for the first time since learning his trade Haakon found himself wondering whether his time was up. He hadn't really thought about his own death at the hands of a successor, but he knew that he wasn't prepared to die just yet.

The time had come to gather his own information. Haakon and Faustus had known that a spy was watching them that night he had walked with Alexis, who hopefully had told his co-conspirators that Haakon was gone from the clan house, so now the advantage lay with Haakon.

Both moons were obscured by thick clouds. Haakon emerged from his hiding place from the infirmary where Faustus had hidden him. The iridescent fish created moving shadows through the room, bathing Latasha's still form in colored light. Since she had been here, Latasha hadn't moved or uttered a single sound. Of course, Haakon talked to her daily. He had taken over the duties of cleaning her, turning her to prevent bed sores, and trying to exercise her muscles through small movements to help stop muscle wastage, even though Faustus had told him it was pointless.

Haakon donned his night gear. It had been cycles since he had needed it, yet the clothes were immaculately cared for as were the weapons. Haakon offered a quick prayer to The Death Jester, then he placed on a slim belt that held various weapons and pouches. Finally Haakon tied his sword across his back; it had been given to him by the oldest member to ever serve the clan many years ago. The sword had no name because it was said that the blade owned the user, not the other way round. Haakon had refused to name it in respect for the long line of wielders that had come before him since the clan had been founded.

With a last look at Latasha, Haakon opened the small trap door in the floor that was used to empty the chamber pot. The door was too small for most people to climb through, but Haakon wasn't concerned by this. He lowered his legs through, straightened one arm above his head, then lowered himself down slowly to just below his broad shoulder with one arm tucked alongside his body. Ever since he had been a young boy Haakon had grossed out his family and friends by dislocating his joints, especially his shoulders. The ability to do it had come in useful many times. Now he breathed slowly, then with a sudden jerk his left shoulder slipped out and down allowing him to slide the shoulder down beneath the lip of the floor. From there it was easy to just slide down into a squatting position beneath the infirmary. Grasping his left arm Haakon slammed the joint back in place with a well-placed shove that took his breath away before bringing relief. His shoulders were becoming weak from the wear and tear from previous dislocations, and he knew it would ache for days.

Haakon stayed motionless as his eyes adjusted to the gloom. The night was alive with calipo frogs along with the tell-tale tikot noise the forest lizards made. Slowly Haakon eased onto his stomach. He could see the two guard's boots at the front of the infirmary as well as smell the cheap tobacco they smoked. He knew his guards would also be vigilant around the clan base. They might be involved in the plotting to kill him, but while he still ruled here his men would fear the repercussions he would deliver them if their security was found wanting. And this night, it would be. Haakon pulled himself to the embankment where he paused again. In his mind, he ran over the message Faustus had passed to him earlier that day that had alerted him that Alexis had been meeting with a select group of the clan who wanted Haakon removed. They had been meeting secretly in one of the outer observation posts that looked out towards Culchar. Haakon counted back from ten slowly as a patrol of three came down the walkway to his left scouring the area with hooded lanterns. The arcs of light passed over him once, then the guard stopped.

'Joss, you scaly skinned jowl wobbling ass, are you going to stand there all night?'

'Come here, I got that whisky I owe you.'

The light flashed away from Haakon again.

'Bout time, you ol' donkey, I thought you would still be rutting with the crazies at junk town.' Loud laughter followed, and Haakon used the distraction to roll to his feet, sprint down the path, then slide out of view again amongst the trees. It took Haakon the better part of a chime to reach the outpost. He had to admit that his men were good with their patrols and came close to discovering him several times.

The outpost was a small timber cabin built alongside a tower that supplied not only shelter for the sentries but the only entrance to the tower's highest observation point. From where Haakon lay he could make out four figures from the shadows they cast in the oily light within the cabin. Haakon guessed there was one more on guard up the tower, but he had yet to see anyone from his vantage point. Haakon stayed silent and unmoving acknowledging the inkling of intuition that snaked through his mind as moments later two figures moved out of the bushes onto the pathway. One of them hocked up phlegm then spat.

'What the heck, Rasp, you asshole!'

'Let's go in, fuck waiting any longer. They are all here by my count, and there's a brew with my name on it.'

Haakon watched as Rasp knocked then muttered some password as they were challenged from inside. Momentarily the smell of roasting fowl wafted out before the door shut behind them, leaving Haakon alone again. Haakon kept still for the moment. As he lay there he continued to think on a course of action other than slaughtering the usurpers, but he couldn't come to any other conclusion. To show weakness now would be inviting a swift death from these enemies who had now shown their hand against him.

Faustus had begged Haakon to take a small crew of men with him, but that had never been Haakon's style. He had been good to these men who now plotted his downfall, he had brought them in, given them a home, and raised them as his family within the clan, some from childhood. The last thing he owed them was death at his hands. The day he wasn't prepared to do his own dirty work was the day he would no longer see himself as clan lord.

Deciding enough time had passed, he moved swiftly to the side of the cabin where it connected to the outpost tower. By the sounds coming from inside he could tell they were sharing a meal, the perfect time for him to move. He only had to pray that the sentry in the tower would be eating with them.

Haakon strapped on metal climbing claws from his belt then he started climbing slowly up the tower to the room at the top; he moved slower than he needed to, hesitating every few feet to listen for sounds of discovery. When Haakon reached the top he pulled himself over into the empty covered area. A trapdoor in the floor led down into the cabin. So much for security. Haakon tested the trapdoor, pulling it up enough to determine it wasn't locked from within. He waited above the unknowing conspirators as they made boisterous toasts towards returning the clan to the status of the most feared assassins in the known world.

The young voice of Alexis drifted up between the boards of his hiding place.

'In the past, we have spoken of the disillusionment we feel regarding the direction the clan is heading. You all know as well as I do that Haakon has led us well since murdering his predecessor Christof. His leadership has been unforgiving but unwavering in doing the best for the clan above his own needs and desires. However, the Kenzu were once feared and could strike fear into a man's very soul at their mention. Now we have become weak, unknown and leaderless.'

Murmurs of agreement followed this, and Haakon smiled grimly, patting a pouch that hung around his neck to be sure his trump card was still where he had put it.

Someone else was talking softly even elegantly with perfect diction, and so Haakon knew that the elderly Grant was among his enemies.

'Alexis, while I congratulate you on your commitment towards the Kenzu, we are aware of the reason for our clan's divergence from its past. It wasn't just any clan that was chosen to protect the coterie, it was the Kenzu! Have you forgotten the heritage of our famed brotherhood that you are so willing to dismiss possibly the most important contracts of our lives, maybe even our clan's existence?'

'A contract that is based in myth more so than reality,' said a clear voice that Haakon didn't recognize. It cut through the rest of the chatter below. 'All this talk of magic and yet in neither mine nor my father's and his father's lifetimes has magic existed besides supposedly within these five coterie members. And we are to protect them until such a time as they deem it suitable to return magic to our world. Does it really exist, or are we wasting time chasing shadows? I think the magic has died, that these five are no longer or maybe never even been in contact with this mysterious magic at all.'

'Shut ya trap, Jarl, you also have heard the stories supposedly of magic being witnessed once again in Culchar.'

'Aye, I admit to that, but let's be practical; they are only rumours.'

Then Alexis was talking again. 'Mark my words, the magic was and I believe still is real and the coterie are still entwined with its power. I am not here to argue the existence of magic but to merely suggest that under Haakon's rule we have become solely focused on that. If indeed magic will be returning then at least some of our resources need to be spent securing our future for such a time of upheaval as the powers and nations and rival clans fight to come out on top.'

'You may say that, Alexis, but until the day comes that I witness this magic with my own eyes, then I will continue to doubt its existence,' Jarl said. We must set up the clan for the future, but without us taking out other contracts. Our resources are wasted and slowly deteriorating. There is fighting amongst our men who crave the excitement to test their skills once again, and who knows, maybe we can use those very skills to manipulate the clan into a favourable position.'

'Have you all forgotten the heritage of our famed brotherhood that you are willing to dismiss the most important contracts of our clan's existence?' Grant spoke up, maybe he wasn't an enemy after all.

'Well as we all agree the clan's resources are being wasted, there is just the small matter of what we do about Haakon and his inhuman bitch.'

'Haakon has served the clan well,' called out Grant.

'Not only did he save the clan from destruction, but he also relocated us here.'

'Yeah but straight to the middle of a flaming forest along with the mossies and frogs to live in a fallen castle, which is just the location for a powerful clan.' There came the sound of spitting at that.

'Enough, Jarl. You think anyone would be happy to open their town or city to a clan like ours?' There came the sound of something breaking then Jarl spoke up: It's been Latasha who has blinded Haakon to the clan's wellbeing; since he took over as leader he has followed her around sniffing like a dog on heat.'

Haakon had heard enough. He removed the vial of purple liquid from his pouch. He could see through the cracks in the wooden trapdoor that the table had been conveniently placed below where he lay. The outer watchtowers like this one were decaying since the timbers used were untreated against damp. Slowly he raised the trapdoor. Sloppy work indeed, Alexis. Not only were they traitors but lazy, which would someday get them killed, maybe today. At any moment Haakon thought he would be discovered as he eased the trapdoor open, but below him his men were already heavily into their cups except Alexis, who didn't drink. As they slammed down their cups, he jumped landing squarely on the table and knocking its contents and the men seated there men back off their chairs and onto the floor.

$$\text{Chapter 52}$$

His men tried to scramble to their, feet but Haakon held up the small vial for everyone to see. Made from the thinnest silken glass, it would shatter if dropped, releasing the deadly purple liquid and its hellish fumes.

'Good evening, it seems you were planning to have all the fun without me,' said Haakon, his voice a veritable growl. 'In this vial are the fumes of the pyre bird whose noxious breath melts away the flesh from the bones of any caught within it. Let's be civil and throw all your weapons on the remains of the table there to avoid any accidents.'

The five men once considered amongst his closest men began carefully placing, their swords, daggers and other weapons onto the smashed table in front of them making quite a pile. They all looked worried except Alexis who had the gall to look amused.

'It seems we have some issues to discuss. Personally it would have been much easier to have this discussion under better circumstances, but certain parties, being you five, elected to leave your clan master out of it.'

Alexis started to speak, but Haakon cut him off brusquely.

'I don't doubt that the future use of our resources needs to be discussed; however, it is not for the likes of you cowards to decide when that should be. Since none of you are currently directly involved with the coterie, you wouldn't be aware of the situation at present, so let me inform you directly. One is dead already, and so is her sentinel, who also is one of our own. Of the other four, two are accounted for while two have yet to be heard from. Due to extensive injuries to my energy body, I am unable to access the astral and so communication between us is a problem, which I had hoped to correct with your help. Since the Kenzu took on this contract, all we have been called on to do is protect them from harm, which has been pretty much non-existent until now.

'Latasha was my last hope of finding out whether the identities of the coterie were known to our enemies, and with Brianna's death it would seem so. Nearly three hundred years of inaction, now comes to this when we must act to fulfil our commitment to our contracts and do as we are sworn to do. Instead, I must take valuable time away from organizing our plans to deal with the five of you, who seek to do myself and the lady Meldoriel harm.'

'Haakon may I stand to address you?'

'No, you may not, Alexis. I prefer the five of you at my feet like hounds except I would expect more loyalty from such.'

'Haakon, I have approached you recently regarding the feelings of many of our clan, myself included, but you blew me off like some wastrel. I am the trusted collector of records, chosen to do so by your very hand. If you don't heed your closest advisors, master, then how am I to continue treating you with respect?'

Old Grant spoke then, ale and food still clinging to his long beard.

'Haakon, you have been unreachable since Latasha was injured. At a time when you said that the clan has bigger concerns, you have lost yourself in feelings for that…ahhh…woman, who seems to have addled your brain somewhat. Let the whole clan be a part of what comes next and later we can decide these other issues. Your men are well trained-killers with a myriad of skills too good to keep wasting like this. Many criticized you for murdering Christof but I stood by your side and still do. This here is no rebellion, just concerned leaders.'

'Don't give me that crap, Grant, rebellion is certainly what this is, and I can forgive you all but one.' Haakon turned to Alexis, who sat mouth open looking suddenly like the youngster he was.

'Alexis, you were chosen as you say by my hand to collect and keep the records of our clan. This is a respectable position, and yet here you sit with co-conspirators plotting my downfall and ways to deal with Latasha Meldoriel, whose importance you should know of by now. As your master I invoke my right to duel you since you wish to challenge my leadership. The choice of weapon is yours.'

Alexis went very pale as he sat looking up at the formidable form of Haakon, leader of the Kenzu.

'Haakon, there is no need for this, he is just a boy!'

'Yes, that's true, Grant, he is a boy, one that has been foolish enough to try and rise above his station. We are the Kenzu, and this is how challenges have been dealt with for thousands of years, so he will get up like the man he pretends to be and fight me for the leadership of the Kenzu.'

Alexis stayed on the floor, looking up uncertainly.

'Come, Alexis, lets duel, you were earlier saying how we need to become the most ruthless clan of assassins once again so here is your chance. Kill me and run the clan as you like, or die like a man and show you have some backbone.'

That sparked something in Alexis, who climbed to his feet, hands clenched in fury.

'I choose knives.'

'So be it then,' Haakon replied. He removed his shirt, revealing his well-muscled torso.

The three other men moved back, clearing a space around Alexis and Haakon.

Alexis removed his own shirt, his pale skin a direct contrast to Haakon's tan. Haakon withdrew two knives from his boots, tossing one next to Alexis's feet.

'When you're ready boy.'

He barely got the words out before Alexis nimbly leapt in towards him, knife extended. Haakon also lunged, batting the attack from Alexis away with his forearm. The knife took Alexis in the right eye with such force it threw his head back before he collapsed to the floor. The cabin was silent as Haakon walked to Alexis, turning him over with his boot, and removed his knife before wiping the blood off on Alexis's trousers. He then closed the dead boy's eyes.

'I knew him from birth,' he began as Grant, Jarl, Rasp, and Torc looked on.

'His mother was dying when we took her and her baby in. They had been attacked by soldiers who killed his father and would have done worse to his mother had our men not happened along when they did. He was a good boy, always curious and quick to learn, but he always wanted more, never satisfied with what he was given. That was what killed him this day. I was merely the instrument, and you all know I had no choice in the matter, the stupid bastard forced my hand.'

Haakon wiped the back of a hand across his eyes where tears fell unashamedly down his cheeks. He turned to the remaining three men. 'Are you satisfied now that a life has been lost?'

No one answered him or met his gaze, for they knew to do so would be foolish.

'What is to become of us Haakon?' asked Grant as he used the wall to help steady himself. Next to him Torc and Rasp had begun edging towards the door, their eyes locked on Haakon's.

'Nothing, my old friend; enough blood has been spilt this night. What say you that we bury Alexis then return to the clan house?' The look of relief on the men's faces was comical.

Jarl sighed audibly. 'I truly thought you meant to kill us all, Haakon,' He bent to retrieve his sword from the debris. He didn't see Haakon move until it was too late. Haakon's sword sliced down.

Torc grabbed the door to wrench it open, but it was locked, so he turned diving for a weapon as Rasp snatched up a dagger. Haakon stepped in, perfectly timing his kick to catch the big man squarely in the face. Torc toppled with a thump, then Haakon bought the pommel of his sword down on the back of Rasp's head.

Grant was at the door now, fumbling with a key on a chain around his neck and trying desperately to fit it in the lock as he wept.

'Grant?'

Grant ignored the approaching Haakon as he managed to get the key to slide into place, but then it fell from his nervous fingers to the floor and when he looked up Haakon was standing beside him.

'Grant, you should have known better. You knew this would happen.'

Through gut-wrenching sobs Grant tried to speak but could only manage one word.

'Sorry.'

Haakon slammed the knife into the old man's chest. His eyes never left Grant's until the light had extinguished, then he let his body fall to the floor. He picked up the key and opened the door. The three dying men behind him filled the cabin with their gasps and flowing blood. Stepping over the choking Grant, he grabbed a flask of swamp juice, which was the nearly undrinkable spirits his men made from potatoes. This he poured over the dying men and the debris around them, then he unclasped the hooded lantern that illuminated the carnage and at the door once again Haakon smashed the lantern on the floor. Hungry flames spread across the room. Haakon closed and locked the cabin then moved away to sit back against the trunk of a tree. He drank from the remaining swamp juice and settled down to watch the cabin burn.

Chapter 53

That night Dalwyn sat at the top of a hill looking back in the direction of Culchar. When Tamul was at its rightful place he cut his left forearm then clenched his fist to pump the blood faster from the wound.

'Escindre, in your absence we still deign to do your work. In any way or form we ask your blessing for the strike we now level upon your foes. Witness the bloodshed in your name knowing your followers send you this sacrifice.'

With the prayer done he stood motionless looking back at the city almost completely lost in the distance. For a long while there was nothing to be seen, but then a faint glow could be discerned lighting up the night. A broad grin spread over his face at the sight. It felt good to strike back at his foes and he burst into laughter that wouldn't stop; it kept pouring out until in pain and clutching his back he fell to the ground wiping the tears from his eyes.

The lumbering form of Knuckles emerged from the darkness to tower over him.

'Evry thin alrite sir?'

'Yes, Knuckles,' I was just enjoying the show that's all.'

'Fire?'

'Yes, Knuckles, Culchar is burning, which is a good thing indeed. C'mon let's celebrate, my friend. Tomorrow we head for Acclaro.'

Acclaro towered majestically over the surrounding towns. It was the only remaining symbol of the ancient kingdom of Thantos to survive the Severing. They had called Acclaro the Crown of the World during times when all the countries had recognized this king's rule over their lands. The king Jordan Touville had been a most humble charismatic leader famed for his ability to defuse tense situations that otherwise would have ended in bloodshed.

Those times are gone now, thought Dalwyn as his party rode slowly down the winding road towards the city of Acclaro. The new king, Chez Touville, the most recent of the royal lineage to continue in the rebuilding of the great city. Now new outer city walls that stood hundreds of feet high had been made from white stone. Their tops formed peaks that again rose higher, still ending with towers joined by sky bridges that could only be accessed within the interior of the great wall or castle. From outside the city it looked like one gigantic white crown with glittering spires.

'It truly is a magnificent piece of work, master.'

Dalwyn turned to look at the young soldier beside him.

'Indeed, it is, Loren but even for all its magnificence it can never recreate what the city used to be at its peak before the Severing.'

'Can't that be said for all countries, cities, towns across the lands?'

'To a degree, yes, but besides wealth, which obviously the royal family still has plenty of, they have no allies. The Touville family was so desperate for help to rid the city of the infernals' nest unearthed during its cleansing that Arman, the current king of that time tore up all his vassal's oaths of fealty in return for their aid to wipe this threat from its deep roots within the capital. Something is still wrong with the city; everyone feels it once they enter its gates. I would bet a thousand cetas that if not for the Severing a great gate to the Infernal lands would open like the maw of some great beast where this city is. Something is wrong with Acclaro.'

'Wrong, you say, Dalwyn yet here we are the ones consorting with Infernals...'

Dalwyn cut Loren, off tiring of the man's shallow thoughts.

'It's deeper than that, Loren. It's darker than anything demonic we deal with. Something holds this city under its sway as its tendrils snake through the population, bending the people under its despair as if sucking the life from them. You shall experience its pull for yourself very soon.'

Eventually Dalwyn's party made it through the congested roads of the surrounding town and came to the main gate of Acclaro which bustled with activity. The wide gates were swollen with the large number of wagons and people. Dalwyn noticed most of the traffic was leaving the city. Strange.

Unlike Culchar, entry to Acclaro was easy now that they had an invitation from the Soldano family upon request by Tia Urvile. The crowd moved fast, which meant that they were on their way to hot meal and a meeting with Zacriel in no time. The roads were wider than Dalwyn remembered. He wondered whether they still salted the site where the old castle had stood when the Infernals had been cleansed from the city. The new castle had been built in front of the old site, but he had heard that King Chez had extended it to include the old area.

Dalwyn turned in his saddle and urged Loren closer.

'How are you feeling now, Loren? Can you sense it?'

'I feel tired like everything takes a little more effort, as though there is no point to what we are doing.'

'That's what I mean, boy. The city takes its toll, dulls the senses, life here seem sluggish, difficult, and pointless. But why?'

They continued the slow wind through the busy streets where people quietly went about their business. Gone was the ordinary laughter, haggling din of a busy city that was replaced by an almost eerie silence that muted everyday sounds into a hollow, empty beat. When the party arrived at the Soldano manor, they were ushered inside for warm baths as pages took their horses to be stabled.

❧❧❧

Chapter 54

Following his glorious bath Dalwyn dressed to impress their hosts. Knuckles had polished Dalwyn's white leather boots to a shine that matched perfectly with the white cloak upon his shoulders. The severely cut black suit he wore beneath the cloak finished off a smart look that would emphasize his confident natural authority. As Dalwyn stood admiring himself in the mirror, there came a loud rapping on the door.

'Enter.'

'Master we be invited to have food with Lord Soldano who waits for you.'

With a few final adjustments, Dalwyn turned to Knuckles.

'Come along, Knuckles, it would be rude to keep the lord of the house waiting.'

The dining room was sickly in its opulence. The golden hardwood table was ornately carved with an encompassing picture of Arrowhead Lake and Acclaro, in the background. Matching chairs whose backs were inlaid with silver completed the furniture. The red walls and elaborate torch sconces added a touch of gaudiness that made Dalwyn feel uncomfortable. The curtains were drawn, leaving the chamber stuffy and overbearing. Lord Claude Soldano sat at the tables end slouched back in a puffy, purple outfit. His balding pate had been combed over to hide its demise. His sunken face had deep, dark bags beneath eyes that listlessly examined a plate of grapes as he sucked the juice from one before spitting the seeds into a bowl. At his side, his wife Christine sat stiffly sipping from a tall glass of

283

golden ale;- her heavily made up face and long chestnut hair gave her a doll-like look along with her voluminous turquoise gown, from which her massive bosom was attempting to burst.

'Good day to you Lord and Lady Soldano, I would like firstly to thank you for accepting us here within your estate; your kindness is truly appreciated.'

Claude Soldano chuckled then spat a half-eaten grape onto the table.

'Firstly…ahhh…'

'Dalwyn, Lord Soldano, please call me Dalwyn.'

'Firstly, Dalwyn, we are not happy at this imposition upon our hospitality. If not for the fact that we owed our close friend the Lady of Urvile a favor, then you would never have set foot within our estate. Your presence here confuses me since we personally are not acquainted with you or ever heard of you. So if you would be so kind to enlighten us to what possible reason you would have need of our kindness when such good accommodation could be purchased by a man of such means as you appear to pretend to be?'

'All in good time, Lord Soldano. May I sit?'

'No, you may not. Here in Acclaro a lesser man may not make requests of those superior to him, especially within his own home.'

Moving quicker than someone his size should be able to, Knuckles lurched forward towards the Soldano lord, growling loudly and causing Christine to spill the contents of her drink down her cleavage. There was a ring of swords leaving scabbards as the Soldano soldiers pushed in front of their lord and lady to protect them. The main door to the room behind Dalwyn also burst open, revealing six more armed soldiers with hands on sword hilts.

'Knuckles, stop! The lord of the house is right. I have obviously hit a nerve by being here so everyone just put your blades away so I can explain what possible benefit to the Soldano family that our appearance here can bring.'

'Dalwyn, if your brute of a bodyguard steps towards me in anger again, both your lives are forfeit. My patience is waning.'

'Lord Soldano, to put it simply, we have a common problem that can be resolved if we work together, but since I am a generous man you will also receive a considerable reward.'

Before Dalwyn could continue there came the sound of yelling within the manor followed by a shrill scream. The commotion continued to come closer, and the guards at the door turned to the new threat. Claude pushed through the dining room behind the soldiers at the door.

'By the gods, what the damn is happening here?' he thundered.

As they watched, a tall figure emerged from a side staircase then strode down the hallway towards the room, a gray cloak covering the figure's head and trailing out behind it. The figure had one hand chained to a young girl who stumbled behind him as she was practically dragged along by her captor.

Two servants stepped in front of the tall figure only to be roughly shoved aside.

'Step aside, scum don't you know how to treat your guests?'

A guard stepped forward slashing with his sword only to meet with the chain, which cracked against his temple and smashed him into a motionless heap against the wall.

The unusual pair stopped before the swords pointed at them by the other guards.

Claude Soldano was almost bursting with anger now, his face beet red.

'Guards, kill this intruder.'

'Wait!' Dalwyn's voice easily carried over the commotion, ringing with authority that stilled the moment.

'My lord once again I must apologize. This man is one of my party and if you peruse the invitation you will find his name there also. He is known as Zacriel.'

The sound of boots thundered through the house as more guards crowded the hall behind the intruders.

'Guards, seize them all.'

Dalwyn was grabbed roughly by the shoulders then forced to the ground while Knuckles was buried beneath five soldiers who struggled to hold him down until one slammed his sword hilt three times into the brute's head and he ceased struggling.

In the hall, the girl looked around blankly as if waking up. Her skin was dirty and her once fine yellow dress soiled. Beside her the figure threw off its hooded cloak, revealing burnt arms and a face covered in scar tissue that made the left eye bulge and twisted the mouth into a sneer beneath the barely recognizable remains of its nose. At its back cartilage protruded from between shoulder blades.

'Come no closer or I will take you with me to the Infernal lands.'

There was a shocked pause, then Claude turned to Dalwyn.

'You dare bring an Infernal into my home, into a city where they are killed on sight?'

Claude drew a stiletto knife and held it against Dalwyn's neck.

'Do you know nothing of this city's history imbecile?'

Dalwyn could barely speak beneath the knife blade that already drew a crimson trickle from his neck, but he managed to choke out some words none-the-less.

'Harm me further and not only will you never receive the inheritance your wife is due but the king will be told of your crimes against the crown.'

Dalwyn locked gazes with Claude, whose face was steadily turning darker with fury.

'I'm serious, Soldano, unless you release all of us now your manor will be swarming with the King's men. I'm sure he will be happy to know one of his closest advisors has been defrauding him for a rather large sum.' Dalwyn knew he had them then once the words registered on Claude's face. If his spies could be trusted, then the king already knew about the crime that the Soldano family had been committing but for their own reasons the royal family hadn't moved against them. The Soldano fools didn't need to know this, though.

'Don't kill him yet, Claude. I wish to ask him something.'

Christina Soldano moved over to Dalwyn, looking up into his face as she still dabbed away at her breasts where the drink had spilt.

'You mentioned an inheritance, Dalwyn, what do you speak of?'

'Ah, I have your attention now, don't I? I will say no more of the matter until your husband removes the blade from my throat as well as releasing my companions. Then we can do business like respectable civilized folk.'

Chapter 55

Ishmael sneezed again. The dust from the wagons was causing havoc with him. Trust them to get stuck with the last wagon. Four of the five wagons were fully laden with eggs. They were wrapped to keep tomorrows sunlight from the supposedly frail things. But why eggs?

'Manu, you said that the Jewelled one may be the last alive, their queen maybe?'

'It's quite possible that we will be the last humans to ever see a Jewelled one,' Manu answered. 'With its release it will be wary of being caught again and will no doubt return to its allies, the Harlequin. Without it as a prisoner the Jingtalla tribe and the citizens of Illume are in even more danger now. The Jewelled one has had centuries to dream about vengeance. These eggs are hers and we take them to Acclaro to be sold for obscene profits.'

'So why do they fetch such high prices?'

'Delicacies, Ishmael, for the rich to dine on in order to display their opulent lifestyles. I hear they are very tasteful, but I'm afraid it's not high on my list of foods to try.'

'What about babies?'

'Oh they die before hatching time, scoffed by snotty noble men. I'm sure they don't feel a thing.'

'That's terrible, Manu. So you are saying that for hundreds of years since she was caught her eggs have been stolen and sold. No wonder she is angry.'

'Yes it's not hard to see why but think of the other side Ishmael. What would happen to the eggs otherwise? Should they be allowed to hatch?'

'No, but surely even with such alien creatures there could be compromise.'

'That was compromise, Ishmael. The Jewelled ones and even the Harlequin will never compromise by choice. The Jewelled lands are their home and we are the invaders.'

Ishmael lay back to ponder this, and as the rumbling carts moved ever so slowly towards Acclaro he sought solace in sleep away, from the growing sense of foreboding around seeing his family again.

'Wish I could just fall asleep like that,' said Zahra.

'Yeah me too, that's why the brandy helps… helps me forget my past.'

'So what now, Manu? Don't tell me you are going to just melt away into the life of a tavern bum when we get to the capital.'

'For the first time in my life, Zahra, I am free from any obligation with nowhere to go or be, and I am enjoying it. I am content to see what happens in Acclaro and then decide on whether my path continues with yours. I dream more and more of my home lately, but that is not somewhere I can ever return.'

They stayed quiet for a while, and Manu let the slow rolling movement of the cart carry him into sleep.

Zahra knew she was close to the Kenzu clan house. If she was to leave now she could be there in less than a day and a half. The grove that surrounded the clan house was a place of superstition due to fabricated stories spread by the Kenzu. Of course, Haakon had personally dealt with King Chez to be allowed to clean out the current bandits who claimed the grove as theirs. Chez was happy just to have one less problem to fix and had readily agreed to Haakon's terms of acting as an outpost for any direct threat to the Thantos Empire especially from the king of Scuttle. The secrecy that the grove provided enabled them to help create the fear surrounding the clan house, and any foolish enough to go there never returned.

Zahra jumped from the cart and ran forward to clamber up beside Good man Bonwick who eyed her suspiciously.

'What, you not sleeping, lass?'

'Never could sleep while travelling. Do you live in the capital?'

'Ha, you got to be joking! The capital, if you could call it that is like a fading flower that shrivels and soon will die.'

'Why such a bleak view of Acclaro?'

'The king doesn't care for his people and is out of his depth, relying more and more on his advisors. His father used to walk the streets of the city just to talk with his people and get a feel for their lives, but not Chez. Let's face it, the time of Thantos is finished, we have lost our vassals and alienated allies who now sit along with our considerable enemies, content to watch us crumble.'

'You a cart driver, knows all this?' Zahra asked sceptically.

'Don't judge me on my current occupation, girl, it shows nothing of my previous life. To answer your question, I was on the trader council of Acclaro but the rich control the trade now and my family who isn't privy to their inner circle was frozen out. When my wife's brother became ill and could no longer drive the routes I opted for a change, and here I am enjoying the freedom away from politics.'

'Is it true what they say about the capital now?'

'What, that it's still a cess-pit of corruption collapsing in on its self?'

Zahra smiled at that. 'No, that Infernals fly from the castle, there is a curfew in effect and that the king is dead?'

'Bah, mere stories except for the curfew in effect.'

'So you've seen the king then? Attended great parties for visiting leaders or officials in the true Acclaro spirit?'

He was silent for a time. 'It's true that visitors to the king are few, but what can you expect when you are forced to release your vassals and have advisors who care for nothing but lining their own pockets?'

Zahra persisted. 'And the king?'

'He rarely emerges from the castle and was ever the sickly child, but still it would be wrong to assume he is dead.'

'The Jingtalla shaman showed us the Infernals flying about the castle earlier tonight.'

'You sure they're not just birds? It's not as if you can see clearly from a day's travel away is it.'

Zahra could sense Good man Bonwick had had enough of the conversation, so she left him in peace.

Ishmael only half followed their ambling journey through the villages that lined the Winding River. They melded together into one long town that followed the river to Arrowhead Lake, on whose banks Acclaro was built. The area was known as the Drake due to the tail-like shape of the river running into Arrowhead Lake. The lake's beauty was once the crowning glory of the capital. Ishmael climbed up beside Good man Bonwick on the first cart.

'Finally awake then, Master Ishmael?'

'I thought we would be at the city gate by now.'

'Normally yes, but with the bulwar beetles nothing happens quickly, which is why many people dislike them'

'If that is so then why do you use them?'

'You see lad, the bulwar need very little food or water and can travel days without resting if pushed. And they will make a good account of themselves if attacked.'

'Can you tell me if the hall of records still stands?'

'It does indeed, although it has started to fall into disrepair like most of the city. The validity of information from the hall is now questionable. Before the Severing, acolytes of Aeon the goddess of time were tasked with tracking family names; however, since the Severing they lost their god like all the religions. Who are you looking for?'

'My mother. I was parted from my family when I was a child and hope to meet with my mother and sisters if they are still alive and living in the city.'

'Master Ishmael, may I suggest you try the savant's tower? It is where most go if they need to track people or families down.'

Ishmael placed his hand on Good man Bonwick's shoulder. 'You mean the idiot boy, don't you? We used to call him Mumbles.'

'Yes, that is the boy. He now lives with relatives but has used his own money to build a tower which he fills with information he collects on the city. If anyone can find your relatives, it is he.'

They reached the gigantic gates just before dusk when traffic was at its lowest. The guards knew Bonwick so they ushered him through then set about checking their travel papers. Within the chime they were checking into a small inn just inside the gate that was looked respectable. Eating a warm meal of stew in the common room, Ishmael told Manu and Zahra of his plan to visit the savant tower, and they agreed to come along with him.

The next morning, they made their way to the savant tower. The base of the tower was a shop-front selling information the savant collected. A wizened man sat rocking in a chair, pipe glowing in his mouth, and his eyes followed Ishmael and the others as they entered. The area behind the counter showed several bags packed as if for travelling.

'Good morning, friend, we are looking for someone,' Ishmael said.

The man's pipe clacked against his teeth. 'Yep, most who come here are. Here, write down the names you are looking for and any information as to relatives, last known address or anything that might help. We will send for you when we complete the search, but first pay a ceta for the research.'

'We were kind of hoping to see the savant this morning,' said Zahra, running her hands through her hair.

'What you hope for and what we can provide are different things, my lady. Can't you tell that we are set to leave for a while?'

'Pa, send them up to me, I can see them now.'

'Well, don't take too long, the coach will be here.'

'Looks like he will see us now,' Manu said with a grin, heading for the stairs.

'If you please, the gold first.'

The tower had three levels above the shop front. The first was a bedroom and living area and the second was a library overflowing with papers, inks, maps of which many were jammed into bags. They found Mumbles on the top floor which had a glass dome ceiling and walls allowing complete views of the city. A metal rail had been built around the edge of the chamber. Mumbles sat in a chair and used his feet to push him along as he gazed down in the city through a long eye-glass. Ishmael had heard of them but never seen one until now.

Maybe this was a waste of time, thought Ishmael as they waited for the savant to notice of them.

Mumbles stood up then turned to them, bowing low. Even though he had a slight hunch, he was a tall man. His clothes were too short for him and an armless vest showed ink work covering the length of his arms. His long blonde hair was tied back, and he was clean shaven.

He smiled at them, and any tension Ishmael felt melted away.

'Hello there, do you need my help to find somebody?'

'Yes, Mumbles, I do,' said Ishmael.

'What did you call me?'

'I called you Mumbles, which is what we called you when I was in school with you. I am sorry if I offended you.'

'It's fine I just haven't heard that name since those days, that's all. What is your name?'

'Ishmael Shantari.'

Mumbles seemed to go inside himself and turned his back to look over the city.

'Shantari let me see. Ah yes, Shantari. Was a family who used to trade between here and Illume, three children if I recall rightly. You, Christine, and the younger sister, Lucille?'

'Yes, that's my family.'

'Mother named Elaine, father named Tom, who died from a heart condition when you were still young.'

'Yes, that's right.'

Mumbles held his hands clasped before his chest and turned in quiet circles as he spoke. 'Your mother lost the family estate after Tom died. Lucille married a blacksmith then moved to Whaleson with him. As I recall, you were taken to Illume to become a brother, and by looking at you this appears to be true.'

'What about my older sister and mother?'

'So impatient, Ishmael, just wait, it sometimes takes a while for things to clear in my head.

Christine Shantari is still in the city. She married a noble whose name escapes me. Your mother, Elaine, ran a shop selling cloth until…'

'Until she was committed to the asylum,' finished the old man from down-stairs, now standing in the doorway.

'Yes, you are right father, the asylum.' Mumbles shivered.

The old man shuffled over to Ishmael. 'Your older sister, Christine, came here maybe five days ago to leave a message for her brother. I would have forgotten, but Shantari is not a common name.'

'What? My sister left a message for you to contact her if I should visit you here?'

'Yes, Ishmael. She said that she felt you were looking for her and would be coming to the capital. She paid a handsome amount to see you get her scroll.'

Mumbles ran to the second floor and returned shortly, breathless. 'Here, here it is.'

The scroll was small, sealed with a ribbon instead of wax and had Ishmael's name scribed on it. Ishmael opened it and sat on a chair to read it.

'It says here that Christine had tried to contact me in the monastery but no reply was forthcoming. Then news of the attack came and she worried for me and hoped I might come here. Says she knew I would return to my family and to send a messenger to the Soldano residence when I get this.'

'Doesn't sound like a coincidence,' said Zahra, and Ishmael had to agree. Something strange was going on, but he needed to see Christine and their mother so at least this had saved him some time. They paid another gold ceta then turned to leave.

'Ishmael, before you go, I need to tell you that it is no longer safe in the city. I don't know why I'm telling you this, but I feel you are good people. We are leaving the city and so should you. I have seen things that should never be seen in this beautiful place.'

'Like Infernals flying from the castle,' said Ishmael.

Mumbles jumped in glee. 'See, Father I'm not crazy, Ishmael has seen them too. Dire times, I'm afraid. People going missing suddenly and no help from the authorities. Curfew and murder in the streets after dark and, as you say, strange creatures flying from the castle walls. Blood, blood, blood everywhere.' Mumbles now held his hair in both hands and was tugging at it as he spoke, clumps pulling free in his hands.

'Son, stop this, stop it,' Mumble's Father said urgently. 'It's going to be fine we are leaving this place it will be fine now.' He pried his son's hands from his head and attempted to soothe the man.

'I'm afraid it's all been too much for my son. You can see he is, ahh sensitive to such bad tidings. I want you to leave now.'

There was nothing left but to leave. As the three withdrew they could hear screams from the top floor still out in the street.

Chapter 56

They sent a messenger to the Soldano residence the next morning, and Manu used his spare time to visit the moon temple of Aspre. Zahra restocked her supply of daggers and renewed her leather vest while Ishmael stayed in his room, trying to meditate and do the exercises to control the magic within him. He couldn't eat or sleep and felt wound tight with fear about his coming reunion.

It was the mid-afternoon chime before a reply was delivered to Ishmael's door.

The message simply said, 'Meet me at the Wheel in two chimes for ale and we shall talk.'

The Wheel was a quaint drinking house in the city center where the nobility drank, and the three of them stood out among the elitist crowd who seemed to find their presence either amusing or insulting. They purchased ale and waited.

Then Ishmael saw his older sister walking towards them; she was his height with her long chestnut curls drooping around a face heavily made up with pinks. She wore a long gown and a shawl to cover her chest and shoulders. She had grown into a lovely woman.

'There she is,' said Ishmael, a note of trepidation in his voice as he stood waving her over.

'Looks like your sister is doing all right for herself,' said Zahra, but Manu shushed her with a glare.

Ishmael went to hug Christine as she approached.

'Oh no, dear brother that is so yesterday to hug, but it's good to see you.'

'Sorry, it's just I haven't seen you since we were children and I thought…'

'You thought wrong, dear brother, but never mind. Here, send one of your lackeys to get us ale,' she said, throwing down three silver ketches on the table.

'They are not lackeys.'

'It's all right, Ishmael, I will go.' Manu scooped the money up and pushed his way to the bar.

'Christine, this is Zahra. Zahra this is Christine my sister I told you about.'

'Charmed, I'm sure,' said Christine, looking Zahra up and down and wrinkling her nose.

'She is my travelling companion, and so is Manu.'

'So you and Zahra here are together?'

'Like Ishmael said. We are companions for the road and nothing more, Christine,' Zahra said.

'That is well and good, then. I would be mortified if you had married a commoner,' Christine told her brother.

Zahra rose with a hand on her belt of daggers.

'Zahra, please. Not here. She is my sister.'

Manu returned with ale for them all, and they sipped quietly over small talk.

'Is it true mother is in the asylum, Chris?'

'She never recovered from the loss of father, and then Lucille and I married and left. Her decline has been steady, and I have made sure she is well looked after, but money only goes so far.'

'But father left a considerable sum of riches behind which should keep our dear mother living comfortably.'

'Before he passed he deposited the majority of the money with the money lending guild here in Acclaro, which Mama wasn't aware of until too late. Anyhow, the only other person who can sign this credit note is you. The conditions state that the oldest child whilst living, may once proven gain access to the funds. Due to Mama's condition she is unable to do this herself, and since I'm not the eldest living child it falls to you to help end Mama's suffering as much as possible so that all our lives may be simplified and you can rest well assured that she is getting the care she deserves.

Christine paused. 'I have been hesitant to ask you about this delicate matter because I was sure you would have no need or desire to help your family out after the terrible way you were treated by Mother.'

'Not just Mother, you and Lucille were a part of it as well, or have you forgotten how you helped drag me outside to leave me homeless on the streets?'

'We were children too, Ishmael, just children confused and grieving over our father's death and fed lies about you from our very own mother. You know what she's like Ishmael. I have been lucky enough to marry into some wealth, but tough times have befallen our household, which I won't go into right now, but let's just say that we no longer have the money required for the continuing care of Mother.

Mama has been in the asylum for nearly five long cycles, of which we paid to have her in level one accommodation. Now she is being forced to endure hardship in communal cells without access to the medical treatments necessary for her recovery. My family have done this out of our deep love for her, but love cannot give her what she needs and deserves. Who knows what may have happened if you hadn't shown up here.'

Zahra laughed and shook her head. 'Christine, it looks as if you already have plenty of coin, and yet here you are waiting to get greedy hands on more. Ishmael hoped for a reunion, but to me it seems you just want his help for your own needs.'

'Don't judge your betters, commoner,' Christine snapped. 'My family is very important here in Acclaro, and I have achieved great things unlike you. I wouldn't be surprised to find out you are a whore.'

Ale went flying then as Zahra lurched across the table and tried to smash a fist into Christine's face, grazing her chin.

Manu grabbed Zahra as Christine screamed and shrank away. Two burly guards came over to the disturbance as onlookers looked on curiously.

'Remove this scum,' Christine cried, 'she attacked me, a noble lady!'

'No need,' said Ishmael rising. 'We were just leaving.

When do we go visit mother then?'

'The sooner the better, Ishmael. Let's meet three chimes after dawn at the gate. I would say this meeting has been a pleasure, but I would be lying,' spat Christine as Manu pulled Zahra away from the table.

The asylum had withstood the test of time and was one of the few original buildings of Acclaro still standing. Ishmael had expected after all this time it would look run down and in a state of ill repair. To his surprise they turned onto a winding road flanked with fruit trees and surrounded by well-tended sprawling gardens with shaped hedges and bright flower beds. In places people sat on benches or walked along the paths as they visited what would have to be the more sane residents of the asylum, The asylum was a large rectangular building of stone that had four wings spread out one from each side like a cross. It seemed a prison more than an asylum, but then again, thought Ishmael, there is sometimes no difference between the two. The wings were a new addition since Ishmael had seen it last. Someone had put real effort into trying to make the place look friendlier with a new coat of paint.

The foyer was sparkling from the tiles to the heavy candelabra hanging from the ceiling. Christine led the companions to the nurse's station, where they were met by an older lady whose face split into a wide smile when she saw Christine.

'My lady Chris, it's so good to see you. I trust you've been well? We haven't seen you for some time.'

'Dolores, I find these days all my time is consumed by persistent trivial problems within our large household. Without family here it becomes tricky to always visit Mother but by the gods I try.'

'Which is more than most, believe me, Chris. Your mama will be so pleased to see you; she was convinced you had abandoned her here with the other crazies, and you know how much she loves being allowed out into the gardens.' The receptionist shook her head. 'Sorry, listen to me waffling on like an old nut, eh. Now let me just get the names of the other visitors, then I will have her bought out to you in the usual spot.'

Chris led the way down a garden path parallel to the outside of the closest wing of patient rooms. All the rooms had a view of the therapeutic gardens and courtyard surrounding them. As they walked the patients lined their cages to look, jeer, even howl at them as they passed. One even kept shouting out, 'My pretty, for you, my pretty,' as he serviced himself, which was thankfully hidden from view.

'Chris, you said that the inmates live in terrible conditions, but the cells even have courtyards and these patients around us look quite well considering,' Ishmael said.

'Ishmael, what you see now is considered level one accommodation, which, believe me, costs a small fortune. Mama is housed in a different wing that holds mixed accommodation with four to a cell and no courtyard, of course.'

A tall man wearing a fine suit and looking very out of place came striding over to them.

'Ishmael, this is Mr. Bellouse, who kindly agreed to meet us here. He is an employer of the money lenders' guild who I asked to come here in order to verify that you are who we say you are.'

From nearby Zahra gave a throaty laugh. 'Well, it's all starting to come together, this little plan of yours, isn't it, Christine. You certainly don't waste time when it comes to money. I just can't help but wonder why it took you so long. I mean, it's such an amazing coincidence that we show up here to find you waiting for your long-lost brother.'

Christine turned to Zahra; some of the noble lady's heavy make-up was starting to melt from the sun.

'Sarah your insinuations are not welcome. Servants like yourself should just stay quiet!'

'We know what you're up to Chris, and it's Zahra.'

Before she could continue Manu pulled her away from them over to a bench. Ishmael could see them arguing, but he turned his attention to Mr. Bellouse.

Mr. Bellouse wiped a wayward blossom from his suit.

'As much as I would like to dally in such grand scenery, I lack the time to stand around being subjected to pathetic family squabbles.'

'Please, Mr. Bellouse, here she comes now, you have my word it won't take long, and I apologize for the interruption. You know how servants are…'

'They are my companions, not servants, Chris! Mr. Bellouse, exactly how will you decide if I am able to sign the release of these funds to my sister?'

'I already have the word of your sister plus the birth records, so if your mother identifies you as her son, then that's sufficient evidence for me.'

'Look, here she comes now,' said Chris excitedly.

Two assistants walked either side of the woman who could only be Ishmael's mother. Once she had been a tall shapely woman whose lustrous blonde hair and shapely hips had turned many heads. Now all that remained was a sorry old woman with white knotted hair, but those eyes were the eyes of his mother. He would never forget them.

As she walked she extended her arms.

'I'm free, I'm free, out of my cage at last. Chris where have you been, my love? You said you would help me, Chris, take me home, dear, I don't like it here'

'I am helping you, Mother and that's why I have bought someone to see you.'

Her eyes darted here and there before locking onto Ishmael, then they widened and with a cry she bought her hands to her mouth.

'No, it cannot be.' She turned to Chris in wonder, and Ishmael felt a twist of hope come to life inside him.

His mother walked up to him cupping her hands on his face.

'It can't be you, I saw you die! But it's you, and you're here. Tom, take me home. Tom, I don't understand why you haven't come to get me sooner. Tom, they hurt me here.' She embraced Ishmael tightly as over her shoulder Christine whispered to him.

'Tell her, Ishmael.'

'Why, why did you leave me, Tom darling, to just show up here after all this time?' She was sobbing now as she weakly beat her fists against his chest.

Grabbing his mother's arms gently, Ishmael held her in front of him.

'I'm not Tom,' he said trying to sound strong but he had become choked up and felt the need to repeat it.

'I'm not Tom, but I am his and your son, Ishmael.'

'No you're my Tom, I would know you anywhere.'

'Ma, Tom is dead, we both know that.'

'But you look just like my Tom.' Her voice trailed off.

'I'm Ishmael, you're first born. Do you remember me now?'

His mother tore free of his grasp muttering to herself.

'Ishmael, yes, I remember you son.'

When their eyes met again, she was looking at him with undisguised hatred unchanged by years of separation.

'You dare come here after what you did, killing my Tom, your very own father?'

Ishmael stepped towards her palms outward pleadingly.

'I did nothing to father, it was the magic that caused his death, so will you stop blaming me for everything?'

'Stay away, you filth, you're nothing but filth, Ishmael. Your father loved you more than you ever deserved, and you repaid his love with murder.' She flung herself at him screaming in rage, arms flailing, trying to scratch out his eyes but only managing to scratch his cheek. She was weak, and he easily held her away from him.

Ishmael called to the two assistants, who watched impassively.

'Take her back, please, this woman is lost to me.'

As they grabbed his mother, Elaine, by the arms, she continued to struggle, but they lifted her easily and carried her away.

Ishmael shouted after his mother. 'I loved him too!'

He walked over to the bench, catching Chris grinning at him before she turned away.

Ishmael sat down drained by the encounter. He had thought that things could be different now, but she still hated him. Coming here had been a mistake, but he had found the closure he was looking for, which now numbed his heart causing damage far worse than anything physical could have.

He felt an arm around his shoulder. It was Zahra.

'Don't take it personally, Ishmael, she might be your mother but she doesn't know you or who you have become. You are a good person, and you need to be stronger than ever before because we need you. The whole world needs you, even if your own mother doesn't.'

Manu, who had been talking to Chris, moved over to Ishmael and Zahra.

'Ishmael, there is still the matter of the signature. It seems that Mr. Bellouse was satisfied of your claim and now the only thing left to do is sign the papers at the manor, then we can be on our way.'

Ishmael just nodded then rose and started the walk back to the asylum, truly aware now that he had no family. They started back towards the Soldano manor as the lengthening late afternoon shadows began chasing away the heat of the day.

Chapter 57

'Ishmael, dear brother, don't take it so seriously. It's not as if mother ever liked you.'

'Yeah, Chris, but sometimes you feel like there is hope for something better, to start again.'

'My, oh my, Ishmael, you do tend towards flights of fancy. Please tell me you're not that stupid.'

Zahra leaned in towards Chris from the opposite seat.

'Are you always a bitch? If you so much as open your whore's mouth again, I will smash your teeth out.'

Chris shrank away from Zahra's threatening gaze.

'She's right, Zahra. She may be a bitch of a sister, I've always known, but in this case, she is right. I really shouldn't have come here,' Ishmael said. 'So here is what's going to happen, Chris, when we get to this manor of yours I will sign your damn bank note and then will leave your god forsaken life forever, but until then if you so much as try to talk to me I will kill you myself.'

The remainder of the carriage ride was thankfully quiet, and Ishmael was relieved for the reprieve. Manu, who sat opposite him, winked then gave a smile while Zahra looked blankly out the carriage window.

Ishmael felt deeply embarrassed about what had happened back at the asylum. It had only proved what he already had known. The sooner they left this strange place the better. Coming here had only wasted valuable time on getting to the safe house, and yet Manu and Zahra had allowed him to come. The carriage turned from the road onto a long winding driveway to the manor. The grounds and gardens followed a spiral design outward from a large statue of a soldier drawing his blade. It was beautiful, yet deep in his gut there was a persistent feeling of wrongness about not just this place but the whole city. The carriage pulled up outside a huge two-story white stone house complete with balconies and large glass windows.

Manu felt sick to his core, the carriage ride through the city had been ruined by a sudden headache that made him want to vomit. Sweat soaked his forehead, hands, and feet. What is going on with me? Zahra punched him in the shoulder softly.

'C'mon old boy, let's get out of this claustrophobic shell so we can finish this bullshit before I kill his damn sister myself.'

Manu smiled weakly then heaved himself off the seat into the day again where a nice breeze cooled the sweat on his brow. He wasn't sick, so what the heck was going on? Chris of all people noticed his discomfort.

'You are so pale that you look like one of the undead, sweating too; here, come inside so I can get you all refreshments.'

They were briskly escorted up some stairs, through a hall, and into a large dining room. The room was decorated in gold and silver, which would have been nice but for severe red walls that did nothing for the pain in his head. They were introduced to a man sitting rigidly at the end of the table with a shit-eating grin and an obvious hair piece. A lord Soldano or someone to that effect. Mopping his brow again, Manu tried to keep up with the conversation but the pain was getting worse.

He pulled his shirt up to wipe his lips, and that was when he noticed the soft white glow coming from his skin that no one else would be able notice. It had been so long since it had happened but he knew the signs and it was all making sense now. There would be no hiding what he was now from anyone here but that was of little consequence, they were in danger.

Zahra thought the house looked strangely empty for such an obviously important family. There were no servants rushing around attending to chores or guards, which she had expected. Chris and her rich husband could be just very trusting, but from just the excursion to the asylum she knew Ishmael's sister was spoilt, calculating, and maybe even cruel, if the smug glances she had thrown Ishmael following his mother's breakdown had been anything to go by. Manu had been acting strange since the wagon ride and leaned heavily against the banister rail of the staircase to assist him in his ascent. They entered a disgusting dining room whose walls looked like a massacre.

Chris introduced her husband Claude Soldano to them after she gave him a long kiss. Zahra ignored the hand that the balding smug faced man proffered her and slumped in a chair. The double door they came in had been the main entry, she noticed, while the windows that opened to a balcony along with the smaller door behind the head of the table where lord of Soldano sat, were the other escape points. All this occurred to her with a brief look upon entering the room. It was just instinct now that always had her evaluating anywhere she went for possible escape routes.

Ishmael found his sister's manor repulsive. Inside it was over decorated especially the tragic dining room, where he met Christina's husband, Claude. His soft handshake gave Ishmael a repulsive chill.

'So you're the Ishmael that Chris has told me so much about, eh?'

'That would appear to be so, sir.'

Christina passed him over a quill and ink.

'Sign here, dear brother, and then you are free of us.' Her small beady eyes were lit with greed. The papers had already been signed by Mr. Bellouse who had accompanied his sister to the asylum. Apparently, he was happy that all the abuse his mother had thrown at him was enough to prove who he was, thus making it possible to release the money. That's strange, thought Ishmael, if the banker had signed at the asylum why wouldn't Chris have Ishmael sign them there as well?

Manu, who had been sitting, rose unsteadily to his feet from the other side of the table, his face shining with perspiration that gave him a faint glow. He groaned loudly then whispered,

'There are Infernals here!'

Then everything happened simultaneously as the door behind Claude was thrown open so hard the hinges were torn off. A screaming, grotesquely scarred man came through the wreckage, darkness seemingly gathering around him. His own sister had betrayed him again.

Chapter 58

The monstrosity focused its attention on Manu. 'Raheem it's really you. I had hoped you had taken your own life in shame when you failed to protect Alysia from me. I know your smell Archon.'

Claude jumped to his feet to get away only to be swept aside by a back-fisted swing of the Infernal's arm as it strode past him, holding a long sword in one hand.

Christina, who stood open mouthed with Ishmael, snatched the papers from the table then swung her other hand that now grasped a sharp knife towards Ishmael's chest but Zahra swiftly stepped in front of him.

Zahra chopped a hand into Christina's throat, making her drop the blade and stagger away, coughing. An old white-haired man climbed through the ruined doorway, pulling a girl with him who was chained to his wrist. Zahra, who had her sword out now, was pushing him back away towards the double doors behind them.

Manu, bathed in bright light, stood grasping the Infernal's forearms to prevent the scarred monster from completing its downward strike with the long sword. Above and around the two, Manu's Light clashed against the Infernal's darkness, creating an eerie twilight in the room while behind them the girl stood screaming. 'Stop, Zacriel, please stop!'

Manu twisted his arms and stepped in close to the Infernal. He smashed his forehead into the scarred nose then kicked him in the

308

stomach, which threw back the scarred man with a crash through the balcony windows. Manu drew his own sword then glanced back to Ishmael and Zahra.

'Get him away from here; I will hold them.' Manu stepped towards the old man, who ducked beneath his swing, and the blade took a soldier in the throat as he was coming through the doorway. Zahra pulled Ishmael by the shoulder, the old man's eyes locked onto Ishmael's and he came face to face with Brianna's murderer, whose hungry gaze never wavered from his own.

'Get the boy, don't let him escape,' snarled the old man.

Ishmael's breath was coming hard, and as he ran with Zahra two guards appeared at the door trying to prevent their escape but were too slow. Zahra's perfectly thrown knife struck one in the face with the hilt while the other fumbled with his blade as he forgot the doors in order to defend himself. Ishmael slammed into him, pushing him into the opposite wall then kicked the man hard in the groin. He dropped instantly with a scream.

They needed an exit. Ishmael and Zahra turned to use the sweeping staircase they were met by a score of ascending guard's. They kept running down the hall past closed doors; up ahead a maid squealed then disappeared into a small doorway. A servant's passage?

'This way, Ishmael, follow that maid.' Zahra turned through the doorway just before Ishmael, and the both of them barely managed to keep their feet as they found themselves on a steep staircase down to the ground floor. Somehow, they navigated the stairs without injury then burst through another room into the kitchens. Cooks and servants alike stood mouths agape at them.

'Where is the exit?' Zahra shrieked as she grabbed one of the kitchen wenches. Ishmael pushed a chopping table against the stair doorway before Zahra grabbed his arm dragging him down the scullery through another door into a small courtyard.

'Over there, the horses,' said Ishmael, breaking into a run towards the stables with Zahra just behind him. There was a lot of yelling coming from the kitchen now as the guards broke through the barrier, but by then Ishmael and Zahra were through to the stables where a lone man was combing down an impressive stallion. The man dropped the brush and backed away while the grey spotted white stallion rolled its eyes nervously at them.

'Whoa, girl easy,' said Ishmael, extending his hand for the horse to smell, then he gently rubbed its neck and continued to talk softly to the beast.

'Ishmael, they are, coming let's go.'

Ishmael grabbed the horse's mane and pulled himself up onto its back. Except for a whinny the horse stayed put so Ishmael reached down then pulled Zahra up behind him.

A crossbow bolt shot past them to imbed itself into a door, with a yah they were off straight at the guards that had been hot on their heels. One slower than the rest was trampled beneath them before they burst past and out onto the path as bolts sizzled past them.

⸻ ❧ ⸻

Manu was in trouble. The moments it had taken to get over the shock at Zacriel's appearance were over. He never had expected to see the this Infernal again since that day long ago when it had broken into their camp then murdered Alysia the angelic host leader in the epic conflict that had preceded the Severing. Manu had been her protector but had failed her on that bleak day. Dishonoured, he had quit the life as a bodyguard then set out alone, cutting himself away from his kind.

Now was his only chance to exact any kind of revenge for the atrocity Zacriel had committed. Zacriel was climbing to his feet after Manu had kicked him through the glass and onto the balcony. Reacting by instinct to a movement to his right, Manu lashed out with his blade. He barely missed the old man's head as he dared to try and sneak past. Manu then bought his blade back around just in time to deflect a powerful blow from Zacriel that numbed his hands momentarily. Panting with the strain of wielding the blade, Manu cursed himself for his lack of practice, which might prove to be fatal. To gain precious time he retreated to a position in front of the double doors. The guards made a semi-circle around him.

'Leave him alone, he is mine to kill!'

Zacriel pushed through the half ring of guards smiling wickedly. Jagged bits of glass protruded from his body in various places, but he didn't seem to notice. Behind Zacriel, Manu noticed the old man had climbed atop the table with the girl, forcing her to watch the fight.

Manu raised his blade to a defensive stance as Zacriel approached, but the Infernal paused just out of reach.

'Did you know she called for you as I killed her as if expecting you to save her from death? I looked into her eyes, Raheem, to see her life drain away, it was such an intimate moment.'

Manu nearly snapped then but managed to breathe his anger down. It was more important now to give his companions time to escape.

Zacriel stepped in with a powerful thrust towards Manu's chest, but he leant to the side and the blade stuck deep into the oak door behind him. Zacriel tried to jerk the blade free; however, it was stuck fast so Manu lashed his own blade at Zacriel's exposed torso. The Infernal was fast and stepped in against the strike, effectively crowding Manu's blade. Manu felt his nose smash upon his face as his head smacked against the door behind him and his blade was wrenched away. Dazed, he knew what was coming and could only pray he had given Ishmael and Zahra the head start they needed to escape. Manu felt himself lifted by the shirt up against the door. He could hardly breathe due to his broken nose and could only vaguely see out of his eyes that had begun closing up.

Zacriel pressed his face against Manu's, who gagged at the fetid breath of the Infernal. 'Raheem, it seems you are destined to miss the return of magic to this world, the gates are closed, so your soul cannot return to the heavens to be reborn. You will die knowing only failure.'

Manu started laughing then, one long belly laugh, and when he had recovered he looked straight into the face of Zacriel. 'By the gods, Zacriel you are one ugly son of a bitch now.' Then the laughter erupted out of him wild, and free.

Manu felt the sword enter his stomach as Zacriel jammed the blade through and pinned him to the door; it slid slowly through his entrails, popping something important before puncturing out his back., The pain was immense but strangely he seemed separate from it, and a sense of peace flowed over him.

Chapter 59

Zahra and Ishmael raced up the long drive towards the entry gatehouse, leaving the guards behind. As they rode Zahra looked back towards the mansion and spotted two figures standing on the balcony and peering after them. The first was the old man, his white hair giving him away easily. Alongside him was the girl Nina, who had led Zahra and Ishmael out of the mountain. It upset Zahra to see that the girl had not escaped this mess. The old man's eyes stared back at Zahra, and she knew he would create a lot of trouble for them in the future unless they did something about the old bastard. From behind them three short blasts on a trumpet broke the late afternoon silence. An alarm, but to what? Then peering past Ishmael who she clung to tightly, she understood.

'The gate, Ishmael, they are trying to close the gate!'

Ishmael directed the horse off the path, trampling the well-manicured garden. Three guards had spilled from the small gatehouse and two were pulling down hard on the gate winch, slowly winding it shut. The third stood facing them with a bow in hand, arrow nocked in their direction. Twang, the first arrow zipped past them narrowly missing Ishmael's shoulder; it was quickly followed by a second that grazed along the stallion's flank before ricocheting off the saddle and away. As the archer prepared to fire a third, his bravery gave out and he ran back inside the guardhouse to avoid being trampled. The two remaining guards were forced to leave the gate still open to face Ishmael and Zahra.

As the two turned, drawing their blades, Ishmael's kick caught one under the chin dropping him hard while Zahra leaned around Ishmael slashing wickedly with Moonbite so hard the guard spun around in a mist of blood. Then they were past the gates and out into the street, the horse's hooves slipping on the cobblestones as Ishmael directed them down a street empty except for a group of boys playing marbles who scattered, yelling as they got out of the way. Ishmael could feel the power building up within his abdomen. He became aware that Zahra was shouting into his ear to turn into the side road coming up, and the moment he managed to latch onto her voice his senses began to calm, but the heat was building within him and it was all he could do to breathe slowly, forcing his fear down along with the worry about Manu and Zahra. From what seemed a way off, he could hear Zahra directing him.

'Ishmael, we need to get to a safe house, turn left here.'

Then he was falling.

'Zahra cursed as Ishmael slipped sideways from the horse to clatter onto the cobblestones. The street here was almost dark beneath the shadow of the two-storied houses that framed the road, but a light began to flow out from Ishmael's pack where the Earth crystal was. Not wishing to draw any more attention than needed, Zahra slung Ishmael's pack onto her back so the spare blanket hid away the light that was seeping out. Ishmael was a different challenge, though. He lay there emitting a ghostly nimbus from his skin.

'Ishmael, get up, we have to move.'

'Give me the crystal.'

From around the nearby corner Zahra could hear the shouts of guards calling out to one another trying to locate their quarry. Zahra hoisted Ishmael to his feet, holding him up as she guided his slow steps, and they staggered onwards. Zahra knew they were close to a safe house she had stayed in cycles ago, she just needed to see the correct signs.

The alleyways in Acclaro were the brightest aspect of the city these days. The artists' guild had successfully lobbied to be allowed to cover the unseemly city areas with painted murals, and it was in one of these famed pieces of art that Zahra sought out the image of a metallic cat. She dragged Ishmael, who was muttering incoherently as she looked. The mural here depicted a scene where a rampaging pack of hounds snapping at their heels of two children running in front of them. 'There must be a cat here somewhere.' Then she saw it three houses up painted onto the base of a set of stairs.

'Give me the crystal, Zahra, now.'

Zahra, not used to the serious tone of Ishmael's voice, pulled it from the pack, handing it to Ishmael.

'Have you checked this alley, Swartz?'

'Nah, not yet, Del, we can do it together.'

The two voices came closer, and Zahra pulled Ishmael up against her body in a corner. She tugged down her laced top baring a shoulder and breast as the two guards turned the corner.

'Ahhhh!' shrieked Zahra, quickly turning away in an effort to cover herself up.

'Nothing here but a whore Swartz you wanna have some fun with her?'

'Excuse me, kind guardsmen, I am no whore, I make my living in an honest way.'

'Oh shut up, slag, you know the laws regarding whoring in these streets, so just let us have a good look at you and your friend then you can be on your way before curfew kicks in,' one of the guards said.

Zahra didn't recognize the guards from the house, but they would know hers and Ishmael's descriptions.

The guard named Del stepped forwards and sniffed deeply.

'It's them Swartz, I can smell him.'

For a moment Zahra thought she had misheard, and then she looked closer at the one called Swartz, seeing thin scales covering his neck and face. These weren't guardsmen they were Infernals.

Ishmael was burning up, the magic inside of him slowly pouring through his being; when the guards had approached he had grabbed the crystal to hide its glow beneath his tunic. With one arm he pushed Zahra behind him as Del came forward. The light reflected off silvery-scaled arms and as the Infernal's blade descended Ishmael screamed and raised the crystal to intercept it.

The alleyway exploded in light that forced him to close his eyes. When the light subsided, he looked about him to Zahra, who stood hair blown back and clothes torn gazing at him open mouthed. Of Swartz and Del there was nothing but their smouldering remains at Ishmael's feet. The walls of the surrounding buildings had been scorched clean, giving the cobblestones a bleached appearance. The castle's central tower had stood unlit since the Severing, but now even from all the way down in the city Ishmael and Zahra could see an intense blue light emanating from the windows of the tower.

Zahra grabbed him by the shoulder; her lips were moving but Ishmael couldn't understand a word she was saying. The concussion of the release of power had deafened him. The Earth crystal appeared undamaged, so he put it in the backpack. 'Need rest,' he managed to blurt out, half walking as Zahra tried to carry most of his weight towards the house she now pointed out to him.

Zahra got Ishmael to the stairs as from the surrounding streets cries of alarm and shouting could be heard. Nearby shutters cautiously opened and some occupants came outside their homes onto the narrow road looking around in confusion as the white glow that still bathed the whole alley slowly began fading away. Zahra was forced to carry Ishmael up the remaining steps to the door where she stood, taking deep steadying breaths. She began searching for the false panel of the door as she also listened to the conversations going on below her in the street.

'Look Mommy, do you think it was Celestials?'

'Not Celestials, darling, but magic.'

'Don't go filling her head with bullshit, Maria, there has been no magic since the Severing.'

'Mommy, what about up there. See that blue light in the tower? It's never been there before.

Mommy what are that lady and man doing on the stairs?'

Zahra turned to where the young boy stood with his mother pointing at her.

'It's fine,' she called down to them,' we are the owner's friends just using the place for a night is all.'

The lady looked suspicious but nodded, and as Zahra turned back to the door she imagined she could feel the stare of the woman hot on her back.

Her hands passed over the door panels, seeking out any indentation. Soon the guards would be here and they would be undone. There was only a certain amount of luck one could hope for.

'Look, Mommy here comes the watch! Are we in trouble?'

'No, baby, they're just wondering what happened too.'

Her hand found the indentation, and she pushed, nearly falling over in relief as her fingers grasped the iron key inside the panel. The key worked and the door clicked open, allowing her to drag Ishmael inside where he was unceremoniously dumped to the floor as her strength gave out and she collapsed beside him, chest heaving.

Chapter 60

Zahra locked the door then sat with her back to it listening intently as the guards arrived outside.

'What are you all doing out here when it's nearly curfew?'

'Sorry, sir, we meant no harm, we just heard the explosion then saw the whole street covered in white light and thought we should investigate.'

'Well, go inside, good lady and leave the investigating up to us.'

'Hey, wait up. Not so hasty, soldier. I would question the miss some more first,' said the second guard.

'Miss, besides the light and explosion, did you see anything unusual?'

'Like what do you mean, sir?'

'We are looking for two people, a woman with short black hair wearing travelling clothes and with her a young man with short blonde hair and tanned skin. They had a horse but now may be on foot. They are very dangerous, and you will be well rewarded for any information regarding their whereabouts.'

'I seen something,' came the child's voice.

'You only saw the light, now go on inside, Damien I will be in shortly.'

'But Mommy, it's so exciting.'

'Damien, inside now!'

There came the sound of a door closing then the voices continued.

'No, sir all we heard was an almighty explosion, it shook the very walls it did. Then as we lay there waiting, listening the whole area lights up as if it's daybreak again. The most unusual thing I've seen, I tell you. Do you think it was magic?'

'Can't tell you, miss, I haven't ever seen magic. So you saw no one here then is that right?'

'Yes, that's right, sir.'

'Well, we need to come in and check your home to be sure the dangerous individuals we are seeking are not in there, then we will be on your way.'

'No problem, sir your men can go on in. We have nothing to hide from you.'

'The house next door, does anyone live there?'

'Not since the old lady that owns the place died, sir. Apparently her family still owns the residence and plan to move here sometime soon, but it is currently empty. That's why the windows are boarded up.'

'Yes, yes, I can see that.

Come on, men, check the other houses now, they could be hiding anywhere, the night is coming and I want to be in my cups by then.'

'Sarge, I think I have found Del and Swartz… or what remains of them.'

Zahra sighed, looked over to Ishmael who was sleeping soundly. Then she heard footsteps coming up the stairs and drew Moonbite from its scabbard. The door handle turned with a squeak but didn't budge, and Zahra wished she had been clever enough to place the iron bar across the door as well, but it was too late for that.

The handle turned again then was pulled hard but stayed put. Zahra stood with her back against the door, sword in hand, barely daring to breathe. The footsteps moved along the small balcony where the large window was boarded up, and Zahra could hear as someone tested the boards. They must have been satisfied since the footsteps then retreated down the staircase and away down the street.

Moving over to Ishmael, Zahra checked his pulse which was steady;

his color was fine as well and his breathing calm. She forced herself to her feet then with blade drawn Zahra explored the safe house. The place was only two bedrooms with a kitchen and washroom so it didn't take long for Zahra to complete the search. She found a barrel of water along with dry stores of tea and herbs but no fresh food. Soon she would have to head out to find some, but not until night fell, which would place the city under curfew.

In the kitchen Zahra started a small fire in the hearth, enough to boil water for hot tea. As she worked she tried to ignore the shaking of her hands and her mind turned to Manu. Zahra burst into tears.

Manu may have lived and been taken prisoner, she muttered, but she knew that the Infernal she thought died beneath Illume City was intent on killing Manu whom the Infernal had called by some other name. Manu may have lived, but she doubted it.

Zahra had just finished the tea and was boiling more water to use for bathing her and Ishmael's wounds when she saw movement to her side from the doorway. Zahra sprang to her feet, upending the water, which sizzled out most of the small fire.

Ishmael stood in the doorway, palms out in front of him apologetically.

'Sorry, Zahra, I didn't mean to surprise you. I'm so tired but can't sleep anymore.'

'Accepted.' Zahra grabbed the small pot handing it out to Ishmael. 'Through the back there is a barrel of water, refill it since you made me spill it everywhere, will you.'

Ishmael took it and went to fill it.

As they sat waiting for the tea to boil, Ishmael watched Zahra sharpen and oil her remaining knives. She emptied her backpack, making an inventory of their supplies left, and by the look of things it wasn't promising.

'Zahra, do you think Manu is alive?'

'He sacrificed himself to save us, Ishmael, and the Manu I know wouldn't have given up. He was stubborn beyond belief, and this ah,

Zacriel I think Manu called it…was seemingly an old enemy. I knew Manu had a secret but I would never had guessed he was a Celestial. I just wish I had of known earlier.'

'Why did he hide it from us, Zahra?'

She shrugged then busied herself with unwrapping a particular herb that she crumbled into the pot then began putting the other herbs back into her pack.

'Is that dream tangle root, the one that's bluish?'

Zahra looked up at him. 'You know herbs? Was it a part of your training at the monastery?'

'One of the elders liked to think of himself as a physician, but I learnt about herbs through the library and helped maintain the gardens while I was there. So why do you think he hid it from us?'

She handed Ishmael a steaming mug of tea, taking a long slurp of her own, then sighed.

'My mother used to say to me and my brother that tea can ease all things. She was wrong, Ish, it can't fix anything. But certainly helps. To answer your question, I didn't even know he was a Celestial until I saw that light spilling from him. He obviously didn't want to be recognized, and I'm sure he had his reasons, but I will miss the old fool. We shared some history and there aren't too many people whom I can say that about.'

'What happened back there Ishmael?'

'When I was a toddler my father began teaching me a series of exercises which I only learnt after he died that they were for controlling the magic I would inherit. The exercises were designed to strengthen the energy centers that keep the magic coiled within me in a relaxed manner. You see, what the sorcerers who caused the Severing didn't count on was the fact that the magic is like a living beast that seeks to be free of any prison and return to its natural state. Without a way to keep that magic in check, the coterie would burn up from the inside out. The exercises worked very well until recently. Now we have the Earth crystal from the Harlequin, and since then it's as if the magic coiled inside me has grown stronger. It is very important that we find the other crystals as soon as possible.

The Mother showed me that the death of the coterie or release of magic before the right time will have disastrous effects.'

'What is it like, is it painful?'

He sipped his tea thinking for a moment then smiled. 'It's like an itch you can't scratch, like a snake coiled around the base of my spine that during any mental or emotional upheaval. It surges upwards through my body threatening to blow me apart until all I want to do is scream. The crystal the Harlequin gave me seems to causes these surges more easily, but until tonight the magic has never been released. That may have been because of the crystal being struck with the Infernal's sword. When the feeling came tonight it was like severe sea sickness where I couldn't stand or sit up and so fell from the horse. I still knew what was happening around us and when the two guards showed their true selves all I could think to do was use the stone to deflect the blade.'

'I was truly afraid when you fell. Then the guards came and I expected the worst to happen.'

From outside came the loud sounds of bells ringing that went on for some time.

'Curfew,' Zahra rose to her feet shaking the dust from her clothes. 'Wait here for me. I need to find us supplies and an escape route before we leave the city.'

For a moment Ishmael thought about saying he would accompany her, but he realized she would be better without having to worry about him alerting the guards to their location, so he nodded.

'I will clean the house and make dinner.'

Zahra laughed then strapped the sword to her back and headed to the back door of the house which he unlocked for her and watched her disappear up the drain pipe and onto the slated roof above him.

Chapter 61

Ishmael locked the door then returned to place some kindling on the small fire. Settling down to watch the flames slowly dance over the tinder, he let his mind relax. He began breathing short, deep, fast breaths to raise his energy as he tried to contact the coterie. It was easier to contact them since he had received the Earth crystal. Ishmael held the crystal in his hands and followed the laughter he knew belonged to Selene. There was a moment of confusion then recognition as he entered her mind, which opened easily to allow him in.

'You are getting better at that, Ishmael,' came her voice within his head. He looked from her eyes around her to the large fire that lit the night as a group of what looked like travelling musicians played jovial music while some beast slowly roasted over the fire.

'Where are you, and who are these people?'

'Ansar thought it would be best to travel in numbers, so we hired on with a troupe until we get to the safe house. They aren't a bad lot for land lovers.' Selene brought a mug of what turned out to be wine to her lips, drinking deeply.

A man sidled up to sit beside her with a flask in one hand.

'Here you go, my lady, more wine for you?'

'Many thanks,' she replied, holding the mug out.

'Are you drunk, Selene?'

'You are so observant, Ishmael, and yes, I am drunk, because then I won't think about the ocean so much.'

'Is it truly so hard for you to be away from it?' Ishmael asked.

'Yes, it is, my land legs have only just settled, but I feel lost here.'

'We need to speak to Raul and Jona. There have been developments I need to share with all of you. I know what we need to do now, Selene. Tomorrow night at sundown meet us in the tree chamber, all right?'

'Tomorrow night it is,' she said, rising to her feet then wavering alarmingly. Ishmael withdrew noticing for the first time the parts of her mind that he felt fleetingly and could have pushed into if he had wanted but he didn't because he was her friend. Back in the house the fire had nearly burnt out; he had no idea how much time had passed, so he busied himself finding more timber as he awaited Zahra's return.

Chapter 62

Dalwyn was beyond furious-the idiots had allowed Ishmael and his assassin to escape. Not only had Zacriel barged through the door too early, but the guards who were supposed to seal the double doors to the dining room failed to do so in time. The Celestial had been a surprise, but he was dead so of no use to Dalwyn. The girl Nina began screaming once the Angelic died, and he tried to shut her up, but she appeared to be having a breakdown of some sort. He raised his hand to slap the child back to reality but something caught it.

Dalwyn looked up into the hateful eyes of Zacriel whose voice cracked with the effort to speak.

'You touch her, old man, you die!'

Dalwyn wanted so much to make Zacriel pay for touching him but realized that Zacriel would tear him apart before his guards could even get to him.

'Take your play thing, Zacriel, you sick bastard.'

Zacriel was still full of bloodlust from killing his oldest enemy. It should have been a great day, but instead he felt tainted from the violence. The screams of Nina had snapped him from his reverie, and he had managed to stop Dalwyn from hitting her. Nina lay curled up on the tabletop. It seemed that at any sign of distress Nina retreated from the world so as not to get hurt anymore. Such weakness. Stupid child, he would have to teach her a better way to deal with problems.

Zacriel felt a pulling from deep inside his body, a pulsing that called to what he was. He had known the city was doomed as soon as he had entered its gates and felt the pall that had fallen over Acclaro. It had been marked by the Infernal lords. Zacriel had thought he would be able to capture Ishmael and leave without being caught up in what was to come, but he was too late. The pull was his connection to one of the Infernal lords who could send the call to all their kind within a certain distance and was known as the blood summons. The summons thrummed through his body, awakening the need for slaughter that his nature had no way of refusing. The blood of Infernals calls to its own, he recited as if still learning the blood trade.

'One of the four Infernal lords is in the city. Dalwyn, Acclaro is about to become a slaughterhouse. If you want to survive this night then you must leave this place, no human is safe within these walls,' said Zacriel trying hard to control his building rage.

Zacriel had to give the old man credit as he stood unflinching before Zacriel.

'You are making no sense, Zacriel, so tell me again.'

'I know you remember the cleansing,' Zacriel said through clenched teeth. Well, this is the same except this time you humans are the vermin. One of the four Infernal lords is here, and tonight he will unleash his force in the city, taking it as his own. The blood calls me to follow and join in the slaughter, and I suggest you leave while you can.'

Dalwyn tugged Nina's chain violently towards him causing her to fall and cry out, but before Zacriel could stop him the old man had a wickedly sharp blade across Nina's throat.

'Tell you what, spawn, I have a better idea and if you want to see your little toy survive then you had better listen to me.'

Zacriel wanted nothing better than to rip Dalwyn to shreds except he knew Dalwyn would cut Nina's throat. The fight as well as the cost of defying the blood pull was sapping his energy, and he was in no condition for another fight.

Knuckles, who was eyeballing Zacriel, smashed his fist onto the table, splitting the hard wood through the center.

'Spawn, want to die?'

Zacriel ignored the brute and recovered his sword from the floor, causing a terrified Claude and Christine to scuttle away from where they cowered on the floor amidst the debris.

'If we are to stay in the city, then we need to know what is happening. I will take this time to scout out the situation. I will return within the chime.'

'I'm afraid that's not going to happen, Zacriel. We will be coming with you right after this business with the Soldanos is concluded.' He grinned down at where they cowered on the floor.

Chapter 63

Dalwyn stared down at Claude of the house Soldano, who could barely meet his gaze for long. Knuckles had returned to his side, a large bruise darkening his forehead and his hair matted with blood.

Claude Soldano got to his feet and wiped the dust from his trousers then stepped carefully over the broken furniture and bodies littering the room.

'Dalwyn, I will need recompense for the damage done here; it is simply unacceptable.'

'Yes, the matter of recompense now where is it. Here it is,' Dalwyn reached into a belt pouch, counting out ten ceta's as Claude's eyed goggled. Christine had suddenly appeared beside her husband, laughing throatily.

'Knuckles, kindly bring Claude here.'

With a squawk Claude was dragged in close to Dalwyn until he sat before him, head held back by Knuckles.

'What are you doing to Claude. Leave him-I order you to'

There was a smacking sound and a crash as Knuckles backhanded Chris into the wall.

Claude Soldano tried to complain, but as he opened his mouth Dalwyn crammed something hard into it. When Claude opened his mouth to gasp in pain another gleaming ceta was forced inside. 'Here is your precious gold, Master Soldano!' Dalwyn forced yet another coin inside the greedy bastard's mouth, smiling at the sound of breaking teeth. Claude struggled mightily to escape but was no match to the strength of Knuckles, who laughed heartily each time a coin was added. They only got to seven coins before Claude began choking. Knuckles held his hand over Claude's nose and mouth until the man's body stiffened and went limp in his arms. As Claude's body fell against the table, a few cetas clanged to the floor.

Christine made a run for the doors, wailing.

'Chris, you forgot your money, my dear.'

Dalwyn passed the money pouch to Knuckles who, grinning broadly, hefted the bag then threw it. The pouch smacked into the back of Chris's head, knocking her to the ground. As she began to rise unsteadily to her feet, Knuckles hoisted her over his shoulder then carried her back inside the dining room. Dalwyn tied her to the chair with a length of tablecloth he cut free. He noticed Zacriel now standing on the balcony, trembling as he looked out at the lake.

'There we go, Chris, please don't be frightened. We are going to have ourselves a little talk about what you know of your brother. Knuckles, lock the doors, will you?'

⁂

Chapter 64

Zahra paused on the roof to orient herself. During the day she had questioned one of the Soldano servants regarding the curfew, which had only recently been implemented. The city guard had come under attack while attempting to enforce the increasingly stringent laws, and that had led to a group of ex-soldiers and business owners breaching the palace gate then fighting the king's men all the way to the throne room. The following day, curfew had been implemented, which had caused more division between the king and his subjects, and the mercenaries hadn't been heard of since they disappeared inside the castle.

Zahra advanced along the spine of the roof, careful to avoid knocking any tiles off. She was too far from where she needed to be to reach any shops with supplies she recognized the barracks of the city guard. Curfew would mean at least for the first few chimes the night watch would be busy completing patrols. A strange drumming rumble had begun from somewhere in the city. Zahra turned about slowly to gauge what was going on in the city around her, she stopped when she was facing the castle. As Zahra watched, the gigantic portcullis rose, slowly emitting a procession of guardsman that streamed down into the streets, their boots making a low rumble of dread. A loud grating note warbled out from somewhere three times. A call to war, thought Zahra. Amongst the soldiers marched abominations clearly not human as their eerie, twisted forms danced a marching jig accompanied by strange laughter and cries of glee. So the Infernals planned to take the capital.

The need for a swift search was of utmost importance now. If there was one place she could find weapons, medical supplies, and food, it would be at the barracks. She moved quickly down the street, ducking into the shadows of eaves, chimneys of the rooftops to stay hidden. When she reached the end of the rooftops Zahra climbed down into a small park area thanks to an overhanging branch. Swinging to the ground, she landed softly then cursed as she realized someone was standing there.

It was a guard who had been relieving himself. He opened his mouth to sound the alarm, but Zahra chopped her hand into his throat twice, dropping him instantly before choking him until he was quiet. The man's skin was wet with a slimy substance that made Zahra retch, and she wiped her hands on the grass at the base of the tree before collecting the hooded lantern beside the bushes. Zahra adjusted the shutter slightly to illuminate the dead guard who appeared human but for the thick slime that covered him. As luck had it, Zahra was close to the same size as the dead guard, so she wiggled into his uniform ignoring the slime and its reek as best she could then she hid her clothes in the bushes nearby.

As she edged towards the gatehouse she stopped to survey the area, expecting it to have stationed guards, but it appeared empty. Zahra burst from her cover, sprinting across the street, ducking behind bushes where possible. But when she got to the gatehouse, it was empty. She ran through the yard towards a building that showed the symbol of Helene, watcher of soldiers. The door was unlocked, so she crept into the nursing area but once again found it empty. Everything here was covered in a thin layer of dust.

Shaking off her uneasiness, Zahra grabbed a medical bag she found then began filling it with bandages, salves, and anything they might need. She moved deeper into the dark building but was forced to backtrack briefly to the entrance as her lantern faded. Zahra found a half-burnt torch and lit it from the fading lantern. The strange thing was, why weren't these facilities being used, and where were the guards to watch over them?

The next room was full of hospital beds for patients made up to a military standard with a fine layer of dust coating them. The silence was unnerving. Zahra could cross this room heading to what was most likely the kitchens and waste area, but the musty room brought her memory back to the monastery where she had witnessed the demonic child almost kill Ishmael. Outside a mist was taking shape in the night, not uncommon at this time of cycle. At least the mist would cover most of her movements this night, but it would also benefit her enemies. Backtracking to another exit Zahra had passed earlier, she left the medical area in a crouching run, zig-zagging across the yard to the mess hall kindly shown by a sign of a plate holding a roast chicken upon it. Inside the mess hall everything was neat and orderly, no one had eaten here recently. Zahra lit a new torch in one of the wall brackets then went into the kitchen itself. Somewhere here there was a cool room for the food. She added a few jars of honeyed fruit and pickled vegetables from shelves to the bag but couldn't find any sign of meat. The kitchen had a narrow staircase leading down to a double-barred door. Placing her bag on the steps, Zahra knelt beside the door, a strong stench of rancid meat seemed the only thing of interest.

Zahra stood to leave and stopped as the door rattled from the other side.

Chapter 65

'Hello, is that you Captain Morsen, Cap?'

'Too bad if it's frigging not the cap, you dumb ass.'

'Well you can see the light beneath the door as well as I can, Dandy, there is someone there all right.'

Zahra knelt again. 'It's not your captain here, I am scavenging for food.'

There came nervous laughing from the other side of the door.

'Told you someone would come rescue us, didn't I?'

Zahra gave the door a few knocks to get the attention of whoever was there.

'Hey no one mentioned rescue yet I don't know who you are and you outnumber me so until I am satisfied with an explanation you aren't going anywhere yet.'

'Listen here, woman there is no time for stories now. If you don't let us out, they will be back for the next one of us. I am Lieutenant Fyfe, and the city is in danger!'

'Haha did you figure that out all by yourself then?' Zahra asked.

'The Infernal ones have replaced the city guard with their own spawn while we humans have become food for them.'

Zahra couldn't say anything as she sat there, and yet the signs had been there. The mad shaman near the Unkta Falls when he had pointed out the circling Infernals flying around the Acclaro Kings Palace, the gloom that had set over the city, the guardsmen from earlier that night had turned out to be Infernals as well. Even the curfew that would allow any number of Infernals to be smuggled into the city by night-a masterstroke, really.

'Are you still there? Maybe she's gone and left us here?'

'Just shut up, Dandy. If she was gone the light would be too.'

'I'm still here, now listen up closely, I believe you, but when I open this door no one is to rush out. Stay where you are arms above your heads. I am armed, and if I have to kill you then I will, have you got that?'

'Just get us out of here and we will do as you ask.'

Zahra took the two iron bars off the door, pulled her sword free, and then unbolted the door, holding the torch out into the darkness as she pulled the door slowly open. The flames of the torch danced over four grimy figures squinting up at her. One fell to Zahra's feet sobbing.

'Thank the gods, thank you so much.'

Zahra, embarrassed, stepped back to distance herself from the prone guard.

A stout man stepped forward then thought better of it as Zahra raised her blade.

'Well met, your timing couldn't have been any better. I'm Lieutenant Fyfe.' He then turned to the soldier still crying and knelt beside her. 'Pixie, it's time to be strong now like we talked about. If we are to escape we need to know we can trust you not to fall apart. Can I trust you, Pixie?'

'Yes, su… sure thing sir.'

He patted her shoulder reassuringly then helped her to her feet.

Zahra was getting nervous now. She hated groups when her life depended on remaining unseen. She motioned to Fyfe to join her.

'All you need to know of me is that I am also hunted by these Infernals,' she began. 'So we share a common goal to get out of the city. If we find you all weapons, get food, then we can leave this place together. Someone needs to see the king…'

The one called Dandy pushed in beside Fyfe and Zahra.

'You don't know do you? The king is the one who began this in the first place by bringing down the curse on the city. They cleansed the city of Infernals, but no one would have guessed something went wrong. They don't tell you that the palace was never properly cleansed, that something happened to the king that night. None of us even know if the current King Chez is even alive or if something else rules in the palace now. But I will tell you one thing that my grand papa told me, okay? This city was not cleansed of the Infernals. They have nested somewhere in the castle to rebuild and take our capital. Now I don't care what the rest of you are doing, but I'm getting back to my family then at first light we are leaving this evil place.' Zahra caught his sleeve as Dandy moved to leave.

'On my way here I saw Infernal guardsmen marching into the city from the castle. If what your grand papa says is true then Acclaro will fall. As soon as I get supplies I then plan to flee the city also. Is there some way we can leave the city unnoticed?'

' Most likely the gates are barred, so your best bet would be to get down to the docks then slip out by boat onto the lake, but they may have thought of that too. I wish you all luck but I'm leaving, anyone coming with me?' The fourth man who had been locked in the cool room hadn't said a word to this point but stepped forward. 'By the sound out there I would say the city has gone to shit. I'm with you, Dandy.' With that the two guards jogged away towards the exit. Pixie and Fyfe peered out one of the windows, watching as their two friends sprinted towards the street.

Zahra moved away with Fyfe to finish a quick search while Pixie stood guard at the window. Zahra managed to find enough salted beef for three or four days which she quickly added to her backpack. As they paused to open the second room a scream came from outside somewhere, male and lingering like someone terribly wounded. Pixie came running to them out of the darkness, nearly catching Zahra's sword through her gut as she arrived unannounced.

'They got Russ, one of them shot him with a crossbow when he reached the road, but Dandy escaped as far as I could see. Parts of the city are burning-it's the cleansing all over again.'

'Yeah, except this time it's the Infernals cleansing the city of us humans.' Zahra pulled the bolt open to the next cool room. The torch was pretty much useless now but allowed a small amount of radiance for the three of them to see a crowd of terrified faces looking up at them. This room was full of soldiers who looked almost too weak to stand; many had died, and Zahra noted that many of the dead had gnaw marks torn out of their flesh.

Chapter 66

Zahra left the soldiers with their comrades before quickly scouting the remaining area finding nothing but a rear exit. From farther inside she could hear the excited chatting of the rescued guards. They were making too much noise back there. If the Infernal that killed Russ decided to investigate, then this was not the place she wanted to be. She needed to get herself and Ishmael out of this place. It seemed like she was always running lately. Zahra wanted to stay and fight these enemies, but her mission was Ishmael.

After all Haakon had done for her there was no way she would fail to protect Ishmael this time. Zahra decided in that moment to leave the others, they reduced her chances of survival greatly and lingering here served no purpose since she had the supplies they needed. Zahra edged into the night once her eyes had adjusted, pushing away the brief feeling she was deserting the soldiers she had freed…at least she had given them a fighting chance, which was better than what they had before.

There would be no time to dally now with danger all around them. Zahra sprinted to the small park where earlier she had killed the guard. She grabbed her clothing from the bushes, but before she could change a high, piercing voice screamed from down the street.

'There's one there, it's mine.'

Not bothering to look, Zahra threw the sack onto the roof then scrambled up the tree as below and behind her a laughing, sing-song voice carried to her above the nearby screams and fighting.

'Better run harder; you can run, but I'm faster. It's just a matter of time before I take your soul along with the others.'

Zahra swung up onto the roof of the house, sprinting away.

From up high the city sounded and looked like the scene from a war. Houses were burning as monstrous Infernals dragged out their occupants to torment them in the streets. The sounds of fighting rang out throughout the city. Some resistance, then; well, at least that's something, she thought as she ran, scanning the roof ahead for the drainpipe she had used to climb up previously. At the corner she saw it; grabbing the pipe Zahra turned to descend feet first but stopped as she saw the nightmarish creature bearing down on her.

Through thick, twisted, yellow lips grating words slipped out around a blue, swollen tongue.

'Where are you going, mortal, don't you want to hang around and see what we have organized for your people?'

Zahra dropped her backpack to the tiles then drew Moonbite, its blade shining brightly as if answering the light of the moons high above the city.

'Just remember, spawn, you also are mortal here in my world!' The Infernal rose to its full height to tower over Zahra. Its long arms and legs were covered in carapace with jagged edges along the shins and forearms like the shells of those giant crabs she had once eaten by the lake of tears with her family. In revulsion Zahra saw the creature had a second face on its chest which now started screaming gibberish from its toothy maw.

Zahra wasted no more time and stabbed at the face on the chest. The blade struck true, and orange ichor poured from the wound as the face screamed. A flailing swipe of those long arms knocked Zahra from her feet, but she managed to hold onto her blade. The Infernal tried to stomp her face through the tiles as she lay there, and that's when she struck with the blade at the supporting leg, slicing into its thigh.

It fell atop her, both mouths desperately gnawing at her body;

Zahra managed to grab its greasy hair, forcing the face away from her neck. She could feel the other face snapping away at her stomach as her sword arm lay trapped beneath the Infernal. Zahra pulled the Infernal's hair to the side and smashed her elbow down, breaking its face. As it tried to pull away she turned, using her hips to half toss it off her and off the roof. She watched it fall arms, wind milling before it broke apart on the cobbles below. Zahra painfully rolled to her feet inspecting her stomach but relieved to see that the creature's second mouth had only managed to inflict superficial wounds to her midsection. Grabbing the backpack she quickly descended the pipe to the back door where Ishmael was hiding. Knocking twice, Zahra waited anxiously for Ishmael as images of him being dragged from the house by Infernals fought their way to the front of her mind. Then his face appeared at the dirty window of the door, looking too pale in the night.

Ishmael opened the door and started to speak, but she stopped him with a finger to his lips.

'Please, first water, then I will speak.' Zahra began peeling the slimy uniform from her body. It wouldn't matter who she appeared to be now, she was human and they were all hunted.

'Oh, sure, sorry, I wasn't thinking, it's just that I'm so damned happy to see you.'

Zahra couldn't remember the last time someone had said something like that to her. The look he gave her made her feel uneasy. She broke the look they shared to guzzle down water, choking as she drank, then when she had recovered she began.

'The Jingtalla shaman was right: the city is lost, Ishmael. While the world busied itself with its own affairs, the Infernals have been nesting here in Acclaro. The cleansing which was called a success was a farce, and since then they have bided their time breeding in the shadows waiting to strike. Well, tonight the Infernals of Acclaro have begun their own cleansing.'

'What did you see?' asked Ishmael breathlessly.

'From the castle, an army of Infernals marched into the city, killing anybody they could find, torching houses. There appears to be some resistance, but it would seem the city gates remain locked to any chance of escape.'

Ishmael ran his fingers over his short hair. 'Zahra you aren't going to like this, but I can't leave here yet. You saw the blue light that even now is shining bright from the castle tower? It is another of the crystals we need.'

Zahra groaned with exasperation. 'Are you sure? Have you even listened to what I said, Ishmael? The city is a slaughter yard, and you want to go straight to its heart.'

'You think I'm not terrified of going to the castle?' Ishmael asked. 'While you were gone, I could do nothing but listen to the terror that was taking place all around me. I don't want to go there, Zahra, but my duty is to the Earth Mother, and she has shown me in visions the crystals. One of earth, one of air, one of water, one of fire, and one of spirit.'

'My duty, in case you forgot, Ishmael, is to keep your stupid ass alive, which might I add is getting harder and harder.'

'Zahra, as I recall, your duty is to keep me alive so I may fulfill the task given to me by the Earth Mother, which is to release the magic when the time is right. If we run now then we have already failed. I nearly failed once, but thanks to you I am here able to try again.' He looked intently at her. 'Don't let your efforts go to waste now.'

Chapter 67

From the street came a series of crashes. They both ran to the window to peer between the boarded up panes. Ishmael saw soldiers, some human looking others reptilian, kicking in a door across the street. As it splintered, screams broke out from inside and the soldiers were soon dragging out the occupants. One soldier questioned an elderly couple but received only sobbing in return as they huddled arms wrapped around each other.

With a snarl the one in charge said something they couldn't hear, then the Infernal soldiers fell on the couple with weapons. Zahra turned away, seething with anger. 'We need to leave now, Ishmael.'

With a nod he followed her back to the kitchen.

They gathered their supplies quickly. Ishmael strapped his sword onto his hip, then they were ready.

'Ishmael, we need to move fast towards the lake front where the barges are kept, then we can decide our next move. Let's go.'

But he shook his head.

'I told you, Zahra, I need to get up that tower of the castle. With or without you, that's where I am going.' With that Ishmael sprinted in a crouch down the alley behind a large pile of stacked barrels.

'You're a damned fool,' she hissed after him, but he was gone moving again, leaving her behind. Zahra pulled the mask up over her face. She was the chosen of her clan trusted to protect Ishmael, so that was what she must do without letting anything stop them escaping this mess.

Ishmael didn't wait to see if Zahra was following him; he knew she would. Now outside he was acutely aware of the sounds that filled the city around him with screams and gibbering madness that was sweeping the streets. Ishmael ran to the corner of the street where a shop was engulfed in flames making him ward his face with his arms. He heard the soft foot falls as Zahra caught up.

Then the shop windows blew out and they were knocked to the ground. Ishmael lay there covered in glass, flames all around him.

Zahra pulled him to his feet. She had covered her face with the assassin garb now, and it might have been in his mind, but she seemed different.

'C'mon, let's move, it's too open here,' and as if to emphasize her point a mob of screaming citizens armed with daily tools of knives and tools were marching towards them. The guardsman at their lead was bare chested with a terrible injury that left parts of his skull open. When he saw Ishmael and Zahra he called for the others to follow then warily approached.

'The alleys we came from are unsafe, the city guard are kicking in the doors and pulling out the citizens down there, it's safer to move towards the castle,' Ishmael told the group.

'Bah, running away more like it. Well, this is our home and we mean to keep it, we cleansed the Infernal swine once already, but this time I swear it will be done right. Join us now, we just need to join up with the other pockets of resistance we find as we go then we head to the gate.'

Zahra shook her head.

'The gates are barred, the draw chains have been locked. I saw it happening myself from the rooftops. The phoenix gate has become a killing field, and if you go there you will also be slaughtered. Your best chance of escape is the barge docks.'

'You don't understand! It's our home and we are not leaving it,' the injured man stated. Now we know the cause of the despair that has hung here for so long we shall drive it from our home.'

The mob moved on with a roar as a family broke from cover to run across the square closely pursued by a group of hooting creatures. Zahra motioned Ishmael onwards through the destruction past piles of corpses lying in the gutters, torn from their ordinary lives and never suspecting the danger they had lived with. Ishmael's plan now seemed to be the better choice, Zahra admitted, the horde was making its way across the city and having already passed through this part, all that was left was destruction. From somewhere a child wailed but Zahra forced herself to ignore it.

Chapter 68

They emerged from the smoke and carnage to the king's road that led to the open castle. The cries of torment still carried to them from the city below as the gigantic gate beckoned.

'It's too easy; we are just walking straight into a trap, Ishmael, and we don't even know where we are going.'

'My father was a mason, Zahra, he once showed me plans of the castle where the throne room was and how it looked over the city from a private balcony. That tower where the blue light emanates is above the personal chambers of the king, where he entertains visitors to his realms. I think I remember the lay out.'

They moved quickly, hugging the wall as they entered the outer gatehouse into the barbican, a long tunnel with walls lined with arrow slits and murder holes that could trap attackers. However the defences were laid open to them. Maybe the king or whomever had taken over the rule of this cursed place felt no reason to close the defences or this was a trap they were walking into, like Zahra thought. The great fortifications made Zahra feel as a fly must when it finds itself in the company of spiders. Something was waiting for them she knew, but what?

Ishmael led Zahra through to the inner courtyard, which should have been alive with the bustle of servants. All they found was debris and malformed corpses of Infernals. Probably those killed as the horde impatiently waited to unleash itself on the unsuspecting citizens of Acclaro.

As they moved Ishmael became more aware of the taint here amongst the darkness where the only light was the subdued glow of the Earth crystal he carried within the backpack. The despair of this place was accentuated by the silence that now had drowned out the sound of death enveloping the city below. He had been on hallowed ground and felt its direct effects, and now he experienced the opposite: the castle had become tainted, a place of power and unhallowed ground, a beacon for evil. They reached the winding staircase that swept up each side of the inner gatehouse to the great hall. Once carefully painted portraits of the royal linage hung from these walls. Only one remained, and that was of Chez and it had been defaced with demonic symbols. The great throne was still embedded with priceless jewels, the hard wood engraved with scenes from the rise of the empire of Thantos. Before beginning the long climb that the tower promised, Ishmael withdrew a water bag. They rested out on the balcony silently watching as the city below struggled to survive, its inhabitants being systematically rounded up and slaughtered.

The repercussions of these events would reverberate across the known world. Seizing the city would give the Infernals a base that even the most formidable army would struggle to break down.

Their thirst sated, they both walked side by side up the long climb of stairs ahead of them.

For what seemed an eternity they toiled up the steep stairs, eventually arriving at the top landing where a white and gold door stood closed. Knowing they could not put off the inevitable any longer, Zahra turned the handle.

※

Chapter 69

The smell of roasting meat hit them the moment Zahra opened the door, calling to their hunger. This room was immaculately clean, the mosaic scene of the thriving empire etched into the polished stone looked as if it hadn't aged a day since its setting. In the middle of the chamber a long lounge faced the fireplace where sat a dreadfully thin, naked man so emaciated that his organs seemed to bulge from the flimsy skin covering them. He turned something on a spit.

On the thick cushioned ivory lounge a woman reclined with her back to them.

'You sure know how to keep a lady waiting,' she said. 'Lucky, I have time to kill, amongst other things.'

Ishmael cautiously moved to where he could see the woman better. The balcony was open, but still the room was overheated. Sweat ran freely in rivulets down their faces from the long climb up the steps and the cloying heat of the room. Fitting, I suppose, thought Ishmael, since it houses one of the Infernal lords.

He moved around to the front of the lounge and noticed the thick chain connected to an iron ring beneath the lounge; that ran out to four collars on which three men and one woman were chained like dogs. They lay at her feet silently, watching Ishmael and Zahra. Zahra still had her blade drawn and Ishmael could feel the disgust rolling off her amongst the bubbling anger he had come to expect when she had her back up. The skeletal person at the hearth drew a long thin blade then began carving flesh from the roasting meat.

Looking closer, Ishmael realized the roasting meat was a person, blackened and leaking juices. The flesh was heaped on a plate then carried in jerky movements past the human hounds to the woman on the lounge, who took it daintily after placing a cloth across her knees.

'You say that you have been waiting for me but how do you know who I am or what I have come for?' asked Ishmael feeling sick from the heat and the smell of human flesh.

Slowly she forked a piece of flesh into her mouth, closing her eyes, lost in the moment that a truly delicious piece of food will bring. Her eyes then opened and settled on Ishmael. Zahra stood just staring at the Infernal lord her hatred written on her face.

'You actually still think that we don't know who you and your coterie of the Heart are?' She wiped the corners of her mouth with a serviette.

'Which one are you?'

'As you know names are power, you will never get mine.'

A long throaty laugh was her reply.

'All right then since you have no manners at all, I will begin with my story. I am known as the Lady of Whispers. It is I that whispers in the dead of night for you to investigate that strange noise. It is I that whispers in the ear of the mother to cave in the baby's head to stop it crying. It is I that whispers in the king's ear how to destroy his empire. I have caused the rise and fall of empires, but this one has been the most memorable. Maybe it's because with the absence of my true power I have had to rely on my wits to achieve its final downfall.

After the Severing, we Infernals scattered across the lands, hiding where we could. We were hunted and our nests were destroyed, but we hid and waited for the time when our exile would end. Acclaro, the once capital of the famed Empire of Thantos, cleansed us from these walls, but the king was weak. He allowed the sadness of his dead wife who I personally threw from this balcony behind me to cloud his thoughts. I of course planned his downfall perfectly, visiting him often as one of his maids, listening to his despair and gently directing him when I could. I told him, "It's not your fault that your wife killed herself," but he started to spiral down into self-pity then despair. Personally I thought his mind would be hard to break, but the minds of you mortals are flimsy. My whispers told him how his allies and the houses of Acclaro were moving against him. King Arman signed the agreed terms of release for their vassals as reward since they had assisted in the initial cleanse of the city, but he really did it because of the seeds of mistrust I planted in his mind. I became his advisor, mistress, friend, and nurse for his son, taking refuge as Arman's mind slowly rotted under my care. He no longer wanted the responsibility of the throne, the plotting and backstabbing. The deaths of his closest friends and family as well as the loss of the support from other rulers left him isolated and vulnerable and that was how he died.

'I know you must be thinking the worst of me, but I am not devoid of compassion. I took Chez and made an imbecile a king. You see, even amongst all my plotting I grew fond of him, and don't let appearances fool you, he sure knows how to make a lady happy beneath the sheets. We are a team, even had a wedding pronouncing me as his queen.' She held up a ruby encrusted ring. 'When the city is stable again I will be unveiled as the queen of Thantos, then we shall start reclaiming our lands and power from those who shunned us.'

'You talk as if the king is still alive; if that is so, then where is he?' spat Zahra.

That laugh again bubbled up.

'You mean you don't recognize him? Come here, Chez.'

The man, if you could call him that, turning the meat in the fireplace scurried over to the Lady of Whispers.

'Chez, darling, our guests didn't recognize, you can you believe that? I think it's because you are not wearing your crown, so run along and get it, darling.' The grossly emaciated man scrambled away again, looking around the chamber and muttering mindlessly to himself as he went.

'Please excuse Chez, he has been through a lot lately and I fear he is not himself.

Now where was I? Ahhh that's right. Once King Arman, who I'm sure you are aware is the father of Chez, had overseen the cleansing, he sat down in the throne room with his devotees pandering to him over his self-importance.'

Chez came running back then with his crown on his head, smiling childishly at the lady's admiring smile.

'Chez, darling, you found it, and what a king you make, hey?'

Chez clapped his hands together three times then came to sit alongside the Lady of Whispers who stroked his hair before beginning again.

'Well, as Arman sat there he received a mysterious visitor, Chez says it was one of the ancients long thought to have been extinct. This ancient had such presence about her that it is said she spent three whole days with Arman in this very chamber, where she revealed to Arman that he was needed to safe guard an item that one day would help return magic to the world. Then she gave him a rough orb of deep blue crystal.

'Three days ago that blue crystal started to glow, which got me to thinking what it all meant. So I placed the crystal in the tower where it would be seen and prepared to take the city as my own. Chez, bless his heart, stood in that tower just waiting for some sign of why. Tonight you revealed yourself to us when the crystal I know you carry burst into flame in answer to the one I hold.'

Zahra cut in.

'So you allowed us to march in here with the intention of taking the crystal we have in order to collect them all for yourself?'

The Lady of Whispers gave Zahra a patronizing glance.

'I let you march in here without being bothered because I know that amongst you are one of five who hold the world's magic within you, but without the crystals you cannot return magic. It may shock you mortals, but I would prefer to be home rather than trapped here any longer than necessary.'

'Who told you I was here?' asked Ishmael.

'I did.'

From the balcony two figures entered the chamber. It was the old man, Dalwyn from the manor, his cruel eyes smiling. Alongside him the scarred Infernal that had fought Manu and called himself Zacriel.

Chapter 70

Zahra grabbed Ishmael, hauling him back towards the door as a large shadow moved to block the entrance. The man was almost as large as the doorway and slabbed with muscle, an axe in one hand as he laughed at them.

As Zahra faced the brute with Moonbite ready, Ishmael turned back to the two who had relentlessly hunted him to this place.

'Can't you see we want the same thing, the release of magic, just let me leave with the crystals? No one needs to get hurt, and we are the only ones who can bring the magic back.'

'It's a little too late for that. You destroyed my wings, and now I will have vengeance.'

Dalwyn pushed in front of Zacriel, still looking grandfatherly.

'Ishmael, why would we wait while you run around collecting crystals when just killing the coterie would release it anyway? I have seen the magic being released with my own eyes, and so have you.'

'I agree, but if it isn't returned in the correct manner then the power will be unpredictable and could turn this world into a nightmare. If Earth isn't ready for the magic, then the effects will be catastrophic, and as I'm sure you are aware there are no mages to save us this time.'

Ishmael could see his words were having no effect. It was looking more and more like the decision to come here wasn't so smart after all. With Zahra's back to him he held his sword angled up towards Zacriel. The old man withdrew a stiletto knife with a pearl handle. Ishmael had watched this man use it to skin Brianna Dusk.

'Stay back, the both of you,' he said, but a waver in his voice betrayed his fear as the Infernal stalked closer.

'Zacriel there will be no killing here. It is my desire that these two are left to leave the city with both the crystals,' the Lady of Whispers said.

Zacriel turned to her.

'We finally catch them and you intend on letting them just leave? Did you even hear a thing we told you? It is my right to avenge myself!'

The Lady of Whispers rose to her full height, and Chez hid behind the lounge.

'The boy is right, there is a balance that needs to be respected, this cannot be rushed, and it is no simple matter where magic is concerned.'

'It is not up to you to decide this, lady,' said Dalwyn facing her now.

The Lady of Whispers walked towards him, but he didn't flinch away.

'My family were once very powerful in the arts, but this was taken from us and now I will do what I must to restore our honor. You don't have the right to decide for anyone but yourself what must happen. Here, now, you are weak like us.'

'Dalwyn, we both know that you have never felt magic running through your body,' she said. You are no more than a child playing make believe.'

Chez returned to her side and Ishmael saw he held in both hands a loaded crossbow that he had trained on Dalwyn.

'Zahra, things are getting dangerous; what do we do?'

'If it turns to fighting, go up the stairs. I will follow if I can, but I don't think my big friend is keen on letting me go anywhere, he seems to have taken a liking to me.'

The lady turned back to Zacriel.

'It seems you have forgotten who you stand before. If you think for one moment that you are important to our cause, then you are more delusional than Chez here. You are fodder, nothing else, and the one thing you need to show is your obedience.'

Zacriel stared at the Lady of Whispers then knelt with one hand on the floor and the other on his forehead.

'That's much better,' she said, turning away.

His sword thrust forward, piercing through the lady's back and briefly out her chest before sliding back out. The Lady of Whispers gave a long sigh then collapsed.

Chez fired the crossbow, and the bolt embedded itself deep in Zacriel's shoulder, throwing him onto his back.

'Run now,' Zahra yelled as she pushed Ishmael towards the stairs.

The giant charged towards her. Zahra stood her ground, slicing viciously at his stomach, which he easily caught against the haft of the axe, battering her to the side. Turning the fall into a roll, Zahra paused as her assailant rushed past her clattering into Chez, who was trying to reload the crossbow.

Dalwyn's old man nice act had disappeared, leaving hatred painted across his face as he stepped over to the fallen Lady of Whispers. Dalwyn pulled her neck back, straddling her from behind. He whispered something in her ear then drew his knife across her throat.

Zahra glimpsed Ishmael sprint up the stairs but she kept her eyes on the scene before her. She would wait for him here while he looked for the crystal.

Chez squealed as the giant slashed his axe at him, only just managing to dodge behind the lounge. Zacriel staggered to his feet then kicked the Lady of Whispers before snapping the bolt in half that jutted from his shoulder. He saw Zahra on the stairs and moved towards her.

'It's time to pay, assassin.'

As Zacriel passed, the giant wrapped the haft of his axe around his throat then pulled him tight against his chest, lifting him from the floor in a choke hold.

Zahra saw that this took Zacriel completely by surprise-he had been betrayed. She glanced up the staircase, but it was empty.

From the balcony Zahra saw someone enter the chamber near the fireplace where the four slaves squatted in terror. It was Nina, holding a large roasting fork, and she crept up behind the giant as Dalwyn stood calmly talking to the choking Zacriel.

'Your usefulness has come to an end, Zacriel. We can't allow any more mistakes from you.'

Nina plunged the blade in the back of the giant's knee, who howled as his leg collapsed, and Zacriel twisted out of the giant's choke, kicking out at Dalwyn as he went. Nina ducked past to stand between the old man and Zacriel with the fork, stabbing out and barely missing Dalwyn's leg.

'You little bitch.'

Nina lunged forwards again, keeping Dalwyn away from Zacriel with the fork. The giant reached for her, but she skipped aside. Zacriel slashed at the giant, who caught and pulled the blade from Zacriel's grasp, and they both began to wrestle, trying to get the upper hand.

The dark rings that shadowed Nina's eyes gave her a look beyond death.

'No more killing,' Nina screamed, her words breaking the moment.

From where Zahra stood she could see Dalwyn still clasped his knife; she came up behind him then smashed the hilt of her blade to the back of his head. He collapsed without a sound at Nina's feet.

Ishmael reached the top chamber, which had no door. A large, impressive altar was in the center and the walls had chest-height stone windows. On the altar, the blue orb sat on a stand. Bathing the chamber in its blue glow. From the windows Ishmael could see the inferno that Acclaro had become

Pain pulsed through Ishmael's skull, and he used the altar to steady himself from the vertigo as his mind was barraged with the invasion of Selena, Jona, and briefly Raul.

'Ishmael, whatever is happening, we know you are in danger. Maybe we can help.'

'Are you all looking through my eyes now?'

'Yes, we are, Ishmael.'

'Raul? Are you here?'

No answer came even though Ishmael could detect Raul's presence.

'The city you see below me is Acclaro, and it's been breached from within by Infernals. The great cleansing failed and they have nested here until tonight.'

Jona sobbed; Ishmael knew it was her city of birth. 'I'm sorry, Jona but the city is lost.

This blue crystal you see in front of me is the second one I have been led to. The first was one gifted to me from the Harlequin from the Jewelled lands, and they referred to it as the Earth crystal. The Infernal lord that had this one told me it's the Air crystal so that leaves three.'

'What are these crystals you speak of?' asked Selene.

'I will explain all to you later when I get to safety.'

The sounds of fighting carried to Ishmael, and he knew he had to get back to Zahra.

Ishmael walled the others from his mind, not entirely sure how he did it. He was learning new things all the time now.

Ishmael slid the orb off the pedestal and into a satchel, being careful not to touch it since he had no way of knowing what could happen. This wasn't the right time to mess around. He had to get back to Zahra before they became trapped.

Chapter 72

Zahra reached out to Nina.

'Come on, we have to leave, come with us.' Nina shook her leg, which rattled with the attached chain. Behind her Zacriel still struggled with the giant, who was slowly dragging the Infernal to the ground.

Zahra turned at the sounds of footsteps behind her to see Ishmael, holding a leather satchel.

'I have it, Zahra. Nina?' Though he had never seen the girl he had heard how she led them from the caverns, but how was she here?

'Nina, where is the key?' Zahra asked.

The girl was distraught. There is no time, you have to go now, I will be fine.' Tears flooded down her face.

Ishmael grabbed Zahra's arm.

'No Ishmael I can't leave Nina here, we need to take her with us.'

'No, we can't, Zahra, if you stay we all die! Go to the stable; there are the two Lout mounts there, just get out of the city,' begged the girl.

Zahra and Ishmael raced down the stairs as fast as they dared. When they reached the first landing Zahra halted Ishmael with a hand to his chest.

'Something isn't right! The torches are all out from here on down.'

Zahra was right, realized Ishmael, they had all been lit on the way up.

They continued into the gloom that seemed to gather with the only reprieve from the dark the sword Moonbite. Snarling could be heard from the darkness below, and on the edge of the blade's illumination a thick tentacle slithered along the wall. Behind it a figure shuffled into view, humanoid but with tentacles sprouting from its torso, its gaze fixed on them; and the monstrosity emitted a sound like the clashing of stones. The sight of them caused it to speed up its ascension of the stairs.

'Damn it! Quickly back up the stairs, Ishmael.'

They ran back up and past the chamber where Zacriel knelt, and beside him stood Nina, who held a knife in one hand. The old man lay in his own blood across from them, and King Chez whom Ishmael had thought was dead, was crawling towards the exit, his face blue and grey with bruising and blood stained his chest and shoulders.

Ishmael beckoned Zahra. 'Follow me up to the tower, the balcony is too risky.' When they reached the top, Ishmael paused to get his breath back. Any prolonged physical effort was hard for him still, and his breathing came in labored gasps.

'Suck it up, Ishmael we can rest when we're dead.'

Zahra looked out the window and saw another below her, maybe forty feet away, and to the right in the adjoining tower a balcony. She just had to figure out how to reach it.

'The curtains, we can tie them together then climb down,' said Ishmael.

A scuffle of noise came from the entrance, and they both whirled, ready to attack.

Standing in the doorway was King Chez.

'The back of the altar is false, and a ladder leads down to the stables. That's the only way out.' He looked back down the stairs behind him then turned and hobbled towards them.

'We don't have long.'

Ishmael found the false panel and pulled it free, and just like Chez had said there was a round opening with an iron ladder.

Zahra grabbed Chez and pushed a dagger up against his thin throat.

'Why should we trust you, who have sold your people and kingdom to the Infernals?'

'I am weak and will die a coward! This is my one chance to redeem a small part of myself that would have made my father proud.'

'Where does it lead?'

'To the stables, where a larger tunnel will take you beyond the wall to the Glyph grasslands.'

'Then you first, and don't forget I'm right behind you.'

Chez descended and disappeared into the darkness, the only sign of his presence the sound of his boots on the ladder rungs. They followed Chez, and the stench of damp stone and mildew was strong as they pushed through thick webs and heard critters scuttle in the darkness. When the ring of light from the tower disappeared, plunging them into total darkness, Zahra, who was last, knew their pursuer had found their escape route.

'Hurry up, it's at the top of the ladder, hurry!'

It was a relief when they reached the bottom.

'We need light,' wheezed Chez in his nasally voice.

Ishmael removed his pack and pulled forth the Earth crystal, letting its illuminate their surroundings. They saw only dust and rodent's bones among the damp stone. Holding it up they looked back up the ladder to see the monster that pursued them descending head first with its tentacles lowering it down the ladder.

'It's still coming, move!'

'This way,' said Chez, scrambling off as they followed. Ishmael noticed Chez left bloody footprints as he went. They came to a wall, and Chez located some sort of hidden lever that swung a doorway open to a stall empty except for hay. Exiting into the main stable, they found dead livestock littering the corral, either eaten by the Infernals or lying gaunt and shrivelled from starvation. In a section of the stable two Lout's were tied, just as Nina said. The creatures looked similar to their distant cousins the grasshoppers except these were the size of horses. They had grey bodies with pale green heads and powerful hind leg shanks darkening to scarlet at their ends. The Louts' hind wings fluttered as they were approached, and Zahra was relieved to see that both were saddled. Surrounded by vegetation and grass, they were the only beasts that had survived.

'I will open the tunnel,' called Chez as he ran to another wall.

'How do we ride them? Ishmael asked.

'Like horses, but first we need to get them to stay together, and we need water for that,' said Zahra, scooping some water from a trough. He watched as Zahra sprinkled the water on top of the heads of the Louts. 'Water especially rain binds them together. It causes the release of a hormone that attracts them.'

The Louts seemed to delight in the water; they gently butted together, their wings, buzzing in bursts, long legs straightening then bending to crouch again.

'Mount up, Ishmael, then follow my lead. Your mount will follow mine, so just hold on.'

Ishmael carefully mounted the beast, its antennae twitched as he did, its clear eyes turning to watch him making him uneasy.

Zahra untied the reins and leant back to look at Ishmael.

'Use the reins and your legs just like a horse and don't panic when we jump. Make sure the harness is tight'

Chez reappeared, beckoning them to a tunnel opening.

'What about Chez? Asked Ishmael, but the strange king had already run forwards into the tunnel.

Ishmael's Lout bounded after Zahra's, and they quickly caught up to Chez and overtook him. Ishmael pulled up to a stop.

'Chez, climb up behind me.'

From behind the emaciated king a tentacle emerged, slapping him against the wall, and another wrapped around his fallen form then dragged him screaming out of Ishmael's sight.

'It got Chez, go, Zahra!'

They moved fast through the winding tunnel which ended at a rotting door which they barged through and into what appeared to be a barn.

The events of the day had worn Ishmael down, he needed sustenance and rest, but they had to find another place to hide. They left the barn and bounded in long jumps through the grasslands until they came to coming to a river that flowed from Acclaro Lake heading towards Brimmerland. They followed the river for half a chime and found a windmill.

They led the chirruping Louts around the back of the structure, where they tied them to the building with enough room to feed on the grass by the river as well as drink from the slow flowing water way.

The door was locked, but the rusty lock soon broke as they busted it open with Ishmael's sword. Warily the two of them entered the darkness the building, using the crystal once again as a light source. There was the smell of mice amongst the bags of grain and barrels of water. They climbed a ladder to the loft, where the floor was dry and relatively clean. Ishmael began unpacking some stringy meat and wine. When Zahra wasn't looking he added a pinch of powder to her wine then served the food and drink which they consumed in silence.

Dalwyn could feel the warm flow of blood on his scalp as he lay there gathering his thoughts. Had he been knocked unconscious it would have been the end for him, but somehow he had stayed conscious. Maybe it was that Escindre still favored him from wherever the god now resided. It must have been the assassin who struck him down, which meant things had gone terribly wrong. Zacriel should have been dead by now and Ishmael his captive, but instead Ishmael had fled again with the assassin along with the blue orb, and Zacriel was alive with the help Nina. Dalwyn's latest bodyguard Knuckles lay unmoving not five feet from where Dalwyn lay feigning his own death.

He waited and listened as Zacriel and Nina moved around the chamber.

'Are you all right Zacriel? You have a hole straight through the shoulder and out the back. We have to go, that thing with the tentacles could come here.

'I will be fine, girl, just help me up. I need to make sure this is finished. Zacriel paused. 'Why did you help me after all that has happened?'

'I helped you because you have tried to be kind to me and I have no one else. My life is in your hands.'

From half-lidded eyes Dalwyn watched as Zacriel bent then broke the neck of Knuckles.

'Do you have to do that?' Nina asked. 'Isn't it enough that they are beaten and can be our prisoners?'

'Ha, you don't know the old man like I do, girl. Anyhow, we have no need of prisoners while we are hunting Ishmael.'

'You could just let them go as well as me, Zacriel. You don't need any of us. Is it worth all this just for revenge?'

'It is not just revenge, Nina, it is more than that!'

As he listened, Dalwyn followed the clink of the girl's chains as she moved closer. She poked him with a foot then bent down beside him. Stupid child.

He snatched her by the throat and held his knife against her throat. She kicked him and punched him but was too weak to do any real damage as her piteous scream echoed around the chamber.

Zacriel looked up, a low growl coming from his throat, but he stopped where he was when Dalwyn dug the blade deeper into Nina's skin.

'Stay there, Zac, you know I will do it. The girl is nothing to me, so if you want her death on your conscience then take that one step towards me.'

'Our alliance ended when you betrayed me and had your bodyguard attempt to kill me. Do you think you can just walk away from here now?' Zacriel asked.

'I can and will walk away, but with your little plaything here, unless we can come to an understanding. My men will be here soon, then we shall see who is in a position to dictate what happens.'

'Did you somehow forget, Dalwyn that the city has fallen to us Infernals?'

As Dalwyn and Nina watched, Zacriel bent down and took something from the dead body of the Lady of Whispers. He held it up for them.

'This is the Rod of an Infernal lord. The Severing stole its magical enhancements, but it is still recognized by all Infernal creatures as an item of power that proves ruler-ship over them.' He reached down again to the dead Lady of Whispers and tore open her bodice where a rose of metal hung over her heart. It came free with a sucking noise as he tugged on it and root like tendrils dangled from its base. 'With this brooch, all those creatures from your worst nightmares that are gorging themselves on the slaughter of Acclaro will know they have a new ruler. At my command, they will tear you to pieces should I wish that, so how do you propose to talk your way out of this mess you have created, Dalwyn?'

Zacriel opened his tunic then pushed the broach against his heart. He began screaming as blood flowed down his chest and abdomen.

'Why would I need to talk my way out of it?' asked Dalwyn.

'I have one of the two things that you desire, so if you truly value Nina's life so little then kill me now. However, I think that won't be necessary; you see, we both still need one another. I need you with your new army to help me get to the safe house where the coterie of the heart is headed, and you need me if Nina is to survive and your vengeance on Ishmael is to be realized. It's your choice Zacriel.'

The sounds of heavy feet upon the stairs that could be heard for some time now stopped as at least a dozen warriors burst into the chamber.

They were Dalwyn's men.

Dalwyn smiled as he looked back to Zacriel, then motioned for his men to halt.

'Zacriel, old friend, surely you can see that we are stuck with each other for some time yet.'

He began laughing softly, which turned into an uncontrollable belly laugh as tears striped down his face at the anger twisting Zacriel's face when he grasped that he was beaten. At some point Zacriel began laughing too, until both of them were lost in their mirth.

Nina wasn't laughing. She was scared and now had become a game piece to be played between these two monsters that now would have an army of Infernals. Nina thought of her father then, who never gave up even when facing impossible odds, and she knew that even if her life was this terrible a chance would come to restore her family name and have a normal life of her own again.

Chapter 76

As Haakon made his way back to the clan house, a voice called out.

'Halt where you are and identify yourself!'

He ignored it and kept on walking, even when a shrill whistle sounded, and the sound of swords being drawn nearby carried to him. As he walked farther he reached the illumination of the lamps where he stopped with his hands open, palms facing forwards.

'Stay there and don't move.'

Footfalls to the front and left side of him let him know he was being approached by his guards.

'Lower your weapons, its Haakon.'

'You are covered in blood, Haakon, are you hurt?'

He ignored the question and walked into camp along with the soldiers to where a group, including Faustus had started gathering.

They all stood staring at him as if he had just marched straight up out of the Infernal lands themselves.

'Have no fear for my safety,' Haakon said. 'The blood is not mine.'

'Then why are you even out there alone? Someone called out.

'This blood that covers me is the blood of traitors. I will not mention their names. That is the only respect I shall give their memories. By their absence you will soon know who they are.

I ask you all here now to remember this one thing. We are bound together in a task that was entrusted to us, and the time is now upon us to show why we were trusted with such an important role. The coterie of the heart are in danger, and the nations are gathering their forces for war. The time is now upon us as a clan to act, and the time is upon us as individuals to choose. I call you all family, so I feel I must offer you this one chance to leave. Any of you who disagree with my actions or the direction of the clan are free to go. You have 'til daybreak to be out of the camp and good luck go with you, for there are tough times coming.

'I would like to think you will all be here come tomorrow, but I understand there are those among you who view my leadership as inadequate. Tomorrow you are either with this clan or against us, so choose now. No one moved or made a sound as he walked between them to the room where Latasha lay. Once inside he saw the covers were twisted, and half of them lay on the floor, as he bent to retrieve them he stopped. Latasha was in a coma; how would they have ended up on the floor? Haakon reached over and uncovered the tank of sun blazer fish. As the green-blue luminescence dispelled the shadows from the room, the light found Latasha's face.

Her eyes were open.